ON THE TRAIL OF A KILLER

"You know what this means, don't you?" Jacob asked.

"It means somebody has been getting away with murder for the past twenty-five years," Dallas said. "And not just one or two murders, but over twenty murders, possibly more."

"He could have killed other women whose bodies were never found." Holding the papers tightly in his right hand, Jacob slapped the faxed documents against his left palm. "It's got to be the same guy. It's the exact same MO. All the victims were redheads. Either prostitutes or reputed to be bad girls. They were all raped, strangled with a black braided ribbon—left around their necks—and their naked bodies dumped in either a river or a lake or a creek."

"When I spoke to Teri, she said that with the evidence she's compiled, the Bureau will definitely want to become involved, but she's given us twenty-four hours to get our act together before she reports what she's found."

"Did she get Linc to come up with a profile of this killer?"

"Yeah. And Linc says our guy is definitely the organized type," Dallas said. "High IQ, possibly college educated. Could have been a mama's boy or at least the family favorite. And there's a good chance he suffered some type of either physical or mental abuse as a child. And Teri said that Linc suspects some traumatic experience involving a red-haired woman was the catalyst that brought out his killer instinct. In Linc's opinion, this guy is probably a psychopath . . ."

Books by Beverly Barton

AFTER DARK

EVERY MOVE SHE
MAKES

WHAT SHE
DOESN'T KNOW

THE FIFTH VICTIM

THE LAST TO DIE

AS GOOD
AS DEAD

KILLING HER
SOFTLY

CLOSE ENOUGH
TO KILL

MOST LIKELY
TO DIE

THE DYING
GAME

THE MURDER
GAME

COLD HEARTED

SILENT KILLER

DEAD
BY MIDNIGHT

DON'T CRY

DEAD
BY MORNING

DEAD
BY NIGHTFALL

DON'T SAY
A WORD

JUST THE WAY
YOU ARE

THE RIGHT WIFE
(available as an e-book)

Published by Kensington Publishing Corporation

As GOOD As DEAD

BEVERLY BARTON

PINNACLE BOOKS
Kensington Publishing Corp.
www.kensingtonbooks.com

PINNACLE BOOKS are published by

Kensington Publishing Corp.
119 West 40th Street
New York, NY 10018

Copyright © 2004 Beverly Beaver

All Kensington titles, imprints, and distributed lines are available at special quantity discounts for bulk purchases for sales promotions, premiums, fund-raising, educational, or institutional use. Special book excerpts or customized printings can also be created to fit specific needs. For details, write or phone the office of the Kensington sales manager: Kensington Publishing Corp., 119 West 40th Street, New York, NY 10018, attn: Sales Department; phone 1-800-221-2647.

This book is a work of fiction. Names, characters, businesses, organizations, places, events, and incidents either are the product of the author's imagination or are used fictitiously. Any resemblance to actual persons, living or dead, events, or locales is entirely coincidental.

PINNACLE BOOKS and the Pinnacle logo are Reg. U.S. Pat. & TM Off.

ISBN-13: 978-0-7860-4102-2
ISBN-10: 0-7860-4102-1

First Zebra mass market paperback printing: September 2004
First Pinnacle mass market paperback printing: August 2018

18 17 16 15 14 13 12 11 10

Printed in the United States of America

In memory of my father, a man with a kind and generous heart, a mind that thirsted for knowledge and a truly good soul destined for eternal happiness. This one is for you, Dee Jr., my daddy.

PROLOGUE

Kat Baker applied the dark pink lipstick to her mouth, tossed the plastic wand onto the dressing table and stood up to view herself in the full-length mirror. Studying her image, she decided she looked damn good, despite her hair color, an outrageous shade of dark red. She'd been a brunette since childhood and had gone blonde in her early twenties, but never had she considered dyeing her long, glossy mane red. However, being a working girl whose livelihood depended upon pleasing her clientele, she did whatever the men in her life requested. And this new man had the money to pay for the exclusive rights to her whenever he was in town.

Tonight would mark their fourth "date." When he'd telephoned two days ago, he'd given her specific instructions on how to dress and where to meet him, just as he'd done on two previous occasions. He called himself Harry—no last name—but she knew that wasn't his real name. Few of her clients ever divulged their true identities and she couldn't blame them, although some used their real given names. They seemed to want to hear her cry out their name when she came. And she was good at faking those earth-shattering orgasms many men tried so hard to give her.

But Harry wasn't like that. He didn't seem to give a damn whether or not she got off, just as long as he did. A shudder passed through her as she recalled the last time he'd been in town. He'd come here the first time, as most of her johns did, to this small Knoxville apartment she rented strictly for her business dealings. She kept another place—her own private home—across town in a nicer neighborhood where no one knew what she did for a living. The first two times with Harry, he'd been aggressive and demanding, but hadn't requested anything out of the ordinary. But the third time had been different. And truth be told, if he hadn't offered her such an exorbitant amount of money to be available whenever he came to Knoxville, she'd never see him again. She could deal with rough sex, even with mild S&M, but Harry had come damn near close to choking her. When she'd managed to breathe again, she had tried to get away from him, but he'd held her down and fucked her like crazy.

Before he'd left that night, he'd given her a huge sum in cash, instructed her to dye her hair red and to wear a black corded ribbon around her neck the next time they were together. He'd even pulled the ribbon from his pocket and handed it to her. The guy gave her the creeps, but she'd convinced herself that he hadn't really hurt her—just scared the shit out of her—and the money was three times what she usually made. A woman in her business who was over thirty had to think about her future, didn't she?

Kat opened the middle drawer in her dressing table, reached inside and pulled out the black ribbon. As she tied it at the back of her neck, she wondered just what it was about this strip of black braided satin that turned Harry on. Probably some freaky thing from his past. Something to do with his mommy or his nanny or his teenage sweetheart.

Grabbing her purple leather jacket from the closet where she kept her working clothes, she thought ahead to her appointment and wondered what Harry would do to her tonight. Whatever it was, she was sure she'd earn her pay.

* * *

Kat's eyelids fluttered as she tried to open her eyes, but the lids were heavy. So heavy. Her head throbbed something awful. Where was she? What had happened to her? Why couldn't she remember?

She heard an odd noise rumbling in her ears and realized it was the sound of her own groans. Wake up, Kat. Dammit, girl, wake up.

Something odd was going on. Had somebody drugged her? Think. Try to remember. She'd had an appointment with Harry tonight. Oh, God, that was it! The last thing she remembered was having drinks with Harry. Wine. She hated wine, but he'd insisted, telling her that it was a very expensive bottle he'd bought especially for them.

Suddenly she felt something brush over her breasts. Hands. Large hands. A man's hands. But those hands felt strange, as if they were covered in plastic.

She tried again to open her eyes, but without success. Then she tried to speak, but all she managed was a hoarse moan.

"You're beautiful, Dinah," a man said, his hands caressing her body with gentle force.

Who the hell was Dinah?

Kat moaned and tried again to open her eyes. When she gazed up at the man hovering over her, she recognized him. It was Harry.

Harry looked down at her and smiled as he rammed into her. "You're always a good fuck, Dinah. The best."

"Har . . . ree . . . ?" She couldn't manage to keep her eyes open.

"You shouldn't be waking up, my love. But it doesn't matter. It'll soon be over. For this time."

For this time? Her mind was still so foggy she couldn't think straight. She knew she was with Harry, knew he was screwing her and suspected he had drugged her. But why had he drugged her? He'd paid her for her services. She'd do anything he wanted. He knew that. Hell, maybe he got off fucking a woman while she was unconscious. You never knew what turned a guy on.

He pumped into her, his thrusts increasing in speed. She lifted her arms, intending to caress him, to urge him on, but her arms felt as if they weighed a hundred pounds each. That must have been some strong drug he'd put in her wine.

She forced her eyes open again only moments before Harry came. Grunting and shivering, he moaned into her ear. "Dinah . . . my Dinah."

He lifted himself up and off Kat, then slid backward out of the car. Kat managed to halfway sit up. That's when she realized they were in a parked car. She peeked out the window. Darkness. She stared at Harry, who stood just outside the open back door. He carefully removed the condom from his penis and placed it in a plastic bag.

How odd was that? Maybe the guy's a neat freak.

After laying the bag on the floor board beside her, he zipped up his pants, which couldn't have been an easy task with gloves on.

Gloves?

Why was Harry wearing plastic gloves?

Glancing at her, he smiled again. He reached out, shoved her back down on the seat, then caressed the black satin ribbon around her neck.

"Harry? What—"

"Hush, sweet Dinah. Don't talk. It's not part of our game."

"What game?"

He laughed and the sound sent chilling ripples up her spine.

Harry untied the satin cord, then grasped the ends.

When Kat saw the wild look in his eyes, she panicked. She knew in that very instant that he was playing a deadly game.

"No . . . don't," she pleaded. "I—I don't want to play this game."

"I told you not to talk."

He tightened the ribbon around her neck.

Grasping his hands, she struggled against him.

"Please . . ." *Is he going to kill me?*

He slowly tightened the ribbon more and more.

She could barely breathe. God help her, he was choking her to death.

Don't kill me, she pleaded silently. *I don't want to die.*

Allowing the good feelings to linger inside him for a few minutes, he looked up at the dark night sky and laughed aloud. God, he felt great! When he'd come, when he'd finished humping Dinah as he'd dreamed of doing, a great sense of satisfaction had claimed him completely. She had denied him, snickered at him, made him feel like a fool. But in the end, she'd given in and allowed him to make love to her.

He focused his gaze inside the car at the lovely redheaded woman lying on the backseat. Moonlight illuminated her luscious naked body—her parted thighs, her full, round breasts, her slightly open mouth. Power surged through him, every nerve in his body electrified by the dark energy flowing through him. He could taste her—all that lush sweetness. He intensified the pressure as he pulled the cord until it cut into her neck. As he squeezed the life out of her, the pressure from the ribbon burned into his palms and heat suffused his body. This was the defining moment, the pleasure almost unbearable.

It took only seconds for her to die. Or at least that was the way it seemed to him.

But she would not stay dead. She never did.

He had to act quickly, remove her body and dispose of it so that he could put this incident behind him and live in peace for a while. Until she returned to him.

Slipping his arm beneath the plastic sheet he had used to protect the car seat, he pulled her into a sitting position, wrapped the sheet around her and dragged her toward him.

He didn't especially like the scent of death, but it didn't repulse him, either. Actually, the odor reassured him that he had accomplished his goal.

Resting there passively cocooned in the sheet, like a limp dishrag, she made no protest when he scooped her up into his arms. Although she wasn't a large woman, she felt heavy, as if she weighed two hundred pounds.

Dead weight, he thought.

Carrying Dinah with great care, he tromped down the dark, isolated dirt road. He could hear the soft rush of the river nearby, a melodic lull carrying quietly through the woods. When he neared the edge of the embankment, he paused, leaned over and opened the sheet enough to expose her face, then leaned down and kissed her good-bye. Sighing heavily, he tossed her into the Tennessee River and stood watching while the current carried her body downstream.

Farewell, my love.

There, that was done. Now he could go home, return to his normal life and put her out of his mind. At least temporarily. Of course, it was only a matter of time before she would come back. To taunt him. To entice him. To drive him crazy until he possessed her again. Each time she left, a part of him hoped—even prayed— that she would stay away for good. But his prayers were never answered. She always came back. At first it had been years between her reappearances, but gradually she'd begun returning more frequently. Often she returned within a year or less, but most recently she had shown up again in a little over six months.

He wondered how long she would stay away this time.

CHAPTER 1

Reve Sorrell closed the lid on her suitcase, lifted it off the foot of her bed and set it on the floor. She'd been up for over an hour, after waking at three, unable to sleep. Her decision to return to Cherokee Pointe had been made after a great deal of deliberation. She'd spent months unable to put Jazzy Talbot out of her mind. Back in the spring she'd driven up to the mountains to seek out the woman Jamie Upton had told her was her spitting image, a woman who looked enough like her to be her twin. She'd met Jamie at a party here in Chattanooga, back before Christmas last year. He'd been a charming jerk, the type of man she usually avoided. But he had piqued her curiosity when he'd mentioned that his teenage sweetheart, a bar and restaurant owner in Cherokee Pointe, could easily pass for Reve's twin.

If she hadn't been an abandoned child, adopted in infancy by wealthy socialites, Spencer and Lesley Sorrell, she'd have passed off Jamie's comments without a second thought. But since she knew nothing about her birth parents, she'd wondered if it was possible that this Jasmine Talbot Jamie had mentioned could be her sister. So she'd disregarded what her common sense had told her—not to go digging around in the past—and had gone to Cherokee Pointe.

Her first encounter with Jazzy had been less than pleasant. She'd found the woman to be rather crude and vulgar. They had disliked each other on sight. And Reve would have returned home that very day, if she hadn't been involved in a minor car accident.

As if wrecking her Jag hadn't been bad enough, following the accident, the local sheriff had treated her abysmally. Sheriff Jacob Butler was an old friend of Jazzy's and took offense at an offhand comment Reve made about the woman. It had seemed to Reve as if half the men in town were Jazzy's friends, a fact Reve had learned both firsthand and from local gossip.

To complicate matters now that she was returning to Cherokee Pointe, she'd been plagued by thoughts of the big, surly, half-breed sheriff. He was a thoroughly unpleasant sort. A real ruffian. After their initial encounter, she had hoped she would never see the man again. But when Jamie Upton was murdered while she was still in town and a witness identified a woman fitting Jazzy's description—and therefore her description—as having been seen with Jamie shortly before his death, Sheriff Butler had come knocking on her door. He'd had the gall to practically accuse her of the murder, had in fact assumed—erroneously—that Jamie and she had been lovers. Naturally, it hadn't taken the authorities long to realize she wasn't involved in the crime, so she had, thankfully, been able to escape from Cherokee Pointe and the watchful eyes of the Neanderthal sheriff.

Upon returning to Chattanooga, to her home on Lookout Mountain and her own set of friends and business associates, she'd tried to put her less than pleasant experiences in Cherokee Pointe behind her. She hadn't wanted to think about Jazzy or the fact that they did in fact resemble each other in a way only twins did. But try as she might, she hadn't been able to erase from her mind the image of her double, a woman of dubious character.

Reve sighed heavily. Would she regret going back to Cherokee Pointe and joining forces with Jazzy to seek the truth about their possible sisterhood? They had spoken on the phone several times recently. Somewhat reluctantly, Reve had made that first call. Thirty years ago, someone had thrown her into a Dumpster in Sevierville and left her for dead. She'd been an infant, possibly only days or weeks old at the time. However, Jazzy's Aunt Sally, who had raised her from a baby, swore that her sister Corrine had given birth to only one child. Was Sally Talbot lying? Or was there some other explanation? Reve knew she'd never have any peace of mind until she found out the truth—the whole truth.

She hadn't intended to leave Chattanooga this early. It wasn't quite four-thirty. But why not go ahead and get on the road? If she left now, she'd be in Cherokee Pointe by the time Jasmine's opened and she could have breakfast at the restaurant before meeting Jazzy at Dr. MacNair's office around nine. They had agreed that DNA testing was the first step in discovering the truth about their past.

Not wanting to bother any of the servants at this ungodly hour, she heaved her suitcase off the bed. As she walked through the house and out to the garage, she couldn't help wondering if she was making a monumental mistake. She and Jazzy Talbot had nothing in common, other than a strong physical resemblance—and possibly the same birth parents. Did she really want to form a familial connection with this woman who was, by all standards, socially beneath her and morally inferior? *God, Reve, listen to yourself. You sound like the biggest snob in the world.* All right, maybe she was a snob. No maybe about it. She was a snob. But she'd been trained by her parents and peers to look down her nose at her inferiors. *There you go again, assuming just because she grew up poor, has a reputation as the town tramp and owns a honky-tonk, that Jazzy isn't your equal.*

Reve unlocked the trunk of her Jaguar, dumped the suitcase inside, then slid behind the wheel and started the car.

Even if Jazzy and she turned out to be twin sisters, that didn't mean they had to become friends. She seriously doubted that Jazzy wanted to build a relationship with her anymore than she wanted one with Jazzy. But there was a need deep inside her to find out the truth—who had thrown her in that Dumpster and why? Had her birth mother thrown her away? If so, why had she disposed of one baby and not both? And if she and Jazzy were twin sisters, why had Jazzy's Aunt Sally lied to her all these years? After the DNA testing confirmed their relationship, the likely place to start their search for the truth was with Sally Talbot. And what a place to start—with a nutty old woman the whole town thought of as a kook.

Reve hit the button to open the garage door, backed out and then closed the door. As she entered the street, she stopped the Jag and took a long, hard look at her home. This house had belonged to her grandparents, Spencer Sorrel's parents, and the plush mansion held only happy memories for Reve. If only she weren't adopted. If only the Sorrells had been her biological mother and father. But her adoptive mother had pointed out to her on numerous occasions that she *was* a true Sorrell in every way that counted. Except by blood.

As she drove along the steep, twisting street leading off Lookout Mountain, Reve compared the similarities between this road and the one where she'd had her car accident outside Cherokee Pointe. Damn! Why had she thought about that wreck again? Automatically her mind brought Sheriff Butler to the forefront—a vivid image of his hulking six-five frame, his green eyes, his hawk nose, his fierce frown. She intended to do her best to avoid Jacob Butler while she was in Cherokee Pointe. Not only did the man annoy her, but he unnerved her. His nature was a bit too savage to suit her. He'd been more than just downright unfriendly toward her; he'd shown no respect whatsoever for who she was—one of the richest and most powerful women in the state of Tennessee.

* * *

Jazzy's orgasm exploded inside her, eliciting a loud, guttural moan from deep in her throat. The powerful sensations went on and on until they finally tapered off into delicious aftershocks. Hot, damp, completely sated, she smothered Caleb with deliriously exuberant kisses. He toppled her off him and onto the bed, his hard penis slipping out of her during the maneuver. Before she had a chance to catch her breath, he thrust up into her. Deep and hard. Once. Twice. And then he came.

Roaring like the male animal he was, Caleb shuddered with release. Moments later, their bodies damp with sex-induced sweat, they lay on their backs, their bodies not touching, only their entwined fingers.

She loved holding hands with Caleb. A sweet, sentimental gesture, but it said so much about their relationship. About who she was when she was with him. About the type of man Caleb McCord was.

Jazzy looked up at the ceiling, stretched languidly and smiled. Sex with Caleb was always like this—explosive and fully satisfying. But there was so much more to their relationship than great sex. They were friends as well as lovers. And they were madly in love, too. Honest to goodness in love.

She didn't know what she'd done to deserve a fabulous guy like Caleb, but she thanked God for him. And with each passing day, she trusted Caleb and the love they shared more and more. Maybe one of these days soon she would be able to accept his marriage proposal. He had asked her to marry him so many times, it had almost become a joke between them.

Almost.

Even now, months after Jamie Upton's death, his memory haunted her. But not in the way Caleb thought it did. On some basic, totally masculine level Caleb was still jealous of Jamie, of the fact that he'd been her first love and her first lover. There was no reason for him to be jealous. She didn't love Jamie. Only the distrust and fear Jamie had instilled in her kept him alive and allowed him to stand between her and Caleb, between her and happiness.

"Jazzy?" Caleb said her name in that lazy, sexy Memphis drawl she loved so well.

"Hm-mm?" She turned sideways and looked at the silhouette of his long, lean body there in the semidarkness of her bedroom. She knew his body as well as she knew her own.

"Marry me."

Her smile widened. She reached over and ran her fingertips up and down his body, from throat to navel.

He grabbed her hand. "I mean it. Marry me. Let's get a license tomorrow and just do it. We'll elope. No fanfare, no—"

"No Miss Reba throwing a hissy fit until it's over and done."

"Do not bring my grandmother into this equation. I've told you a thousand times that I don't give a damn what she thinks." Totally naked, Caleb jumped out of bed and grabbed his jeans up off the floor.

Damn it, she'd hurt his feelings by questioning his loyalty to her. Her mind told her that he would never do as Jamie had done and allow Miss Reba to dictate who he could and couldn't marry. But her heart had been broken once by an Upton heir, by the charming, worthless, womanizing Jamie. And her heart was afraid to trust, afraid to believe that Miss Reba didn't wield the same power over Caleb that she had over her other grandson.

"What are you doing?"

"I'm putting on my clothes," Caleb told her.

"Why? You aren't leaving, are you? Please, Caleb, don't go."

He pulled on his jeans, then felt around on the floor until he found his shirt. "I'm just going outside for a few minutes. I need some early morning air to clear my head. I'll be back in a little while."

"I'm sorry."

"It's okay," he said. "Just remember, I'm not Jamie. I'm not walking out on you or giving up on us. Not now or ever. You couldn't beat me off with a stick, honey."

"I know you're not Jamie." When she sat up, the sheet dropped to her waist, exposing her breasts.

"Then stop assuming I'm going to treat you the way he did. I can't stand it when you project his actions onto me."

Caleb turned from her and hastily left the room. Jazzy flipped on the bedside lamp, then got up and headed for the bathroom. Usually they didn't get up this early—and seven-thirty was early for people who didn't go to bed until two in the morning—but she had an appointment to meet Reve Sorrell in Dr. MacNair's office at nine. Galvin had explained to them that the results of the DNA test might take a few weeks, but Reve had informed him that she would pay any extra costs necessary to facilitate a speedy response.

Jazzy turned on the water, waited a couple of minutes for it to heat, and then stepped under the showerhead. As the warm spray doused her, she thought about her future. Her first concern was Caleb. She couldn't keep putting him off. Sooner or later he'd get tired of waiting for her to marry him. The thought of losing him was too terrible to consider, yet she wasn't ready to say yes. There were too many unanswered questions in her life, too many loose ends she had to tie up before she could build a solid future with the man she loved. And she did love Caleb. More than she'd ever thought possible to love a man. But she had to convince him that he was the only man she loved. In order to do that, she had to let go of Jamie completely.

Since Caleb spent most nights at her apartment above Jazzy's Joint, they usually closed the bar together and came upstairs for a late-night meal and then went to bed. She loved being with him, making love with him, sharing her life with him.

So why don't you marry the guy? she heard Lacy Fallon's voice inside her head. Lacy, the bartender at Jazzy's Joint, treated Jazzy like a kid sister, giving her advice and watching out for her.

Don't let what Jamie did to you keep you from finding

happiness with Caleb, Jazzy's best friend, Genny Sloan, had told her repeatedly.

Even her own heart advised her to reach out and grab the happiness Caleb offered.

Jazzy bathed hurriedly, washed her hair and emerged from the shower, fresh and clean and clear-headed. By the time she dried her hair and dressed, Caleb would probably be back in the apartment and in the kitchen fixing their breakfast. She smiled to herself. Her Caleb was a man of many talents.

The telephone rang. *Who on earth would be calling so early?* Everyone knew they slept late. After wrapping a towel around her, Jazzy rushed into the bedroom to answer the phone.

"Hello."

"Jazzy, this is Reve Sorrell. I got an early start so I'm already in town. I'm over at Jasmine's and have just ordered breakfast. Any chance you can join me?"

"Ah . . . I just stepped out of the shower, but—" Maybe it was a good idea to touch base with Reve before they went to see Galvin. After all, if it turned out they really were twin sisters, as they suspected, they'd be spending a great deal of time together in the upcoming weeks. They had agreed that if the DNA tests proved they were siblings, they would work together to discover the truth about their parentage.

"If you'd rather not—" Reve said.

"No, it's okay. I'll hurry and dress." Jazzy peeked through the open bedroom door and into the living room. No sign of Caleb. She listened for any sound of him in the kitchen. None.

"It's okay if I bring Caleb along, isn't it?"

"Sure. After all, he is your fiancé, right?"

"He most certainly is. Unofficially."

"Have you two set a date?"

"Not yet." Everyone assumed that sooner or later she'd accept Caleb's proposal—everyone except Caleb's grandmother, one of Cherokee County's grande dames, Reba Upton.

Damn the old bitch!

"Bring him along," Reve said. "I'll go ahead and eat, then have coffee when y'all arrive. Or would you like for me to order for you two and wait?"

"Yes, do that. Just tell Tiffany that Caleb and I will be eating at the restaurant this morning. She knows our usual order."

"See you soon."

"Mm-hm." The dial tone hummed in Jazzy's ear.

Reve Sorrell had been pleasant enough, but not overly friendly. The woman had erected some sort of emotional barrier around herself, one that effectively kept people at bay. If they were twin sisters, how was it possible that their personalities were as different as night is from day? She supposed it all boiled down to the old question about which dominated a person's physical, mental and emotional makeup more—nurture or nature.

Reve Sorrell was a class act. A real lady. Jazzy Talbot was a dame, a broad, a good old gal.

"Jazzy?" Caleb called to her as he entered the living room.

"Huh?"

"Want me to put on some coffee?"

Caleb might get upset with her, he might storm off in a rage, but he always came back. He never left her for more than a few minutes, an hour or two on a few occasions. He meant what he'd said about not ever leaving her. Not the way Jamie had done, time and time again.

"Reve Sorrell just called," Jazzy said. "She wants us to meet her for breakfast over at Jasmine's."

"She got in early, didn't she?"

"Yeah, she did. I guess she's as anxious as I am to get our DNA samples sent off to the lab."

Caleb appeared in the bedroom doorway. "Give me a couple of minutes to grab a quick shower." As he moved past her, he paused, leaned over and kissed her cheek, then yanked off her towel before he went into the bathroom.

Jazzy hugged herself and sighed contentedly. Reve Sorrell

might be a lady—a very rich and important lady—but who
cared? Caleb didn't. And it didn't matter to him that Jazzy
wasn't some blue-blood with a lily-white reputation. He loved
her just the way she was. And Caleb's opinion was all that
mattered.

Sally Talbot stood on her front porch, a tasty chaw of tobacco in her mouth. Peter and Paul, her old bloodhounds,
lounged lazily under the porch, their heads barely peeking
out as they snored. She wished she could sleep as easy as
them two varmints did, but if they had the worries she had,
they wouldn't be sleeping so soundly either. After spitting a
spray of brown juice out into the yard, Sally wiped her
mouth and took a deep breath of autumn mountain air. There
weren't nothing like autumn in the Appalachians. The crisp,
clean morning air. The bright colors nature painted the earth
this time of year. No, sirree, weren't no place on earth as
near God's heaven as these here mountains.

All her life—some seventy-one years now—she'd spent
here in Cherokee County, most of it in this same old house
her pa had built for her ma before he up and died of TB back
in forty-nine. And all these years she'd been an oddball, different from folks hereabout. Not crazy, mind you, but not
quite all there either. She had book learning. She could read
and write and add up figures. And she knew these hills as well
as anybody, better than most. She'd always been poor and
hadn't never cared a hoot about money. Not until Jazzy came
into her life. She'd wanted to give that gal everything her little heart desired, but she'd failed miserably. She'd done the
best she could. If she'd had a man bringing in a living, things
might have been better, but she and Jazzy had made out all
right. They'd had a roof over their heads and they'd never
gone hungry. Jazzy had grown up to be a fine woman, a real
smart woman who'd done all right for herself. Her gal owned
a restaurant and a bar in Cherokee Pointe and she was a part-

ner with some other people in Cherokee Cabin Rentals. Yep, she was damn proud of her niece.

A chill racked Sally's body. "Winter's coming," she said to no one in particular.

But it wasn't the cool morning breeze that had chilled Sally. It was thoughts of Jazzy. Her little Jasmine. She'd named Jazzy for them beautiful flowers that her sister Corrine had loved so. When she'd put Jasmine in Corrine's arms thirty years ago, she'd never dreamed that within a few months Corrine would be dead—her and her lover—and she'd be left to raise Jazzy all alone. But there hadn't been a day passed that she hadn't thanked the good Lord for that gal. She loved Jazzy as if she were her own, and Jazzy loved her like a mother.

"God, forgive me and please help me," Sally said softly. "You know I didn't have no idea there was another baby, that Jazzy had a sister."

Reve Sorrell might not be her sister, Sally told herself. *Could just be a coincidence that they look so much alike.* But if that DNA test they was having done proved them to be twins, then Jazzy was going to be asking a lot more questions. She'd want to know how it was possible that her aunt Sally hadn't known nothing about another baby.

All the lies she'd told Jazzy from the time she'd been a little girl would come back to haunt her—if that Sorrell gal turned out to be Jazzy's sister. She knew what Jazzy would say to her, could almost hear her.

"You told me that my mama came back home to you right before I was born, that her boyfriend had run out on her and she had no place else to go. You told me that you delivered me and that you sent for old Doc Webster a few days later to record my birth and check me and Mama to make sure we were all right. Isn't that so? Tell me, Aunt Sally, did you or did you not deliver another baby? Were you the one who threw my sister away?"

Them there DNA tests wouldn't lie. If they proved them

gals to be sisters, then Sally had some explaining to do. *If I tell Jazzy the truth, will she hate me? I just couldn't bear it if that gal hated me.*

Genny Sloan stopped suddenly on her morning trek from the greenhouse to her back porch. Although she'd seldom been able to control the visions that came to her, she had learned what signs to expect, signs that forewarned her.

Drudwyn paused at her side, then licked her hand.

"It's all right, boy. I think I can make it to the porch." Genny stroked the half-wolf dog's head. "But if I don't make it, you let Dallas know that I need him."

Drudwyn hurried ahead of her, then paused and waited at the door. Genny made it to the porch. Barely. She slumped down on the back steps and closed her eyes. She'd been born with the gift of sight, a God-given talent inherited from her grandma. More times than not, she'd found the gift could be a curse.

Lights swirled inside her head. Colors. Bright, warm colors. And then she heard Jazzy's laughter mixing with softer laughter. Another woman's laughter. Happiness. Beautiful happiness. Genny sensed a togetherness, a oneness, almost as if Jazzy and this other woman were a single entity. As that knowledge filled Genny's consciousness, she understood she was receiving energy from Jazzy and from Reve Sorrell. She didn't need to see the results of a DNA test to know they were twins. Identical twins. Individuals, yet forever linked from the moment of conception.

Suddenly the bright, cheerful lights inside Genny's mind darkened. Black clouds swirled about in her consciousness, completely obliterating the beauty and happiness. Fear. Anger. Hatred. Jealousy! An evil mind concealed by a mask of normalcy.

Danger! Jazzy and Reve were in terrible danger.

But from whom? Who possessed this dark, viciously

cruel heart? Who feared the truth? Who was willing to do anything—even kill—to keep the truth hidden?

Genny delved deeper into the black abyss, seeking the identity of this person, searching for any link between this evil and her dearest friend, Jazzy.

Oh, God, the hatred. Pure, wicked hatred.

"Genny!"

She heard Dallas's voice as if it came from far away.

"Damn it, Genny, come out of it. Now! You're going in too deep."

He shook her soundly.

Genny groaned. Her eyelids flew open. She gasped for air.

Dallas pulled her into his arms. "What the hell happened? I thought you promised me that you wouldn't go in that deep without my being there to—"

"I had to go as far as I could," she said as she rested her head on her husband's chest and wrapped her arms around his waist. "I had a vision about Jazzy and Reve Sorrell. I know they're twins." She lifted her head and looked at Dallas. "That was a vision filled with joy and light and beauty. But suddenly the darkness came. I—I'm not sure if there's a connection between Jazzy and Reve and the evil I sensed."

"The two visions might have nothing to do with each other," Dallas told her as he caressed her cheek with the back of his hand.

"Maybe not, but usually, when two visions overlap that way, they're somehow connected."

"But not always."

"No, not always."

Dallas lifted Genny into his arms and carried her into the house. She snuggled close, loving the protective feel of this man she loved above all others, more than life itself.

"You're awfully quiet," Dallas said. "Are you sure you're all right?"

"Yes, I'm all right. But Jazzy and Reve may be in grave danger."

CHAPTER 2

Veda MacKinnon had a slight hangover this morning, the second one this week. She'd realized months ago that she was drinking too much and had tried her best to cut back on the amount of alcohol she consumed. She had been succeeding to some extent, but twice this week she had succumbed to stress and worry. Outsiders might well wonder what she had to worry about considering she was married to one of the two richest men in Cherokee County. But her husband was one of her worries, as was their son and her husband's brother. And truth be told, her own brother had lately given her a reason for concern. If only she'd had a daughter, someone who could understand, could see her side of situations. But she was a lone female in a family of men—unless you counted the servants, and she didn't.

Donning her satin robe, Veda glanced at herself in the cheval mirror in her bedroom. God, she looked a fright. Dark circles under her eyes. Her mouth drooped with age. And without makeup, she looked every day of her sixty-eight years. She supposed she could do as Reba Upton did and have a facelift every five or six years, but instead she had opted to grow old gracefully.

Veda laughed softly.

Gracefully?

There had been a time when that adverb described the way she did everything. With grace and flair, with pomp and ceremony. When Farlan had brought her, as his bride, home to his parents' Victorian mansion in Cherokee Pointe, she'd been twenty-two. Slender. Beautiful. Charming. An Atlanta debutante. And Farlan MacKinnon had been the envy of every man in town.

Here she was forty-six years later, fat and wrinkled, with a husband who no longer loved her—if he ever had. A son who was sad and lonely, despite his successful career running MacKinnon Media. His childless marriage had ended in a bitter divorce years ago. She suspected that her brother, Dodd, was on the verge of ruining his life—over a woman! And then there was Wallace. God, there had always been Wallace. Poor old soul. The first time she'd met him, she'd actually been afraid of him. But it hadn't been her fault. After all, her husband's younger brother had been the first mentally handicapped person she'd ever known. Wallace had the IQ of a six-year-old and the sweet innocence, too.

Studying herself in the mirror, Veda decided she needed her hair cut. The ends were a bit frizzy and weren't curling under the way she liked. She'd worn her hair in the same neat chin-length pageboy most of her life, not changing as her hair went from dark brown to gray. And she really should lose a few pounds before the holidays. She tended to put on at least five pounds between Thanksgiving and New Year's every year and had to struggle half the year to shed those unwanted extra pounds. Of course on a woman who weighed in at one-ninety-five and stood barely five-three, what was five more pounds one way or the other?

Five pounds would mean weighing two hundred, she reminded herself. She'd sworn she'd never reach that two-hundred pound mark.

Veda made a detour into her dressing room. After running

a brush through her salt-and-pepper hair, she applied a touch
of blush and lipstick. *There, that's better,* she thought, then a
moment later wondered why she'd bothered. It wasn't as if
Farlan would notice. He hadn't paid much attention to her in
years. They shared the same bedroom, the same bed, but he
had not been a real husband to her in going on two years.
She could remember the exact date they'd last made love. It
had been on her sixty-sixth birthday.

If she didn't know better, she'd think he kept a mistress.
But not Farlan. Since that one woman, years ago, he'd been
as faithful as an old dog. To this day she blamed Dodd for
Farlan's one and only indiscretion. But that was the past,
water under the bridge. Best forgotten. After all, when she
had strayed a couple of times after she hit forty, Farlan had
forgiven her and they'd gone on as if nothing had happened.

As Veda made her way down the hall, she listened to the
familiar sounds of morning in her home. Although this enormous house had seemed alien to her when she'd come here
as Farlan's bride, she had soon renovated the place and made
it her own. Everything in this house—from the crystal and
china in the dining room to the imported soap in the bath-
rooms, from the landscaped grounds to the wicker furniture
in the sunroom—had Veda's personal stamp on it. She ruled
this house as if she were a queen. And she was. Queen Veda.
Everyone in Cherokee Pointe either respected her or feared
her just a little. She was known for being a vengeful bitch,
and that pleased her. Let that silly, skinny, blond Reba Upton
be the social grande dame. Who cared? She certainly didn't.
She much preferred being a power to be reckoned with. No
one crossed Veda Parnell MacKinnon without paying a steep
price.

When she entered the dining room, Farlan glanced up from
the morning paper. The *Knoxville News-Sentinel,* she noted,
not MacKinnon Media's local *Cherokee Pointe Herald.* He
made a habit of checking out other East Tennessee newspapers almost daily, such as the *News-Sentinel,* the *Cleveland*

Daily Banner, the *Chattanooga Times Free Press,* and the *Maysville Ledger Independent*.

"Good morning, my dear," Farlan said, his gaze quickly returning to the newspaper.

Brian rose from his chair and assisted her as she sat on the opposite end of the long dining table from her husband. Her son leaned down and kissed her cheek.

"You're looking lovely this morning, Mother."

She offered Brian a fragile smile. She loved her only child with all her heart. If only there was something she could do to make him happy. But he'd always been rather gloomy, even as a boy. Her father had been like that—a stern, gloomy man who had wandered in and out of her life after her parents' scandalous divorce when she was an infant. Then, when she was fourteen, he'd killed himself. Veda had been the one who'd found his body, there in her mother and step-father's library in their Atlanta home.

"Thank you." Veda patted Brian's ruddy cheek. Her son resembled her a great deal, which meant he was a handsome man. But the older he became, the more he looked like her father. Sometimes when she caught a glimpse of him out of the corner of her eye, she'd shiver, somehow feeling as if she had just seen a ghost.

"Something interesting in the News-Sentinel?" Brian asked Farlan as he returned to his seat.

Farlan grunted. "Nothing much."

"You seem quite absorbed in nothing much," Veda said, knowing her comment would evoke a reaction from her husband. It seemed the only way he'd talk to her these days was if she provoked him.

Farlan folded the newspaper and laid it on the table beside his plate, which was empty except for biscuit crumbs. He glanced at Veda, a somber expression on his face, his faded brown eyes skimming over her quickly before his gaze settled on his coffee cup. He seldom smiled at her anymore. In fact, he seldom smiled at all.

"The news seems to remain the same, just the people and places change," Farlan said. "A fire in a low-rent apartment complex in Oak Ridge, two policemen accused of racial profiling in Cleveland, the mayor in Harriman fighting with the city council and a prostitute's body fished from the river outside Loudon."

"Another one?" Veda said. "I seem to recall that about six or seven months ago, they found a prostitute's body in the river south of here. I don't remember where."

"Downstream from Watts Bar, I believe." Brian picked up his fork and speared the scrambled eggs in his plate.

"You have an excellent memory," Farlan said. "I used to. Never forgot anything. But lately . . . I suppose it comes with growing old."

Veda motioned to Abra, their cook, to pour her a cup of coffee. Abra Trumbo had been with the family for the past twenty-five years and was the only servant who actually lived on the premises; all the others, even the new housekeeper, Viv Lokey, chose to come in at seven each morning and required Sundays off. Servants just weren't what they used to be.

"You blame everything on old age," Veda said, her tone scolding. She didn't mean to always be so critical, but couldn't stop herself where Farlan was concerned. Over the past few years, it seemed they brought out the worst in each other. Perhaps they always had. She wasn't sure.

"Old age is—" Farlan began, but was interrupted by the rumble of thundering footsteps.

Wallace MacKinnon, a towering bear of a man, came barreling out of the kitchen and into the dining room, his eyes bright, his fat cheeks pink from having been exposed to the cool morning air. He still wore his heavy gray sweater, the one Veda had thrown away several times only to have him drag it out of the garbage again and again. With his faded overalls, ratty sweater and scuffed leather boots, her brother-in-law looked like a bum.

"She's here!" Wallace clapped his huge, calloused hands together, the way an excited child might do when exclaiming he'd just seen Santa Claus.

"Calm down," Farlan said. "Who's here?"

"Miss Jazzy's sister. I told you she was coming in from Chattanooga today, didn't I?" Wallace grinned. "I saw her over at the restaurant. She and Miss Jazzy were eating breakfast together. They look just alike."

"For the life of me, I can't understand why you go into town to eat breakfast at that restaurant so often when you could eat at home with your family." Veda frowned disapprovingly.

"Let him be," Farlan said. "He enjoys the company at Jasmine's. He's especially fond of Miss Jazzy, who he tells me is always very nice to him. And he gets a chance to run into all sorts of interesting people."

"Interesting indeed. As I recall, this Jazzy person is the town trollop." Like most other Cherokee County residents, Veda knew all about that woman's shameful reputation. "She was accused of killing Jamie Upton a few months back, wasn't she?"

"Jazzy Talbot didn't kill him. You know *as well* as I do that it turned out she was innocent." Farlan stood and walked over to his brother. "Take off your sweater and have a seat. Tell us all about seeing Jazzy and her sister." With Farlan's assistance, Wallace removed his heavy sweater, handed it to Abra and then sat next to Brian.

"They're twins. They look just alike," Wallace repeated. "Except Miss Jazzy's got short hair and Miss Reve's got long. Only she wears it done up. Everybody at the restaurant was talking about them and saying that they had to be sisters, that two people don't look that much alike unless they're twins."

Veda reached over and patted Wallace's hand. "Have you already eaten, dear? Or should I have Abra—"

"I ate over at the restaurant," Wallce replied. "I had pancakes."

"Very well, do go on with what you were saying." Veda offered her brother-in-law an approving smile.

"Must we hear all of this? You shouldn't encourage him, Mother," Brian said. "It's just the latest Cherokee Pointe gossip. Jazzy Talbot and some woman named Reve Sorrell may turn out to be long-lost sisters. Why should this concern us?"

"Why indeed?" Veda agreed.

"Reve Sorrell is Spencer Sorrell's daughter," Farlan said. "The Sorrels have been stockholders in MacKinnon Media for decades. I knew Sorrell slightly, but I never met his wife or his daughter. The man died ten years, ago and his wife took control of the family business, which his daughter now owns."

"If this woman is Spencer Sorrell's daughter, why on earth would she want to claim Jazzy Talbot as a long-lost sister?" Veda asked.

Brian scooted back his chair and stood. "As much as I hate to leave in the middle of such scintillating conversation, I'm afraid I need to go or I'll be late getting into the office this morning."

"Are you working on a Saturday morning?" Farlan asked.

"You often did, didn't you, Father?" Brian said. "I wouldn't want you to think I'm a slacker."

"Will you be home for dinner?" Veda smiled warmly at her son.

"I'll phone if I make other plans."

Once Brian had left the dining room, Veda sipped on her coffee and half listened to Wallace as he launched into a blow-by-blow account of his early morning venture into town, where he went almost every day to eat breakfast at Jasmine's. Her brother-in-law knew everyone in Cherokee County and associated with people of every social class. Since his teens, Wallace had spent his weekdays working up in the mountains at the Cherokee Pointe Nursery, now operated by the original owner's granddaughter, that odd young woman,

Genny Madoc, who'd recently married Dallas Sloan, the new chief of police. The girl was lovely—dark and exotic, a quarter-breed Cherokee. And said to possess the gift of sight, as her grandmother, the old witch woman, had.

"Veda? Veda!'"

Hearing Farlan calling her name, she snapped to attention and stared at her husband. "Yes, what is it?"

"Do you think perhaps we should invite Ms. Sorrell to stay with us while she's in Cherokee Pointe?"

"What?"

"I'm simply thinking along the same lines you were," he told her. "After all, Spencer Sorrell was a business associate, if not a friend. And his daughter is unlikely to find anyone, other than the Uptons, in these parts who are her social equal. She'll have no place to stay other than one of those dreadful cabins. I hardly think she'll choose to stay with Jazzy Talbot, at least not unless they do find out they're siblings."

"How old is Ms. Sorrell?" Veda asked.

"How old? I have no idea. The same age as Jazzy Talbot, I suppose, if they believe they're twins." Farlan rubbed his chin. "I'd say Jazzy is in her late twenties, early thirties." He eyed Veda speculatively. "What sort of crazy notions have you got going on in that silly head of yours?"

"I don't think it's silly to want to see our son married and providing us with grandchildren, do you?"

"If you decide to invite Ms. Sorrell to stay with us, do not"—he stressed the word *not*—"try to play matchmaker for Brian and her. Do I make myself clear?"

"Brian needs a girlfriend," Wallace piped in. "Ever since Miss Genny got married, he's been so sad. He doesn't like Miss Jazzy, but I think Veda's right—Brian might like Miss Reve. She's awfully pretty. Not quite as friendly as Miss Jazzy, but—"

Farlan shot to his feet, the move silencing his brother and bringing a soft gasp from Veda. "God help me!"

Farlan marched out of the room and went straight to his

study. Veda knew without following him where he'd gone. He holed up in what he considered his private domain every morning and she'd yet to work up the courage to interrupt him. Though a good man at heart, her husband had a terrible temper.

"Is Farlan mad at me?" Wallace asked.

Veda patted his hand again. "No, dear, no. He's upset with me. But he never stays angry with me, so don't you worry about it." Although she felt more like crying, she smiled. "Later on, why don't you come outside with me and we'll work in the flower garden. I always count on you to help me. You've learned so much about gardening over the years. First from Melva Mae Butler and in recent years from Genny."

Veda loved gardening. It was one of the few passions left her in life. She'd been born with the proverbial green thumb, as had her brother-in-law. Most of the time, she considered Wallace a nuisance, a burden she and Farlan had to bear. But she genuinely enjoyed his company when they worked together in the yard.

"Veda, how's it possible for Miss Jazzy and Miss Reve to be twin sisters and not grow up together or even know each other?" Wallace asked.

"That's a complicated question with a very complicated answer."

"If you explained, do you think I'd understand?"

"Probably. It's just that I really don't know anything about it. Let's just say that when they were born—twins are usually born within minutes of each other—for some reason their mother couldn't keep them . . ." Veda grew silent as ancient memories invaded her thoughts. Painful memories.

"Yeah, go on. If their mother couldn't keep them, what?"

Veda cleared her throat. "The girls would have been given to other people, people who couldn't have their own child and wanted a baby to raise."

Wallace's face screwed up in a pondering frown. "Is that what folks call adoption?"

"Yes, that's right."

"Miss Jazzy ain't adopted," Wallace said. "But I heard somebody say that Miss Reve's mama and papa adopted her when she was a baby."

Not wanting to continue the conversation about babies—twins in particular—Veda rose from her chair. "I'm suddenly not very hungry. I—I think I'll take my coffee"— she lifted the cup and saucer —"into the parlor and catch the morning news on WMMK."

"I'm sorry, Veda," Wallace said, his voice trembling with emotion. "I just remembered that talking about babies makes you sad."

"It's all right, dear. I—I'm perfectly fine. I'll see you after a while. We'll work in the garden together later this morning."

She escaped from her brother-in-law's scrutiny as quickly as she could. She hated the way he often stared at her with such pity in his eyes. The poor old fool had such a kind heart. Wallace wasn't very bright, but he wasn't totally stupid either. Since he'd always lived with them, he'd been around when she had suffered miscarriage after miscarriage, trying again and again to have another child, not wanting Brian to be raised without at least one sibling. Perhaps if he'd had younger brothers and sisters, if she'd been able to fill this house with more joy and laughter, her son wouldn't be such an unhappy man now. And maybe her husband would still love her.

The mention of the word twins shouldn't bother me the way it does. After all, just because Jazzy Talbot and Reve Sorrell might turn out to be long-lost twin sisters really has nothing to do with me, with what happened thirty years ago.

Are you sure? Are you one hundred percent sure?

No, I'm not sure. And that's the problem. I don't have any idea exactly how old Jazzy Talbot is, and I need to know. If she's older or younger than thirty, then I can breathe a sigh of relief. However, if she's the right age, perhaps I should find out more about her and Reve Sorrell.

Do you think they could be those twin girls?

Of course not. Those twins are dead. They've been dead for thirty years.

You didn't see them dead, did you? You didn't actually kill them yourself.

No, but—

You trusted someone else to dispose of them. You should have done the job yourself. That way you could have been certain.

They're dead. They have to be dead.

And if they're not? What if Jazzy and Reve Sorrell turn out to be those twins?

Then I'll have no choice but to kill them. No one can ever find out the truth.

CHAPTER 3

The DNA samples had been taken quickly and easily—just a swab in the mouth. Such a simple thing that would determine if she and Reve Sorrell were indeed sisters. If it turned out to be true—that they were twins—the fact would irrevocably change their lives. Everything she had believed since she was a child would prove to be lies. How could she deal with knowing her aunt Sally had been deliberately lying to her all her life? How was that possible? She knew, deep inside her, that Aunt Sally loved her with all her heart. The two of them shared a mother/daughter bond stronger than most.

Don't get ahead of yourself. Wait for the results. And even if you two are twins, maybe Aunt Sally will have an explanation as to why she never told you about having a sister.

But could there be a good reason for throwing away a baby, for tossing her into a Dumpster and leaving her for dead?

The few times since she'd met Reve that she'd brought up the subject to Aunt Sally, her aunt had sworn to her that Corrine Talbot had given birth to only one child, one baby girl, and that baby was Jazzy.

"I'm told we should have the results within a week," Galvin MacNair said as he walked with them into the waiting room. He smiled warmly at Jazzy and then at Reve. "Your paying for a private lab to do the test will speed things up immeasurably."

"What good is money if you can't use it?" Reve said, but she didn't smile.

Jazzy had been raised dirt poor, watching Aunt Sally scratch and scrape for every dime, so she'd grown up thinking all of life's problems could be solved with money. She had longed to be rich. Rich like the Uptons and the MacKinnons, Cherokee County's two families worth multi-millions. There had been a time when her dream had been to marry Jamie Upton, the heir to a vast fortune, but that dream had never come true. Thank God!

Jamie's wealth had not made him happy, and it certainly hadn't helped make him a better man than those without so much money. He'd been a heartless bastard. And now here she was practically engaged to his cousin, the new heir to the Upton fortune. But Caleb McCord was as different from Jamie as night from day. He hadn't been raised in the lap of luxury, hadn't even known about his mother's wealthy family when he'd grown up on the streets of Memphis. But now he'd been crowned the heir apparent by his grandparents— by Big Jim and Miss Reba. As much as she wanted to believe that Caleb's new station in life wouldn't change him, she lived in fear that it would.

Jazzy glanced at Reve and wondered if she was happy with all her millions. She sure didn't act like a happy person. To her way of thinking, her might-be twin was an uptight, bossy snob. How was it possible that two people who shared the same genes were nothing alike?

But looking at Reve, Jazzy once again got that gut-tightening reaction. The woman was her spitting image. Except for a few minor differences. Reve was slightly taller, maybe fifteen or twenty pounds heavier and she didn't wear green-colored contacts over her brown eyes or dye her auburn hair a bright red.

"You'll call us the minute you receive the results," Reve said, her words a commanding statement, not a question.

"I certainly will," Dr. MacNair assured her.

"Thank you." Reve shook hands with Galvin, then turned to leave.

"Thanks," Jazzy added and rushed to catch up with her sister.

Damn, don't do this. She'd already begun thinking of Reve Sorrell as her sister. And it was apparent to anyone with the least bit of perception that the last thing Ms. Sorrell wanted was to find out she was biologically linked to a person like Jazzy Talbot.

"Hold up, will you?" Jazzy grabbed Reve's arm just as she headed out the door of the Cherokee Pointe Clinic.

Reve skewered her with a narrowed gaze. "What?"

"Are you staying in town until we get the results or—"

"I'm staying."

Jazzy released her hold on Reve's arm. "Where?"

"I reserved one of your cabins."

Jazzy shrugged. "I see. You could have stayed with me."

"I didn't want to inconvenience you."

Reve wasn't a very good liar. Just a hint of color darkened her cheeks. Jazzy knew right away that her look-alike hadn't even entertained the idea of staying with her.

"If you need anything while you're here—"

"I think we need to become better acquainted," Reve said. "Perhaps we should have lunch together today and figure out the best way to approach this problem."

Jazzy swung open the door and held it. "You first."

Just as Reve exited the clinic and set foot on the sidewalk, Jazzy directly behind her, she came face to face with the one person in Cherokee Pointe she'd told Jazzy she hoped she would never see again.

Jacob Butler, all six-feet, five-inches of him, blocked Reve's path. The man's size alone was intimidating, but adding to his tough-guy image were the hard, chiseled features, the pensive green eyes and the long black hair. His appearance screamed dangerous savage.

"Morning, Jacob." Jazzy tried to control the grin spreading across her face. She glanced from Reve to Jacob. She wasn't sure whose expression conveyed more shocked dismay. These two had despised each other on sight when they'd met back last spring. "You remember Reve Sorrell, don't you?"

Jacob tipped his Stetson. "Ma'am."

Reve's spine stiffened. "Sheriff."

When Jacob tried to walk past them, Jazzy jumped in front of him. "What's your hurry?"

"I need to talk to Dr. MacNair. I've got an appointment."

"Are you sick?"

"You sure are nosey," Jacob said.

"You know me—always concerned about my fellow man."

Jacob's lips twitched in a hint of a smile. Ever since they'd been kids, she'd been able to make Jacob smile, even when Genny couldn't. And he loved Genny more than anybody on earth, her being his cousin who'd been raised like a sister to him.

"I'm setting up a time for flu shots for all my employees," Jacob explained. "It's getting to be that time of year. With the small force I have at the sheriff's department, I can't afford to have anybody laid up with the flu for a week."

"I hear your staff is going to be decreasing by one pretty soon," Jazzy said. "Just as soon as Tewanda gets her law degree and passes the bar."

Jacob nodded. "Yeah, and we're all right proud of her, but we're sure going to miss her. She's been a topnotch deputy."

"Hey, if you're not doing anything special for lunch today, why don't you come over to Jasmine's and join Reve and me." She swallowed a chuckle and clamped her teeth together to keep from laughing out loud. "We're going to get acquainted.

You know . . . just in case we turn out to be sisters. You could fill her in on what I was like as a kid. And you could give her some insight into me as a woman." She turned to Reve. "You know Jacob and I even dated for a while, and I'm here to tell you that this man"— Jazzy wound her arm around Jacob's arm —"is one great kisser."

Reve gasped. Jazzy laughed. Jacob seared Jazzy with his tight gaze.

"Ah, lighten up, you two," Jazzy told them. "Relax. I'm just having some fun with y'all."

"I'm afraid I don't see the humor in this situation," Reve said.

"Look, I don't know why you two decided instantly that you can't stand each other, but we need to do something to change this. Right now. If Reve *is* my sister, I can't have one of my oldest and dearest friends and my newly found twin hating each other."

"I haven't got time for this," Jacob said and tried to move past Jazzy.

She stood stubbornly in his way. "Agree to have lunch with us and I'll—"

"I have other plans for lunch," he said.

"Then supper tonight—you two with Caleb and me."

"Don't do this," Jacob told her, a strained expression on his face.

"I'm not available for dinner," Reve said.

Jazzy heaved a deep sigh. "Okay, I give up. For now. But don't think this is the end of it." She moved aside and allowed Jacob to pass.

Once they were alone, Reve snapped around and glared at Jazzy. "I do not—under any circumstances—wish to be engaged socially with Sheriff Butler. I'd appreciate it if you'd give up any plans you have that involve my becoming better acquainted with that man."

Jazzy let out a long, low whistle. "He really punched all your buttons, didn't he?"

"All the wrong buttons."

Jazzy shook her head. "I just can't figure it out. I've never seen Jacob have a negative effect on a woman before. Usually, a woman takes one look at him and swoons at his feet. After all, honey, let's face it—the man is to die for."

"I'm afraid I fail to see whatever it is that makes him so irresistible."

"You're kidding, right?"

"Let's end this ridiculous conversation." Reve started walking toward her Jaguar in the side parking lot next to the clinic. "I can drop you back by Jasmine's, if you'd like. I made plans for an early check-in at my cabin. I'd like to get settled and freshen up before lunch."

"I'll walk," Jazzy said. "It's only a few blocks."

"Very well. What time shall I meet you for lunch?"

"How about one o'clock?"

Reve nodded agreement.

Jazzy didn't press the matter—getting Reve and Jacob together—but she had no intention of letting it drop. She suspected that although Reve disliked Jacob and probably found him intimidating, she wasn't as immune to his obvious masculine charms as she professed to be. Maybe Reve just didn't know how to deal with unwanted sexual attraction. And unless she missed her guess, that was what was going on between Jacob and Reve.

Jazzy couldn't contain her laughter, amused at the thought of sexual sparks igniting between Jacob and Reve. Talk about a mismatched couple.

"Dare I ask what you find so amusing?" Reve asked.

"Nothing really. I was just thinking how you stick out like a sore thumb around here. Unless you hobnob with the Uptons or the MacKinnons, all you're going to run across around here are just common folks. Hill people. Rednecks. And a few breeds, like Jacob and Genny."

"I suspected the sheriff was part Native American. Doesn't he mind being referred to as a breed?"

"He and Genny are both a quarter Cherokee and damn proud of it. And I'm practically family to them, so my referring to them that way is the same as the two of them calling themselves breeds."

"At least they know their heritage. Whereas you and I . . ." Reve let the sentence trail off into silence.

"You really are worried about it, aren't you? Poor Reve. What if you find out I'm your twin and that our parents were really white trash? Me, I've got nothing to lose. I've always been white trash. But you—"

"I am a Sorrell, regardless of my genetic heritage."

"Yeah, I guess you are, aren't you?"

Jazzy turned and walked away, not glancing back, but sensing that Reve was watching her. She wanted to be friends with this woman, to find some common bond between them other than the likelihood they were sisters. But the chances of that happening appeared to fall into the snowball's chance in hell category.

Becky Olmstead had graduated from high school in the spring and was working as a gofer at MacKinnon Media headquarters to earn enough money to pay for college. At least, that was what she'd told her mother. But she had no intention of going to college, and her job here was just a smoke screen to keep her old lady off her back. Combining what she earned here with what she picked up at night on her other job, she should be able to leave Cherokee Pointe before New Year's and begin a new life in Nashville. More than anything, she wanted to get away from home—from her nagging mother and her mean, drunken stepfather. If anyone had told her two years ago that she would have gone from being a teenager who just liked to have fun, to one of half a dozen hookers in Cherokee Pointe, she wouldn't have believed it. But when, at sixteen, she'd been offered fifty bucks to go down on a guy, she hadn't been able to refuse such easy money.

If folks knew the men she'd screwed during the past couple of years, they'd be surprised. Hell, they'd be shocked. Her first john, the one who'd given her fifty bucks to give him a blow job, was old enough to be her grandfather and was a prominent citizen. He still came to her occasionally, but not so often lately. As a matter of fact, she hadn't serviced him in nearly two months. But he wasn't the only big spender. Not by a long shot. Actually, if she wasn't just a little bit afraid of getting into some bad trouble, she'd try blackmail. She sure could ruin a few lives if she named names.

Nah, better not go that route, she told herself. She'd been saving steadily for her big escape, and pretty soon she'd have a sizable nest egg, enough to live on until she could hook up with the right people in Music City. Who knew, could be she'd wind up married to some famous country singer and get to live in one of those fancy mansions that would put the Upton house and the MacKinnon house to shame.

"Becky! Go over to Jasmine's and pick up Mr. MacKinnon's lunch, right now!" Glenda Motte, Brian MacKinnon's secretary, called out to her.

"Right away, Ms. Motte."

Becky hurried to the employee's lounge, where she'd left her jacket that morning, and glanced at the wall clock above the coffeemaker. She hoped the meal was ready when she got to Jasmine's; otherwise, Mr. MacKinnon would take a strip off Ms. Motte's hide. The man was a tyrant. She figured that nobody who worked for him really liked him. But who had the balls to tell the man to go to hell? He ruled over MacKinnon Media like a damned dictator, and if anybody crossed him, he saw to it that they lost their job. Since starting work here in June, she'd had to run errands throughout the complex that housed the *Cherokee Pointe Herald* as well as WMMK TV and radio stations, so she'd heard plenty of grumbling about the big boss.

"He's not half the man his father is."

"Farlan MacKinnon is one of the best men I know. A fair and honest man. Brian runs a poor second best to his father."

"Brian is such a shithead. Too bad he's not more like the old man. Or even more like that loony uncle of his. At least Wallace MacKinnon is likable."

Becky buttoned up her jacket as she rode the elevator from the fifth floor to the first. The MacKinnon Building was the tallest building in town, with the boss's office taking up a large section of the fifth floor. When she went outside, the autumn sun warmed her despite the chilly north wind stirring up leaves from the sidewalk and scattering debris. She quickened her pace as she sauntered up the street.

He watched Becky Olmstead as she strode up the street, her slender hips swaying seductively in her skin-tight jeans. The girl was a tramp. None of her fellow employees at MacKinnon Media knew what she did to earn extra money at night. But he knew. He knew all about her. For months now, he'd made a point of learning everything he could about Becky without drawing any attention to himself.

He didn't intend to do anything about his attraction to her, even though he couldn't stop himself from thinking about her, from watching her. Of course, the first thing he'd noticed about her had been her red hair. It wasn't quite the same shade as Dinah's, but then again, she didn't always choose to come back as a redhead. However, when she came back as a blonde or a brunette, he always asked her to dye her hair. And she always obliged.

If Becky didn't live here in Cherokee County, he would approach her, get to know her and see if there was a possibility that Dinah might come back through her this time. Dinah always came to him in the bodies of women who reminded him of her, women who attracted him physically. But whenever he was drawn to a hometown woman, he never acted on that attraction. He didn't want to run the risk of becoming involved with someone this close to home. Over the years, he'd always found Dinah outside Cherokee County. In Knoxville. In Sevierville. In Johnson City. In Kingsport. In Oak Ridge. Even down in Cleveland and Chattanooga. And once as far east as Asheville, North Carolina.

But watching Becky, his gaze focused on the sexy way she walked, his penis grew hard. He closed his eyes and imagined what it would feel like to be inside her. He ran his hand over the fly of his slacks and sighed.

He'd have to make another trip out of town soon and see if he could find Dinah. If he couldn't find her, he could at least ease the ache with some other whore. But it was never the same with another woman. Never as satisfying. He could fuck a dozen other women and still be hungry for what only Dinah could give him.

He ran the tip of his tongue over his lips, imagining what Becky Olmstead would taste like if he kissed her, if he sucked her tits, if he delved his tongue between her parted thighs.

Groaning inwardly, he turned around and looked the other way. After taking several deep breaths, he managed to control the raging hunger inside him. He would have to wait for satisfaction. There was no way he could leave town again so soon, but at the first opportunity, he'd go back to Knoxville and find himself a willing woman.

And if he was very lucky, he'd find Dinah again.

CHAPTER 4

Dora opened the front door of the Uptons' antebellum mansion situated a half mile off the winding road leading up the mountain. She offered Caleb a warm, welcoming smile when he entered the massive black-and-white marble-floored foyer.

Although both Miss Reba and Big Jim had accepted him as their grandson and had invited him to move in with them, Caleb still didn't feel as if he really belonged—in this house or to the Upton family. He'd been born and raised in Memphis, never knowing his father and somehow managing to survive as the child of a drug-addicted mother. It wasn't until Melanie Upton was dying that she told Caleb who her parents were and where they lived. She'd begged him to go to the Uptons then, when he'd been sixteen. But back then, he hadn't wanted anything to do with people he didn't know. Up until then he'd been taking care of himself by cheating, lying and stealing, doing whatever it took to stay alive and keep just below the child welfare department's radar. Despite all his mother's faults, he'd loved her and had done whatever he thought was necessary not only to stay with her, but to take care of her. In their case, the parental roles had become reversed when Caleb was about seven.

"They're waiting for you in the breakfast room. Go on in. I've made a big pot of chicken stew and baked a carrot cake, fresh this morning."

Dora, the Uptons' faithful housekeeper, had taken an immediate liking to Caleb the first time Big Jim had brought him home. But on their very first meeting, she'd issued him a warning. "That Jamie was a no-good devil, but we loved him. Miss Reba most of all. He broke her heart over and over again. I suspect you ain't nothing like Jamie. But I'm telling you now, if you ever hurt Miss Reba, you'll have to answer to me."

The last thing he ever wanted to do was hurt either of his newly found grandparents. But he'd realized right off the bat that his grandmother was a master manipulator, a strong-willed woman who liked to rule the roost. Although Big Jim was more laid-back, not as snooty or judgmental, the old man was used to running things his way. Caleb guessed that kind of authoritarian mind-set came from being born rich and powerful.

"One thing I've found out since I've been getting to know the grandparents is that their most valuable asset is you, Dora."

Giggling like a child, Dora blushed, then swatted Caleb on the arm and said, "You do have that in common with your cousin Jamie—you know how to flatter a woman."

"My flattery is sincere," Caleb assured her, hating to be compared to his late cousin in any way, shape, form or fashion.

"Yes, I believe it is. And that's the difference. One of many that makes you a far better man."

While Caleb headed toward the breakfast room, Dora turned and went into the kitchen. The moment Miss Reba saw him, her face lit up, her lips curving into a broad smile and her eyes bright with excitement. Big Jim eased up from his chair and threw out his hand.

"We're delighted you could join us today," Miss Reba said.

"Good to see you, son. Good to see you." Big Jim took Caleb's hand in a firm, man-to-man shake.

"You just don't come around nearly enough." His grandmother's tone was friendly yet scolding. "I do wish you'd reconsider coming here to live with us. We've got so much room. You could have your own suite. We'd redo Jamie's old rooms for you or—"

"Leave the boy be." Big Jim indicated one of the large oak chairs at the table. "Sit, sit. Dora's fixed some of her world famous chicken stew. You're in for a real treat."

Caleb sat between his grandparents at the large oak table. "I'll do my best to visit more often, Miss Reba. But I have a job and a girlfriend that both require a great deal of my time."

He sensed rather than saw his grandmother stiffen at the mention of a girlfriend. Reba Upton had forbidden her grandson, Jamie, to marry Jazzy when they'd been teenagers and he'd gotten Jazzy pregnant. And although Jazzy had miscarried the child and Jamie had allowed his grandmother to dictate who he could and could not marry, Jamie and Jazzy had continued an on-again, off-again affair for years. Not only did his grandmother's disapproval stand between Jazzy and Caleb, but so did his cousin's memory. Yet he hoped that with each passing day, Jazzy's memories of Jamie would dim and the time would come when she would trust him with her heart. Jamie had used her and disappointed her so often that Jazzy was afraid to believe in another man, especially another Upton heir. The fact that Miss Reba staunchly opposed his and Jazzy's relationship sure didn't help his efforts to convince Jazzy to marry him.

"You shouldn't be wasting your time working as a bouncer in that awful place," Miss Reba told him. "Jim is eager to have you come into the family business. He should have retired completely years ago. Someday in the not too distant future, Upton Dairies will be yours, so you should be learning the business now."

That was another thing he hadn't quite gotten used to—

being the only heir to a fortune worth at least fifty or sixty million, maybe more. The Uptons had originally been dairy farmers, and he supposed that's what they still were. But right after World War I, Big Jim's grandfather and father had expanded the local business, and by the time World War II ended, Upton Dairies was the biggest producer of milk and dairy products in the state of Tennessee. With shrewd investments and by branching out, the family's wealth had increased immeasurably over the years. Big Jim had recently taken Caleb aside and explained all this to him.

"Good God, woman, will you stop pressuring the boy. Let him get used to being our grandson before you start trying to run his life."

Reba gasped dramatically. "I'm offended that you'd accuse me of such a thing. I'd never try to—"

Big Jim laughed, the sound deep and robust. "Lord love you, honey, you honestly can't see your own faults. Never could." Not giving his wife time for a quick rebuttal, Jim reached out and slapped Caleb on the arm. "Something tells me that this young man won't be so easily manipulated. From what I've seen, he has a mind and a will of his own. He'll do whatever the hell he pleases—about Upton Dairies and about Jazzy Talbot."

"How is Jasmine?" Miss Reba asked, her voice strained.

Caleb was genuinely surprised that his grandmother had even inquired about Jazzy. He knew how much effort it had taken her to say Jazzy's name in a civil manner, considering how she—no matter how irrational the idea was—held Jazzy partly responsible for Jamie's death.

"Jazzy's just fine," Caleb replied. "Thank you for asking, Miss Reba."

"I do wish you'd call me Big Mama."

"I feel more comfortable calling you Miss Reba, at least for now."

"Miss Reba and Big Jim are fine with us," Jim said. "So, Jazzy's doing fine, huh? You'll have to bring her out here to dinner one evening." He shot Reba a warning glare. "Won't he, honey? We'd be pleased to have her."

Caleb glanced at his grandmother and barely restrained the laughter bubbling up in his throat. Miss Reba had gone ghost white, her perfect pink mouth formed a startled oval and her big blue eyes widened as round as saucers.

"I doubt Jasmine Talbot would accept an invitation to dine with us," Reba said. "Considering our past history."

"She might." Caleb looked pleadingly at his grandmother. "If you telephoned her and invited her yourself."

Miss Reba swallowed, took a deep breath and offered him a weak smile. "Would you like that, dear? Would it please you?"

"Yes, ma'am. It would please me a great deal. I'd very much like it if the woman I love and my grandmother could get along."

"You—you love her?"

"Yes, ma'am, I do."

"I see."

Jim sat quietly, watching and listening. And apparently waiting to find out what the outcome of this exchange would be.

"You might as well know that sooner or later, I'll wear Jazzy down and she'll agree to marry me." Caleb kept his gaze fixed determinedly on his grandmother's pale face. "And there's nothing anyone can say or do to stop me from making her my wife. Do you understand what I'm saying, Miss Reba?"

"Yes, I understand perfectly."

"I hope you do because I wouldn't want to ever have to choose between you and her. I've just found you and Big Jim. I'd sure hate to lose you."

"You aren't going to lose me—lose us," Miss Reba said with firm conviction. "I'll telephone Jasmine later today and invite her to Sunday dinner tomorrow."

Grinning, feeling as if he'd won a major battle, Caleb got

up, walked over to his grandmother and kissed her on the cheek. "Thank you."

Tears glistened in Miss Reba's eyes. Curling her small hand around his arm, she pursed her lips and returned his kiss.

"Oh, by the way, you might want to invite Reve Sorrell, too," Caleb said. "She arrived in Cherokee Pointe earlier today and is going to be staying for a while. Dr. MacNair took DNA samples this morning and sent them off. We should know within a week if Jazzy and Reve are twins."

"That's a mighty peculiar thing," Big Jim said. "Those two gals finding out that they could be sisters. Has Jazzy questioned her aunt Sally again about the circumstances surrounding her birth?"

"No, not lately, but the old woman has sworn that Jazzy was the only baby born to her sister, Corrine."

"Where is Ms. Sorrell staying?" Reba asked. "Surely not with Jasmine. I mean, the two hardly know each other and certainly have nothing in common."

Caleb pulled away from his grandmother and returned to his seat. "No, she and Jazzy haven't reached the sisterly bonding point. Yet. Reve is renting a place from Cherokee Cabin Rentals."

"I should invite her to stay here," Reba said and elicited surprised looks from Caleb and Big Jim.

"Why ever would you do that?" Jim asked.

"Because Ms. Sorrell was a friend of Jamie's. And her parents were part of the same social circle as the Wallaces and the Grambrells. Eileen Wallace and I were sorority sisters. Anna Lee Grambrell and I have served on numerous Republican fund raisers statewide. And I'm almost certain that I met Lesley Sorrell not only at a couple of those fundraisers, but at Eileen's daughter's wedding, too."

"Then by all means, considering how closely our families are connected, you must call Ms. Sorrell immediately and invite her to stay with us." Big Jim chuckled, quite pleased with his own sarcastically humorous assessment of the situation.

"I don't appreciate your facetious comment," Reba told her husband. "I'd be remiss in my duties as a social leader in Cherokee County if I didn't extend an invitation to Ms. Sorrell." She eyed Caleb quizzically. "Do Reve Sorrell and Jasmine Talbot look just alike?"

Caleb grinned. "Yes, except for a few superficial differences. Why do you ask?"

"Oh, no reason." Reba sighed, then a genuine smile spread across her face. "I'll telephone Jasmine and invite her and Ms. Sorrell to join us for Sunday dinner. Tomorrow, when they're here, I'll issue Ms. Sorrell an invitation to stay with us. I'm sure she'll find living here preferable to staying in one of those dinky little cabins. A lady of her breeding must find roughing it quite intolerable."

Big Jim chuckled under his breath, then winked at Caleb before looking directly at his wife. "I know you, Reba Upton. You're up to something. You wouldn't by any chance think that since those two gals look just alike, they could be interchangeable as far as Caleb is concerned, would you?"

"I have no idea what you're talking about." She feigned innocence.

"I'm talking about your thinking Reve Sorrell is socially acceptable and would make a suitable granddaughter-in-law."

"Why, Jim, what a thing to say."

Caleb reached out and grasped his grandmother's hand. "I'm sure you'd never believe something so foolish, would you, Miss Reba? I'm in love with Jazzy, with everything about her. And that includes a lot more than her physical appearance. You could parade a dozen look-alikes in front of me and not one of them would ever measure up to Jazzy. After all, if a man who looked just like Big Jim showed up, you wouldn't automatically fall out of love with Big Jim and in love with this other man, would you?"

"No, of course not. I—"

Dora came bustling into the breakfast room, placed a china soup cauldron on the table, then hurried back to the kitchen and returned with a plate of cornbread and a pitcher of iced tea. "Save room for dessert."

"Let's enjoy our lunch," Big Jim said. "This afternoon, while you're issuing invitations"—he smiled at Miss Reba—"I want to show Caleb around the stables and maybe the two of us will take a ride out over the farm."

"A ride as in a horseback ride?" Caleb asked.

"Have you never been horseback riding, son?" Jim cocked his eyebrows ever so slightly.

"Nope. I was raised a city boy. I spent a lot of time riding a motorcycle, but I've never been on a horse."

"Then it's high time you learned how," Jim said. "The best way in the world for a man to look over his land is from horseback."

Caleb groaned inwardly. This business of being the Upton heir was going to take some getting used to. He just hoped he could find a way to make his grandparents' golden years happy and still live his life on his own terms.

On the ride up the mountain, Reve let Jazzy do most of the talking, just as she had during their lunch together at Jazzy's downtown Cherokee Pointe restaurant, Jasmine's. This was yet another striking difference between them—Jazzy was an extrovert, who could and did talk nonstop. Apparently the woman never met a stranger. On the other hand, Reve was more of an introvert; and although she enjoyed good conversation, she never talked just to be talking.

Reve wished she could relax around Jazzy, wished she could look at the woman and not cringe at the thought that they were probably twin sisters. Jazzy had done nothing to make Reve dislike her. The exact opposite was true. She seemed determined to make Reve feel comfortable about their potential relationship as siblings and was working over-time to achieve that goal.

Maybe she could learn to like her. She really haven't given her a chance. Whenever she looked at Jazzy, all she saw was the woman's wild, bright red hair, her abundance of dangling jewelry and her rock star clothes. And listening to Jazzy's silly, nonstop chatter about nothing that she could even vaguely relate to made Reve assume Jazzy was unsophisticated and uncouth. The words redneck, hillbilly and white trash instantly came to mind. Besides, Reve couldn't quite get past her private investigator's initial report that concluded Jasmine Talbot was considered the town tramp. However, Reve had learned at an early age that some things were not what they seemed. She couldn't shake the feeling that Jazzy was sorely misjudged by the local populace. *Is that really a gut feeling?* she asked herself. *Or is it that you just want to believe Jazzy isn't a slut?*

As Jazzy maneuvered her red Jeep up the steep driveway to the side of Genny Sloan's house, Reve took in her sur-roundings. The large old farmhouse sat way up off the road on a rise, nestled into the mountain. Woods surrounded the place on three sides. Colorful, towering trees reached high into the clear blue sky. An old rock-wall fence marked the front yard and rock steps led from the road to the rock side-walk. Already, in mid-October, the foliage had begun chang-ing from green to deep, vivid shades of red, yellow and orange. Leaves covered the ground and pine cones dotted the land-scape. Jazzy pulled her vehicle alongside the SUV parked in the drive.

"There's Genny," Jazzy said. "She's expecting us. You'll like her. Everybody does."

"She's the . . . the psychic, isn't she?" Glancing through the windshield, Reve saw Genny standing on the wide front porch, waiting for them. "She's lovely."

The woman was breathtakingly exotic, with creamy tan skin, long, straight, jet-black hair and a small, slender body.

"Yeah, Genny's a beauty." Jazzy opened the driver's door. "She and Jacob have similar coloring, but Genny looks a lot like her Granny Butler and I'm told Jacob looks a great deal like their Grandpa Butler."

"Oh, yes, I'd almost forgotten that Genny and the sheriff are first cousins." *Don't dislike Genny Sloan just because she's Sheriff Butler's cousin,* Reve told herself. It wouldn't be fair to assume this woman was anything like her unpleasant relative.

"Actually, they're more like brother and sister. They were raised together after their mothers were killed in a car wreck when they were just kids." Jazzy got out of the Jeep, then motioned to Reve. "Come on. Genny's eager to meet you."

Reluctantly, Reve emerged from the vehicle. She had tried to beg off making this trip up the mountain to meet Jazzy's best friend, but Jazzy had insisted. "I've asked her to give us a reading," Jazzy had said. "She might be able to pick up on whether or not we're twins. And if she can, I'm hoping she'll be able to help us find out what happened when we were born."

Reve was not looking forward to this visit—to becoming acquainted with a backwoods witch. For the sake of civility, she'd do her best not to voice her opinion on people who professed to have a sixth sense. But if Genny started foretelling her future, she'd have to find a courteous way to let Genny know she wasn't interested in any predictions or prophecies.

"Come on. Don't drag your feet," Jazzy said. She reached out and grabbed Reve's arm. "You act like you're going to your own hanging. I promise you won't regret coming here with me today."

"I'll hold you to that." Reve tugged free, but let her look-alike lead the way.

Genny scurried off the porch and met them in the yard. She hugged Jazzy with great affection. "It's turned out to be such a gorgeous day, I've set up apple cider and tea on the porch. And I baked one of Granny's apple dapple cakes. I'll bring some out later."

"Genny, this is Reve Sorrell." Jazzy presented Reve as if she were introducing her to royalty. "Reve, this is my dearest friend on earth, Genny Madoc Sloan."

Reve extended her hand. "Nice to meet you, Mrs. Sloan."

"My goodness, you two do look remarkably alike." Genny grasped Reve's hand firmly. "Please, call me Genny." She shook Reve's hand, then held it for a brief moment.

Reve jerked her hand away.

"Sorry, I didn't mean . . ." Genny smiled. "Most people don't mind if I probe just a little. And I must admit that I'm curious about you."

"Did you pick up on anything?" Jazzy asked.

Reve glared at Jazzy. She wanted to beg them not to include her in any of their forays into the psychic world, a world in which Reve did not believe.

"Only that Ms. Sorrell isn't comfortable making this visit." Genny spread her arm out in invitation. "Why don't we go sit on the porch and relax?"

Be polite, Reve told herself. *Make an effort to get along with these people.* "Genny, you must call me Reve. And I apologize for—"

"No need to apologize," Genny said. "You don't know me and you're skeptical. You have every right to be. I don't expect you to accept my gift of sight as a natural, God-given talent. Nor do I expect you to like me instantly just because Jazzy and I are best friends."

An odd feeling of relief eased Reve's tension. She wasn't quite sure why or how it happened. There was something strangely comforting about Genny's voice. She projected a gentleness that seemed to encompass everything around her.

Once the three were seated in big wooden rockers, Genny's chair turned so that she could face the other two, Genny asked, "Tea or cider, Reve?"

"Neither, thank you."

Genny poured hot liquid from an earthenware teapot that looked hand-painted, then gave Jazzy a cup. "Well, I'm going to come right out and say it. I had a vision this morning."

Reve sighed. *Here we go,* she thought.

"Was it about us? About Reve and me?" Jazzy asked.

"Part of it was. The good part. The happy part."

"Tell us," Jazzy all but begged.

"I sensed laughter," Genny said. "And wonderful happiness. A oneness as if the two of you were a single entity. You are separate and yet together. Individuals, but linked from birth."

"Then you sensed that we're twins, didn't you?" Jazzy asked.

Genny smiled at her friend, but Reve picked up on something not quite right about the smile. She sensed a sadness in Genny. *Stop doing that!* Reve scolded herself. *You're playing right into Genny's hands by letting your imagination play tricks on you.*

"Yes, I believe you and Reve are twin sisters," Genny said. "I have no doubt about it."

"That's good enough for me." Jazzy looked at Reve as if she expected her to respond by grabbing her, proclaiming them sisters and hugging her. Instead Reve stiffened her spine and sat up straighter in her chair.

"I believe I prefer to wait for the DNA test results." Reve hated that she'd been unable to mask the coolness in her voice, but she simply could not accept some hillbilly psychic's sixth sense.

Jazzy glared at Reve, then fixed her gaze on Genny. "You said that was the good part of your vision. What was the bad part?"

Genny hesitated, as if she didn't want to tell them more. Was her hesitancy real or was it a way to dramatize the moment? Reve wondered. She could not—would not—take Genny's psychic abilities at face value.

"I sensed evil." Genny's voice barely rose above a whisper. "And danger."

"Danger for Reve and me?"

"I'm not sure. But . . . y'all must be very careful."

"This is nonsense!" Reve shot out of her chair.

"Why must you be such an uptight, unfeeling, unhappy bitch?" Jazzy stood and faced her. "Believe me, I'm having as much trouble accepting our being sisters as you are. For all your millions and hoity-toity ways, you're no grand prize yourself, you know."

Reve felt as if she'd been slapped. Taken back by Jazzy's outburst, she stared at her look-alike, then smiled. "You're quite right. I'm not a grand prize, am I? I'm sure you'd never have chosen me to be your sister. I'm rich, well-educated, socially prominent and yet I don't have one single close friend. And not one man has ever cared about me just for me, whereas men seem to fall at your feet."

"Well, well, well." Jazzy laughed. "You are human after all."

"Oh, yes, only too human." Reve turned her gaze on Genny. "I don't believe in hocus-pocus stuff. But I apologize if I've been rude. And if letting you do a reading, as Jazzy calls it, will make her happy, then by all means—"

"You are not what you seem," Genny said, her dark eyes pinning Reve with their intensity. "You and Jazzy are two halves of a whole, and very soon both of you will begin sensing your oneness."

Reve wasn't sure how to react. Genny wasn't telling her anything that couldn't be true about any set of identical twins. But the way Genny stared at her, as if she could see beyond her body and into her spirit, unnerved Reve.

"You're very lonely," Genny said. "That loneliness will soon end. I see you surrounded by family. You will never be lonely again."

CHAPTER 5

The Cherokee Country Club was just barely within the city limits of Cherokee Pointe. The two-story frame Federal-style house had once been home to a wealthy banker who'd lost a fortune in the Crash of 1929 and shot himself in one of the upstairs bedrooms. His widow had taken her children and returned home to Mississippi several years later, letting the house go for back taxes. Farlan MacKinnon's father had purchased the house and surrounding twenty acres for a song. He'd been a young husband with a wife growing increasingly unhappy living with her in-laws, so he'd packed up his wife and two young sons and moved into the old Watley house in 1936. Farlan supposed that was the reason he felt so at home here, because he'd lived in this house as a boy, before he'd been shipped off to military school in Chattanooga.

When, over forty years ago, the most prominent citizens in the county had decided they needed a country club, Farlan had offered this house, which by then had been empty for a good many years, except for a few odds and ends of furniture his mother had left when she'd run off. Farlan had been eighteen at the time of his mother's great escape and had been preparing to enter college that fall. Moonshiners used to run rampant in the hills, and that summer the federal agents had swarmed the county in search of stills. He remembered Agent Rogers—a robust, devil-may-care bachelor who'd set local feminine hearts aflutter. But never had he imagined that the woman who could capture Agent Rogers's heart would be Farlan's forty-year-old mother. Helene MacKinnon had run away with her lover, leaving behind her two sons and their heartbroken father. Farlan never saw his mother again, although he did attend her funeral in Baltimore many years later, where he'd met his young half-sister.

Water under the bridge. The past should stay in the past, he'd told himself countless times. He could no more change anything that happened in the past than he could stem the tide of the Tennessee River, although the Tennessee Valley Authority had done their best to control the raging river with their numerous dams.

A man shouldn't look back, Farlan reminded himself. But it was hard not to think about what might have been, especially when a man's present life was less than satisfactory. He supposed there were others worse off and knew he should count his blessings. The only problem was, his blessings were few. Being filthy rich was, he supposed, a blessing. But when had it ever brought him happiness? In their youths, he and Jim Upton had both offered sweet Melva Mae everything money could buy and she'd turned them both down flat. She'd married a penniless quarter-breed and lived happily ever after. He supposed he'd come out of that ill-fated love triangle far better than old Jim Upton because Jimmy had been madly in love with Melva Mae and never did quite get over losing her.

Farlan, on the other hand, had fallen deeply in love again— with the prettiest little Atlanta debutante who'd ever come out. Veda Parnell had taken his breath away the first moment he laid eyes on her. They dated less than six months before he proposed, but at first she'd been reluctant to accept and leave the social whirl of Atlanta behind. Eventually he'd won her over and they married, but she never seemed really happy. Having her younger half-brother move to Cherokee Pointe when he finished law school had helped her finally adjust to life in the small mountain town. But the young, vibrant girl he'd married soon disappeared and was replaced by a melancholy woman he'd never been able to please.

He wasn't sure when he'd come to realize that something wasn't quite right about Veda. Looking back, he supposed he could have figured it out sooner if he hadn't been so besotted with her.

Cyrus, the waiter who had worked at the country club since it opened and had before that been a groom at the MacKinnon stables, entered the library. His appearance interrupted Farlan's less than pleasant thoughts about his wife. This room in the old Watley home—Farlan's favorite at the club—housed the Watley family's books as well as numerous additions club members had made over the years.

"Judge Keefer and Mr. Fennel have arrived, sir," Cyrus said.

"Show them in," Farlan replied. "And as soon as my son and Mr. Truman complete their game, send them on in." Brian and the county's Democratic district attorney, Wade Truman, played golf together almost every Saturday afternoon. Farlan liked young Truman and had hopes of helping put the boy in the governor's mansion when the time was right.

"Yes, sir. Will that be all?"

"Pour up some of my best bourbon for Dodd and Max." Farlan swirled the liquor in the glass he held. "And make sure no one else disturbs us."

Cyrus nodded, then discreetly disappeared, leaving the pocket doors open. Max entered first, a big grin on his round, full face. Maxwell Fennel was Farlan's first cousin, once removed. Max's grandmother had been Farlan's mother's elder sister. Always dapper in his three-piece suits, Max considered himself somewhat of a ladies' man, even at the age of fifty-nine. He kept his hair dyed dark brown, and Farlan suspected he'd had a few nips and tucks to keep his face from succumbing to the ravages of time.

"Glad you set the meeting up for this afternoon," Max said, a mischievous twinkle in his hazel eyes. "I have an engagement with a mighty fine young lady tonight."

"Not too young, I hope," Dodd Keefer said as he followed Max into the library. "You wouldn't want your penchant for sweet young things to mar your sterling reputation, now would you?"

Max's smile dissolved into a solemn frown. "Why do you insist on bringing up that one indiscretion? It was years ago. And the girl told me she was eighteen."

"A married man should be faithful to his wife and not out chasing young girls." Dodd glared at Max.

"Something you learned from experience," Max shot back without blinking an eye.

Cyrus appeared in the doorway, a tray of drinks in his hand. Farlan cleared his throat, cautioning his guests to watch what they said, then motioned for Cyrus to enter.

"Is this some of that fine bourbon I'm so fond of?" Max asked as he lifted his glass from the silver tray Cyrus carried.

"Yes, sir." Cyrus offered Dodd the other glass.

"Thank you." Dodd lifted the crystal tumbler and took a sip of the corn mash whiskey.

Farlan studied his brother-in-law, a tall, slender, elegant gentleman. Dodd was now, as he'd been for many years, Farlan's best friend. It never ceased to amaze him how different he was from his older half-sister. As different as daylight is from dark, Dodd shared none of Veda's mental and emotional problems. He was highly intelligent, soft spoken and easy to get along with. Farlan had always liked him. Physically, Dodd and Veda shared the same pensive blue eyes—the color inherited from the mother they shared—but Dodd's once sandy hair was now a multi-colored brown and gray mix. At sixty-four, Dodd lived alone and had since his wife's death ten years ago.

"Have a seat and we'll get started." Farlan motioned to two tufted leather chairs flanking the fireplace. "Brian and Wade will join us when they finish their game."

After the two men sat, Farlan eased down on the over-stuffed couch that faced them. He took a final swig of his liquor and set the glass atop a coaster on the sofa table behind him.

"Well, don't keep us on pins and needles. What's this meeting about?" Max lifted his glass to his lips.

"Politics. Our sheriff, our DA and our two circuit court judges are all Democrats, but we've still got a damn Republican mayor," Farlan reminded them. "I want us to get a jump start on the next mayoral election by finding ourselves a suitable candidate before the first of the year. We want to spend time building him up, letting the folks in Cherokee Pointe know there's a better man for the job than Big Jim's man, Jerry Lee Todd."

"You got somebody in mind, Farlan?" Dodd gazed down into his glass as if studying its contents.

"A few names come to mind. But the reason for this meeting is so we can put our heads together and see if the same name keeps coming up. If it does, we'll know we've got the right man."

"What about George Wyatt?" Max asked.

"He's better off left on the city council," Dodd said. "My recommendation is Joe Duffy. He's a good age—forty—and he's married with two children. He attends church every Sunday, and since he has a thriving feed and seed business, he wouldn't be put off by the pittance we're able to pay our mayor."

Farlan nodded. "That's one of the names that keeps popping up in my mind." Farlan turned to Max. "Do you know of any dirt in his past that might jump up and bite him in the ass during a campaign?"

Max shook his head. "Not that I know of, and I've known Joe since he was born. He's lived here all his life, except for four years away at UT. And he married a local girl, Emily Patrick."

"So, are you saying you'd okay Duffy for our choice as a mayoral candidate?" Farlan asked.

"I suppose so."

"Good. But before we make a definite decision, I want to hear what Brian and Wade have to say. They're closer to Duffy's age and probably know him better than any of us." Farlan relaxed into the comfort of the familiar old sofa, crossing his legs and motioning for Cyrus to bring him another drink.

By the time Brian and Wade joined the older men in the library, they'd each polished off their third bourbon and even Dodd Keefer's usually soft voice was a little louder than normal. They had discussed various subjects of interest to three wealthy, successful men, albeit neither Max nor Dodd possessed the sizable fortune Farlan did. As the afternoon wore on, they'd laughed and talked and enjoyed their whiskey. For the life of him Farlan couldn't remember who'd brought up the subject of the article in this morning's *Knoxville News-Sentinel* about the prostitute's body being dragged out of the river near Loudon. But he figured it must have been Max, who had a tendency to talk too much, a quality shared by many in his profession.

"Good riddance to bad rubbish, I say." Dodd downed the last drops of his third drink.

"Do you mean to say you think it's all right for someone to murder prostitutes?" Max asked, rather indignantly.

"No, of course not." Dodd's olive complexion splotched with pink. "I spoke without thinking." Dodd stood, set his whiskey glass aside and walked over to the floor-to-ceiling windows that overlooked the massive front lawn.

"I hear it's going to frost tonight." Farlan quickly changed the subject, hoping to ease Dodd's discomfort. His brother-in-law was a sensitive, emotional man. A good man.

An apologetic look crossed Max's face. He glanced from Dodd, who stood with his back to them, to Farlan, then nodded agreeably. "Yes, sir, cold weather is just around the corner."

Farlan studied Dodd's drooping shoulders, his bowed head. If they were alone, he'd bring up that old taboo subject that haunted them both; and they would discuss it again, as they occasionally did when the burden of guilt and regret overcame them. But they weren't alone and that shameful part of their pasts wasn't something they ever discussed with anyone else, not even Max, whom they both trusted implicitly. That particular time in their lives was something Farlan would rather forget. And usually he was able to keep it buried deep inside, but occasionally he wondered if he should have done things differently. If he had, would his life now be better or worse?

Apparently sensing he'd inadvertently upset Dodd, Max began talking about this and that, doing his best to lighten the mood. Maxwell presented a jovial face to the world, even to family and friends. Farlan knew Max as few others did, knew the demons that plagued him.

"What are you jabbering about, Max?" Brian asked teasingly as he and Wade walked in, both ruddy-cheeked from having played a round of golf in the crisp October weather.

"Did I hear someone say something about another prostitute being found in the Tennessee River?" Wade inquired.

Farlan looked at the young man and thought not for the first time that the boy was too damned good-looking. Too pretty to be a man. "The prostitute's murder was just something Max mentioned in passing. We've been shooting the bull for a couple of hours waiting on you boys to show up."

Wade meandered over toward the windows where Dodd still stood with his back to the room. "How are you, Judge?"

"Well enough," Dodd replied in a quiet, stilted voice.

"What did you mean when you said another prostitute?" Max asked. "Has there been more than one murdered?"

Wade turned around and faced the others. "Several in the past couple of years. All in the eastern part of the state, all the bodies dumped into the river. One was as recent as six months ago. That body was recovered downstream from Watts Barr. I believe I took note of a similar case for the first time only a couple of years ago, and if I recall correctly, there have been four cases with practically the same MO."

"And that MO would be?" Brian asked as he turned to accept a glass of bourbon from Cyrus, who'd just offered him a drink.

Dodd whirled around, his eyes overly bright, his facial features drawn. "If y'all will excuse me, I'm not feeling well."

"Do you need me to drive you home?" Farlan asked.

"No need for that," Dodd replied. "I'll just go to the men's room and throw a little cold water in my face, then I'll see if Cyrus can rustle me up a bite to eat. I skipped lunch. I'm sure that's the problem."

Poor Dodd. Brilliant man, but far too sensitive. People said that combination made him an excellent judge.

Once Dodd left the room, Farlan motioned for Wade and Brian to sit. "As much as y'all find the gruesome murders of several young women fascinating, let's set aside the gossip and get down to business."

Brian shrugged. "And that business would be?"

"Choosing a new Democratic candidate for mayor."

"Joe Duffy," Wade and Brian said practically simultaneously.

Chuckling, Farlan eyed Max, who nodded. It would seem this meeting was over before it began. By unanimous agreement, they had their candidate. All that remained was putting the idea into Duffy's head and promising him not only Farlan's full support, but the backing of MacKinnon Media.

Genny sensed Reve Sorrell's uneasiness and did all she could to make the woman feel comfortable. Although Reve had eventually drunk a cup of tea and eaten a slice of cake, she still seemed tense, as if she were afraid of something.

What was she so afraid of? The moment the question came to Genny's mind, the answer appeared seconds later. The wealthy and powerful Ms. Sorrell was afraid of being taken advantage of, afraid of being used. She believed that anyone professing to possess a sixth sense had to be a fake. Was that what vast wealth had done to her? Made her distrust everyone? How sad, Genny thought, and decided at that very moment to make this lonely woman her friend.

"I'd love for y'all to stay for supper," Genny said, while the threesome sat around the kitchen table, their crumb-dappled plates and empty, tea-stained cups sitting in front of them. "And I will not take no for an answer." Not giving Reve a chance to refuse, she turned to Jazzy. "Call Caleb and tell him to grab a ride in from town with Dallas."

"That's a wonderful idea." Jazzy lifted her small red-leather shoulder bag from where she'd hung it on the back of her chair. "I'll call him right now. This supper will give Reve a chance to get better acquainted with the most important people in my life."

"I'm not sure—" Reve looked like an animal caught in a trap, her brown eyes wide open and filled with uncertainty.

"As I said, I won't take no for an answer." Genny scooted back her chair. "Have you ever done any cooking, Reve?"

"No, not really," she replied. "When I was a child, I occasionally watched our cook when she prepared dinner. And sometimes she allowed me to help her frost a cake or bake cookies."

"Well, I intend to put you and Jazzy to work helping me fix tonight's supper. Nothing fancy. Just some fried chicken, fried potatoes, butter beans, cornbread and deviled eggs." Genny eyed the glass-domed cake plate sitting atop an antique sideboard at the far end of the room. "We still have plenty of cake left for dessert. And I froze a half gallon of homemade vanilla ice cream the last time we made some, so there should be more than enough for a couple of scoops each."

Jazzy punched in Caleb's cell number and while the phone

rang, she asked Genny, "Will we have time for you to give us a reading before we start supper?"

"I really don't want to participate in any kind of reading," Reve said.

Jazzy frowned, but quickly recovered from the disappointment. "Okay, then, just give me a reading. Reve can be an observer."

"If you're sure that's what you want." Genny didn't often give readings, only under special circumstances and for special people. She had learned that most people only thought they wanted to delve into the supernatural realm, and when confronted by predications they didn't like, they wanted to shoot the messenger.

"I'm sure it's what I want." Jazzy slid back her chair, stood and gathered up their empty plates, stacked them and put them in the sink at the same time Genny picked up their cups. "Do we need to go into Granny Butler's room the way we did the last time?"

"I'd prefer to do it there. I always feel closer to Granny and her powers in her old room."

Out of the corner of her eye, Genny caught a glimpse of Reve's furrowed brow, her wrinkled nose, her pursed lips. The expression of skepticism and disapproval. "Give me a couple of minutes to prepare, then you two come on up." She looked right at Reve. "I know you don't believe, but come upstairs anyway. Consider it an adventure. Or perhaps a learning experience."

"She'll become a believer," Jazzy said. "Just give her time."

Genny offered them both an understanding smile, then left them to go upstairs. The moment she entered the semi-dark bedroom, the scent of roses assailed her. Granny had always worn rose-scented powder, and although she'd been gone for a good many years, her scent lingered. Of course there were times, when the scent was very strong the way it was today, that Genny felt her grandmother's presence.

You're here, aren't you? She didn't expect a reply.

Hurriedly she lit the array of white candles situated throughout the room, then pulled the curtains to darken the room completely, except for the positive light given off by the candles. After arranging two chairs at a small, antique table, she sat in one of the chairs, folded her hands in her lap and waited, her mind settling into a meditative state. Readings were not like visions. During a vision, the images were clearer, sometimes so clear it was as if she were watching them through the lens of a movie camera. But when she did a reading, she seldom received clear pictures. She usually simply felt things, sensed things and sometimes heard a voice inside her head.

While she waited for Jazzy and Reve—she knew that despite her misgivings, Reve would come—Genny concentrated, all her thoughts on the look-alike redheads. Almost immediately she sensed a deep yearning to protect the twins. Protect the babies.

Babies?

Pure white light surrounded Genny. The innocence of newborn babies. Completely void of any evil. Love. Maternal love. A desire to nurture and protect.

Whoever had given birth to the twins had wanted them, loved them and believed she had to protect them. But from what? From whom?

Genny focused on Jazzy and Reve again instead of the mother, willing herself to move forward into the present and out of the past. She couldn't even be certain that it was the real past she sensed, anymore than she knew for certain it was a past that Jazzy and Reve had shared. But her instincts, which were seldom wrong, told her that the two women were twins and the powerful maternal love she sensed did indeed come from their birth mother.

"Are you ready for us . . . for me?" Jazzy asked.

Genny opened her eyes. Jazzy stood in the doorway, Reve directly behind her.

"Yes, please come in." She motioned to the chair on the

opposite side of the antique table. "Sit here, Jazzy." She nodded to a rocker in the corner. "You may sit there, Reve."

Both women did as Genny had instructed. The vibrations from the sisters—the twin sisters—bombarded Genny. Jazzy was eager, hopeful, almost giddy with excitement. On the other hand, Reve was anxious, uncertain, fearful.

Genny laid her hands, palm up, on the table, closed her eyes and repeated the name "Jasmine" several times. By using that one name, she hoped her gift of sight would connect only with that one person.

"Happiness. Love. A rejoicing over good news," Genny said.

"That means the DNA tests will prove we're sisters." Jazzy sneaked a peek at Reve.

"Two who are one. Forever linked. A bond that cannot be severed." Suddenly the bright, clear light in her mind grew dim, darkened. Gray shadows filled Genny's consciousness. She tried to will the negative thoughts away, but they persisted. Grew stronger. "Fear. Fear of discovery. Anger."

"Who's afraid of being discovered?" Jazzy asked. "Is it Aunt Sally? Has she been lying to me all my life?"

"No, I don't believe it's Sally."

"Then who?"

The gray mist within Genny's mind turned black. Black swirls of malevolence. "I sense a strong combination of love and hatred, of desire and rage." Genny tried to see who emitted such powerful emotions, but she could not pin them down, couldn't even discern if the person was male or female. But she did know—without a doubt—that these disturbing feelings were connected with Jazzy. And with Reve. The twins. "There's danger. Great danger."

"Stop. Please, stop. Don't do this." Reve jumped up from the rocking chair.

"Who's in danger?" Jazzy asked. "Reve and me?"

"Yes, both of you. But—Oh, God! Jazzy, I sense the greatest danger for you." Genny gasped, then slumped over, her head dropping to the table, cushioned by her cupped hands.

CHAPTER 6

He stood alone in the shadows of autumn twilight, the sky overcast with gold, and thought about Dinah. In the beginning, after she'd gone away that first time, it had been years before she came back to him. Years he'd been able to live in relative peace. And then she had reappeared unexpectedly, still as beautiful and alluring as ever. He had stupidly thought they had been given a second chance to be together and that this time she would really love him. She had pretended not to know him, but he'd understood that she was simply playing a game. Being the whore she was, she'd made him pay her for her favors. He'd paid her handsomely those first few times, but unfortunately found the sex less than satisfactory. That was when he came to understand what he had to do. Only by repeating the past could he achieve the fulfillment he craved, the pleasure only Dinah could give him. So they had played out the same scenario that time and then again and again with every return visit, both of them acting out their parts from memory.

After half a dozen recurrences, he had considered keeping a diary, marking down the dates and places But he'd thought better of the idea, and the only record he kept was in his head. If anyone had ever accidently come across such a diary, they might not have understood. The police wouldn't understand. They would think he had killed numerous women—over twenty in all—when he'd actually killed only one woman. Dinah. The authorities wouldn't care that he'd been justified in killing her. They wouldn't believe that it really hadn't been murder. No one would understand that he had to keep killing her over and over again because she wouldn't stay dead.

For the past few hours, he had been unable to get Becky Olmstead out of his mind, despite his best efforts to forget her. He always went with his heart in these matters, because his heart always knew when the woman he desired was Dinah. But allowing his mind to rule his emotions when it came to protecting himself was what had kept him safe all these years. No one had ever connected him with any of the bodies found in the river. Thankfully, Dinah had never come back to him in Cherokee Pointe, and he'd never sought her out in his home area. But he feared that things had changed, that Dinah had chosen to tempt him beyond all reason in his own backyard. He had hoped Becky wouldn't turn out to be Dinah, but he was beginning to believe she was. Dared he risk going to her and confronting her?

What choice did he have? Once Dinah came back to him, she wouldn't leave him alone. What he didn't understand was why she'd returned so quickly, only a matter of days since they'd last been together.

Soon—very soon—he would have to seek Becky out. Once he'd fucked her, he'd know for sure whether or not she was Dinah.

Reba Upton parked her black Mercedes at the back of the mountaintop chalet so that anyone who happened to drive past wouldn't see it. As nervous butterflies jittered in her stomach, she flipped down the sun visor and inspected her face in the mirror. She had taken special care with her hair and makeup and had worn her pink cashmere sweater set with a pair of winter white slacks. He'd told her she looked especially lovely in pink. She'd been wearing a pink silk bed jacket the first time he'd visited her in the hospital while she was recovering from her heart attack this past spring. That visit had been the beginning for them. Odd that she had known him for years, had been friends of a sort with his late wife, and yet she'd never thought of him as more than an acquaintance. In all the years Jim and she had been married, she hadn't looked at another man, despite knowing Jim cheated on her frequently. She'd been so in love with her husband, so totally, devotedly in love.

Reba opened the door and got out of the car, then glanced at her wristwatch. She was early. But once Jim had left the house, supposedly to go to the club to have dinner with some of his political cronies, she'd been so eager that she'd dressed and left less than half an hour after he had. She suspected he wasn't going to the country club. In fact, she was ninety-nine percent sure he was driving straight to Erin Mercer's cabin, straight into the arms of his latest mistress.

But Erin wasn't just another in a long line of women her husband had bedded. No, she was different and the way Jim felt about her wasn't just lust. He was in love with this woman. He loved Erin as he had never loved her, his wife of over fifty years. She suspected that Erin was the first and only woman he'd truly loved since he'd been a very young man and mad about Melva Mae. She supposed that was why, when Dodd Keefer had begun showing an interest in her, she hadn't rejected his advances. Oh, there had been nothing more than friendship between them at first, all during the spring and summer. He had come to the house several times on this or that pretense, and she'd shown up in various places she'd known he would be. After losing her grandson Jamie, she had desperately needed comfort. Although Jim and she had tried to offer each other comfort, they had both needed more. Jim had soon turned back to Erin, and once again she'd been alone. So alone. Then right after Labor Day, Dodd had made a confession that prompted her to search her heart.

"I find that I'm falling in love with you, Reba," he'd said.

She'd stared at him, surprised by his admission, but strangely, giddily happy. "I'm flattered, Dodd, really I am," she'd told him. "But surely you've mistaken a deep liking for love. After all, I'm several years older than you and I—I am a married woman. Besides, a man like you could have his pick of women."

"I've picked you." He had caressed her face tenderly. "I've admired you from afar for many years and when you almost died, I promised myself that I would go to you and—"

"Don't say anything else. Please."

She had tried to stay away from him, tried to concentrate on the joy of having a new grandson in her life, tried to remain faithful to her unfaithful husband. During the past six weeks, whenever Dodd had called her, she'd put him off, telling him she wasn't ready for an affair. But a few days ago, she realized that her feelings for Dodd Keefer were stronger than her will to resist infidelity. She wasn't quite sure when it had happened or how, but she had fallen out of love with Jim and in love with Dodd.

Reba owned a rustic chateau high in the mountains. This had been a place where her son, Jim, Jr., and his young friends used to come to let off steam, and then later on he and his wife had used it for weekend getaways. After their deaths, Reba had thought about selling it, but instead she'd handed it over to a Realtor to lease as a rental property. Then this past summer, when she'd been recuperating, she'd hired a contractor to update and remodel the A-frame mountain house. They had finished up a few days ago, so the place hadn't been rented again.

After fishing the key from her purse, Reba climbed the wooden steps to the front entrance, unlocked the door, opened it and walked into the two-story great room. A shiver of un-

certainty mixed with a large dose of anticipation rippled up
her spine. Could she do this? Could she really follow through
with her plans for an intimate tryst with Dodd? She hadn't
been with a man in years. Knowing about all of Jim's affairs,
she had finally reached a point where she couldn't bear for
him to touch her and had requested they have separate bedrooms. What if when Dodd made love to her, she couldn't
respond? What if she couldn't feel anything sexual? After
all, she was past seventy and those fiery hormones of youth
had long ago died down. What she didn't know was if her
sexual desire was now cold ashes or simply dying embers
waiting to be stoked back to life.

The room was cold. She felt the chill even through her
white wool coat. Originally there had been a wood-burning
fireplace in the chateau, but ten years ago, on her Realtor's
advice, she'd had it converted to propane gas. A fire would
add a touch of romance. If she'd had more time to prepare,
she'd have brought candles and champagne. Maybe next
time.

If there was a next time.

Nervously, Reba shed her coat, tossed it onto a plaid arm-
chair and quickly reset the thermostat on the heating unit
and turned on the gas logs in the fireplace. Glancing around,
she decided that if she was going to spend any time here in
the future, she needed to make some changes. The decor was
much too rustic country to suit her tastes, but tourists who
rented the cabins and chateaus in the mountains often preferred this old-timey look—at least that's what the Knoxville
decorator she'd hired had told her.

Going through the selection of CDs stacked beside the
entertainment center, she found that it was comprised of
mostly older country hits. She didn't care much for country
music and doubted seriously if Dodd did. As she continued
perusing the stack, her gaze stopped on one particular CD
that stood out from the rest. *The Romantic Piano*. She removed it from the stack, opened it and inserted it in the

player. When she heard the soft , sweet strains of Schuman's "Dreaming," she sighed.

Only moments after she relaxed on the sofa, she heard a car outside. Her heartbeat accelerated. Forcing herself not to jump up and run to the door, she rose from the sofa and walked slowly toward the entrance. By the time she reached the door, she heard footsteps on the porch. She took a deep breath and opened the door.

Dodd Keefer was an elegantly handsome man, his grayish-brown hair neatly styled, his attire a sports coat, dress slacks and lightweight turtleneck sweater. He paused the moment he saw her and smiled. His sparkling blue eyes devoured her. A tingle of some sort fluttered in her belly. Suddenly she felt like a young girl meeting secretly with her first beau.

He held up a bottle of wine. "I brought champagne. Dom Perignon. It's been chilled, but we might want to—"

Reba boldly grasped his free hand and tugged, urging him toward her. Lowering his hand holding the bottle to his side, he stepped over the threshold and eased the door closed behind him. Acting purely on instinct, she stood on tiptoe and kissed him fully on the mouth. He responded instantly, returning the kiss with gentle force. A feeling of pure euphoria filled her body, unlike anything she'd experienced in ages.

Dodd ended the kiss somewhat reluctantly. Reba gazed up at him. He smiled.

"I've been wanting to do that for a very long time," she admitted, then took a step back, putting some space between them.

"So have I." He studied her for a moment. "This isn't something we have to rush. I'll be perfectly content this evening to sit here in front of the fire with you and drink champagne, listen to music and talk."

She nodded. "I'd like that very much." He's a rare man, she thought, a man who understood that she wasn't quite ready to make that big step into a full-fledged affair.

"And perhaps you'll allow me to kiss you again."

"I'll be disappointed if you don't kiss me. Several more times."

Reve found herself at Genny Sloan's kitchen sink removing the shells from a dozen boiled eggs. If her Chattanooga friends could see her now, they'd be shocked. Reve Sorrell doing a menial task! She had rolled up the sleeves of her silk blouse and donned a white apron her hostess had provided, then had listened carefully as Genny explained how to prepare deviled eggs. It had seemed simple enough, but she was having more than a little difficulty. Some of the eggs shed their shells without a problem, but some shells stuck as if they were glued on, and the only way to remove them was to tear the egg apart.

"I'm afraid I'm not very good at this." Holding one of the tattered eggs in her hand, Reve glanced across the kitchen to Genny, who was lifting pieces of fried chicken from the heavy iron skillet filled with hot grease.

"Oh, you're doing fine," Genny told her. "The whites that mess up, just save for Drudwyn. That dog loves eggs. And put the yolks with the other ones. I always like to have more yolks than whites. It makes for overflowing deviled eggs."

Reve forced a smile. She felt as out of place here in this old mountain farmhouse helping prepare dinner as Genny and Jazzy would probably feel at one of her elaborate dinner parties. And it's not dinner here in Cherokee County, she reminded herself. These people call the evening meal supper.

These people? Watch out, Reve, your snobbery is showing again. These people are two very kind women who have done their best to make you feel as if you fit in. Since that crazy "reading" Genny had done a couple of hours ago, both Genny and Jazzy had bent over backward to soothe Reve's ragged nerves. Considering how she'd reacted to Genny's dire prediction that both she and Jazzy were in grave danger, Reve supposed she was lucky they hadn't asked her to leave and never come back. She had jumped up from her chair in the corner of the darkened bedroom and screamed for them to stop.

"This is total insanity and I want no part of it!" After yelling this, she had run from the room, leaving Jazzy to deal with Genny, who had either fainted or had done a great job of acting as if she had. As skeptical as Reve was about Genny's sixth-sense abilities, she didn't think the woman was a fake. Maybe sometime in Genny's childhood, her crazy old witch woman grandmother had convinced her she was psychic. It seemed obvious that Genny truly believed she was gifted.

Later on, the two women had found her outside on the porch. Neither mentioned the "reading" or Reve's outburst. Instead, Genny suggested she give Reve a tour of her greenhouses, which turned out to be a rather interesting excursion. It seemed that Genny owned a successful local nursery and specialized in herbs she also sold by mail order.

As soon as Jazzy removed a skillet of cornbread from the oven and turned it out onto a brown earthenware plate, she came over and eased the hot skillet down into the soapy water on the left side of the double sink. The minute the skillet hit the water, it emitted a sizzling sound.

"Need some help?" Jazzy asked Reve.

"Yes, I'm afraid I do."

"Looks like you've managed to keep about six of the whites intact." Jazzy lifted a tray from the counter and set it down to Reve's right. "Clean your hands and then arrange the whites on the tray in a circle. While you do that, I'll prepare the yolks."

Reve sighed with relief. "Thanks."

Jazzy patted her on the back. "It's okay. Really. You're just new to this kind of stuff. Any time I try something new, I feel as if I'm all thumbs."

Before Jazzy could take over, a phone rang. Reve knew instantly from the musical ring that it wasn't her cell phone or Genny's residential line.

"That's mine." Jazzy wiped her hands on her apron, then grabbed her purse from the back of the kitchen chair and retrieved her cell phone. "Hello." Jazzy's eyes widened in surprise. "I'm doing just fine, Miss Reba. How are you?"

Genny stopped dead still and looked inquiringly at Jazzy, who shrugged and grinned. Genny eased up beside Reve and whispered, "That's Caleb's grandmother. She's always hated Jazzy. I can't imagine why she's calling her."

"Lunch tomorrow?" Jazzy asked. "I—yes, I suppose so. Hold on just a sec, will you?" Jazzy looked at Reve. "Miss Reba has invited us to Sunday dinner. What do you say? Want to go?"

Not really, Reve thought, but when she noted the hopeful expression on Jazzy's face, she replied, "Yes, certainly, if you'd like to go."

"Miss Reba, we'll be there." Jazzy sucked in a deep breath and slowly released it. "And thank you."

The minute she hit the off button on her phone, Jazzy whirled around, grabbed Reve and hugged her. Reve stiffened. She was unaccustomed to physical displays of emotion. Her parents had been kind and caring, but neither of them had been the type to shower hugs and kisses on anyone, not even their only child.

"Hot damn!" Jazzy released Reve and danced jubilantly around the room. "I guess hell has done froze over, gals. Miss Reba not only was civil to me, she honest-to-God invited me to Sunday dinner."

The sound of a dog's friendly barks alerted them that someone was outside several minutes before they heard tromping on the back porch. The kitchen door swung open, and a huge wolf-looking dog came barreling in, followed by Caleb McCord and Dallas Sloan. The dog came straight to Reve and sniffed her. Oddly enough, she wasn't afraid of him, even though she'd never owned a pet. When he finished sniffing, the dog lifted his head and stared at her with golden eyes.

"I believe Drudwyn likes you," Genny said. "You should take that as a compliment. He's usually a very good judge of character."

Chief Sloan slid his arm around his wife's waist, leaned down and kissed her on the mouth. Reve glanced away, somehow feeling as if she was a voyeur. Her line of vision just happened to turn to Jazzy, who was in the middle of an equally loving exchange with Caleb. Reve's cheeks burned with an embarrassing blush.

Don't be ridiculous, she told herself, *you have nothing to be embarrassed about and you know it.* If people chose to make spectacles of themselves, she was hardly to blame. Not once had she ever seen her parents kiss each other. They considered such public displays of affection vulgar and low class.

With shaky hands, Reve placed the halved boiled egg whites in a circle on the plate, deliberately avoiding making eye contact with anyone else in the room.

"You'll never guess in a million years who called and invited Reve and me to dinner tomorrow," Jazzy said.

"My grandmother," Caleb responded.

"You did it, didn't you? Somehow you twisted her arm into—"

"Didn't do any arm-twisting," Caleb said. "I simply told Miss Reba that I loved you and intended to marry you and it would please me greatly if you two could get along."

"You actually said that to her?"

"Sure did. And I mentioned that I'd hate to think she'd force me to choose between the woman I loved and my grandmother because I'd choose the woman I loved."

Reve glanced up just in time to see Jazzy throw her arms around Caleb's neck and kiss him again.

"You're the most wonderful man in the world," Jazzy told him.

"Then why don't you accept my proposal? Say you'll marry me."

Jazzy pulled away from him, but held on to both of his hands. With tears misting her eyes, she looked right at him and said, "I'll marry you."

"Glory hallelujah." Genny clasped her hands together in a prayer-like gesture.

Reve grew more uncomfortable with each passing minute. She should never have agreed to come here with Jazzy today. It had been a mistake from the very beginning. These people were little more than strangers to her, and yet here she was, not only helping prepare a meal they would soon share, but being privy to a marriage proposal and acceptance.

These two couples were close friends. She was an outsider who was unaccustomed to feeling out of place. Even if she and Jazzy were twin sisters, she doubted she'd ever be able to fit into Jazzy's world. No more than Jazzy could fit into hers.

While the foursome were sharing this happy moment, Reve eased toward the back door. She could hardly escape and go back into town to her rental cabin, considering she'd ridden out here with Jazzy. Besides, none of them would understand why she felt so uncomfortable around them. But she needed a few moments alone, to compose her thoughts. She could step out on the back porch. Just for a couple of minutes. Several deep breaths of cool evening air might do her nerves a world of good. She seriously doubted anyone would miss her, at least not immediately.

Reaching the door without being noticed, Reve grasped the knob. Just as she opened the door and took her first step, she came face-to-throat with a wide-shouldered man wearing a brown suede jacket. Her heart all but stopped when she lifted her gaze and looked into the slanting green eyes of her worst nightmare—Sheriff Jacob Butler.

CHAPTER 7

When his father left the country club to drive home shortly
after six, Brian had told him that he wouldn't be in until late.
And when Farlan had asked—hopefully—if he had a date,
Brian had smiled and said yes, but that it was a first date and
he preferred keeping the lady's identity to himself in case
things didn't work out between them. It was far from the first
lie he'd told his father, and it certainly wouldn't be the last.
Lying had become second nature to him. Sometimes he
thought it easier to fabricate a lie than to tell the truth. Besides,
what did his father expect after the example he'd set? Both
of Brian's parents were adept liars and apparently felt little
or no guilt when they didn't tell the truth. He'd been a kid,
barely twelve, when he'd discovered that his beloved father,
his idol, had feet of clay. And although he'd always adored
his mother and, in a way, still did, he'd known since childhood that she was emotionally unstable.

Here he was, at forty-two, still living with his parents.
He'd tried living on his own, during his years away at college
and during his brief marriage to Phyllis, but he preferred the
family residence in the heart of Cherokee Pointe. The Mac-
Kinnon mansion made a statement. It shouted, "The people

who live here are rich and powerful and important." He enjoyed being a MacKinnon, with all that entailed. And someday the entire family fortune would be his and his alone. If his nutty Uncle Wallace outlived Veda and Farlan, he'd have the old man put away somewhere. A nice facility where he'd be taken good care of, but where he'd be out of Brian's hair. His uncle had been an embarrassment to him all his life, but neither of his parents would hear of institutionalizing him. His father truly loved his only brother, but he suspected his mother's concern for her brother-in-law was more self-serving. After all, she had to know that on any given day, she, too, might be a candidate for the looney bin.

His parents had made it perfectly clear to him that they expected him to remarry and sire at least one child, to provide the family with a MacKinnon heir. Although he seriously doubted he could endure the dullness of a monogamous relationship for more than a few months, he realized he needed to get married. A man in his position should have a family. Otherwise, people talked. They wondered about his sexual orientation. And they whispered that maybe his first wife had broken his heart so badly that he could never love again. Some probably even speculated that he'd been too much of a mama's boy growing up to be able to completely sever her apron strings.

What did he care? Let the tongues wag. For now. When he did remarry, that would shut them all up fast enough. And he *would* get married again. It was just a matter of time. He'd thought he had found the perfect woman to be his wife. Genny Madoc. Lovely beyond words. Gentle and kind. And she'd been a virgin. He'd courted her, turned himself inside out to please her, and yet the minute that burly blond FBI agent had shown up in Cherokee County, Genny had proven herself to be no different from most other women. She'd given her precious innocence to a man unworthy of her, a man who could never have appreciated the priceless gift the way Brian would have.

Even now the thought of tutoring Genny in the ways to please him aroused him unbearably.

Brian had driven his Porche this afternoon, not only to impress Wade Truman, but because he had known he'd be picking up a companion for the evening. Ladies—and he used the term loosely—always appreciated riding in an expensive car. He'd never used a local prostitute before and even now, on his way to pick up his "date," he felt uneasy. What if someone saw him with this woman? How would he ever explain? When the need to be with a woman drove him hard, he usually made a trip to Knoxville, but he'd been assured by Mr. Timmons that the girl he was sending Brian tonight would fulfill all his fantasies. All he required in a woman was that she be agreeable to a little S&M.

Farlan didn't want to go home. His life had reached that sad state where he'd rather be anywhere than with his own wife. If the guilt of a long-ago indiscretion hadn't weighed heavily on his shoulders—a love affair with another woman that had pushed his unstable wife over the edge—he would have sought a divorce twenty years ago. But Veda had never completely recovered from the nervous breakdown she had suffered when she found out about his mistress. She had gone so far as to try to kill herself and threatened to try again if Farlan ever left her. Since then he'd been shackled to her with a ball and chain formed out of guilt and regret.

Poor Brian had been only twelve at the time Veda tried to commit suicide, and Farlan would never forgive himself for the upheaval he and Veda had created in their son's young life. After Veda's botched suicide attempt, Brian had become unruly and occasionally violent. But when Farlan had mentioned seeking psychiatric help for both his wife and his son, Veda had gone berserk, saying she'd rather die than be subjected to such humiliation for herself and their child. Looking back, Farlan realized that he'd made a mistake by giving in to her threats. But at the time, it had been easier to let Veda have her way. If he could turn back the clock and do everything all over again, he wouldn't take the easy way out. Not with Veda and Brian. And not with—

No, don't even think her name, he told himself. *After she went away, you swore to yourself that you wouldn't go after her. Not ever. And you wouldn't let her memory drive you mad.* But how could a man ever completely forget what it was like to have a woman love him with her whole heart, to light up the moment he walked into a room, to lie in his arms and make him feel like a king?

Before he knew what he was doing, Farlan parked his Bentley down the street from Jazzy's Joint, the local honky-tonk. It had been over a year since he'd ventured inside—since Max's last birthday when he'd asked his buddies to meet him there for an all-male celebration. After parking, Farlan called home on his cell phone and left a message with Abra.

"Tell Miss Veda that I won't be home for supper. I'm staying late at the club."

What was one more lie between them, after a lifetime of lies?

The minute he entered Jazzy's Joint, the roadhouse ambience put him at ease. In this place he wasn't Farlan MacKinnon, Chairman of the Board of MacKinnon Media. In here, he was just another man looking for a glass of beer and a quiet corner where he could drown his sorrows. Of course, he'd already drowned quite a few sorrows with three glasses of bourbon at the club, but the numbing effect of that liquor had begun to wear off. He needed to renew that languid feeling only alcohol produced.

Surrounded by loud music and smoky air, Farlan walked up to the bar and ordered. The bartender wasn't especially busy since this early in the evening there was only a handful of patrons. A couple of guys in the back shooting pool, one sitting at the other end of the bar and another man at a nearby table, nursing a glass of what looked like whiskey.

"I haven't seen you around here in quite a while," the bartender said.

"You know who I am?"

"Of course. Everybody in Cherokee County knows you, Mr. MacKinnon."

He shrugged. So much for finding anonymity in this place. "You have me at a disadvantage, madam. You know me, but I don't know you."

"Lacy Fallon." The middle-aged bleached blonde offered him a kind smile. "I've been bartending here ever since Jazzy opened up this place."

Farlan nodded, then glanced around the room. "Guess it's a bit early for most folks."

"Yeah, this place doesn't usually start hopping on a Saturday night until after nine."

"Well, that suits me fine. I just came in for a beer. I'm too old for much of anything else."

"You don't look too old to me," a feminine voice behind him said.

The bartender frowned and turned up her nose as if she'd smelled something rotten. Farlan glanced over his shoulder. The girl standing only a few feet away was a pretty little thing and probably not a day over twenty. She wore too much makeup and not enough clothes.

"We don't want your kind in here," Lacy Fallon said, loud and clear. "Jazzy's done sent you packing once. If you'll leave now, I won't call the police."

Farlan glanced back and forth from the young woman to the bartender and realization dawned. The unwanted customer was a prostitute. He hadn't realized there were any in Cherokee Pointe. But then again, he hadn't been in the market for a hooker. Not since . . .

"I'll leave quietly," the girl said, then cozied up to Farlan and whispered, "Want to give me a ride? Or if you'd prefer, I could ride you."

Farlan didn't flinch, but his gut tightened. He inspected

the girl thoroughly, from head to toe. For a split second his old eyes played a trick on him, and he saw the ghost of a pretty young woman from his past.

He paid for his drink, then said, "Why don't I give you a lift home, young lady? You shouldn't be in a place like this. You should be out on a Saturday night date with some nice young man."

Glowering at Farlan, the bartender harrumphed. Hell, let her think whatever she wanted to. He had no intention of taking this girl up on her offer, but he did want to spend a little time with her. And he didn't owe Lacy Fallon or anyone else an explanation.

The young woman curled her arm around his as they walked out of Jazzy's Joint. "I don't have a place of my own, so you'll have to rent us a room somewhere. Or if you'd rather, we can just do it in your car. I give great blow jobs."

Without replying to her offer, Farlan led her out of the bar and down the street to his Bentley. He unlocked the car and helped her in on the passenger's side; then he slid behind the wheel and turned to her. "I don't want sex from you. But I am willing to pay you for an hour or two of your time tonight."

She stared at him, her expression one of doubt. "How much? And what do you want me to do?"

"Would a hundred dollars be sufficient for . . . say, two hours of your time?"

She grinned. "Yeah, I'd say a hundred is just fine, depending on what I have to do to earn the money."

"Take a ride with me. Talk to me. Tell me about your hopes and dreams."

She looked at him as if she thought he was crazy. "That's it. That's all you want from me?" she asked.

"Yes, that's all."

"You're kidding, right?"

"No, I'm perfectly serious. You see, I'm a lonely old man with only a few truly happy memories. Some of those memories are about another pretty young woman who had so many hopes and dreams for her future."

She shrugged. "Sure, if talk is all you want. I can talk all night for fifty bucks an hour. And if you change your mind about the blow job or—"

"I won't change my mind. I know what I want."

She'd told him she was eighteen. He'd asked to see her driver's license. Sure enough, she was legal. Just barely. Despite his penchant for tasty young things, he couldn't risk screwing around with jail bait. He'd learned his lesson ten years ago when a certain fifteen-year-old gal's daddy had come after him with a shotgun. If Farlan hadn't had the law in his hip pocket back then—both the sheriff and the chief of police—things might have gotten nasty. But once Farlan paid her father fifty thousand not to press charges, the whole ugly mess simply went away. Not one word had ever been printed in the local paper, thanks to the fact that MacKinnon Media had a monopoly on the press in Cherokee County. Max couldn't help shivering just a bit whenever he thought about the whole situation and how close he'd come to ruining his life. He owed Farlan a debt he could never fully repay.

Max lay in bed, naked as the day he was born, and let her remove his soiled condom. When she got up, he swatted her smooth, round backside. Glancing over her shoulder, she smiled at him, then disappeared into the bathroom. With the heat of passion fading, he felt a sudden chill, so he dragged the sheet and blanket up to his waist.

He had needed this evening's entertainment, needed it the way he needed air to breathe. Sex with his wife—which he got about once a month, if he was lucky—had never been great, not in years. Not after she got a little older and more demanding. He liked 'em young. So sue him. If all men would admit the truth, most of them would prefer a sixteen-year-old to a thirty-year-old.

Hell, he wasn't a damn pedophile. Little girls didn't turn him on. They had to be mature enough to have tits and a furry pussy before he was interested. Somebody between fourteen and twenty. He'd enjoyed his share of the younger ones in the past, until he'd picked the wrong gal. Ever since then, he'd made sure they were either legal age or in an illegal profession. Lately most of his pickups were the later. Young prostitutes.

When she came out of the bathroom, she started putting on her clothes. Max patted the bed and motioned to her.

"If you want more, it'll cost you," she told him.

"That's fine by me." Max whipped back the covers and slid to the side of the bed. "I'll be good to go pretty soon, sugar. I took my Viagra today."

She let her jeans drop back on the floor and came toward him, her slender hips swaying and her small, perky breasts begging for his mouth.

Wade Truman threw back his head and groaned deep in his throat as he came. Shudders of release racked his body. A minute later, as the aftershocks rippled through him, his partner came. God, she was loud, he thought, as he listened to her scream in his ear. Sweaty and exhausted, he rolled off her and onto the bed. While he lay there, gazing up at the ceiling, she cuddled up against him. If he didn't have plans for her later, he'd get up now, wash off, put on his clothes and leave. He'd bought her dinner; they'd talked and laughed and danced. He'd been charming and attentive, giving her what most women wanted, ladies and sluts alike. At thirty-five, he had yet to meet a woman he really wanted that he couldn't talk into his bed.

Don't lie to yourself. There was one. That fiery redhead who told you flat out no. And for the life of him he didn't understand why, not when she'd probably spread her legs for half the men in Cherokee County.

Looking back, he figured he'd just approached her at the wrong time, one of the times Jamie Upton had been in town. Everybody knew that Jazzy Talbot had been hog wild crazy about the bastard. And now that Jamie was dead, she'd latched on to the new heir apparent to the Upton fortune, Caleb McCord. Lucky son of a bitch. What he'd give to be in that guy's shoes. Wade chuckled to himself, thinking what he'd give to be in Caleb's bed, on top of Jazzy, buried to the hilt inside her.

He was an idiot! A damn fool. Hell, even his ex-wife had reminded him of Jazzy. Not as buxom. Not as tall and leggy. Not as wild. But a pretty redheaded lady who had made him a good wife. Too bad she'd been as boring as hell and completely dull in bed. Three years of having to beg her for sex and then pretend to be grateful afterward had been three years too many. He'd been footloose and fancy free for the past two years, so he'd been making up for lost time by screwing around every chance he got. Because of his political aspirations, he stayed away from married women. And he did his best to keep his affairs discreet. He didn't make promises and tried not to break any hearts, despite being a strictly love 'em and leave 'em type.

Things would have been different with Jazzy.

Shit, man, get over it. Get over her. Even if she wanted him—which she didn't—he could never marry her. No way in hell could he ever run for political office again if he had a wife like Jazzy. He kept reminding himself that the world was full of pretty women. Pretty redheads who didn't say no. Just because he'd had a thing for Jazzy as long as he could remember didn't mean he had to spend the rest of his life mooning over her.

"Wade, honey . . ." She nuzzled his neck, then kissed his jaw. "You're awfully quiet. What are you thinking about?"

He groaned inwardly. What was it with women—all women—always wanting to know what a man was thinking? If he told her that he'd been thinking about another woman, she'd not only be hurt, but she'd get pissed.

"I'm thinking about you," he lied. "About all the things I'd like to do to you."

She giggled.

He pulled away from her and slid out of bed. After his feet hit the floor, he grabbed his tan slacks off the back of the nearby chair where he'd neatly hung them and then pulled them on. "I'm going to get myself a glass of wine. Do you want one?"

She crinkled her nose. "I don't much care for wine. Do you happen to have a beer?"

"Sure, I'll bring you back a beer."

Wade grinned. His date tonight was no more the type you'd bring home to Mama than Jazzy was, but she sure made a man's blood boil. And his dick get hard and stay that way.

She'd pulled a fast one on him. That's what she'd done. Jacob Butler finished off his second piece of apple dapple cake and washed it down with his third cup of coffee. If he'd had any idea that Reve Sorrell would be here tonight, he'd have declined Genny's invitation to supper. When Genny had called earlier in the day, she'd mentioned that Jazzy and Caleb would be joining them this evening, but she hadn't mentioned Jazzy's guest. Ms. Sorrell, the might-be twin sister from Chattanooga. The rich bitch who looked down her nose at other folks, him in particular. The first time they met, she'd called him a big country hick Cochise wannabe. In one sentence she'd insulted his body, his place of residence and his ethnic heritage. And the worst part of her caustic remark had been that she'd felt totally justified in verbally abusing the Cherokee County sheriff.

For the past hour he'd done his best not to even look at her, but Genny had made that damn near impossible. She'd sat them across the table from each other and then proceeded to draw them both into every conversation. If he didn't know better, he'd swear Genny was trying to match him up with this dang-fool woman. But Genny wouldn't do that knowing how much he disliked Ms. Sorrell.

He wasn't sure who'd been the most surprised when she'd opened the back door when he first arrived and had all but run right into him. Instinctively, he'd reached out and grabbed her shoulders to prevent them from colliding. For just a second, she'd stood there staring up at him, her mouth hanging open and her eyes as big as half dollars. Then she'd jerked away from him as if he were the boogie man himself. They'd glared at each other, neither of them backing down, and that was when he'd taken a really good look at her. She sure as shoot looked like Jazzy. Definitely enough to be her twin. But she was taller than Jazzy, maybe by a couple of inches, which meant she was probably at least five-ten. And although she wasn't built too bad—if you could actually tell her exact proportions under her loose-fitting slacks and baggy sweater—she was rounder and fuller than Jazzy. Not fat, but definitely not slim. She was every bit as pretty as Jazzy, maybe prettier because she didn't cover up her flawless complexion with a layer of makeup.

"Would you care for another piece of cake, Reve?" Genny asked.

"It was delicious, but no, thank you," she replied. "Besides, I doubt there's any cake left." She glanced directly at Jacob when she spoke.

Dallas and Caleb both chuckled. Jacob shot them both scurrilous glares, damning them with only a look.

"I guess you're watching your weight anyway, aren't you, Ms. Sorrell?" Jacob ran his gaze over her. "Why is it that you plump girls are the ones always dieting and the skinny ones eat whatever they want?"

Reve gasped. When Jacob noted the hurt look on her face, he halfway wished the words back. Usually he didn't intentionally hurt anybody's feelings, and certainly never a lady's, but damn it, this particular lady made him want to instantly go for the jugular.

A hushed silence fell over the room. Genny gave Jacob a condemning look, then said loudly, "Well, if everyone's fin- ished, why don't we go into the living room and visit for a while. We can all have a glass of Ludie's muscadine wine to celebrate Jazzy and Caleb's engagement."

Caleb and Jazzy scooted back their chairs and stood.

"It won't be official until she's wearing my ring." Caleb put his arm around Jazzy's shoulders. "But I'm all for some of that wine before we head into town." He glanced down at Reve and smiled. "Have you ever tasted muscadine wine, Reve?"

She shook her head. "No, I'm afraid that's one experience I've missed."

"You men go on," Jazzy said. "Reve and I will help Genny clean up in here."

"Why don't we all go on into the living room now." Dallas slipped his arm around his wife's waist. "I'll help Genny clean up in here later."

"I really ought to be going." Jacob had no intention of spending the rest of the evening with Reve Sorrell. He didn't care if she did turn out to be Jazzy's twin, there was no way the two of them would ever be friends.

Jacob got up, but before he could make his getaway, Genny grabbed his arm. "Don't be silly. You never leave this early when you're not on duty."

"Maybe I've got a late date," Jacob told her.

"Do you?" she asked.

Why he glanced over at Reve about that time, he didn't know, but when he did he caught her glaring at him. He wanted to lie and say yes, that he had a hot late date. But he'd never lied to Genny and he sure as hell wasn't going to start now.

"Nope. No late date. But I've got a ton of paperwork I need to catch up on."

The others meandered out of the kitchen, while Jacob re- mained there with Genny, who kept a tight hold on him. The minute they were alone, she said in a low, quiet voice, "I want you to stop being hateful to Reve."

"Damn, Genny, the woman gets on my last nerve."

"Shush. Don't talk so loud. I think you've insulted her enough for one evening."

He grimaced. "Yeah, I guess I shouldn't have said what I did about her being plump, but whenever I'm around that woman, I want to strangle her. She's such a snooty bitch."

"She is not what she seems."

"And just what does that mean?"

"She is afraid to trust others, so she has built this strong protective shield around herself. But deep inside she is a lonely woman who longs for true friends and longs to be loved for herself alone."

"Why tell me all this?" Jacob's gut tightened painfully. Not a good sign.

"Because she is in danger. Both she and Jazzy."

"What sort of danger?"

"I'm not sure. But I believe there is someone out there who would harm them in order to keep a terrible secret from being revealed." Genny released her tenacious hold on Jacob's arm. "I gave Jazzy a reading today and although I sensed that it is a good thing that she and Reve are sisters, they're both in grave danger. And I sense the danger is greatest for Jazzy, at least at the present."

"As the sheriff and as Jazzy's friend, I'll do whatever—"

"I know that, and I pray we can keep her from harm. But Jazzy has Caleb. He would die to protect her."

Jacob didn't like the way this conversation was going.

Genny trapped him with her dark, pensive gaze. "Reve has no one. She needs you, Jacob."

No way in hell. He wasn't taking on the job of being Reve Sorrell's private protector. "Let her hire a bodyguard. God knows she's got enough money to hire an army to protect her."

"She doesn't need an army. She just needs one good man."

"Well, I'm here to tell you, honey, I'm not that man."

"Yes, you are." Standing on tiptoe, she kissed his cheek, then stepped back and stared at him, a knowing look in her black eyes. "So there's no need to fight Fate."

Feeling as if a noose had just tightened around his windpipe, Jacob rubbed his throat. Genny was seldom wrong in her predictions, and he usually paid heed to them. But not this time. Even if Genny believed he was destined to be the one man who could take care of Reve Sorrell, he had every intention of fighting Fate, tooth and nail.

Jeremy Timmons's eyes bulged from his head, wide open and glazed by death. The guy had been an easy kill because he'd been stoned out of his mind.

He could still sense the feeling he'd experienced when his hands tightened around Timmons's throat. The man had been a toad, a worthless piece of trash, and the world was better off without him. Killing the vermin had given him no pleasure, but he'd had to do it. Dead men tell no tales. With Timmons dead, there was no way anyone could connect him to Becky Olmstead.

God knew he'd tried his best to stay away from her, but she had tempted him beyond all reason. He had suspected, once the obsession took him over, that it wasn't really Becky Olmstead in that young, nubile body. It wasn't Becky's thoughts and feelings ruling her actions. No, it was Dinah. She'd come back immediately, giving him no time for any peace of mind. He'd had to make sure she was really Dinah, hadn't he? And now that he knew, he would seek her out again and send her back to hell where she belonged.

Perhaps later tonight. The sooner the better.

But for now he needed to search Timmons's body and his house to make sure he didn't keep any kind of records about the clientele his whores serviced. And he had to be very careful that he left behind no clues that would link him with

Timmons's murder. He'd been careful to wear gloves. No fingerprints. Later he'd burn the gloves, as well as every article of clothing he was wearing.

With expert ease, he riffled through Timmons's pockets. Then, finding nothing, he went through all the drawers, closets and cabinets in the house, but came up empty-handed. He couldn't afford to stay here much longer. The longer he remained at the crime scene, the greater the likelihood he'd get caught.

Cracking the door several inches, he peered outside and saw no one. Good. Maybe he could make it to his car, which he'd parked down the road, without being seen by any nosy neighbors. The fact that there weren't any streetlights outside of town meant the only source of illumination at night came from the moon. His arrival and departure were less likely to be observed out here than on a well-lit street. And the houses were separated by acres instead of feet, some sitting a good ways off the road. But on the off chance someone did see him, he'd have to think up a reasonable excuse for being in this area. He wasn't worried. He was a smart man. He'd think of something.

Becky knocked on the motel room door.

"It's unlocked," he said.

She opened the door and found the room dark, the only light coming from the neon motel sign flickering outside the window. This john was her second for the night, which wasn't unusual for a Saturday, but when Jeremy had told her to meet this guy at the Cloud View, she'd come close to saying no. She hated this creepy old motel that had been used primarily by tourists back in the sixties, long before she was born. Now, the place was a rathole and the customers were mostly drug addicts and other scum of the earth types. This was only her third time here and she dreaded spending even an hour in one of the beds. The last time she'd been here, she'd killed a roach the size of a half dollar as it crawled across the bathroom floor.

"Come inside and close the door."

What was wrong with this guy's voice? He sounded like he had a cold or something.

An odd feeling shivered through her as she entered the room and closed the door behind her. The room was not only dark, but chilly. Either this guy liked the cold or the heat wasn't working.

"Mind if I turn on a light?" she asked.

"Leave the lights off," he said in that strange, husky voice.

"Sure." Her gut instinct warned her that something wasn't quite right about this guy, but then again she'd felt this way before. Half the men she serviced were oddballs. But what the hell, a buck was a buck. "So what do you want? Jeremy didn't say whether you wanted a blow job or—"

"I want you to take off your clothes and lie down on the bed," he told her.

"You won't be able to see much with the lights off," she said. "If you want to get your money's worth—"

"Oh, don't worry, I'll get what I paid for . . . and then some."

What the hell did he mean by that? And then some?

"Hey, I should warn you that I'm not into anything too kinky. You can spank me or ass fuck me or piss on me, but that's it. Understand?"

He chuckled, then tossed something through the air. It landed at her feet. She looked down, then bent over and felt around until her hand encountered a corded string of some kind. After picking it up, she held it up to the window and saw it was a dark satin ribbon.

"Tie it around your neck," he said. "That's not too kinky, is it?"

Becky tied the ribbon around her neck, then moved toward the bed. As she stripped out of her clothes, she watched the shadow in the corner of the room and knew that he was staring at her. She could feel his gaze raking over her, almost as if he was touching her.

"I'm ready," she said.

"Are you?"

"I'm naked, in the bed, and I've got the ribbon tied around my neck. Anything else you want, just tell me."

"Look on the nightstand," he said. "There's a glass of wine there. I'd like for you to drink it."

"You want me to drink alone?"

"I have my glass here with me." He tapped the side of the flute he held.

"Okay, sure."

He couldn't see her clearly in the semidarkness, but he could make out her form and the bright red highlights in her hair. The neon sign outside provided just enough light for him to maneuver in the room without giving Becky a good look at him. He couldn't let her see him clearly, because she would recognize him and possibly balk.

As she sipped the wine, he set his empty glass on the floor and moved closer to the bed, but kept himself in the shadows.

"Finish it off, then we'll get down to business," he said.

"I'll take a few more sips, she said. "But I really hate the taste of wine."

"Just a few more sips will be fine." She didn't have to be unconscious, just subdued enough so that she wouldn't fight him. He'd learned, early on, that Dinah would fight him every time, if he didn't drug her, so he'd realized that that was exactly what she'd wanted him to do. She'd been the one to set in place so many of the rules for the little game they played each time he killed her.

After she'd taken a few more sips of the wine, he walked over and stood by the side of the bed. "How are you feeling?" he asked.

"A little groggy," she said. "I'm not used to wine. I guess that's why I feel so funny."

"Yeah, that's probably why."

She crawled into the bed, atop the covers, and held out her arms to him. "If you don't have any condoms, I've got some. Just check the pockets of my jeans."

"I have my own, thank you."

"What's your pleasure? Got a favorite position?"

"Turn over. We'll do it from the rear the first time. I want to butt-fuck you."

"You're paying for more than once?" she asked. "Did you okay that with Jeremy? I think he's lined up a third 'date' for me tonight."

"I took care of everything with Jeremy."

Oh, he'd taken care of Jeremy all right. That slimy little bastard wouldn't be sending any other whores out on assignments tonight or tomorrow night or ever. He'd had no choice but to use Timmons to secure Becky's services tonight. He'd known all along that he'd have to kill Timmons. He never left any loose ends. That's why he'd been able to find Dinah and kill her, over and over again. Because he outsmarted the law. Every time.

At first Becky had wondered why those few sips of wine had gotten her so drunk, but then she'd figured it out pretty damn quick. The asshole had drugged the wine. Had he thought she'd put up a fuss when he'd wanted to ass fuck her the first time?

Afterward, she must have fallen asleep for a while, something she never did. He was feeling her up again now, his hands on her tits, squeezing. But there was something odd about the way he was touching her. It was his hands. Was he wearing gloves?

Becky's eyelids flew open; she stared up into his face. The blinking light coming through the window hit him, spotlighting his features. Oh, God! She should have known it was him.

"It's you," she said.

"It's me."

He put his hands beneath her hips and lifted her. His hard dick pressed against her pubic hair. She felt the plastic gloves he wore as they scraped over her backside.

"What's with the gloves?" she asked. "Afraid you'll catch something?"

"They're a precaution," he told her. "I always wear them. You know that, Dinah. I can't leave behind any evidence. If the police ever caught me, it would be the end of our games."

"What—what games? And who is Dinah?"

Evidence? The police? What the hell was he talking about—oh, God, no. Please no.

He rammed into her hard and fast. She cried out.

"It is you, Dinah," he said. "I thought it was, but now I'm sure."

Sheer panic encompassed her. This guy was freaking nuts.

"Let me go. I don't want—"

He covered her mouth with his hand. "Don't talk."

She murmured her pleas against his open palm, then tried to bite his hand.

"Why are you fighting me? You want this as much as I do," he said. "You love playing our little game. If you didn't, you wouldn't keep coming back from the dead."

Becky screamed inside her mind. This couldn't be happening. It had to be a horrible dream. She was too young to die.

Don't kill me, she pleaded silently. *Please, don't kill me. Oh, God in heaven, help me!*

CHAPTER 8

Reve smiled and nodded and replied with yes or no to anything the others asked, but she focused on the room itself. She had noted earlier today that Genny Madoc's home was filled with antiques. Every room she had seen evoked images of a bygone era. Some of the furniture was museum quality and would sell for a small fortune. When she inquired about the age of the farmhouse itself this afternoon, Genny had told her that it was well over a hundred years old, built by her great-grandfather, and had replaced an old log cabin constructed by a distant ancestor in the nineteenth century.

A glowing fire shimmered in the large fireplace, the blaze reflected in the glass chimneys of the two oil lamps flanking the sofa. The old, wide plank flooring glistened from the patina of numerous waxings and the wood-paneled, wainscoted walls gleamed with the richness of aged pine. This room—this entire house—expressed a quality and charm no interior decorator could ever reproduce. It possessed warmth and comfort, proclaiming the character of the people who lived here and the generations who had come before. This structure was a home, not merely a house.

Suddenly Reve felt terribly alone, more so than she'd ever felt in her parents' elegant Lookout Mountain mansion, now that she was the sole occupant. And when she heard Jazzy and Caleb laughing at something Dallas had said, she envied how comfortable they were around one another. Friends who had no hidden agendas. Friends who simply enjoyed being together.

And as if she wasn't feeling bad enough at that particular moment, she felt even worse when she saw Jacob following Genny into the living room. Reve groaned. She had hoped he'd already left. Apparently not. Genny must have persuaded him to stay, despite his rush to leave. It had been embarrassingly obvious to everyone that she—the outsider—was the reason he hadn't wanted to stay for a visit with family and friends.

Genny smiled at Reve as she joined the others, but Jacob avoided looking at her as he made his way across the room to stand near the fireplace. Noting the sullen expression on his face, she surmised that he didn't want to be in her company anymore than she wanted to be in his. So why was Genny forcing the issue? Why hadn't she let him leave when he'd wanted to go?

"Dallas, help me get the wine," Genny said.

Her husband followed her to the large cupboard on the far side of the room. Genny opened the double glass doors and removed six wine glasses. Austrian crystal, unless Reve missed her guess. Dallas lifted a glass jug, removed the cork and poured the homemade wine into the glasses, then picked up two and brought one to her and handed Jazzy the other.

Once everyone had a glass, Dallas lifted his and said, "Here's to Jazzy and Caleb. May their upcoming marriage bring them as much happiness as Genny and I have found in ours."

"I'll definitely drink to that," Caleb said.

"That was very sweet, Dallas," Jazzy told him. "Thank you."

When everyone else took a sip of the wine, Reve did, too, and discovered it wasn't half bad. Nothing to compare to a truly excellent vintage, but nevertheless definitely palatable.

"So, what do you think of Ludie's wine?" Dallas asked.

Reve found herself glancing toward Jacob, expecting him to make some acrid remark. And at that exact moment, he looked right at her. Their gazes locked and held. No one said a word. Silence hung heavily over the room. Reve's heartbeat accelerated maddeningly.

"It's quite good," she finally managed to reply and sensed that everyone breathed a sigh of relief.

"You met Ludie, didn't you?" Jazzy asked. "She was the old Cherokee woman who was with Aunt Sally that first day you came to Cherokee Pointe."

"Yes, I met her," Reve said. "She's the woman who makes those delicious desserts for your restaurant, isn't she?"

"That's Ludie. But she's also Aunt Sally's best friend and just like family to me."

Did that mean, if she and Jazzy were sisters, that she'd be expected to consider both Sally Talbot and Ludie as family? For the life of her, she couldn't see herself embracing a nutty old mountain woman who chewed tobacco and her Indian friend as family.

Watch out, Reve, your snobbery is showing again.

During the next hour, Jacob gradually joined the others in conversation and appeared more relaxed, but he didn't speak directly to Reve nor did he ever look right at her again. She tried her best to be friendly, but she realized she was carefully watching everything she said, not wanting to offend anyone, not even Jacob. Unable to fully participate in the camaraderie, she withdrew more and more, a well-learned defense mechanism that she had relied on all her life. In her world, she was respected and deferred to by others, only occasionally running into people who weren't impressed by her wealth and social standing. But as a child, she'd often felt out of place, the odd girl out, with her peers. In those instances, she had retreated into the safety of stubborn shyness.

Jazzy sat on the sofa, Caleb beside her, his arm resting across the sofa back behind Jazzy's head. Genny sat on a round leather ottoman near the fireplace, and Jacob stood behind her, while each took a turn recounting his or her particular take on an event from their shared childhoods.

"You should have seen Granny's face," Genny said.

"Yeah, it was all she could do not to laugh, but she told us, in no uncertain terms, that young ladies didn't run around naked, not even in the summertime." Jazzy looked up at Jacob. "And it was all your fault that we got in trouble because you told on us."

"I swear I didn't tell her that you two eight-year-olds were skinny-dipping in the pond in front of half a dozen other kids. It must have been somebody else. Maybe one of the Winstead boys." The twinkle in Jacob's eyes revealed the uselessness of trying to defend himself from a crime of which he was obviously guilty.

"Yeah, tell that to somebody who'll believe you," Jazzy said. "Neither Aaron nor Miles Winstead would have told on us. Aaron was sweet on me, and Miles would have walked over hot coals for Genny."

"Especially after he saw her naked as a jaybird," Jacob said, then roared with laughter.

"What did your grandmother do?" Caleb asked Genny, once the boisterous laughter died down.

"She gave me a spanking, made Jazzy and me put on our clothes and then she marched Jazzy home, with me in tow, and told Miss Sally what had happened."

"And then I got my butt blistered." Jazzy laughed.

Dallas came over to where Reve stood by the windows, in the same room and yet separate from the others. "Those three grew up together. They're like siblings who share the same memories. It took me a while to begin to fit in, to feel as if I were a part of that golden circle. And Caleb only recently joined the ranks." Dallas spoke quietly so that their conversation remained private.

Reve nodded, not sure what message Dallas was trying to convey.

"Give yourself time and you'll fit in. You'll become one of us," he told her. "If you want to be a part of that closeness, that sense of belonging to a special family, you can be."

Reve wanted to tell him that she had no desire to be a part of Jazzy's extended family, that she could care less about fitting in, in fact she abhorred the idea of being one of these people. But the denial died on her lips. Partly because the comments would have offended, but mostly because she realized her denial wasn't true. Somewhere deep down inside her lonely soul, she envied them all and wanted what Genny had with Dallas and Jazzy had with Caleb.

"I suppose you believe, as Genny does, that Jazzy and I are twins."

"If my wife says she knows it for a fact, then it's a fact," Dallas said with utter conviction. "You and Jazzy are twins. You're family. And if you're Jazzy's family, then you're Genny's, too." He paused, glanced lovingly at his wife and then looked back at Reve. "They're not keeping you out, you know. Jazzy and Genny will welcome you with open arms. All you have to do is reach out to them."

"And what about Jacob?" Reve whispered. "He really doesn't like me." Now why had she said that to Dallas? He'd think she gave a damn about what Jacob Butler thought. And she didn't!

"Genny says she's never seen Jacob take an instant dislike to anybody the way he has you." When Reve gazed at him in disbelief, surprised by his honesty, Dallas laughed softly. "And she also said that you're the first woman she's ever known who didn't swoon at Jacob's feet."

The corners of Reve's mouth twitched, and finally she smiled.

"Give yourself time to get to know him, and I think you'll discover that Jacob is a good man," Dallas said. "Actually, he's one of the finest men I've ever known."

"Really?"

Before Reve had a chance to completely digest Dallas's

high praise of the sheriff, Jazzy and Caleb stood up and each hugged Genny in turn, then Jazzy hugged Jacob.

"We've got to be going. It's nearly eight-thirty and we need to get to Jazzy's Joint by nine, before things get rowdy." Caleb glanced over at Reve. "We can drop you off at your cabin on the way, if you're ready to go."

Reve started to say that she was more than ready to leave, when Genny spoke up hurriedly, "You two go on to work. Reve can stay and visit a while longer. Jacob would be glad to drop her off when he goes back to town later."

Genny's statement created a unanimous silent gasp.

"Why in heaven's name would you—" Jazzy said, only to be interrupted by Jacob himself.

"Yeah, sure, if Ms. Sorrell wants to stay for a while longer, I'll give her a ride back into town." Avoiding making eye contact with Reve, he downed the last drops of the wine he'd been nursing all evening.

Jazzy looked at Genny, who smiled as she gazed steadily at her friend. Suddenly Jazzy's face lit up as if she'd just figured out an intricate puzzle.

"That's mighty nice of you," Jazzy said, a sly smile on her face. Apparently she and Genny shared some cute little secret that the rest of them weren't privy to.

"I'd rather go on now, if you don't mind." Reve looked pleadingly at Jazzy, not sure what was going on, but not wanting to be a part of anything that put her in Jacob's company any longer than necessary.

"Of course we won't force you to stay, but I'd really like it if you would spend some more time getting to know us . . . Dallas and me and Jacob," Genny said. "I'd like for us to be friends."

Reve sighed. She felt Jacob's gaze on her, and when she looked at him, she sensed that he was issuing her a challenge. He thought she didn't have the guts to let him drive her home later. Did he actually believe she was afraid of him? Well, she'd prove him wrong. She'd show him.

"All right," Reve agreed. "It would be unmannerly of me to decline such a generous offer of friendship."

Lesley Sorrell had drilled good manners into Reve from the time she was a small child. Under most circumstances she easily played the part of a modern, wealthy, cultured, genteel southern belle. Occasionally her strong-willed character and her stubbornness injected themselves into situations, especially when she was confronted by the likes of Sheriff Butler.

Jazzy came over to Reve, acting as if she intended to hug her. Reve stepped back to avoid physical contact. Jazzy offered her an understanding smile. "We'll pick you up tomorrow for dinner with Miss Reba and Big Jim. I'll call you in the morning."

"Yes, do that. I'll see you tomorrow."

While Genny and Dallas saw their guests out, Jacob moved in on Reve. Every nerve in her body screamed, every muscle froze. He came up beside her and paused.

"If you'll play nice, I'll play nice," he said. "Genny likes you. For the life of me, I don't know why, but she does. And she's given me strict orders to be on my best behavior around you."

"For Genny's sake, I'm willing to call a truce. At least for tonight."

She glanced up at him. He shook his head.

"What?" she asked.

"Just thinking about Fate."

"What about Fate?"

"It plays odd tricks on us sometimes. Like you and Jazzy for instance. Twins separated at birth, raised in two different worlds and now here y'all are on the verge of turning each other's lives upside down."

Reve glowered at him. "Explain something to me, will you?"

He nodded. "Sure. If I can."

"How is it that, considering Jazzy and I are probably

identical twins, you react in a totally different way to the two of us although we look a great deal alike? I'd think that considering she's your friend, you'd have viewed me in a more favorable light when we first met. But you disliked me instantly."

"That's a damn good question. And when I figure out the answer, Ms. Sorrell, you'll be the first to know."

Dallas held Genny in his arms as they sat alone in front of the living room fireplace, the soft tapping of raindrops on the old metal roof soothing them like a lullaby. He loved moments such as this, just Genny and him. And Drudwyn asleep on the floor. If a year ago somebody had told him that he'd not only be content being a small town sheriff, but that he'd marry a psychic and live a simple life with her in the Tennessee hills, he'd have told them they were crazy. But he would have been wrong. He'd never been as happy or content as he was here with Genny. His wife. His life.

"Do you think I might have pushed too hard?" Genny asked. "I suppose I shouldn't have insisted that Reve stay and that Jacob take her home. I don't know who looked the most miserable when they left here, him or her."

"I'd say it was even-Steven."

"They're not always going to despise each other." Genny maneuvered herself around so that she could keep her head resting on his shoulder and look up at him at the same time. "But maybe I should just let nature take its course."

"What are you talking about?" Sometimes Genny spoke in riddles. And sometimes he instinctively figured out those riddles. But other times, like now, she was a complete puzzle to him. He tried to see into her mind, but couldn't. Had she shut him out or was he just not concentrating hard enough? The latter, he suspected.

"I'm not the only one who sees it," Genny said. "Jazzy picked up on it, too. I don't understand why you didn't."

"I'm lost, honey. What is it that I don't understand?"

"That Reve is the woman for Jacob."

"What?"

"Goodness, Dallas, a person doesn't have to be psychic to pick up on the sexual tension between them. It's so strong it practically has a life of its own."

Dallas laughed, but stopped immediately when he noted the frown on Genny's face.

"Sorry, but all I picked up on between those two was pure, unadulterated hatred."

Genny jerked away from him, crossed her arms over her chest and shot him a disappointed glare. "Okay, so maybe you do have to be psychic—or a woman—to see what's right under your nose. I'm telling you that I know"—she laid her hand over her heart—"Reve and Jacob are meant for each other."

Dallas grasped her hands and tugged on them, toppling her over and into his lap. He nuzzled her ear. "If you say they're meant for each other, then they're meant for each other. I trust your instincts without any doubts."

She draped her arm around his neck. "Why don't we go to bed?" She kissed him.

Dallas's body hardened instantly. He stood, Genny in his arms, and walked out of the living room, up the stairs and straight to their bedroom. His last thought before he concentrated fully on making love to his wife was that he hoped Reve and Jacob didn't kill each other before they discovered they were destined to be lovers.

The rain had slacked off by the time Jacob pulled his Dodge Ram to a halt in front of Reve's rental cabin. On the ride down the mountain, they had managed to remain civil, even without Genny's presence as a deterrent. Of course, neither of them had said more than ten words. He'd turned on the radio for a while, but as soon as he realized she didn't like his taste in music, he'd turned it off. The silence between them had been more deafening than a rock concert. He couldn't ever remember feeling so damn uncomfortable.

When he opened the driver's door, Reve said, "You needn't bother to get out."

Disregarding her statement, he got out, pulled an umbrella from the back and opened it. Holding the bright orange and white UT umbrella over his head, he rounded the hood and opened the passenger door for her. When he offered her his hand, she stared at it as if it was contaminated with leprosy. Reluctantly, as if she knew he had offered her his hand more as a dare than as a gentlemanly gesture, she put her hand in his and allowed him to help her out of the truck.

Once on the ground beside him, she looked him square in the eye and said, "Are you going to walk me to my door or are we going to stand here holding hands all night?"

If she thought that would make him drop her hand like a hot potato, she had another thought coming. He held her hand a little tighter.

"I'll walk you to your door." Keeping the umbrella over them to block the slow drizzle, he urged her into movement. "But don't expect a good-night kiss. Not on a first date."

She cut her eyes upward and gave him a sidelong glance.

"I wouldn't want you to think I'm easy," he said, a smile playing at the corners of his mouth. Maybe the best offense was a good defense, he thought. Taking her off guard with a little humor might work. After all, he had promised Genny that he'd be nice to Reve, hadn't he?

"I doubt you give a damn what I think of you," she said in a very pleasant voice.

When they reached the cabin door, he took the key she held and unlocked the door, then handed the key back to her. "Good night, Ms. Sorrell. Spending an evening with you has been an experience I wouldn't care to repeat anytime soon."

"For once, Sheriff Butler, we're in total agreement." Her smile was as phony as her sweet tone of voice.

He turned and walked away, but when he reached his truck,

he glanced back and found her standing on the doorstep watching him. He waved. She waved.

"And one more thing, just to set the record straight," he said. "You're right, I don't give a rat's ass what you think of me."

Laughing, she shot him a bird, letting him know she felt the same, then turned around, went inside her rental cabin and closed the door.

Jacob chuckled. Damn infuriating woman! He closed the umbrella, tossed it in the back, then hopped up into the cab of his truck. Just as he shut the door, a call came in over the radio.

"Jacob," Tewanda Hardy said. "We've got a homicide on Clinton Road. Moody and Bobby Joe are on their way there now."

"Give me the exact address."

"Two-oh-nine Clinton. It's a rental house."

"Do we know the victim's identity?"

"Jeremy Timmons."

Jacob groaned. Ever since he'd taken office, Jacob had been trying to acquire enough evidence against Timmons, the slimy little bastard, to arrest him. The guy was a pimp who oversaw a stable of five or six working girls, but he'd managed to stay one step ahead of the law. Jacob wasn't surprised that somebody had killed the son of a bitch.

"Who called it in?" Jacob asked.

"A girl named Amber Chaney."

"Have you contacted—"

"The coroner and forensics? Yeah, Pete's on his way. And Burt said he'd go by and pick up Dewayne."

Jacob started the engine, shifted into reverse and backed up, then headed out of town. Just when he'd thought his bad night was over, it had taken a turn for the worse. During his short term in office, there had already been too many murders in Cherokee County. The last thing he or his county needed was another one. Even if Timmons had deserved killing, and he probably had, it was still the sheriff's job to find the murderer and bring him or her to justice. Jacob's guess was that one of Timmons's "girls" had whacked him.

He laid her limp body on the edge of the bed, spread apart her legs and touched her intimately. Desire consumed him, urged him on, forced him to do the unthinkable. He unzipped his pants, freed his penis and rammed himself into the girl.

Pure evil. Black hatred. Passion and anger. A need for sexual gratification and a hunger for power.

He took her with brutal pleasure, coming quickly. But sexual release alone could not satisfy him.

Suddenly he undid the braided black satin ribbon around the girl's smooth neck. In a frenzy of excitement and unparalleled power, he grasped the ribbon and tightened it around her throat. She didn't struggle, couldn't struggle. Within minutes, she stopped breathing.

Genny Madoc screamed.

Dallas came instantly awake, flipped on the bedside lamp and turned to his wife. She lay beside him, thrashing back and forth, her screams tapering off to gasps and sobs. Gently, he slipped his arms around her and lifted her up and into his embrace. While she trembled and wept, he stroked her back lovingly.

Although her mind and spirit were still halfway submerged in the obsidian depths of a precognitive experience, Genny felt Dallas holding her, soothing her. And she sensed his love and concern.

"Slow and easy," Dallas said. "Come back to me, but don't try to rush it. Take your time."

Forcing the dark shadows from her mind, she inched her way steadily back into the realm of reality. Finally she managed to speak. "He strangled her."

"You witnessed a murder?" Dallas asked.

She nodded. "But I don't think it's happened yet."

"Did you see his face? Did you recognize the victim?"

"No, I didn't see his face. Only a hazy glimpse of his hands and his . . . his penis."

"What?" Dallas grasped her shoulders.

"He raped her and then killed her. He enjoyed killing her. It gave him more pleasure than the sex."

Dallas swallowed hard.

"The victim is young and pretty and has curly red hair. I didn't recognize her. I got only a glimpse of her face."

"I'll call Jacob and we'll see if we can stop this murder before it happens. Did you pick up on anything that might help us locate this girl?"

Genny shook her head. "Not really. They were inside, not outside. He laid her on a bed. And—and he choked her to death with a braided black ribbon."

"Will you be okay while I contact Jacob?"

She gave him a gentle shove. "Call him and then fix me some chamomile tea."

Dallas rolled out of bed, dragged on his discarded jeans and reached out for the bedside phone.

Jacob answered on the fifth ring. "Butler here."

"Jacob, it's Dallas. Genny has seen another murder. She believes it hasn't happened yet, so—"

"It has. I'm on the scene now. Pete's examining the body. Please tell me that Genny saw the killer."

"Nope, sorry. She did see the victim however, but didn't recognize her."

"Did you say her?"

"Yeah, why?"

"This victim is a man," Jacob said. "Jeremy Timmons. Looks like somebody strangled him."

"Genny saw a young woman being strangled with a black braided ribbon. She had curly red hair." The wheels in Dallas's mind turned at breakneck speed, resulting in an educated guess. "What do you want to bet that the woman Genny saw murdered is one of Timmons's girls, that their murders are connected?"

"Could be. But there might not be a connection between this murder and the murder Genny saw in her vision."

"Maybe you should find out if one of Timmons's girls has red curly hair."

"I'll do my best to find out, but the odds are against us. The girl—Amber Chaney—who found Timmons's body isn't likely to give me the names and addresses of her colleagues."

"If I'm right, then finding this girl right away might be the only way to save her life. Tell that to Amber Chaney."

CHAPTER 9

Jacob couldn't help feeling sorry for Amber Chaney, despite the fact that she looked anything but sympathetic. Frizzy, jet-black hair—dyed—matched the color of the thick eyeliner splotched by her tears and the knee-high, spike-heeled boots she wore. She'd been puffing on a cigarette when Jacob arrived at Jeremy Timmons's rental house on Clinton Road; and she was smoking now while she waited impatiently at the sheriff's department for him to question her again. At the scene of the crime, she hadn't admitted she worked for Timmons, that he'd been her pimp.

"I know him, that's all," she'd said. "He's a friend of mine."

"Want to give us the names of his other *girlfriends*?" Jacob had asked.

She'd blown smoke in Jacob's face and replied, "I didn't say I was his girlfriend."

Moody Ryan, Jacob's youngest deputy, shook his head. He stood beside Jacob's desk looking into the outer office where Amber sat tapping her foot on the floor and glancing nervously about as if she wanted to get up and run off.

"I knew Amber in school," Moody said. "She was a freshman when I was a junior. She's my kid sister's age. I had no idea she"—he lowered his voice—"was in that line of business. Heck, she's got a little boy, you know. Mike Crouch knocked her up when she was in tenth grade, and he up and joined the Army and left her high and dry. But I heard Amber got her GED and was working somewhere over in Newport."

"Do you think she remembers you?" Jacob asked.

"Maybe. Probably."

"Why don't you go talk to her. Take her a cup of coffee." Jacob inclined his head toward the coffee machine in the corner of his office. "See if you can make her understand that a woman's life might well depend on what she tells us. We need to find this redheaded woman Genny saw in her vision as soon as possible."

"Sure thing. I'll give it a try." Moody, like the rest of Jacob's staff, didn't question Genny's psychic abilities. They'd all seen her in action and knew she was the real McCoy, not some fake out to fool people and take their money.

Just as Moody left the office with a cup of hot coffee in his hand, he met Pete Holt, the county coroner. Jacob motioned for Pete to come on in.

"What do you have for me?" Jacob asked.

Pete sprawled out in a chair to the side of Jacob's desk. "Pretty much what I told you at the site. Cause of death was definitely strangulation. My guess is that while Timmons sat there in a drug-induced fog, our perpetrator came up behind him, took him unaware and wrapped the rope we found at the scene around the guy's neck."

"An up-close and personal kill."

"Yep."

"There were no signs of a forced entry or of a struggle. Amber told us that Timmons usually left his doors unlocked, which means anybody could have walked in on him. But I'd say, considering his profession and the fact that it didn't appear to be a robbery, he probably knew his killer. Right?"

"Yep. That would be my guess."

"Considering how neat the killer was, what are the odds he left any evidence behind, other than the rope?"

"Slim to none. But it's possible Burt and Dwayne will find something."

"Even if they do, I doubt it'll help us stop the second murder. The woman Genny saw being strangled could be with the killer right now."

Jacob got up and walked to the door, cracked it open and took a look at Moody talking to Amber. He wondered if his personable young deputy was having any better luck getting information from Ms. Chaney than he'd had. If Genny was right—and she usually was—out there somewhere was an unsuspecting young redheaded woman who just might meet her Maker before morning.

He watched her body as it disappeared beneath the surface of the lake. He had traveled Highway 321 until it intersected with 411, then he'd driven through Sevierville and from there to Douglas Lake. At this time of the morning—a little after two—there was no one else around, not another soul to see what he'd done. Although this time he'd been forced to kill Dinah in his home area, he had disposed of her miles away. If her body was found, it would probably be weeks from now, and by then identifying the remains would be more difficult. And even if she was found and properly identified, no one could ever connect him to Becky Olmstead, the latest body Dinah had inhabited. Only three people had known about their rendezvous last night. Now two of those people were dead. Timmons would stay dead, slimy bastard that he was. But she would come back. She always did.

He breathed in deeply as satisfaction spread through his body. She was dead. He had vanquished her once again. She had to be stupid to keep coming back, thinking he wouldn't be strong enough to rid himself of her. Any sexual gratification he experienced with other women paled in comparison to fucking Dinah just before he choked the life out of her, while her beautiful body was still warm and soft. The combination of sex followed by death stimulated every fiber of his body and mind. He was never more alive than he was at moments like this. Being with Dinah again so soon, participating in their often repeated ritual within days of the last time, made him understand that despite the risks involved, a part of him hoped she didn't make him wait months for her next return visit. Although he'd often wished her gone forever, he was beginning to doubt he could willingly give her up on a permanent basis.

When the night air chilled him, he sought the warmth of his car. As he sat behind the wheel, he glanced backward toward the trunk. There shouldn't be any evidence back there, hopefully not even the slightest trace. He had transported her body wrapped securely in a plastic sheet, which he would burn later, along with his clothes and gloves.

He shut his eyes, savoring the memory of making love to her and then killing her. The euphoria he felt only with Dinah prolonged his fulfillment. Not just the sexual fulfillment, but the gratification of exerting power over a woman who had once rejected him.

"Aren't you sorry, Dinah?" he said aloud. "Don't you wish you had loved me instead of him?"

Jacob downed the last drops of coffee from his mug. He'd poured a refill less than five minutes ago from the fresh brew he'd recently made. On nights like this, he lived off caffeine, depending on the stimulant to keep him wide awake and alert.

Nobody, not even Moody, had gotten anywhere with Amber Chaney. After hours of being held for questioning, she'd finally asked for a lawyer—Max Fennel in particular. But when they'd been unable to get in touch with Max, she'd agreed to use Max's partner, his nephew, Christopher. Chris Boatwright was Max's wife's sister's son and had grown up in Cherokee

Pointe. The guy had graduated high school the same year as
Jacob, but they'd never been friends, having hung around
with different crowds. Jacob had spoken to him briefly when
he first arrived at the sheriff's department half an hour ago
and had done his best to impress on Chris the importance of
Amber being totally honest with them. A woman's life could
well depend on it.

"You know how Genny's sixth sense has helped local law
enforcement on more than one occasion," Jacob had said.
"Try to make Amber understand that by not telling us who
the other girls that worked for Timmons are, especially any
redheads, she could be preventing us from saving a life."

As he settled behind his desk, Jacob placed the empty
coffee mug on a leather coaster, then glanced at his wristwatch. Two-forty-five. He shut his eyes, spread out his hand
and rubbed his eyes by rotating his thumb and middle finger
over the lids. With his eyes still closed, he tilted his head backward and pivoted his neck from side to side. He was tired. It
had already been a long night, and he figured he might as well
catch a catnap right now since there wasn't much chance of
him getting home to his own bed anytime soon. He'd found
that a ten-minute power nap could mean the difference between keeping mentally alert and fading off into a weary fog.

It usually took only a minute or two for relaxation to
claim him, but tonight, before that comfortable semi-asleep
stage kicked in, a woman's image flashed through his mind.
A warm inviting smile. Arms held open to him. A body clad
in a sheer satin nightgown.

Just looking at her aroused him.

Jacob's eyelids flew open. "Damn!"

The woman who'd given him a hard-on was Reve Sorrell.

*Don't beat yourself up over it. Your subconscious is get-
ting things all mixed up.* He blamed Genny for causing this
problem, for putting the idea in his head that he was destined
to be Reve's protector. Hell, with that highfalutin she-devil
around, he was the one who probably needed protection.

Willing his body under control and doing his best to erase thoughts of a scantily clad, overly friendly Reve from his mind, Jacob didn't hear his office door open. When he saw Chris Boatwright standing in front of his desk, he jerked involuntarily, taken off guard for a split second.

"What the hell? Haven't you ever heard of knocking?" Jacob asked.

"I did knock."

"Oh. Well, what is it? Have you been able to talk any sense into your client?"

"Maybe," Chris replied. "If she admits that Timmons was her boss and names the other girls working for him, will she and the girls be brought up on charges?"

Jacob grunted. "She doesn't have to admit to breaking the law. All I want are the names of Timmons's other girls, starting with the names of any redheads."

"Do I have your word that—"

Jacob waved his hand. "Yeah, yeah, you've got my word."

"There are seven girls, counting Amber, but only two redheads."

"Names? Addresses?"

"April Fowler and Becky Olmstead are the redheads. They both live in Cherokee Pointe. We should be able to find out exactly where without much trouble. Amber thinks April lives with a boyfriend over on Eighth Street, and Becky still lives at home with her folks, but she doesn't know the address."

Jacob stood. "Does she have any idea who April and Becky might have been with tonight?"

"She has no idea," Chris said. "Sometimes men contact Timmons directly to set up something, but often the girls pick up the guys on their own."

"Thanks." Jacob rounded his desk and shook hands with Chris. "Tell Amber she can go on home, but not to leave town. I might need more information from her."

As soon as the lawyer left his office, Jacob got to work tracking down the addresses for the two redheads. Considering what time it was, well into the early morning hours, there was a good chance both women would have gone home by now. He sure hoped they were both home in their beds, safe and sound.

His murky green eyes focused on her face, then moved languidly downward, inspecting every inch of her naked body. Her breath caught in her throat when she looked at him. He was big and hard and overpoweringly male. She knew he was going to touch her. Waiting with anticipation, she offered him a come-hither smile. He ran his fingertips across her cheek, then speared his big fingers through her hair and cupped the back of her head. She gasped with pleasure. He pulled her to him, lowered his head and took her mouth in a hungry, demanding kiss. Desire unlike any she'd ever known spiraled through her body, making her want him desperately.

Reve came awake with a startled cry and sat straight up in bed. Heaven help her! Her nipples were tight, her breasts swollen, her body damp with perspiration and her feminine core throbbing.

Flinging back the covers, she got out of bed, put on her gold satin robe and slipped into the matching satin shoes. Checking the digital clock on the bedside table, she saw that it was nearly four o'clock. She might as well stay up because there was no way she would go back to sleep. Just the thought of having another erotic dream about Jacob Butler was enough to make her want to stay awake for the rest of her life.

What on earth was wrong with her? Why had she dreamed of that rude, crude savage? She didn't even like him, so what had possessed her to dream about him?

She walked through her dark bedroom, lit only by the moonlight shining through the curtains, and opened the door leading into the living room/kitchen of her rental cabin. After making her way to the sink, she flipped on the overhead flourescent light and went about the business of preparing coffee. She'd brought her own preferred brand with her. Drinking gourmet coffee all her life had spoiled her, making most other coffee taste like dirty dishwater.

While the coffee brewed, she peered out the kitchen window at the paved driveway and parking area illuminated by a bright security light. Wet leaves stuck to the pavement, and the black asphalt glistened with rainwater. Looking to the right, she saw the cabin next door and, remembering it was occupied by a middle-aged couple, breathed a sigh of relief. Awakening so abruptly from a nightmare—and dreaming of kissing Jacob Butler was a nightmare!—she felt shaken and a bit on edge. If she'd been at home in Chattanooga, surrounded by the familiar, with two live-in-servants ensconced in the garage apartment and only a quick phone call away, she would feel completely secure.

You could have stayed with Jazzy. She graciously invited you to live with her while you're in Cherokee Pointe, but you chose to rent a cabin and be alone.

Alone. That one word repeated itself in her mind over and over again. That was exactly what she was. Alone. All alone. And had been since her mother's death. Her parents' families consisted of cousins and one elderly uncle on her mother's side, since Lesley had been an only child and Spencer's one sibling, a brother, had died in childhood.

In a way, Reve had been alone all her life, even when both of her parents had been alive. They had adored her, given her everything money could buy, yet they had spent so many years childless and were so devoted to each other that occasionally they seemed to forget that she even existed. They had hired a nurse when she was an infant, then replaced her with a series of nannies, four in all, until Reve was fourteen. Instead of public high school, she had attended GPS, Chattanooga's girl's preparatory school, and dated boys who attended McCallie and Baylor. She had lived the life of a privileged American princess, but had she ever been truly happy?

When the coffee finished brewing, she poured herself a mugful and went into the living room, sat on the sofa and placed her mug on the coffee table in front of her. She picked up the remote control and turned on the TV. As she flipped through the stations, she realized her only choices were a variety of paid advertisements, a couple of old movies and several news stations. She chose one of the movies, having immediately recognized Clark Gable and Greer Garson. Ever since childhood, she had been crazy about old movies, especially romantic movies. Sometimes she'd spend a Sunday afternoon alone, watching movie after movie, feeding her feminine need for romance. The movies from the Thirties and Forties were her absolute favorites.

As she watched while Clark grabbed Greer and kissed the breath out of her, Reve sipped on her delicious gourmet coffee. If she also had a piece of pie or cake or a Danish, she'd be in heaven right now.

Suddenly the actors on the small screen, who were driving into Reno to get married, metamorphosed from Greer and Clark into Reve and Jacob. Reve blinked several times to dissolve the illusion, then glanced back at the TV. She heaved a deep sigh when she saw the old movie stars again.

Get a grip, she told herself in no uncertain terms. She had to stop dreaming about, fantasizing about and thinking about Jacob Butler. If she didn't stop, she'd lose her mind.

You don't like him. He doesn't like you.

He was the last man on earth she'd want.

If that was true, then why couldn't she get him off her mind—awake or asleep?

Jacob Butler said good-bye to Becky Olmstead's mother and stepfather. Their daughter had told them she had a double date Saturday night and planned to stay over with her girlfriend, Amber Chaney, so she wouldn't be home until sometime Sunday morning.

"She promised she'd be home in time for church," Becky's mother had said.

"Yeah, she'll need to go to church all right." The step-father, a grizzly, bleary-eyed loudmouth, glared at Jacob. "She might fool her ma, but not me. She's shacked up with some guy tonight. The girl's got the morals of an alley cat."

Jacob slid behind the wheel of his Dodge Ram and closed the door. Half an hour ago, he'd found April Fowler at home with her latest boyfriend, so that ruled her out as a victim, at least for now. But since Becky's parents hadn't seen her since Saturday afternoon and had no idea where she was—she certainly hadn't spent the night with Amber—then Jacob had to consider her missing. Was Becky the intended victim Genny had seen in her vision? If so, then where did he begin to search for her?

He backed out of the driveway and headed toward the courthouse. If he used the standard means of tracing a missing person, there was little chance he'd find Becky within a few hours or even a few days. If she was lucky, she wasn't with a cold-blooded killer right now and she'd show later this morning, ready to go to church with her mother.

Just as Jacob eased his truck into his designated parking slot at the back of the courthouse, his cell phone rang.

He flipped it open. "Butler here."

"Jacob, it's Dallas."

"I suppose Genny's wanting an update. Tell her we narrowed it down to two women. One's been accounted for, but the other, a young woman named Becky Olmstead, is missing and I have no idea where to start looking for her."

"Start with the nearest creek or lake," Dallas said.

Jacob's stomach knotted painfully. "Genny had another vision."

"Yeah."

"I take it that when we find Becky Olmstead, if she is our victim, she won't be alive."

"I'm afraid not. Genny saw this woman's dead body submerged in deep water somewhere."

"Did she drown?"

"Genny doesn't think so. In this vision, just as in the one she had earlier, she saw a black braided ribbon around the victim's neck. Our guess is the woman was strangled."

Jacob heard the hesitation in Dallas's voice. "And?"

"Whoever the killer is, he's a rapist and a murderer. Genny said the girl was unconscious when he raped her, so that means he either drugged her or knocked her out first."

"Genny saw it happening that way in both visions? Damn, it couldn't have been easy for her to witness something like that. Rape and murder."

"It wasn't. She's in the bathroom right now still throwing up. This vision was a lot more vivid than the last one. She even got a glimpse of the killer's body, at least below the waist."

"And?"

"His John Thomas is a bit on the small size. And the hair surrounding it is brown." Dallas blew out a disgusted breath. "I know that description fits forty percent of men in general and that part of the anatomy isn't normally on view for the world to see, but it's all we've got."

"When I bring in any suspects, I'll be sure to ask them to drop their pants for a thorough inspection," Jacob said sarcastically.

"Yeah, you do that," Dallas replied. "Look, I've got to go. I need to check on Genny and make sure she's all right."

"Hey, ask her if she thinks she can narrow down the area where he dumped the body."

"I will, but not right now. She's too exhausted to be of any help to you. Come by later this morning, after she's had a chance to rest for a while."

After shoving his cell phone back into its belt holster, Jacob slammed his hands down on the steering wheel. Two new murders. One body in the morgue, the other buried in a watery grave. And a killer on the loose. Somebody who got his jollies by balling an unconscious woman, then killing her immediately afterward. A real sicko who had just killed a young, redheaded prostitute.

CHAPTER 10

After being up all night and exhausting every possible source to find Becky Olmstead, Jacob resigned himself to the possibility that the teenage prostitute was the redhead Genny had seen in her visions. If that was the case, her body could be in one of a dozen different locations. Anywhere there was a creek, a stream, a lake or a river. The body might never turn up, so his only hope of capturing her killer might be through solving the Jeremy Timmons murder.

Jacob parked his truck in the driveway, got out, went to the back door and knocked. Dallas opened the door immediately and ushered him into the kitchen.

"You look beat. Want a cup of coffee?" Dallas asked.

Jacob chuckled. "I've drunk a couple of pots during the night, but if you'll throw in some bacon, eggs and biscuits, I'll—"

"I fixed breakfast this morning. Scrambled eggs and toast. Take it or leave it."

Jacob removed his suede jacket and Stetson, hung them on the rack by the door and sat at the table. "How's Genny feeling this morning?"

"She's asleep. Finally. And I don't want to wake her."

Dallas poured coffee into a Blue Willow cup and set it down on the table in front of Jacob.

"The Olmstead girl hasn't shown up," Jacob said.

"Hm—mm." Dallas removed the lid from the skillet on the stove and spooned scrambled eggs onto a Blue Willow plate. He undid the aluminum foil encasing a stack of buttered toast, removed four slices and placed them on the plate, then handed it to Jacob.

"I've got one definite murder and a second possible one. I don't know for sure if the two are related, but my gut instincts tell me they are. I think whoever killed Timmons, killed the Olmstead girl. Why, I don't know. If I knew that, maybe I could figure out who our killer is."

Dallas handed Jacob a knife, a fork and a spoon, then nodded to the two jars of jelly flanked by the salt and pepper shakers in the center of the table. "Strawberry and grape. Take your pick." Dallas poured himself a fresh cup of coffee and sat across from Jacob. "You're certainly earning your stripes the hard way. Since being elected sheriff, you've been faced with a serial killer who almost murdered our Genny, then before the dust settled, you had to deal with a female psycho who tortured her victims to death. And now, just when you thought things were settling down, you've got one—probably two—new murders to solve. And all of this during your first year on the job."

Jacob spread grape jelly onto the four slices of toast. "Two murders are bad enough, but I'll gladly take two isolated murder cases over a series of murders where the body count keeps piling up."

"I hope you're right about these being two isolated murders. It could be that some dissatisfied john did away with Timmons and Becky Olmstead. Either that or Timmons and his girls were somehow involved with drugs. Not a far stretch, considering their line of business." Dallas eyed Jacob over the rim of his cup as he lifted it to his mouth.

Jacob sighed heavily. "But? Just say it. I know you think there's more to the murders."

"A dissatisfied john who's a bit of a nutcase or an angry drug dealer doesn't customarily strangle his victims. With those types, a gun is usually the weapon of choice. A quick, clean kill."

"Strangling a person is far more personal, right?" Jacob speared his scrambled eggs and shoved a forkful into his mouth.

Dallas nodded. "Most of the time. I'd look for a jealous lover. Or . . ."

"Or?"

"Or strangulation could be part of a serial killer's calling card."

Jacob swallowed. "Damn!"

"I didn't say I think we're dealing with another serial killer, but you need to keep an open mind. The type of murder Genny witnessed in her vision was ritualistic. I don't think this killer is a novice."

"We haven't had any murders in Cherokee County similar to the one Genny saw in her vision. Not while I've been sheriff and none that I can recall."

"It could be his first kill in Cherokee County. The other women he's murdered could have lived in neighboring counties, even other states."

"If this is a serial killer and the redhead was his victim, then why would he kill Timmons?" Jacob knew the answer before Dallas replied. It was the only logical explanation.

"To keep Timmons from identifying him. If Timmons set the guy up with one of his girls and she came up missing, then Timmons could ID the guy."

"Man, I hope you're wrong on this one, but you're probably not." Jacob wolfed down the rest of his eggs, polished off the three pieces of toast and washed it all down with coffee.

"I realize that without a body, we can't be certain Becky

Olmstead is dead," Dallas said. "But if we had a picture of her, we'd know if she was the woman Genny saw being strangled. If she is, then unless she shows up, you can at the very least consider her a missing person."

"I have a photo of Becky." Jacob glanced at his suede jacket on the rack by the back door. "Her mother gave me a wallet size of the girl's senior picture. I'd like Genny to take a look at it."

"Yeah. Good. As soon as Genny wakes, we'll show it to her," Dallas said. "In the meantime, why don't we make some phone calls and see if there have been any murders in neighboring counties with the same MO as the one Genny saw in her vision. We'll start with Sevier, Knox, Blount and Loudon."

"I'll take Sevier and Loudon," Jacob said. "I know the sheriffs of both counties."

"Okay. I'll take Knox and Blount."

Jacob had learned a great deal about solving crimes and hunting down criminals from Dallas, who was a former FBI agent. The two of them had become good friends since they first met back in January. They found out, on that very first case, that they worked well together. Jacob had the greatest respect for Genny's husband.

When Farlan MacKinnon had suggested Jacob run for sheriff after he took an early retirement from the Navy and left behind his career as a SEAL, he had been reluctant. After all, his background was as a warrior, not a lawman. But old man MacKinnon and a few other politically minded citizens had persuaded him to run. No one had been more surprised then he when he'd won by a landslide. He'd entered office believing he could do the job since Cherokee County wasn't exactly a hotbed of criminal activity. He should have known that things would change—for the worse—not long after he was elected.

"Let's go over the basic facts of Genny's vision and see if we can put together our killer's MO," Jacob said. "If he does turn out to be a serial killer."

"Let's hear it," Dallas said.

"Okay. He strangles his victims with a black braided ribbon. He kills redheads." Jacob shook his head. "Not just redheads, but redheaded prostitutes or possibly women he perceives as whores."

"Go on."

"Moments before he kills a woman, he screws her. Then he dumps her body in the—" Jacob huffed. "Damn, why didn't I think of it sooner? A prostitute's body was fished out of the Tennessee River near Loudon just a few days ago."

"You're right. I remember reading about it or hearing about it." Dallas nodded to the wall phone. "We'll call the Loudon County sheriff first and find out if their victim was strangled with a black ribbon. And if she was sexually assaulted. If she was, then—"

"Then the odds are we have another serial killer on our hands."

Fifteen minutes later, just as Jacob got off the phone with Loudon County Sheriff Whit Ezell, Genny walked into the kitchen and went straight to Jacob. She placed her hand over his heart and the two exchanged a silent understanding.

"The man who killed this young woman has killed before, and he will kill again," Genny said, her voice a mere whisper.

Dallas came up behind his wife, but didn't touch her. "Did you have another vision?"

She shook her head. "Not exactly a vision. It was more a strong feeling than anything else. I sensed great sorrow. The sorrow of more than one woman. It was such tremendous sadness that it had to come from numerous souls."

"Are you all right?" Dallas turned Genny to him and skimmed his fingertips lovingly over her face.

She offered Dallas a fragile smile and took his hand. "I'm fine. Let's sit down."

Dallas quickly assisted Genny in sitting at the table. After preparing her a cup of hot tea, he sat beside her and then turned to Jacob. "Fill us in on what Sheriff Ezell had to say."

Jacob joined them at the table. "At first he wasn't too thrilled to be disturbed on a Sunday morning."

"I'll bet he wasn't." Dallas grinned.

"Who is Sheriff Ezell and why did you call him?" Genny held the cup to her lips, then took a sip and sighed.

"He's the sheriff over in Loudon County," Jacob replied. "They found a prostitute's body in the river over near the dam a couple of days ago and—"

"You and Dallas thought perhaps that murder was connected to the one I saw in my vision." Genny completed his sentence for him.

Both Dallas and Jacob nodded, then Jacob said, "The woman they found in the river was identified as Kat Baker, a Knoxville call girl. She'd been missing less than a week."

"Did she have red hair?" Genny asked.

"Yeah. Dyed red. But regardless of that fact, technically she was a redhead."

"What about the cause of death?" Dallas asked.

"Strangulation." Jacob looked from Dallas to Genny. "They found a black braided ribbon knotted around her neck."

Genny gasped.

Dallas grunted. "Same MO as the killer in Genny's dream."

"Maybe I was seeing something that had already happened," Genny said. "It could be that the woman I saw was this Kat Baker."

"Possibly," Jacob replied. "But I'd lay odds that the woman you saw was Becky Olmstead, our missing Cherokee Pointe prostitute."

"Let's get busy making some phone calls to other police and sheriff's departments to see if Kat Baker's murder was an isolated incident." Dallas glanced at Genny. "I want you to eat something, then rest for a while. And under no circumstances are you to do anything without me. Understand?"

Genny reached over and patted Dallas's hand. "I understand."

"Promise?"

"I promise."

Jacob emitted a closed-mouth chuckle. "I'm glad to see she finally listens to somebody. Whenever Jazzy or I warned her to take things easy, not to delve too deeply or try to connect to a killer's mind, she didn't pay any attention to us."

"I paid attention," Genny corrected him. "It's just that occasionally I knew what had to be done and did it."

Jacob's cell phone rang. Genny jerked nervously. Standing quickly, Jacob pulled the cell phone from his belt clip and responded.

"Butler here."

"Sheriff, it's possible Becky Olmstead's body has been found," Deputy Bobby Joe Harte said. "A couple of fishermen up at Douglas Lake pulled a woman's body out of the lake about two hours ago."

"Do we have any details?"

"Sketchy. Young female. Apparently the body's pretty fresh."

"Do we have a number for Sheriff Floyd?

"Yeah."

"Give it to me. I'll get in touch with Noland and see what I can find out." Jacob undid the snap on his shirt pocket, retrieved a small notepad and pen and hurriedly jotted down the number. "Thanks."

As soon as Jacob returned his cell phone to the belt clip, he looked over at Dallas. "A couple of fishermen pulled a woman's body out of Douglas Lake this morning. It could be Becky Olmstead."

Both men glanced at Genny.

"I can see if I can pick up anything," she said.

"Maybe you shouldn't." Dallas frowned. "You're already exhausted."

"I won't go in very deep." She closed her eyes and meditated for several minutes.

Taking both of her hands in his, Dallas watched her protectively. Jacob went over and pulled the photo of Becky

Olmstead out of his coat pocket, then walked out of the kitchen and onto the screened back porch. After slipping the wallet-size picture in his shirt pocket, he dialed Sheriff Floyd's number. By the time he went through several deputies and actually had the sheriff on the phone, Dallas eased open the back door and the two men made eye contact.

"Genny says she's certain the woman they found in Douglas Lake is the woman from her vision."

Jacob nodded, then pulled Becky's photo from his pocket and handed it to Dallas. "Ask her if this is the woman."

Dallas took the high school picture and went back into the kitchen. Jacob focused on his phone call.

"Sheriff Floyd, this is Sheriff Jacob Butler over in Cherokee County. I understand you've got a brand-new homicide case."

"Yeah, we do. What's your interest?"

"We've got a missing woman from Cherokee Pointe. Been missing since last night. She's a young prostitute whose pimp was found murdered. Strangled to death."

"Give me a description."

"Like I said, young. Red hair. About five-six. Slender."

"That fits our wet floater's general description. You got someone who can ID the body? Although our coroner says the body probably hasn't been in the water more than ten or twelve hours, she's not a pretty sight."

"Our girl's name is Becky Olmstead. She has a mother and stepfather." Jacob cleared his throat. "On a strictly confidential basis, tell me how she died?"

"She could have drowned, but I figure she was strangled first and then dumped in the lake," Sheriff Floyd replied.

"Did y'all find anything in particular that indicated strangulation?"

"A black braided cord of some kind was still around her neck. That bit of info won't be released, of course. Beneath the cord, there was a straight line bruise on her neck and it looks as if the cord cut into her flesh."

Jacob sucked in a deep breath, then released it slowly. "Ask your coroner to check carefully to see if she was raped."

"I thought you said she was a prostitute."

"If what I suspect is true, the last sex this girl had was not consensual. She could have been drugged, and he probably raped her only moments before killing her."

Veda MacKinnon returned from Sunday services at the Methodist church she had attended since coming to Cherokee Pointe as a young bride. Although she'd been raised Presbyterian, she had soon converted, much to her husband's and his parents' delight. In those early years, she had truly tried to please Farlan and his family. She had longed to fit in, to belong. Although their marriage hadn't been perfect, they had once loved each other. And when she'd given birth to Brian, all the MacKinnons had treated her like a queen. But time had a way of changing things. She had tried unsuccessfully to give her husband more children, but after five miscarriages, the doctors had warned her to never become pregnant again. If only there could have been other children. Perhaps a daughter.

When she entered the foyer, Abra met her and took her coat and purse.

"Has Mr. Farlan come down yet?" Veda asked.

"Yes, ma'am. He's in his study with Wallace."

"What about Mr. Brian?"

"I haven't seen Mr. Brian this morning."

"Thank you." Veda removed her gloves and handed them to the housekeeper. "I'd like dinner served at one-thirty today."

"Yes, ma'am."

Veda glanced up the carpet-covered staircase and wondered if Brian was still in bed. He often stayed out late on the weekends, but usually didn't stay out all night as he'd done last night. When he had moved back in with them after his divorce from Phyllis, he'd remodeled two rooms and a bath on the opposite end of the hallway from his parents' rooms. Under normal circumstances, she wouldn't have been aware of exactly what time he'd come home, wouldn't have known that he'd stayed out until shortly before dawn. But this morning she had been awake and waiting, not for her son, but for her husband. It wasn't like Farlan to stay out all night, although when he made business trips, she had no idea what type of schedule he kept.

Veda had gone to bed at eleven, but had been unable to rest, knowing Farlan hadn't come home. He had telephoned earlier and left a message for her with Abra. At three this morning, she'd gotten out of bed, put on her robe and sat by the windows overlooking the driveway. She'd seen Brian pull his Porsche into the garage, then heard him walk up the back-stairs. Being quiet as a mouse, she'd eased open her bedroom door and watched her son rush down the hall and into his bedroom. Just as his door closed behind him, she'd heard the grandfather clock strike. Five o'clock.

Where her son went and what he did was his own business. He was no longer a boy, but a man of forty-two. He'd probably been with some woman, but that was perfectly un-derstandable. After all, a man had needs. It wasn't her son's needs that concerned her, but her husband's. Sex wasn't a regular part of their lives these days. She had lost interest in sex in her mid-fifties, but had faked passion to satisfy her husband. But as time passed, Farlan's sex drive had also waned, and only recently he'd assured her that at seventy-five, he preferred a good meal to a good fuck.

In all the years since that one ill-fated affair so long ago, Farlan had been faithful to her. At least she was reasonably certain he had been. After all, he'd sworn to her that he would never let another woman come between them. And she had made it abundantly clear that if she ever discovered he'd been unfaithful to her again, she would kill herself. She wasn't sure if she'd actually commit suicide, but that didn't matter as long as she'd convinced Farlan. And apparently she had.

Veda walked down the hall and knocked on the closed study door. "May I come in, please?"

She heard murmurs, then footsteps. The door opened, and Wallace came out, a wide smile on his face. Poor, sweet Wallace smiled most of the time. Smiled as if he knew a secret no one else knew. Perhaps in his childlike mind, he held all kinds of mysterious thoughts.

"I got me a dog," Wallace told her. "I found him this morning, out in the front yard. Farlan says he's a stray, but that if I make him a bed out in the garage, I can keep him. You don't mind, do you, Veda?"

A dog? Veda wasn't overly fond of animals and had never allowed Brian to keep a pet. She had always vetoed the idea of Wallace keeping any of the strays he brought home, something he did quite often. "Well, isn't that nice. A dog."

"I'll keep him outside, and he won't bother you none. I promise. I'm going to name him Spotty since he's white with black spots all over him. Do you think that's a good name?" The more excited Wallace became, the faster he talked. "Farlan says I can ask Abra for some old quilts to make his bed and to tell her to fix him a dish of food."

"Yes, yes, dear. You go along and take care of Spotty."

Wallace barreled past her and lumbered down the hall. He was a bear of a man with a little boy's mind. She squared her shoulders and entered her husband's private domain, but stood just over the threshold until he looked up at her from where he sat in his leather easy chair.

"Come on in and close the door," Farlan said. "I'm sure what you have to say to me needs to be said in private."

Turning around, she closed the door, then pivoted to face her husband. "Do we need privacy for what you have to say to me?" Their gazes met and momentarily locked.

"Don't stand there glaring at me. Come on in and sit

down." He indicated the chair across from him. She broke eye contact as she walked over and sat, her back ramrod straight. "How was Reverend Prater's sermon this morning?"

She folded her hands in her lap. "He asked about you. I told him you were a bit under the weather this morning."

"A socially acceptable white lie."

Hearing the humor in his voice, she glowered at him. "It would have been unnecessary for me to lie if you'd gotten up at a decent hour and attended services with me."

"Don't beat around the bush, Veda, just come right out and ask me."

"Very well." She drew in a deep, hopefully calming breath. "Where were you all night? You didn't come home until after daybreak this morning."

"I drove over to Sevierville and rented a hotel room." His gaze collided with hers. She noted a defiant look in his eyes, one she hadn't seen in years. "And I spent an enjoyable night with a very entertaining young woman."

Veda's face flushed, and her heartbeat drummed deafeningly in her ears. "You say that as if you think I wouldn't care that you broke your promise to me. How could you? And how dare you act so cavalier about it."

"If you intend to kill yourself, my dear, would you mind doing it after Sunday dinner? Abra has prepared prime rib, and you know it's my favorite."

CHAPTER 11

When Jacob entered the kitchen, Genny handed him the high school photo of Becky Olmstead. "You know that in my visions I don't always see everything. And with a person, it's often only the hair or the eyes or—"

Jacob grasped her shoulders lovingly. "What are you trying to tell me, little sister?"

"In my vision, I saw the woman's hair and neck . . . and her legs and hips."

"You saw more."

"Yes. I got a quick look at her face." Genny glanced at the photo Jacob held. "This is the person I saw in my vision. I'm sure."

Jacob's gut tightened. "I'll contact Becky's mother and ask her to drive over to Jefferson County with me."

"I'm sorry," Genny said. "I realize how difficult it will be to tell this woman her daughter is probably dead."

Jacob nodded. "It's part of my job."

"The body being found in Douglas Lake complicates matters some, too, doesn't it," Dallas said. "Not only do you have the Jefferson County sheriff's office involved, you've got the TVA guys and the state boys, too."

"If I know Noland Floyd, he'll cut through all the crap pretty quick. He's an experienced lawman. Been the sheriff over there for nearly twenty years. I'll let him deal with the state. They're not my problem. And I doubt TVA will get involved."

"If there is a serial killer loose in northeast Tennessee, then every law enforcement agency around these parts has a major problem," Dallas said. "But what we need to worry about is whether this guy will strike again in our territory."

"Yeah, I know. And a part of me wants to go on television and issue a warning to all redheads in Cherokee County, but I can't do that. It could cause a panic. Considering that three-fourths of the families in these parts are of Scottish and Irish decent, we have a high percentage of redheads."

"Including Jazzy and Reve," Genny said.

Jacob and Dallas turned and stared at her. Damn, she was right. Why hadn't those two even crossed his mind? Especially Jazzy, considering the fact that she had a less than sterling reputation. Anyone who didn't know her well might think she was a slut. She wasn't. But if the killer listened to local gossip . . .

"Genny, did you pick up on—?" Dallas asked, but Genny cut him off in mid-sentence.

"No, I haven't sensed a connection between the danger I believe lies ahead for Jazzy and Reve and the man who killed Becky Olmstead, but . . ." Genny's black eyes moistened with tears.

"But what?" Jacob knew his cousin often tried to pretend, even to herself, that some of the horrible things she saw in her visions were not real. But time and again, her psychic abilities had proven to be reliable and accurate.

Genny shook her head. "I don't know. It's just an odd feeling that I can't explain. If I could try to connect with the killer's mind—"

"Absolutely not!" Dallas growled the words.

"Perhaps later, after I've rested more. I want to help."

"Maybe later," Jacob said. "But not now. Dallas is right to protect you from your own good intentions." He kissed Genny's cheek. "I'll stop by this evening." He turned to Dallas. "Walk me out."

Dallas followed Jacob onto the porch and into the backyard. Drudwyn, who'd been curled up in a corner on the porch, raised himself on all fours and followed them. The sky was gray and overcast, giving the day a solemn aura. Dallas reached down to stroke the wolf dog's head.

"Make those other calls for me, will you?" Jacob unlocked his truck. "Find out if there have been similar murders anywhere else in northeastern Tennessee. Like you said, this could be the guy's first kill in Cherokee County, but not elsewhere."

"I can do that. And later we need to contact Caleb and tell him to keep a close eye on Jazzy. Just in case."

"He'll ask questions."

"And I'll give him answers."

Reba inspected the dining room table. Everything was in order as she had expected it would be. Dora never let her down, unlike so many others in her life had and still did. Her housekeeper was reliable, trustworthy and highly competent. The china, crystal and silver glistened. The floral arrangement sat low and wide in the center of the antique mahogany Duncan Phyfe table. A delicate hint of their meal wafted from the nearby kitchen, where Dora was putting the finishing touches on Sunday dinner.

If anyone had told her six months ago that she would be entertaining Jasmine Talbot in her home, she'd have called them crazy. Reba disliked the woman. No, dislike was too mild a word. She had despised Jazzy since the woman was sixteen and had deliberately gotten herself pregnant with Jamie's child. It had soon become apparent to everyone that the baby had been nothing more than a trap to snare herself a rich husband. Once Jamie had refused to marry her, she'd gotten an abortion. And until the day Jamie died, she had kept her hooks in him, never setting him free to be happy with someone else.

Reba still mourned Jamie, the grandson she had loved so deeply. He had disappointed her more times than she cared to remember, but she had forgiven him each time he broke her heart. After losing her two children, Jim, Jr., and Melanie, Jamie had been all Jim and she had—he'd been their legacy, the heir to the Upton fortune. When he'd been brutally murdered this past summer, she had thought they'd lost everything. But she'd been wrong. Like a miracle, Caleb had come to them, the grandson they'd never known existed. Melanie's child. And already she understood how different Caleb was from Jamie. He was a better man. Strong and reliable. Trustworthy and caring. But he did share one weakness with his dead cousin—being in love with Jasmine Talbot.

Despite her intense hatred for the woman, Reba had invited her for Sunday dinner today, to please Caleb. She was damned and determined not to make the same mistakes with Caleb that she'd made with Jamie. If Jazzy Talbot was the woman Caleb loved, the woman he intended to marry, then if she wanted to keep her grandson in her life, she'd have to swallow her pride and accept the inevitable.

Of course, if there was any way she could manipulate the situation, she would. If only Caleb would realize how much more suitable Reve Sorrell was for him.

"Everything looks mighty fine," Jim said.

Reba gasped at the sound of her husband's voice. She hadn't realized he'd come downstairs. She turned and smiled at Jim. "I want things to be perfect. For Caleb's sake."

Jim walked over, put his arm around Reba's shoulder and kissed her cheek. "I'm proud of you, old gal. I know this won't be easy for you, but you're doing the right thing. We both learned our lesson with Jamie, didn't we?"

There had been a time when this small show of affection from her husband would have thrilled her, but now it was only moderately satisfying. It wasn't that she didn't love Jim. She did. She probably always would. But she hadn't been in love with him for quite some time. And now there was Dodd. Was she really in love with another man? Yes, she thought perhaps she was. Stealing away to her chalet in the mountains to meet with a lover wasn't something she'd ever done; she had never even entertained the thought. But Dodd was different. He made her feel different. Besides, technically, they weren't lovers. Not yet. Last night they had sat together, drunk champagne, held hands and talked until nearly midnight; then they'd kissed good-bye.

On the way home, she'd wondered what she would tell Jim, if he happened to be at home. He hadn't been. More and more lately, he stayed gone all night. She knew where he was; he was with Erin Mercer. If Jim had been at home, would she have told him the truth—that she'd been with Dodd Keefer, that she was in love with Dodd?

Reba eased away from Jim and moved about the room, pretending to inspect the table, something she'd already done. "You were missed at church this morning."

Jim hadn't been the only one missed this morning— Dodd, too, hadn't attended services. He'd been raised a Presbyterian, but his late wife had been a Congregationalist and he'd converted early in their marriage. She hoped Dodd would call her later today to set up a time when they could meet again. Odd how, at her age, to experience anticipation and giddiness as if she were a young girl with her first boyfriend.

"I apologize for not making it to services today," Jim said.

No further explanation. Not one word of where he'd been all night or with whom he'd spent his time. Perhaps after all these years, all the mistresses, all the nights spent away from home, there really was no need for little white lies between them.

Tilting her head proudly and looking him square in the eyes, she said, "That's all right. No need for apologies. Not between us. Not any longer."

He eyed her speculatively. She smiled secretively. Let him make of that whatever he wanted to. Let him wonder.

Farlan had allowed Veda to fuss and fume and oddly enough actually enjoyed her discomfort. Had it reached the point that he not only no longer loved his wife, but he could derive pleasure from her unhappiness? No, not really. He didn't want Veda miserable, although little he did seemed to make her happy. But in this one instance, he felt justified in turning the screws just a little. After all, she had held the threat of suicide over his head like the proverbial sword of Damocles for thirty years now. He had toed the line out of fear he'd do something to push Veda over the edge. And partly out of guilt. He had betrayed his marriage vows, had not only taken a mistress, but had dared to love the woman.

If only he could turn back the clock three decades. But he couldn't do that; and even if he could find her now, it would be too late for them. She was probably married, with children and possibly grandchildren.

Weeping quietly, her body quivering every so slightly, Veda gazed up at him from where she sat in the leather chair. She looked rather pitiful, like a fat, withered rose, ready to fall apart. Poor old thing. He shouldn't have been so unkind to her, but damn it all, he was seventy-five and didn't have much time left. With little to look forward to, he'd become depressed lately. Paying that girl last night to spend time with him had been like a breath of fresh air in his stale life. Once he'd gotten it through her cute little head that he didn't want sex, she'd relaxed and opened up to him about herself. And he had told her about another young woman who'd been in her line of business, a girl he'd loved and lost.

They had talked and laughed and even cried together. And around midnight, they'd ordered room service. After eating, he'd stretched out on the bed and she'd curled up next to him, the way a man's daughter might do. Innocently. That was how he'd thought of her—as if she were his daughter.

"I don't see how you could have done this to me," Veda said, then sobbed loudly.

"I didn't have sex with her," he explained.

Veda's head popped up. "What?"

"I needed someone to talk to."

"I don't understand. You and I talk every day."

"You're right," he said. "Maybe what I needed was to spend time with someone young and fun and nonjudgmental."

Eyes dry, face scrunched with disapproval and a hint of anger, Veda glared at him. "What you mean is that you wanted to spend time with someone who reminded you of her. That's it, isn't it? You've found yourself another whore to love."

Farlan snorted. "Damn it, woman, I'm not in love with the girl. I spent a few hours with her. We didn't have sex, and I probably won't ever see her again."

"Probably?"

"No probably about it. I won't see her again."

"Do you think about her?" Veda asked.

"I just met the girl last night. Why would I—"

"You know who I mean. Her."

He could lie and swear he'd never given her a thought, not once in all these years. But Veda would know he was lying. "Yes, I think about her sometimes. I wonder where she is. I hope she's happy. I hope she found a nice man, got married and"—he swallowed hard—"had children."

"Other children, you mean."

"Yes, Veda, other children."

"Do you ever think about—"

"Damn it, woman, leave it alone, will you? I've tried my

best to give you what you wanted. I stayed with you, didn't I? We made things work for Brian's sake. The past is dead and buried. Let's leave it at that."

Veda's eyes widened; her face went ashen. What the hell was wrong with her? But before he could ask her what had shaken her so badly, she snapped out of it, rose from the chair and walked toward him. "You're right. I shouldn't bring up the past. I—I won't do it again."

He patted her on the shoulder. "I apologize for being so cruel to you. You know I didn't mean what I said about your killing yourself."

She sighed dramatically. "Yes, dear, I know."

Veda smiled. Triumphantly. Wickedly? She left the study, closing the door behind her. Farlan heaved a deep sigh. He crossed the room, reached up over the fireplace and pulled on the hinges connected to the frame of the painting hanging over the mantel. His personal wall safe appeared. He and he alone knew the combination. Rarely did he open this safe. It contained personal items. With speed and accuracy, he rotated the nob, letting the numbers click into place. The door swung open. He reached inside and removed one item. The photograph of a young woman. A pair of vivid hazel-green eyes stared up at him, and for a moment he drowned in memories of a forbidden love.

Dodd felt as if he had a hangover. Perhaps he'd drunk too much last night, after he'd left Reba. He wasn't sure, couldn't exactly remember. He'd wanted to make love to Reba, to consummate their affair in a physical way, but he realized she wasn't ready for anything that intimate. And he loved her enough to wait until she was ready. If only she weren't married, if only they could build a life together. Neither of them was getting any younger. But would she ever leave Big Jim? Would she ever willingly give up the prestige and privileges associated with being Mrs. James Upton? Could she be content as the wife of a circuit court judge?

If she loved him, truly loved him, she could be.

But that was the question—did she truly love him?

Dodd sat there in Jasmine's Restaurant as he did every Sunday, after church. And he always ordered the same thing—fried chicken. He'd missed church this morning, something he seldom did, but since he hadn't gotten to sleep until dawn, he had slept until nearly eleven. His sleep had been fitful, filled with crazy dreams. No, not dreams. More like nightmares.

What would Reba think of him if she ever learned about what he'd done? Would she understand and forgive him as his wife had? His Beth Ellen had been an extraordinary woman, kind and gentle beyond belief. Until he'd become smitten with Reba, he had thought he'd never love another woman. Most women wouldn't forgive a man for straying. Veda sure hadn't forgiven Farlan. Quite the opposite—she'd made his life a living hell. To this day, Dodd felt guilty. After all, he'd been the one who'd persuaded his brother-in-law to go with him to Knoxville that first time, and it had been Farlan who had paid the highest price for both their sins.

"Afternoon," Max Fennel said as he and his wife approached Dodd's table. "You look as bad as I feel. We really tied one on last night, didn't we?"

Claudia Fennel inspected Dodd as if he was a product she was considering buying. Max stood right behind her, an odd expression on his face. Dodd almost missed the sly wink Max gave him, but quickly realized that his old friend was giving him some sort of signal. No doubt Max wanted to use him as an alibi once again. There was no telling where Max had been last night or who he'd been with or what he'd done. The man was a charming scoundrel, but they'd been buddies for years and this wouldn't be the first time Dodd had covered for him.

"I told Maxwell that I was thoroughly disappointed in him." Claudia's cheeks flushed; her voice held a hint of censure. "I'd think you would be a better influence on him, Dodd. Whoever heard of a judge and a respected lawyer whooping it up together and getting so drunk that they didn't sober up and come home until morning. You're both entirely too old for such shenanigans."

"Now, sweetheart, don't embarrass Dodd." Max hugged Claudia, who cringed at his touch, apparently more than a little upset with him. "We learned our lesson last night, didn't we?" Max's gaze pleaded with Dodd to back him up.

"We most certainly did." Dodd tried his best to smile at Claudia, but all he could manage was not to frown.

Although she was a bit of prude, Claudia was a nice lady and Dodd hated lying to her. But he consoled himself by halfway believing he was sparing her feelings by keeping the truth from her. If he had a wife like Claudia, you wouldn't catch him fooling around. He'd learned infidelity came at too high a price. For everyone involved. There were always consequences. His careless actions years ago had almost cost him the thing he'd treasured most—his sweet Beth Ellen. How men could repeatedly cheat on their good wives, he didn't know. Big Jim Upton was every bit as bad as Max. Both of them were philandering bastards. Reba's husband had gone through a succession of mistresses, and just about everyone in town knew it. How did Reba endure the shame?

"Well, you two have been mighty naughty," Claudia said jokingly. "But I trust y'all to behave in a more gentlemanly manner in the future."

"Come along, sweetie." Max tugged on his wife's arm. "I'm sure Dodd would like to finish his lunch in peace." Max cast Dodd a grateful glance.

Carrying a coffee pot in her hand, Tiffany Reid came over to his table just as Max dragged Claudia away. "Care for another refill, Judge?"

"Yes, thank you. And I'd like a piece of apple pie. I think Sharon forgot that I always have apple pie on Sunday."

"I'll get your pie right away. Sharon got waylaid by a take-out order." Tiffany leaned in closer and said in a quiet voice so she wouldn't be overheard, "Jacob and Dallas have ordered lunch for their people since they had to call a bunch in to work who were supposed to be off today."

"Is there some crisis I haven't heard about?"

Lowering her voice to a whisper, Tiffany said, "Just between us—and I overheard two of the deputies talking so I can't swear it's gospel—it seems we might have us another serial killer in Cherokee County."

Cold, deadly fear slugged Dodd in the pit of his stomach.

"It seems they think a local prostitute's been murdered by some guy hung up on killing whores and dumping them in the river. He dumped this one in Douglas Lake over in Jefferson County."

"How horrible." Suddenly losing his appetite, Dodd laid his napkin on the table and stood. "I think I'll forgo the apple pie today. My stomach's not quite right."

Tiffany gave him a questioning look. "I sure hope you get to feeling better."

He nodded, then headed for the door where he picked up his coat and hat from the long wall rack stationed in the entryway. Once outside, he sucked in a deep breath of cool autumn air. Another serial killer? One who killed prostitutes? He doubted anybody else had been keeping track, as he had, of the reported deaths of prostitutes in northeastern Tennessee. He'd noted the first kill in the *Elizabethton Star* over ten years ago, when he and Beth Ellen had been visiting her family there. The victim had been a young woman from Johnson City. Not a prostitute, but a waitress with a reputation for sleeping around. They had run her photograph on the front page. Pretty. Sweet smile. Auburn-red hair. The reason he'd paid particular attention and had never forgotten was because she had reminded him of another young redheaded girl, someone he and Farlan had known long ago.

After that, he'd started a scrapbook of similar cases. He subscribed to over a dozen northeast Tennessee and neighboring North Carolina newspapers. Whenever an article appeared about such a crime, he cut it out and pasted it into his secret book. Someday he just might write a novel based on these murders. There had been well over a dozen similar crimes in the past decade. Three women had been from the Johnson City area. And each time Dodd read about another "fallen angel," he was forced to face an ugly truth about himself. He wasn't especially sorry that these women had been killed.

CHAPTER 12

Reve felt right at home when she entered the Uptons' antebellum-style mansion, which reminded her a little of her parents' home in Chattanooga. The moment Miss Reba came forward to greet her, she sensed a kindred spirit. A woman of taste and good breeding. Caleb's grandmother was dressed in a camel tan suit, her blond hair was styled to perfection, her makeup was flawless and a strand of pearls around her neck was similar to the one Reve had chosen to wear today with her navy blue dress.

"We're simply delighted that you could join us for Sunday dinner." Reba Upton reached out and grasped Reve's hands. "And before another moment passes, I want to issue you an invitation to stay here with us while you're in Cherokee Pointe. We have loads of room"— she gestured with her hand in a sweeping motion—"and could make you quite comfortable. I'm afraid local accommodations aren't up to your standards."

Realizing that in showering her with attention, Reba was ignoring Jazzy, Reve suddenly felt rather awkward. "I appreciate the invitation, Mrs. Upton, but—"

"Please, call me Reba, my dear girl. You do know that

your late mother and I worked on several Republican statewide committees together, and if that isn't reason enough for me to feel kindly toward you, there is the fact that you were a friend of Jamie's."

Jim Upton practically pushed his wife aside as he made his way to Caleb and Jazzy, who stood to Reve's left. "I can't tell you how happy we are that you two gals are here." Jim laced Jazzy's arm through his, then grabbed Reve's arm and urged them into motion. "Come on into the living room and we'll have a drink before dinner." With Reve and Jazzy in tow, Big Jim glanced over his shoulder and said, "Caleb, escort your grandmother."

The living room was as tastefully decorated as Reve had expected. A combination of expensive new furniture and priceless antiques. Glancing at Jazzy, she realized that Jazzy was as uncomfortable in this house as she was at ease. Reve and the Uptons lived in the same world, breathed the same rarified air, and associated with people of similar backgrounds. Jazzy, on the other hand, was an alien visiting in a foreign land. Even her choice of clothing for today's dinner spotlighted those glaring differences. Reve had chosen a simple, navy blue dress with navy pumps, and her only jewelry was a single strand of pearls and pearl stud earrings. Jazzy wore a broomstick, calf-length skirt in a vivid purple with matching purple boots and a multicolored cotton sweater. Two pairs of large gold hoops dangled from her ears, six bangle bracelets circled her right wrist and a rhinestone wristwatch adorned the other.

Noting how fidgety Jazzy was, Reve actually felt sorry for her and had the strange urge to grab her hand and squeeze it reassuringly. But she resisted the urge. Despite the fact that she was beginning to like Jazzy, she did not want to become emotionally attached to the woman, even if she was her sister.

Once Reba had taken her seat across from the sofa where

Jazzy and Reve sat side by side, she studied them closely for a couple of seconds. "Please forgive me for staring, but you two do look remarkably alike."

"Like two peas in a pod," Big Jim said.

"And yet two very different women." Caleb, who stood directly behind Jazzy, reached down and placed his hands lovingly on her shoulders.

Why was it that Reve felt as if she'd just been unfavorably compared to Jazzy, that Caleb was reminding his grandmother that though look-alikes, the two women weren't interchangeable?

"Yes, looks can be deceiving, can't they?" Reba focused on Jazzy, who bristled, but managed to keep quiet. "Some people are not what they seem to be. They can fool us."

Reve had to bite her tongue to stop herself from reminding Reba Upton that Jazzy was a guest in her home and that it was always poor manners to belittle a guest. And besides that, Reve didn't like to see anyone being mistreated. Yes, Jazzy might be socially inferior to Miss Reba, but that was hardly any reason to be so unkind.

"We should share our good news with my grandparents." Caleb's devilish grin gained his grandmother's full attention.

"Good news?" Reba raised her eyebrows inquiringly.

"Caleb, maybe now's not the time." Jazzy glanced nervously up at her fiancé.

"No time like the present for good news," Big Jim said as he poured white wine into crystal flutes. "If we have something to celebrate, give me a minute to distribute the wine and I'll make a toast."

Caleb came around to the front of the sofa, took Jazzy's hands and assisted her to her feet. While Big Jim handed out the wine, Caleb accepted his flute, put his arm around Jazzy's waist, then lifted his glass and said loudly and distinctly, "Last night Jazzy accepted my marriage proposal and agreed to be my wife."

Silence.

Apparently this bit of news had astonished Caleb's grand-parents so much so that they were at a loss for words.

"Well, congratulations, boy." Big Jim slapped Caleb on the back in a show of approval. He lifted his glass in a salute. "Here's to Jazzy and Caleb. I wish you two all the happiness in the world."

Reve lifted her glass to her lips and sipped the wine just as everyone else did. Everyone except Miss Reba.

"Are you planning on getting married soon?" Reba set her glass on a coaster atop a small mahogany table to her right.

Caleb hugged Jazzy. "I'd marry her today if she'd do it."

"Surely there's no rush," Reba said.

When all eyes settled on her, Reba smiled weakly and added, "Every woman wants a proper wedding, and I'm sure Jasmine will want time to plan the perfect event."

"Do you want a big, elaborate wedding?" Caleb asked Jazzy.

Looking right at Reba, a defiant, I've won/you've lost expression on her face, Jazzy replied, "Yes, as a matter of fact I do."

"If that's what you want, then it's what I want," Caleb said.

"Damn right about that." Big Jim looked at his wife. "A big, fancy wedding with all the trimmings is just what this family needs. Hell, it's what Cherokee County needs. You two plan whatever you want. Spare no expense. Consider this wedding a gift from Reba and me."

"That's very generous of you, Mr. Upton," Jazzy said, but she remained focused on Reba's pale face. "I would absolutely love a Christmas wedding. Miss Reba, do you think we could pull off an elaborate affair like I want in less than two months?"

"I doubt two months will give us enough time," Reba replied. "I believe a June wedding would be more suitable. That would give us eight months. I'd prefer to have a year, but—"

"I can't wait eight months," Caleb said. "I don't want this lady changing her mind."

"Is there any reason for such a rush?" Reba asked.

Deadly silence. Reve sensed the sudden chill that filled the air. And once again she felt terribly sorry for Jazzy, being all too aware of Reba Upton's barely disguised animosity.

"You're wondering if I'm pregnant, aren't you?" Jazzy glared at Reba.

"Good God, Reba, that's none of your business," Big Jim said.

"Jazzy and I are getting married because we love each other and for no other reason," Caleb told them.

"I'm sorry," Reba said. "But under the circumstances, I believe it was a perfectly reasonable question."

"What circumstances?" Caleb dared his grandmother to reply.

Reba blushed. "I didn't intend to bring up the past, but—"

"Then don't!" Big Jim bellowed.

"I'm not pregnant," Jazzy said very calmly. Too calmly. "And I'm not sixteen years old. You don't intimidate me, Miss Reba. Not now. Not ever again."

"Do I need to remind you that I'm not Jamie?" Caleb asked his grandmother. "Nothing and no one is more important to me than Jazzy. Do you understand?" He glanced back and forth from Jazzy to his grandmother. "Do both of you understand that fact?"

Jazzy's eyes moistened with tears. She reached down, took Caleb's hand and held it tightly. "I understand."

Reba stood, lifted her wineglass and held it up; then she cleared her throat and said, "Here's to Caleb and Jasmine. I wish them well."

On the drive back from Jefferson County, Jacob listened to a favorite from his CD collection—*The Best of Jim Reeves*. His tastes were simple. He preferred old country to modern country. Looking back at the past few hours, he sure was glad Becky Olmstead's stepfather had insisted on driving his wife to Jefferson County to identify the body that had been dragged out of Douglas Lake early this morning. If her husband hadn't been at her side, the woman would probably have dropped over in a dead faint when she saw her daughter's body. And who could have blamed her?

Few people ever have to go inside a morgue, where the smell of death overrides the combined scents of astringent cleaner and tissue preservative. And even fewer people had to see their child's dead body on a stainless steel autopsy table.

"That's her," Becky's stepfather had said; then he'd quickly ushered his wife out of the room.

As he drove along Highway 411 heading toward Sevierville, Jacob went over the basic facts Sheriff Floyd had shared with him. The girl had been strangled, presumably with the black braided satin ribbon still tied around her neck when she was dragged out of the lake. When found, she was naked. And there was evidence of sexual intercourse, but the local coroner found no evidence of semen, which meant the killer had used a condom. Law enforcement in Jefferson County was no more prepared to find a serial killer than Cherokee County had been earlier this year. The Knoxville crime lab, with up-to-date equipment and highly trained personnel, could accomplish more than the county sheriffs. But even by using an experienced team and state-of-the-art equipment, this puzzle might remain unsolved.

With his headpiece in place, Jacob punched in Dallas's home number on his cell phone. Dallas answered on the fourth ring and Jacob immediately asked, "Got anything for me?"

"Yeah, and none of it's good."

"Shoot."

"First tell me if the girl found in Douglas Lake—"

"Genny was right. It was Becky Olmstead."

"Too bad."

"Yeah, but what I need to know now is if we've got another serial killer on our hands."

"When I contacted the authorities in each county, I just inquired about the recent past," Dallas said. "I questioned them about any similar crimes in the past few years."

"And?"

"You're not going to like what I found out."

"Damn, Dallas, why do you like to build these things up? You're too fucking dramatic. Just cut to the chase, will you?"

"Sorry. It's a bad habit of mine." Dallas paused a moment, then continued. "Okay, here it is. In the past three years there have been a total of seven murders involving a redheaded woman being strangled with a black ribbon and her body tossed in either a river or a lake, or in one case, a creek. That's seven counting Becky Olmstead and the woman found near Loudon Dam a couple of days ago. And the bad thing is that, until now, nobody had connected these crimes."

"The killer's been moving around, right?" Jacob said. "How many counties are involved?"

"Four of the seven women were Knoxville prostitutes, but each body was dumped in a different location—Loudon, Knox, Blount, to name only three. Two others were Johnson City girls, both with less than sterling reputations. Both were considered easy pickups in any local bar, although neither was a professional. The seventh victim was Cherokee County's own Becky Olmstead."

"Do you figure he made his first kill three years ago?"

"Maybe," Dallas said, "but it's possible that if we dig deeper, we'll find evidence that he's been around even longer. And it's also possible that not all the victims have been found. If he's tossed all of them into bodies of water, could be what's left of some is still at the bottom of the Tennessee River."

"So where do we go from here?"

"Since it's an area-wide problem, covering numerous counties, we're going to need federal help."

Jacob groaned. The Feds tended to take over when they got involved.

"I'll go through the Knoxville field office. Chet Morris is still the special agent in charge there, and as you know, he and I go way back."

"How much do I tell the press?" Jacob didn't like dealing with the local media. Brian MacKinnon had it in for Jacob. The two had never liked each other, but when Jacob had discouraged Brian's romantic interests in Genny before and after she met Dallas, Brian's dislike had turned to hatred.

"Basic facts. Local prostitute murdered. Strangled. Tossed into Douglas Lake."

"Right. Noland Floyd told me he's keeping a tight lid on certain facts—such as her being a redhead, that she was strangled with a black ribbon and that she was raped."

"I suggest you call a press conference as soon as you get back to Cherokee Pointe. Genny and I will drive into town and we'll meet up afterward for supper over at Jasmine's."

"How's Genny feeling?"

"Better. But I've got my hands full. She still wants to try to connect with the killer's mind."

"Sooner or later she'll wear you down," Jacob said. "I know Genny. If she's determined to do something, she eventually does it. Maybe you should quit trying to stop her and just help her."

"Look, she wanted to wait to tell you herself . . . later. But I think you need to know now."

A trickle of uneasiness jingled along Jacob's nerves. "What is it?"

"Genny's pregnant."

"What!"

"About five weeks along. She hasn't even seen a doctor yet. We did one of those home pregnancy tests a few days ago."

Genny, his little sister of the heart, was going to have a baby. A sense of elation swelled up inside Jacob. "Congratulations. This is great news. Genny must be very happy."

"She is. We both are."

"This changes everything. No way in hell can you let her try to psychically connect to the killer. We have no idea how it might affect the baby."

"I agree, but try telling that to Genny."

"I will. At supper tonight."

Reve couldn't remember enduring a social occasion as stressful as this simple Sunday dinner at the Uptons'. Although when Miss Reba had toasted the engaged couple, the tension in the room had waned slightly, and an atmosphere of uneasy truce settled over the assembly. Big Jim did his best to be jovial and went out of his way to compliment Jazzy and make her feel welcome in his home. Caleb hovered over his fiancé as if afraid his grandmother would attack again at any moment. But Reba Upton put on a happy face, even though everyone knew her cheerfulness was fake. However, her interest in Reve seemed genuine, and despite the woman's treatment of Jazzy, Reve found that she liked Caleb's grandmother very much. In fact, she reminded Reve a great deal of her own mother, whom she'd loved dearly.

When Dora served dessert, Reve smiled. "Banana pudding? How wonderful. Cook used to prepare it just for me because she knew it was my favorite."

Dora chuckled. "Mr. Caleb specifically asked me to make banana pudding today because it's Miss Jazzy's favorite."

Reba glanced from Reve to Jazzy. "Have the two of you discovered other similarities? I understand that often twins separated at birth find they have a great deal in common, although with the two of you, I'm sure any similarities will be minor."

"They don't even know for sure they're twins." Jim gave his wife a warning glare.

"I think we are," Jazzy said. "Physically, we're almost identical. We have the same blood type—AB negative. We're the same age, with birthdays the same week."

"And you both like banana pudding," Caleb added, a big grin on his face.

"When do you expect to get the DNA results?" Jim asked.

"Within a week, possibly sooner," Reve replied.

"And what will y'all do if it turns out that you are indeed twin sisters?" Reba asked.

"I want to find out who our parents were," Reve said. "I plan to hire Griffin Powell, who heads an exclusive protection and investigation agency in Knoxville, to unearth the truth about our births."

Reba turned to Jazzy. "What does your aunt have to say about all this?"

"Aunt Sally swears that her sister gave birth to only one baby."

"Well, considering that Sally Talbot is a rather"—Reba paused as if searching for the correct word—"eccentric old woman, it's possible she's confused, that her memory isn't what it should be."

Jazzy nodded. "Yes, that's possible."

"Or she could be out and out lying," Reve said, then wished the words back, realizing how bitter she'd sounded. But she was bitter. Someone had thrown her into a Dumpster, as if she was trash. And that same someone had kept Jazzy. But why? Dear God, why?

"I vaguely remember Corrine Talbot," Jim said. "A right pretty woman, as I recall. She and Sally resembled each other some, but Corrine was younger by ten years and a lot prettier." Jim studied Jazzy's face. "I don't see any resemblance."

"No, I've seen pictures of Corrine and I agree that I look nothing like her," Jazzy said. "Aunt Sally always told me that she thought I must look just like my daddy, whoever the son of a bitch was."

"Have you ever considered the possibility that Corrine Talbot wasn't your mother?" Reba's question gained everyone's attention. When all eyes were on her, she shrugged. "Well, it is possible, isn't it?"

"Then how did I become a part of the Talbot family?" Jazzy's voice quivered. "It's not as if Aunt Sally found me in a cabbage patch."

Corrine Talbot wasn't your mother. Wasn't your mother. Miss Reba's words echoed inside Reve's mind. If it was possible that Sally Talbot's younger sister didn't give birth to Jazzy, then who had? Who gave birth to twin girls thirty years ago? Who handed over one baby to Sally Talbot and tossed the other baby in the trash?

"I think we should talk to your aunt," Reve said. "I'd like to ask her a few questions."

Jazzy gave Reve a puzzled look. "You want to talk to Aunt Sally even before the DNA tests confirm that we're sisters?"

"If you'd prefer to wait, we can. But I think we both know what those DNA results will prove."

"We're twin sisters," Jazzy said.

"Yes, we're twin sisters." Reve admitted the truth to herself as well as to the others, for the first time since she'd laid eyes on Jazzy. "Why wait for the DNA results? You set up a time for us to talk to your aunt as soon as possible. And first thing in the morning, I'll call Griffin Powell and have him instigate an investigation. Someone somewhere knows who our mother was and why she disposed of us the way she did."

CHAPTER 13

Reve had tried to beg off having supper with Caleb and Jazzy, but when they both insisted she join them at Jasmine's, she had reluctantly agreed. Now that they were at the restaurant and she saw how happy and at ease her dinner companions were, she was actually glad she'd tagged along. Even though she had connected on a personal level with Reba Upton this afternoon, their three-hour visit with Caleb's grandparents had been less than pleasant for everyone involved, but especially for Jazzy. And as odd as it felt to Reve, something truly strange seemed to be happening to her. She was beginning to feel protective where Jazzy was concerned, protective in a big-sister kind of way.

You're being foolish, she told herself. *You don't know for certain she's your sister and you're not even sure you like her.* Ah, but she did know Jasmine Talbot was her sister. She knew deep down inside. She knew instinctively, had probably known all along, ever since this past spring when she'd first met Jazzy; but she was only now admitting the truth to herself. Okay, so they were sisters. That didn't mean she was the elder of the two, did it? Yes, it did. She felt that instinctively, too, that she was the one born first.

"What'll it be, folks?" the waitress asked. "Our special tonight is—"

"Denise, I want pork chops, with the works," Jazzy said. "I'm starving. I didn't eat much for lunch today."

"I'll take a hamburger steak, creamed potatoes and green beans," Caleb said. "And don't forget the cornbread."

"And for you, ma'am?" Denise asked Reve.

She glanced up at the young waitress and smiled. "Just a Caesar salad, please."

"Iced tea all around?" Denise asked.

Jazzy and Reve replied affirmatively, but Caleb said, "Coffee for me."

Once Denise was out of earshot, Caleb looked across the table at Reve. "So, what did you think of my grandparents?" He grinned devilishly. "And why didn't you take my grandmother up on her offer to stay there with them?"

He'd certainly put her on the spot, hadn't he? Being known as a blunt-spoken person, Reve saw no reason to shy away from complete honesty.

"I liked them both. Your grandfather has a great sense of humor, and Miss Reba reminds me of my mother."

"Poor you," Jazzy said.

"I beg your pardon?" Reve's gaze connected with Jazzy's.

"Sorry. I'm sure your mother was a lovely person. It's just that—" Jazzy huffed. "Hell, what difference does it make? I should have known that you and Miss Reba would hit it off like a house afire." Glaring at Reve, she continued, "You do know what she was up to with that gracious invitation for you to stay with them, don't you?"

"Yes, I believe I do. And that's the very reason I declined. I don't want to become involved in any of Miss Reba's matchmaking schemes. It's quite obvious that she would prefer for Caleb to be romantically involved with me instead of you."

"Smart lady," Caleb said.

"Thank you." Reve liked Caleb, and if he wasn't madly in love with Jazzy, she might be interested in him. Despite being a little rough around the edges, he was a handsome, intelligent man. And he was almost as rich as she was, or would be someday when he inherited the Upton millions.

Frowning, a slight catch in her voice, Jazzy turned to Caleb. "Miss Reba will do her best to stop us from getting married. You know that, don't you? Trying to use Reve to come between us is only the first item in her bag of tricks. I know her. I've been fighting her since I was sixteen, and she always wins."

"Not this time." Caleb slipped his arm around Jazzy's shoulders.

"Miss Reba has made two mistaken assumptions," Reve said in a matter-of-fact manner. "She actually thought that because Jazzy and I are look-a-likes, you might easily transfer your affections from the unsuitable sister to the suitable one."

Snapping her head around, Jazzy's eyes widened as she glowered at Reve. "Since you seem to know so damn much about Miss Reba, maybe you'd be kind enough to tell us what you think her second mistaken assumption was?"

"Certainly. I'd be glad to. She believes you simply transferred your desire to marry Jamie to Caleb. And you did this simply because he's now the heir to the Upton fortune," Reve said. "But that isn't true, is it?"

Jazzy shook her head. "No, that's not true." She looked at Caleb. "You know that's not true, don't you?"

"Yes, I know." He kissed her on the mouth. A quick yet passionate affirmation.

Reve was so absorbed in Caleb's tender, loving concern for Jazzy that she didn't realize at first that two people were heading toward their table at the back of the restaurant.

"Now I know why y'all are sitting way back here away from the other customers," Dallas Sloan said. "It's easier for you to steal a few kisses without being noticed."

Chuckling as he released Jazzy, Caleb then stood immediately and held out his hand to the chief of police. "What are you two doing in town this evening?"

"We're planning on having dinner out tonight," Genny said.

"Then sit right down here and join us." Jazzy pointed to the empty chairs at their table. "We've got plenty of room."

"We'd love to, if y'all are sure you don't mind?" Genny looked directly at Reve. "Jacob will be joining us shortly, as soon as he finishes with the press conference."

Reve's spine stiffened at the mention of the sheriff's name. And just when she thought she might enjoy this evening, circumstances proved her wrong. Her worst nightmare was probably on his way over here right now.

"Why is Jacob giving a press conference?" Jazzy asked.

"It's an official announcement about the murder of a local girl," Dallas said. "A young prostitute named Becky Olmstead. She'd been missing less than twelve hours when her body was found over in Jefferson County, in Douglas Lake."

"Does this have anything to do with the murder of that man out on Clinton Road last night?" Caleb asked.

"We think so, considering Timmons was her pimp, but we'd prefer—" Dallas stopped talking the moment Denise appeared.

"Do y'all need menus?" Denise asked.

"I don't," Dallas replied. "Do you, honey?"

"No, thanks. I know what I want. I'd like potato soup and a house salad, with lots of crackers," Genny said. "And Thousand Island dressing on the side. And a large glass of milk."

"Make mine chicken and dumplings, with cornbread."

"Tea?" Denise asked.

Dallas nodded, then pulled out a chair for his wife, who sat down beside Reve. He then sat across from her alongside Caleb, leaving the chair on the other side of Reve empty.

"I'd also like hot decaf tea, as well as the milk," Genny replied to Denise's question, then pivoted in her chair so that she faced Reve. "So, how are you?"

"I'm fine, thank you."

Genny spoke directly to Reve, her voice soft and low. "You

were smiling when we first arrived, but I noticed the moment I mentioned that Jacob would be joining us, you got a peculiar look on your face."

Genny Sloan was much too perceptive. *Of course she is,* Reve reminded herself. *The woman is psychic, isn't she?* Reve wasn't sure she believed in psychic powers, but she prided herself on having an open mind. For the time being, perhaps she should give Genny the benefit of the doubt. "I, uh, I'm not sure how to respond to that."

Genny's dark gaze penetrated the barrier Reve kept in place to prevent the world from getting too close. For a split second she sensed someone probing into her mind.

"Sorry," Genny whispered. "I didn't mean for that to happen."

Reve stared at her, startled by the unexpected invasion.

"Sometimes I can't control it," Genny explained.

Slightly shaken by the odd experience, Reve nodded. "The sheriff and I got off on the wrong foot when we first met and nothing has changed. I'm afraid we simply don't like each other."

"That's a slight understatement," Caleb said. "To outside observers, you two seem to despise each other."

Reve hadn't realized the others were listening to her conversation with Genny. She shot Caleb a defensive glare. "I believe despise is too strong a word."

Dallas grinned. "Well, however you feel about him, how about going easy on him this evening? The guy's had a rough twenty-four hours. He hasn't slept since night before last. And today he had to be present when a woman identified her eighteen-year-old daughter's body."

Reve was certain Dallas hadn't meant his statement as a chastisement, but that's how it felt to her. "Perhaps it would be better for Jacob if I simply left now and—"

Genny grasped Reve's arm when Reve started to stand. "Please, don't go."

Reve settled back into her chair.

"Being in the same profession gives Dallas and Jacob a common bond," Genny said. "Other than their relationships with me, of course. Dallas didn't mean to be rude. It's just that he's concerned about Jacob and these new murders."

Reve nodded, but thought it best not to reply verbally. In some dim corner of her mind, the thought of how difficult Jacob Butler's job must be elicited some unwanted sympathy pangs. She did not want to feel anything for the man, least of all warm, kind thoughts.

"I apologize if what I said came off sounding rude." Dallas smiled at Reve. "Lucky for me, I have a diplomatic wife."

Reve forced herself to return Dallas's smile, and everyone at the table breathed a sigh of relief.

"I'm going to share some info with y'all that can't go beyond this table," Dallas said. "And the only reason I'm telling y'all is because . . . well, because both Jazzy and Reve have something in common with our victim."

A heavy knot of unexplained fear tightened in Reve's belly.

"Our victim was a redhead." Dallas leaned over the table and spoke quietly, so his words wouldn't carry beyond their small circle. "She's not the first redhead killed in a similar manner in northeast Tennessee. In the past three years, there have been seven murders in all, that we know about. These redheaded women had one other thing in common—each one was either a prostitute or had a bad reputation."

Reve looked right at Jazzy.

"Well, I guess I'm next up, huh, since I qualify on both counts." Jazzy's sarcastic laugh sent a chill up Reve's spine. "I'm definitely a redhead, and nobody in Cherokee Pointe has a worse reputation than I do."

"An undeserved reputation." Genny reached across the table and grasped Jazzy's hand.

Jazzy squeezed her friend's hand, then glanced around the table at everyone there. "Not entirely undeserved. Let's face it, I'm no saint. And if this nut is killing bad-girl redheads, he won't need to look any farther than"—she tapped the center of her chest—"little old me."

"Nobody's going to hurt you," Caleb vowed.

"That's the reason I'm sharing this strictly confidential info with you," Dallas told Caleb. "I knew you'd keep a close eye on Jazzy. Just in case."

"What about Reve?" Jazzy asked. "Or since she doesn't qualify on both counts, is she safe?"

"Possibly," Dallas replied. "Probably."

"Just to be on the safe side, maybe she needs her own personal protector," Genny said. "I could speak to Jacob about it."

"If I feel the need for a bodyguard, I'll hire one," Reve told them. "But since, as Jazzy pointed out, my reputation is not questionable, I should be safe from this killer. Right?" Why was it that as she made such a confident pronouncement, a sense of foreboding encompassed her, as if a threatening dark cloud had suddenly settled directly over her head?

The minute Jacob arrived at Jasmine's, he gave Denise his order. Then she pointed to the table where Genny and Dallas were sitting. When he noted who their dinner companions were, he knew he'd been set up. Again. After the night and day he'd had, the last thing he needed was being forced to share a meal with Reve Sorrell. He had half a mind to turn around and go back to his office. He could get some peanut butter and crackers and a Coke out of the machine down the hall from the sheriff's department at the courthouse. Yeah, that was what he'd do.

Get the hell out of here, an inner voice warned.

Just as he turned to leave, Genny spotted him, threw up her hand and waved, motioning for him to join them. Great. Just great. He who hesitates, gets caught. Grunting, he shed his Stetson and suede jacket, hung them on the rack by the entrance and trudged grumpily toward the table on the far backside of the restaurant. When he approached the table, he soon realized that the only empty chair was—not surprisingly—beside Reve. He saw Genny's manipulative, matchmaking hand in this whole damn mess. If he didn't love his cousin so much, he'd be tempted to wring her pretty little neck.

"Evening," Jacob managed to say without growling the word.

Genny eyed the chair on the other side of Reve. "Sit down and tell us about the press conference."

He gave Genny an I-know-what-you're-trying-to-do glare. She smiled, her black eyes gleaming with satisfaction and a hint of mischief.

Reluctantly, Jacob sat. He was a big man, with broad shoulders, and it was a tight fit at the table with three people on each side. Inevitably, his arm brushed Reve's when he settled into his chair. He felt her stiffen and thought he heard her gasp. Willing his hot temper under control, he just barely managed to keep from saying, "Look, lady, I don't want to be here any more than you do. And accidently touching you wasn't exactly a thrill for me either."

"We've all ordered," Jazzy said. "Let me call Denise—"

"I gave her my order already," Jacob replied.

"How did the press conference go?" Dallas asked.

"I'm still standing." Jacob harrumphed. "But just barely. The reporters realized that I know more than I told them. And since Brian MacKinnon has made it perfectly clear to both his newspaper and TV reporters that I'm fair game, they bombarded me relentlessly."

"It'll get worse," Dallas said. "Especially if another local woman is murdered."

"I sure would like to know how to prevent that from happening." By moving only slightly, Jacob once again brushed his arm against Reve's. He scooted his chair over as far as it would go toward the end of the table. All of two, maybe three inches. His left shoulder was pressed up against the wall.

"You could let the public know that it seems to be only

redheaded women who are at risk," Reve said, but didn't look at Jacob.

"I shared that info with them in confidence," Dallas explained.

"With all the redheads we have in Cherokee County, that bit of information could cause a real panic." Jacob had been looking forward to a quiet, peaceful dinner with Genny and Dallas, but instead he was doomed to at least an hour of abject discomfort.

"Caleb plans to keep a close watch over Jazzy," Genny said. "Just in case."

"Yeah, since I'm a redheaded slut, I'm probably numero uno on this guy's hit list." Jazzy laughed, but there was no humor in her voice.

"You shouldn't joke about it that way," Reve said.

Jazzy shrugged. "Why not? It's a lot better than biting my nails down to the quick and living in fear. It's not my style to run scared, especially from such a non-specific threat." She eyed Reve insightfully. "Something tells me running isn't your style either."

"You're right. It's not my style," Reve said. "I'm stubborn and determined, and when my fight-or-flight instincts kick in, I tend to stand and fight."

"Another thing you two have in common." Genny glanced from Jazzy to Reve, then leaned in slightly so she could look around Reve at Jacob. "I think perhaps the sheriff's department should check on Reve every night and make sure—"

Reve bristled. "Genny, I told you that if I feel I need protection, I'll hire a bodyguard."

When Jacob glanced over at Reve, he noted a subdued blush on her creamy cheeks. "Yeah, sure, Genny. As a favor to you and"—he looked across the table—"to Jazzy, I'll send one of my deputies around to check on Ms. Sorrell every night."

"That won't be necessary!" Reve's voice rose loud enough so that customers at the nearest table turned and stared at her. Her face turned bright red.

"Here comes our supper," Jazzy said as Denise and Kalinda brought two large serving trays to the table. "Yum, everything looks delicious. We have great food here at Jasmine's, if I do say so myself."

Okay, Jacob thought, he could take the hint and ease up on Ms. Sorrell, if she'd do the same. Participating in a verbal sparring match during a meal wasn't high on his agenda of things to do. Besides, he had the oddest notion that his comment really had offended Reve Sorrell. Unless she was a lot dumber than she looked, she had to know that Genny was playing matchmaker. Her ploy to have Jacob make a nightly check on Reve had to be as repulsive to Reve as it was to him.

And then he did something really stupid. He looked at Reve and caught her looking right back at him. The expression in those big brown eyes reminded him of a deer caught in the glare of oncoming headlights. There was more to her animosity toward him than simply hatred—the woman was afraid of him. Their gazes locked for a second too long, and a hush fell over the table as everyone else seemed aware of their visual Mexican standoff. Thankfully, just about that time, Denise set his bowl of chili down in front of him. He broke eye contact first, picked up his spoon and dug into his meal. But he could feel Reve's heated glare boring into him. *Ignore her*, he told himself.

"This sure does look good," Jacob said, and within seconds everyone breathed again and renewed their conversations.

It was done. A fait accompli. He couldn't go back and undo it; he wouldn't even if he could. After all, it wasn't his fault that after all these years, Dinah had chosen to come back to him in Cherokee County. Of course, in the past, he hadn't searched for her locally, had made a point of looking for her in other places and had once been able to exert some control over her reappearances. But lately, things had changed. And this time, she had forced him to act more impulsively than ever before, making it necessary for him to also kill someone else in order to protect himself.

He'd done what he had to do. This time, he hadn't sought her. She had found him.

She walked right into your life and all but begged you to notice her.

Then the next move had been his. He'd hated going through that bastard Timmons, but it had been the quickest and easiest way to make contact. And killing Timmons had been no more trouble to him than cleaning mud off his shoes.

This time Dinah had resurfaced in the guise of Becky Olmstead, a local prostitute. Once again, she had chosen someone a great deal like herself, someone in whose body she'd felt comfortable. In all her reincarnations, not once had she chosen someone pure and innocent. She probably never would. Nor had she ever chosen anyone who was as beautiful as she had been. Not until now.

He had been aware of this woman for years, had even found himself fascinated by her beauty as all the other men in the county had been. But he had kept his distance from her, not wanting to tempt Dinah into tricking him into killing her in his home territory. But she'd fooled him after all—by not choosing Jazzy Talbot first. She'd used Becky, as she'd used all the others, to seduce him, to lure him into her trap, to force him to destroy her yet again.

He couldn't believe that she was returning so quickly now—three times in less than a week—giving him little peace and no rest whatsoever. Less than a week ago, he'd killed her and dumped her body in the Tennessee River near Loudon Dam. She'd called herself Kat Baker then. He had thought, had hoped, she would stay away for months, as she usually did, sometimes even as long as eight or nine months. But she had come back to him almost overnight in the form of Becky Olmstead. And now, less than twenty-four hours later, she had done what he had always feared she would do someday. He was almost certain that she had come back in Jazzy Talbot's body.

Sitting there tonight at Jasmine's with her friends and current lover, Jazzy had been totally unaware of her fate. Dinah never let her victims know she had possessed them, not until it was too late. Poor Jazzy didn't even suspect that she was as good as dead.

CHAPTER 14

Reve caught a glimpse of her reflection in the shop win-dow she passed on her way to Jasmine's. She was too tall. Her hips were too wide. She needed to lose twenty pounds. Damn, she had to stop berating herself. How could a wealthy, intelligent, reasonably attractive woman waste time worry-ing about her physical appearance? *Because you're human,* she reminded herself. She certainly didn't have any self-esteem problems—except about her body. And if she were honest with herself, she'd admit that those concerns had be-come greatly magnified after meeting Jazzy. They looked al-most alike. *Almost* being the operative word. She was probably two inches taller and at least twenty pounds heavier than the slender, curvy Jazzy. And her twin's hips were in perfect pro-portion to the rest of her sexy body. Okay, so Jazzy was more attractive than she was. Big deal. She possessed qualities her sister didn't. And she wouldn't trade a one of them for a body like her sister's.

Her sister? Yes, her sister. She felt certain the DNA test results would prove what she had already accepted—that she and Jazzy were twins.

Picking up her pace, she hurried down the sidewalk,

avoiding making eye contact with any of the downtown shoppers she passed. The townspeople seemed to be particularly interested in her because she looked so much like Jazzy. According to Genny and Jazzy, apparently everyone in Cherokee County was speculating about their relationship and the consensus was that Jazzy and she were twins. Although some people gawked at her and others merely stole quick glances, no one spoke to her. Thank goodness.

Were these people comparing her to her sister? Were they thinking she was a pale imitation of the real thing? Or did they marvel at how different they were? At the fact that Jazzy was vivacious and flashy and, although extremely friendly, had a kiss-my-ass attitude, whereas Reve appeared well-bred, conservative in her appearance and hopefully mannerly in her demeanor. God knew Lesley Sorrell did her best to drill good manners into her only child.

Just as Reve entered the restaurant, she met Caleb. He grabbed her by the shoulders and kissed her on the cheek.

"Good morning. Isn't it a beautiful morning?" Caleb's grin spread from ear to ear.

"Somebody is certainly in a good mood."

"Jazzy and I just set our wedding date, and I'm on my way over to tell my grandparents."

Reve smiled. "That should be interesting. So when is the big day?"

"December the eighteenth. Jazzy really does want a Christmas wedding."

"Then I hope she gets what she wants."

"Can you keep a secret?" Caleb asked.

Reve widened her eyes in a questioning manner.

"After I tell Miss Reba and Big Jim the news, I'm driving over to Knoxville to pick out an engagement ring. Of course I wouldn't be leaving Jazzy alone, not after what Dallas and Jacob told us last night, but I understand that you two are going to spend the rest of the day together. Just stick together at all times and play it safe."

"We will. You don't have to worry about Jazzy. We can look out for each other."

"You're beginning to like her, aren't you?"

Reve laughed. "Maybe."

"Give her a chance, will you? I think you two can be really good for each other."

"Did she tell you that I've hired Griffin Powell to investigate our past, to try to find out the truth about our births?"

"Yeah, she told me." Caleb's smile softened. "She said you phoned him last night and he's driving in today to meet with y'all. I guess that's what you can do when you've got the Sorrell money and power at your disposal—you can get Griffin Powell to personally take your case."

"Wealth does have its privileges," she said. "Now that you're part of the Upton family, you'll soon find out."

He studied Reve for a moment, then asked, "About being an Upton . . . I've been debating whether to ask my grandfather for a loan so I can buy Jazzy a really impressive diamond. But I'm just not sure. What do you think?"

Why ask me? I hardly know Jazzy, had been the first thought that crossed her mind, but she managed not to voice the question. "I think you know Jazzy better than I do. Do you think she expects an impressive diamond?"

Caleb shrugged. "Maybe. And I know she deserves something spectacular. I just don't want her to think that I think she's marrying me because of the Upton fortune. So, tell me, Ms. Sorrell, if you were going to marry a guy who couldn't afford a huge diamond, what would you want him to do?"

"If I loved a man enough to marry him, I wouldn't care about the size of the diamond." Well, where had that thought come from? Reve wondered. Surely she'd never consider marrying a man who wasn't extremely wealthy in his own right.

Caleb nodded. "Yeah, but you've already got enough expensive jewelry to open up your own jewelry store." He eyed the two-carat diamond studs in her ears and glanced down at the small diamond and gold butterfly pin attached to the collar of her brown jacket. "Jazzy likes flash and sparkle. She's that kind of girl. Nothing about her is subdued, if you know what I mean."

"Then buy her a big, flashy diamond," Reve said. "Something that will knock her socks off with its sparkle and glitter."

Caleb chuckled. "You're right. See, you know Jazzy a lot better than you think you do."

After she wished him luck in finding the perfect engagement ring, Caleb and she said their good-byes and she entered the restaurant. Several customers turned and stared at her. Holding her head high, with just a hint of snobbery in her expression, she ignored them completely.

The hostess on duty, Tiffany Reid, smiled warmly at Reve and said, "Jazzy's expecting you. Go on back to her office."

"Thank you."

"She said to take your lunch order when you got here and we'll serve y'all in her office later, after your meeting with Mr. Powell." Tiffany giggled. "I can't believe that Griffin Powell is coming here. Today. I've seen pictures of him, of course, but I never thought I'd get a chance to see him in the flesh."

"Tiffany, when Mr. Powell arrives, please show him into Jazzy's office immediately. And whatever you do, don't drool all over him."

Tiffany giggled again, the sound slightly irritating. "I'll do my best. I promise. But we're all talking about Griffin Powell. He's a legend around here, you know. Not only is he one of the most famous former UT football players, but now he's the most talked-about man in Tennessee. His picture's always in the newspaper or in magazines whenever his agency is involved with a big case or when he's attending some high society do, like charity balls and stuff like that."

"Yes, well, that may all be true, but today, please see to it that none of the other customers bother him. Usher him straight to Jazzy's office the minute he arrives."

"I will. I swear. Jazzy's already given me my instructions." Reve offered Tiffany an understanding smile. "I'd like soup and salad. Onion soup, if you have it. If not, vegetable will do. And a Caesar salad."

Grinning, Tiffany shook her head.

"Is something wrong?" Reve asked.

"Nope. It's just funny. Jazzy ordered the same thing. Veggie soup and a Caesar salad. Only she added carrot cake. Miss Ludie brought in three fresh-baked carrot cakes early this morning."

Beginning to get used to the idea that she and Jazzy had certain tastes in common, Reve simply said, "Add a slice of carrot cake to my order."

She then made her way to the back of the restaurant. She passed the restrooms and the door leading to the storage area, then stopped and knocked on the closed door to Jazzy's office.

"Come on in," Jazzy called.

Reve opened the door. "Aren't you concerned that I might have been the latest Cherokee County killer, the one murdering redheads?"

"Nope. I wasn't the least bit concerned." Jazzy swirled her swivel office chair around and faced Reve. "I heard your footsteps coming up the hall. Most men don't wear high heels."

Reve walked into the room and shut the door behind her. "Have you contacted your Aunt Sally?"

Jazzy motioned for Reve to take a seat in the empty chair to the left of her desk. The other chair, on the right, was piled high with magazines. "No, I thought it best not to alert Aunt Sally that we're coming to see her later today. She just might decide to take a hike in the woods. Believe me, she is not going to want to talk to us about my mother. Our mother."

"You think she'll stick to the lie that Corrine Talbot gave birth to only one child."

"Every time I've questioned her, she's sworn that it's the truth."

Reve sat, placed her brown leather purse in her lap and rested her clasped hands on top of the purse. "And what if it *is* the truth?" She kicked back in her chair and crossed her arms over her waist.

"How's that possible? I thought we'd both decided, even without the DNA test results, that we're definitely twins."

"We did decide that and I do believe we are twin sisters," Reve said. "But that doesn't mean Corrine Talbot gave birth to us."

Jazzy's eyes widened; her mouth gaped open. "I don't understand. If Corrine isn't our mother, then who is? And how did Aunt Sally get hold of me and not you, too? And if Corrine gave birth to a child, what happened to that baby?"

"Good questions. Ones we need to ask your aunt."

Jazzy stood. "Yeah, you're right. As soon as our meeting with Griffin Powell ends, we'll drive up the mountain to Aunt Sally's place and pay her a surprise visit. And if the old coot tries to run off, I'll tie her to a chair."

Despite the harshness of the comment, Reve heard the underlying affection in Jazzy's voice when she spoke of her aunt. "You love her very much, don't you?"

Jazzy chuckled, then faced Reve with a closed-mouth smile. "Oh, yeah. I love her. She's the only mother I've ever known. Aunt Sally's one brick shy of a load by anybody's standards, but she's a wonderful old woman. She's been awfully good to me my whole life."

"How will it affect your relationship with her if you find out she's been lying to you all these years?"

Jazzy sighed loudly and blew out a huffing breath. "I'm not sure. But I know it won't make me hate her. No matter what, she'll always be my Aunt Sally."

"When my parents told me that I was adopted, I was only six. They made it sound as if being adopted was something special. They made me feel as if I was a chosen one. Then when I was fourteen, I started getting curious about my biological parents and I asked Mother and Father if they knew anything about where I'd come from and why my birth mother had given me away. They swore they didn't know anything."

Reve gritted her teeth in an effort not to cry. Remembering the day her mother had finally confessed the truth to Reve still affected her at a deep emotional level. "When I graduated from college, my mother finally told me about my being found in a Dumpster in Sevierville. She said I'd been little more than a newborn when I was found. But that was all she and my father ever knew about me."

"You know, that's something that makes no sense to me. If our birth mother threw you into a Dumpster, why didn't she toss me in there with you?"

"Another very good question."

Jazzy walked over to Reve and stood above her, looking down at her until she lifted her gaze so that they were staring right at each other. "I guess it makes you feel like shit, doesn't it? Knowing you were thrown away like a piece of garbage."

Reve swallowed, then cleared her throat. "Yes. Yes, it does."

"You know what, sis, maybe she threw us both away. Maybe somebody found me in that Dumpster first and—"

"Your Aunt Sally?"

"Or maybe Corrine Talbot."

"We're making a lot of wild guesses here, none of which may turn out to be correct."

A loud, repetitive knocking on the door ended their conversation.

"Jazzy, Mr. Powell is here," Tiffany called through the closed door.

"Show him in right now." Jazzy turned to greet their visitor.

Reve rose, laid her purse on the chair seat and stood beside Jazzy.

The door opened to reveal a big, wide-shouldered man in a navy blue suit, a crisp white shirt and a burgundy, navy and white striped tie. His white-blond hair was cut short, obviously in an effort to control the curliness that revealed itself despite the style. A pair of dark blue eyes surveyed the room and the two women. Everything about him reeked of money and good taste.

At six-four, with the toned body of an athlete and the aura of a dangerous warrior, Griffin Powell possessed the kind of magnetism that intrigued women and intimated other men. Reve knew the man by reputation only. Although she had used his agency when she'd had Jazzy investigated nearly a year ago, the two had never met. She knew only what everyone else knew about Mr. Powell—that he'd been a poor boy who'd grown up on a farm outside Dayton and had made a name for himself as a star quarterback for the University of Tennessee nearly two decades ago. After graduation, when everyone had been sure he'd turn pro, the man had disappeared off the face of the earth. For ten years, no one had any idea what had happened to him. Then five years ago, he'd come back to Tennessee—rich, powerful and apparently world-weary. He'd opened a private security and investigation agency in Knoxville, catering to an elite clientele, and soon became the state's most famous mystery man.

Powell declined to give interviews, despite public curiosity and the media's quest to unearth his secrets. Over the years, his reputation had become legendary, with half a dozen different scenarios circulating that explained the missing years of his life. Reve had to admit that she was curious, but understanding what it was like to be the focus of that kind of attention, she intended to keep her curiosity in check. And she'd warned Jazzy not to ask him any personal questions when they met.

"Mr. Griffin." Reve extended her hand.

He shook hands with her. A strong, confident exchange. Neither smiled.

Jazzy came forward, her usual glittery personality and sexiness all but oozing from her pores. "I'm Jazzy Talbot. It's really nice to meet you, Mr. Griffin."

"Ladies." He nodded curtly.

"Won't you sit down?" Jazzy rushed to remove the stack of magazines from the chair to her right.

"Why don't we all sit," Griffin suggested.

They all sat, Griffin and Reve in the chairs flanking Jazzy's desk. Jazzy chose to prop herself on the edge of her desk in a rather provocative pose. Reve realized that Jazzy wasn't even aware of what she'd done, that being sexy was second nature to her. She wasn't coming on to Griffin Powell. She was just being herself.

Griffin laid his briefcase on his lap, flipped it open and removed a document. "I ran an initial check on the two of you first thing this morning before I left Knoxville."

"We could have told you anything you wanted to know." Jazzy smiled flirtatiously with Griffin. And once again Reve realized that Jazzy wasn't doing it intentionally.

The corners of Griffin's mouth lifted ever so slightly, as if he was mildly amused by Jazzy. "I like to cut through any sentiment and get down to the bare facts." He looked at Reve. "I've sent an agent to Sevierville to look into the events surrounding your being found in a Dumpster. I want the exact date, and if possible we'll track down any eye witnesses. I'll also want your permission to speak to the attorney who handled your adoption."

"Yes, of course. Winston Carroll is retired now, and when I questioned him myself, he didn't seem to know any more than my mother had already told me."

Griffin nodded, then looked at Jazzy. "I'll want to question your aunt." He glanced down at his report. "Sally Talbot. I believe she raised you after her sister Corrine Talbot's death."

"That's right," Jazzy said.

"We'll find out more about Corrine, too. A good start will be to find records proving she really was pregnant and if she was, whether she gave birth to one baby girl or two. And if she did have twins, were those children the two of you."

"Reve and I had planned to speak to Aunt Sally later today. We're paying her a surprise visit."

"I'd like to go with you. My guess is that Sally Talbot can shed a great deal of light on the matter."

"Oh, I know she can," Jazzy replied. "The problem is, will she tell us the truth? You see, I'm the most important person in the world to Aunt Sally. If she has been lying to me all these years, then she's going to be afraid to tell me the truth, afraid she'll lose me."

"Then perhaps you should assure her that isn't the case." Griffin held out a copy of his report to Jazzy. "Read this over and see if it's correct and if there's any pertinent information that needs to be added."

When Jazzy took the report, he then turned to Reve and handed her a copy. "Would you do the same, Ms. Sorrell?"

Reve took the report, nodded and then scanned the two-page summary. She soon realized that the document was a concise, accurate, condensed account of her life, from when she was adopted by the Sorrells to the present day, including all the known facts that connected her to Jazzy.

Same blood type. AB negative.

Strong physical resemblance. Practically identical.

Sorrell adopted as an infant. Talbot reared by an "aunt."

The two women grew up within a three-hour drive of each other.

"Why not add that our favorite dessert is banana pudding?" Jazzy said, lifting her head after skimming the document.

"Or you could even add that we both prefer Caesar salad to house salad," Reve said and returned Jazzy's instant smile.

Griffin glanced from one to the other. "I take it that you two have already decided that you're sisters. Am I right?"

"You're right," Reve told him. "We believe the DNA test results will only confirm what we already know. That's why I hired you before the results came back. We don't want to waste any more time in tracking down our biological mother and discovering the facts surrounding our births."

"Are you both prepared to learn the truth?" Griffin asked. "Sometimes it's better to not go digging around in the past. You might not like what you find out."

"I assume we won't like what we find out," Reve said. "After all, how could a story that begins with disposing of an infant in the trash possibly wind up reading like a fairy tale?"

CHAPTER 15

They took Jazzy's red Jeep and left Reve's Jaguar parked in town. They had passed the turnoff for the Upton estate several miles back. The road leading from the main highway that wound around and around in its ascent up the mountain was a hazardous, narrow, paved strip, jutted with potholes and protected from deep ravines by low, rusted guardrails. During most of their trip, one country-and-western song after another had blasted from Jazzy's radio. Reve had made herself grin and bear it. She really didn't like country music, especially not the current brand. And all the while the music pulsated through the Jeep, Jazzy had chatted away about first one thing and then another.

"I hope Mr. Powell wasn't offended by my insisting he wait to talk to Aunt Sally until we'd had a chance to talk to her first," had been one of Jazzy's first remarks.

With that topic discussed and dismissed, Jazzy had gone on to comments about her aunt, her poor but filled-with-love childhood, and her aunt's friend Ludie, who was a full-bloodied Cherokee. Reve had wanted to shout "Stop!" Too much information given too quickly. But her sister hadn't paused long enough for Reve to get a word in edgewise.

As Jazzy zipped her shiny red Jeep around one sharp curve after another, Reve held her breath. When they reached a level strip of roadway, Jazzy glanced at Reve. "You look pale. What's wrong? Is it my driving or my choice in music?"

"Truthfully?" Reve asked.

"Yeah, if nothing else, let's promise to always be honest with each other."

"It's both. I don't care for most country music. And although I've been known to drive fast myself, the steep dropoffs on each side of this road unnerve me."

Jazzy immediately slowed down to forty-five miles an hour and turned off the radio. "Better?"

Reve breathed a sigh of relief. "Yes, thank you."

"What kind of music do you like?"

"I have fairly eclectic tastes. There are a few older country songs I like, but for the most part I prefer cool jazz, classical and semi-classical."

"Hm-mm. Jazz is okay. And I like the blues, too." Jazzy kept her eyes focused on the road ahead. "I wonder what else we have in common, other than banana pudding and Caesar salad and liking jazz music."

"My guess would be not much."

Jazzy laughed, the sound deep-throated and entirely genuine. "Do you like movies?"

"Yes, as a matter of fact, I do. I'm addicted to old movies. My favorites are those made in the thirties, forties and early fifties."

"You're shitting me."

Reve looked quizzically at Jazzy.

"Pardon my French, honey," Jazzy said jokingly. "I'm wild for old movies, too, especially love stories."

"It would seem we do have something else in common."

"What about collectibles? Do you collect anything in particular?"

"I collect Hummel figurines. I began collecting them when I was a child."

"I collect salt and pepper shakers," Jazzy said, excitement in her voice. "I have a display case filled with them in my living room."

"Sometime you'll have to show them to me."

Smiling broadly, Jazzy cast Reve a quick glance. "Why don't you have supper with me this evening in my apartment?"

Knowing that Caleb probably wanted to be alone with Jazzy tonight to present her with the engagement ring he'd gone to Knoxville to buy, Reve hesitated.

"It's okay if you don't want to have supper at my place." Jazzy couldn't hide the disappointment in her voice. "I'm probably pushing too hard. I tend to do that. Sorry."

"I'd really like to have dinner with you at your apartment tonight, if you don't think Caleb would mind." *I'm sorry, Caleb, I really am. I just can't let Jazzy think I don't want to get to know her better. I can't hurt her feelings.*

"Why would Caleb mind? He told me that he thinks we'll wind up being really good for each other. He likes you, you know."

"I'll tell you what. I'll come for dinner, but I'll probably leave early. I have some business calls to make before I turn in." That wasn't exactly a lie. She did have to check in with her personal assistant, Paul Welby, who handled her social schedule and her business calendar.

"That's fine. You can leave as early as you need to. There will be other nights. And who knows, one of these days we might plan a sleepover."

Both of them laughed at the thought of thirty-year-old women having a slumber party.

A few minutes later, Jazzy drove the Jeep off the paved road and onto a bumpy dirt lane. Up ahead on a sloping hillside rested a small white structure inside a circular clearing surrounded by dense forest. A dirty black truck—an antique from the looks of it—was parked at the side of the house.

The late afternoon sun hung low in the west, sunset only an hour or so away.

"I had vinyl siding put on Aunt Sally's house a few years ago," Jazzy said. "Her daddy built the house back when she was a young girl. The place used to look a lot like many of the other shacks up here in the mountains. It's just four rooms, a front and back porch and a bathroom. The bathroom was an addition in the late sixties."

When Jazzy stopped the Jeep in front of the house, two old dogs raised their heads from where they lay on the porch. One yawned and lay back down. The other got up and stood there staring at them as they emerged from the vehicle.

"That's Peter and Paul," Jazzy said. "They're Aunt Sally's bloodhounds. They're the best tracking dogs in the county. Sometimes the law uses them to hunt down criminals or search for a missing person."

As she passed the dogs, Jazzy reached out and petted the one standing. Reve stayed on the other side of Jazzy, away from the animals. She liked dogs well enough. She simply wasn't accustomed to being around big, foul-smelling country dogs that lived outside.

Jazzy grasped the doorknob with one hand and knocked with the other. "Remember, let me do all the talking. At least at first," she told Reve.

Reve nodded.

"Aunt Sally? Are you home? It's me, Jazzy. And I've brought somebody with me."

Jazzy entered the house and motioned for Reve to follow. Before she could close the door, both dogs came loping in behind her. The larger of the two almost identical bloodhounds nuzzled her palm. Reve jumped when his cold, damp nose touched her skin.

"Peter, behave yourself," Jazzy scolded.

"Who've you brought with you?" Sally called from the kitchen.

Before Jazzy could reply, Sally Talbot entered what Reve assumed was the living room since it was furnished with an old floral sofa and two seen-better-days chairs. Scanning the area, Reve noted a round table covered with a plaid cloth between the two chairs, an aluminum coffee can on the floor beside one of the chairs and a small, black potbellied stove in the corner. The walls had been covered with inexpensive wood paneling. Three photographs of Jazzy were arranged in a triangle shape over the sofa—all three obviously school photographs. And above the door that led to the kitchen was a framed reproduction of *The Lord's Supper*.

The minute Sally saw Reve, she stopped dead still and her welcoming smile vanished. "You should've called first. Me and Ludie was just fixing to go on over to her place."

As if on cue, a short, squat gray-haired woman appeared. Her expressive black eyes settled on Reve. "We ain't in no hurry. You two come on in. I'll put on a fresh pot of coffee and serve up some peach cobbler I brought over here for Sally."

"Coffee would be great, Ludie," Jazzy said. "But I'll forgo the cobbler. Reve and I both had some of your carrot cake for lunch."

Ludie gave Sally a nudge. "Sit down and visit a while with Jazzy and Ms. Sorrell. I'll go fix that coffee right now."

Sally looked from Reve to Jazzy. "What brings y'all out here?"

"I think you know." Jazzy sat down on the sofa.

"Yeah, I guess I do." She turned to Reve. "Have a seat, gal."

"Thank you." Reve sat beside Jazzy.

Sally walked over to a pile of wood stacked in a rickety old crate, picked up a couple of split logs and carried them over to the cast-iron potbellied stove. After opening the hinged door, she rammed the wood inside and then closed the door. The stove gave off a great deal of heat so the room was toasty warm on this cool autumn day. After wiping her hands on the sides of her faded denim jeans, Sally sat in one of the ragged, slipcovered chairs.

"Reve has hired Griffin Powell to investigate the circumstances surrounding her adoption," Jazzy told Sally. "She wants to find out who tossed her into that Dumpster in Sevierville. She wants to know who her biological parents are."

Sally pulled a square of tobacco from her shirt pocket, bit off a chunk and began chewing. After a few minutes, she said, "I can think of better ways to spend money than paying that highfalutin private dick to meddle in things best left alone."

"Don't you think Reve has a right to know who her birth parents are?"

Sally picked up the coffee tin from the floor beside her chair, brought it to her lips and spit. After wiping her mouth, she narrowed her gaze and glared at Reve. "It seems to me that them Sorrells gave you a mighty good life. I'd think you'd be grateful and not have a hankering to cause other folks trouble."

"For whom am I causing trouble?" Reve asked. "You, Ms. Talbot?"

Sally spit into the can again, then set it on the floor. "I'll tell you what I told my niece. My sister Corrine come home to these hills when she was about ready to deliver her baby. She said her husband deserted her, but I figured she weren't never married. She was still calling herself Corrine Talbot. Anyhow, I delivered her baby. A little girl. One little girl. Not two. Not twins. And a few days later, old Doc Webster come up here to see about my sister and the little one. He recorded Jazzy's birth. Nine pounds, seven ounces. She was a big, healthy youngun."

"Aunt Sally, you know that Reve and I are expecting to get the results of our DNA tests back any day now." Jazzy leaned forward, a pleading look in her eyes. "We fully expect the results to show that we're twin sisters. Why won't you tell us the truth?"

Jumping to her feet, the old rawboned woman's ice-blue eyes burned with indignation. "Are you calling me a liar, gal? Me, your own aunt?"

Jazzy shot off the sofa, rushed over to Sally and grabbed her hands. "Now, you listen here, you crazy old woman—I love you. Do you hear me? No matter what, I love you. And nothing will change that fact."

Tears welled up in Sally's eyes. "I didn't know nothing about no other baby. I swear I didn't."

Jazzy squeezed her aunt's hands tightly. "I believe you. Now, please, tell us . . . tell me the truth. Am I your sister Corrine's baby?"

"Ah, hell, gal." Sally jerked free of Jazzy's tenacious hold. "I couldn't bear it if you hated me. I just couldn't—"

Sally lumbered to the front door, flung it open and went out onto the porch. Jazzy and Reve exchanged nervous glances, then Jazzy followed her aunt outside. By the time Jazzy reached the porch, Sally had already gone out into the yard and was heading for the woods, both old bloodhounds lumbering along behind her.

"Aunt Sally, wait!"

Ludie came scurrying out of the kitchen, shaking her head and wringing her fat little hands. When Ludie hurried onto the porch, Reve got up and followed her. The old woman grabbed Jazzy's arm just as Jazzy headed down the steps. She stopped, turned and glared at Ludie.

"Leave her be," Ludie said. "She ain't going to tell you nothing right now. Give her time. Wait until you got them test results in your hand to show her."

Jazzy hesitated, then nodded. "What do you know, Ludie? And don't you dare tell me you know nothing."

"I know that Sally's been everything a real ma could have

been to you. You're lucky, you know, mighty lucky that she found you and took care of you."

Reve's heartbeat accelerated. Had the old woman said that Sally Talbot had found Jazzy?

"What do you mean she found me?" Jazzy asked.

"I ain't saying no more. It's Sally's place to tell you. Not mine."

"Please, Ludie—"

"All I'll say is this—Sally thought she did the right thing. For you and for her sister Corrine. She didn't know there was another baby. How could she have known?" Ludie glanced back at Reve. "You really was found in a Dumpster over in Sevierville, right?"

"Yes."

Ludie turned back to Jazzy. "You weren't in no Dumpster in Sevierville."

"Are you saying Aunt Sally found me somewhere else, that I'm not Corrine's baby?"

"I can't say. I just can't."

Jazzy covered her mouth with both hands, closed her eyes and took a deep breath. When she opened her eyes, she focused on Ludie and said, "Please, if you'll answer just one more question, I promise I won't ask anything else. And I promise that I'll wait to question Aunt Sally again until the DNA test results come back."

"You swear?"

"Yes, I swear."

"What's the question?" Ludie asked.

"Am I Corrine Talbot's child, and if I'm not, what happened to her baby?"

"That's two questions."

"Please, Ludie."

Ludie didn't reply immediately, instead she seemed to be thinking, considering her options. "You love Sally? You'll never walk away and leave her? Not ever? You promise?"

"Oh, Ludie, you know Aunt Sally will always be my family, no matter what."

Ludie nodded. Her keen black eyes settled on Jazzy. "Corrine's baby was a little girl. Tiny little thing. Never breathed the first breath. The cord was wrapped around her neck. Sally blamed herself, but I told her it weren't her fault that her sister's baby was born dead."

He had to think of a way to get to Jazzy. The problem was, the woman was never alone. Her lover lived with her, and when he wasn't around at Jasmine's or at Jazzy's Joint, other people were. And to complicate matters, now that her long-lost sister had shown up, she seemed to be stuck to the woman like glue. Besides, there was the added problem of Jazzy being friends with both the sheriff and the chief of police. What if they had shared confidences with her? What if they had warned her someone had already killed one red-headed Cherokee Pointe slut?

How could he trick Jazzy into meeting him? Because she knew him, if he just called her up and made an excuse to see her alone, she was bound to tell someone. Calling her was out of the question. There had to be a way of bringing her to him, of luring her into a trap. It was only a matter of time before he figured out what would work, how he could bring Jazzy to him without anyone ever finding out—until it was too late. He had to keep his identity a secret.

He'd never faced a challenge such as this. Knowing that this time there would be heightened danger in killing Dinah excited him unbearably.

He'd been watching Jazzy earlier today when he'd had lunch at Jasmine's and she and Reve Sorrell had walked out of the restaurant with Griffin Powell. According to what he'd overheard the waitresses saying, Ms. Sorrell had hired the renowned investigator to search for her birth mother. A crazy thought had gone through his mind when he'd seen the two women together, but he'd quickly vanquished it. It wasn't possible that Jazzy and Reve had any connection to his past.

Think about the future, he told himself, *about the pleasure that lies in store for you.* She would be his soon. He would tie the black satin ribbon around her neck and tighten it until she couldn't breathe. He would never forget the look in Dinah's eyes the first time he'd strangled her. She'd thought him incapable of such strength, such boldness. He'd proven her wrong. Sometimes he saw her eyes in his dreams. Staring at him, accusing him.

So long ago and yet it often felt as if the first time had been only yesterday.

Allowing those tormenting memories to take him over, he closed his eyes and recalled ripping off her gown, eager to touch her, to suck her large, round breasts. Licking his lips, he could still taste the wet sweetness of her nipples. She had fought him, called him names, even laughed at him. But he had managed not to come before he'd rammed into her. But just barely. He'd jumped on top of her and screwed her like crazy. It had been the best fuck of his life.

Would screwing Dinah while she was in Jazzy's hot, sexy body be as good? If not, only half as good would be good enough.

In his mind, images of Jazzy mixed with his memories of Dinah and soon became one. He lifted a piece of braided satin ribbon out of the drawer and stroked it lovingly.

There had been a tiny gold heart on the black ribbon she wore around her neck. After he'd killed her, he had removed the gold heart and stuck it in his pocket. He still had it, locked away in a safe place.

Standing naked and fully aroused in front of the full-length mirror, he stroked his penis with the ribbon. Ah, the feel of it. His erection grew harder, stronger, just from the touch of the satin against his flesh. If only he could be with Dinah now, if only he could bury himself deep inside her. He tied the satin ribbon around his jutting sex and slid the ribbon back and forth, all the while thinking of Dinah. Dreaming of killing her again. That gentle friction alone almost made him come. Almost.

Think of killing her, he told himself. *Think of thrusting into her hard and fucking her while she's helpless to stop you.*

His hand moved faster and faster. His excitement built to a frenzy.

And then he ejaculated. His cum shot out, covering his hand and dampening the braided ribbon still circling his slowly withering penis.

CHAPTER 16

Reba met Dodd at an out-of-the-way restaurant in Sevierville, hoping they would go unnoticed in the rush of tourists who flocked to the mountains in October, filling hotels, motels and restaurants to capacity. While sitting in her car, waiting for Dodd to arrive, she'd watched the flow of customers arriving and leaving and had felt terribly conspicuous even though no one paid any attention to her. By the time Dodd arrived, exactly at seven-thirty, she was a nervous wreck. How on earth had Jim been able to handle all his affairs, all those clandestine meetings with one mistress after another, not to mention the numerous one-night stands he'd probably had over the years? The answer, of course, was crystal clear. Jim hadn't been burdened by enormous feelings of guilt, while she, on the other hand, had a conscience that bothered her greatly. After all, she was a married woman doing the one thing that she had condemned her husband for doing repeatedly during their long, unhappy marriage.

Dodd reached across the table and clasped Reba's hand. Her first instinct was to jerk away from him. After all, they were in a public place. But their booth was at the back of the large restaurant, and no one was particularly interested in an old couple they probably assumed had been married to each other for ages.

"What's wrong?" Dodd asked. "You're a million miles away."

She looked at him and smiled. Such a dear man. Gentle and kind. And loving in a way Jim had never been. When Dodd merely held her hand, as he was doing now, and gazed tenderly into her eyes, she felt his love for her. In the early years of their marriage, Jim had been an attentive lover and the sex had been quite good. Incredibly good. But all that had changed when Jim, Jr., and Melanie were preschoolers and she had learned about Jim's affair with his then secretary, a woman whose name Reba couldn't even remember now. That woman had simply been the first in a long line of women who had paraded in and out of Jim's life. After that first incident, every time Jim touched her, Reba had cringed, but she'd done her wifely duty and submitted to her husband's sexual needs. But in time, he'd come to her less and less until finally she had requested that they no longer share the same bed. He had protested at first, but eventually he'd moved into a different room. And not once had they ever discussed that decision or the reason that had prompted it.

"Reba!" Dodd called her name loud enough to gain her full attention.

"Oh, Dodd, I'm sorry. My mind really is wandering."

"What's the problem? Is there something I can do to help?"

She squeezed his hand, then eased her hand away and slipped it back into her lap. "Caleb brought Jasmine and Ms. Sorrell to Sunday dinner yesterday." Caleb marrying Jasmine Talbot was a problem, but it wasn't what she'd been thinking about. How could she explain to Dodd that she needed a firm commitment from him before she decided whether or not to end her marriage of more than fifty years? "Caleb has asked Jasmine to marry him and she's accepted. They want a December wedding. And Jim has forbidden me to do anything to interfere. He's afraid that unless we support Caleb's marriage to that woman, we'll lose him."

"I understand how you feel about Jazzy Talbot," Dodd said. "And I hate to agree with Jim, but—"

"She's so unsuitable. She's poorly educated, has no social skills whatsoever and God only knows how many men she's slept with since she was sixteen and tried to trap Jamie into marrying her by getting pregnant."

"Women like Jazzy have a strange kind of power over men. They can make us act like fools, do the unthinkable, betray our—" Dodd stopped mid-sentence, his face solemn, his eyes misted with tears.

"Dodd?" Reba stared at him, not liking what she was thinking. He spoke as if he knew from personal experience what a bad woman could do to a man. No, absolutely not! She refused to believe that Dodd—her sweet, gentle Dodd—would have ever been involved with a woman like that.

"I'm sorry. I'm so sorry." He swallowed several times and refused to make eye contact with her. "I didn't mean to . . . Now isn't the time."

Reba's pulse quickened. Guilt was written all over Dodd's face. She couldn't believe it, but the truth was there in his expression. "Please tell me that you didn't . . . I thought you loved Beth Ellen more than anything. I thought you two were very happy."

With his head hung in shame, Dodd responded. "I did love her. More than life itself. And we had a good marriage, a happy marriage, until the day she died."

"Then I don't understand."

"Please, can't we let this go . . . for now?"

"How can I let it go? If you were unfaithful to your wife, then I have a right to know."

"Yes, you do have a right to know. And I intended to tell you, but just not tonight."

Every nerve in Reba's body tensed. "Tell me. Make me understand."

"It was years ago. I was young and stupid. So stupid."

"You had a mistress?" Was Dodd really no different from Jim? Were all men lying, cheating whoremongers?

"No!" He looked at her then, his gaze begging her for understanding. "It was over thirty years ago. Beth Ellen had found out she could never have a child and she lost interest in . . ." He lowered his voice to a whisper. ". . . sex. It had been over six months since we'd . . . I was a young, healthy man. I wanted my wife, but she wouldn't let me touch her."

"So you found another woman who would let you touch her." Despite her best efforts, Reba couldn't keep the disappointment and disapproval out of her voice.

"I'm ashamed of what I did. I—I went to Knoxville." Dodd hurriedly scanned the tables and booths nearest them, then, keeping his voice low, continued his explanation. "I went through an escort service."

"Are you talking about—?" Reba couldn't bring herself to say the word aloud.

"I went to Knoxville almost weekly and used the services of prostitutes for nearly a year. At first there were different women, but then . . ." He hung his head again.

"Then what?"

Slowly lifting his head, he looked directly at Reba. His eyes were filled with heavy tears. "I became infatuated with one girl in particular."

"Define infatuated."

"At the time, I thought I was in love with her."

Reba felt as if someone had hit her in the stomach and knocked the air out of her.

"Did—did Beth Ellen ever know?" *Or was she luckier than I've been?* Reba thought. *Maybe Dodd's wife never knew about the prostitutes or about that one prostitute in particular. Sometimes Reba wished she'd never known about Jim's other women. What was that old saying? Ignorance is bliss.*

"Yes, Beth Ellen knew. I told her. I confessed everything and begged her to forgive me."

"And she did."

Dodd nodded. "I never betrayed her again. I swear. And I'd never betray you, Reba. I'm very much in love with you. You must know—"

Reba held up her hand to stop him. "Please, don't say any more. Not tonight. I—I need time to think. I'm going to leave now. Please don't call me. When I'm ready to see you again, ready to talk, I'll call you."

When she slid out of the booth, Dodd stood and they faced each other for several moments. She knew he wanted to put his arms around her, to touch her, but she stood stiffly, her body language warning him to keep his distance.

"While you're thinking, consider this—I love you," he told her. "I want more than an affair with you."

"More than an affair?"

"Yes, I want you to divorce Jim and marry me."

A light-headed giddiness exploded inside Reba, like candy gushing from a busted pinata. "You want to marry me?"

"I realize I'm not as wealthy as Jim, that I can't offer you quite as much materially, but—"

She covered his lips with her index finger. He hushed immediately.

"I'll call you soon."

When she turned and walked away, he didn't come after her, but she felt his gaze on her until she was out of his sight. Once in the parking lot, she paused long enough to catch her breath, then dug her keys from her leather purse and hurried to her Mercedes.

This certainly wasn't the way she'd thought her evening would end. Not in a million years would she have guessed that Dodd would confess a thirty-year-old indiscretion or that he would ask her to marry him. What was she going to do? Could she get past his infidelity to Beth Ellen? Did she trust him enough to believe what he'd said? And if she did believe him, did she love him enough to divorce Jim? Could she actually give up the power and prestige of being Mrs. James Upton?

* * *

Jazzy rode him hard. Sweat glistened on her body. She was on fire. Hot and wild.

Caleb suckled one of her breasts while he tormented the nipple of her other breast between his thumb and forefinger. The tension between her thighs built higher and tighter as he caressed her naked buttocks. Her climax blasted through her like dynamite, shattering her into a million pieces of pure pleasure. While she was still convulsing, Caleb flipped her onto her back and hammered into her. When he came, he groaned and writhed, then buried his face in her shoulder.

While the remnants of her orgasm still shuddered through her, Jazzy eased out from under him and lifted the sheet and quilt to cover them. Caleb nuzzled her ear.

"Don't go to sleep. Not yet," he mouthed against her earlobe.

She groaned. "It's after midnight, honey, and—"

He kissed her, then flung back the covers and got out of bed.

"I'd have done this sooner, but Reve was here for supper and then she went with us to work and later I got sidetracked by other things." He grinned at Jazzy, then winked.

With the light from the bathroom casting a long, broad path of illumination into the bedroom, Jazzy was able to enjoy the sight of Caleb in all his naked glory. He went into the bathroom, left the door open and turned on the sink faucets.

"What are you doing?" She sat up in bed and crisscrossed her legs at the ankles.

He removed the condom, tossed it into the wastepaper basket and then washed himself. After wrapping a towel around his waist, he emerged from the bathroom, but didn't come back to bed. Instead he headed out of the room.

"Where are you going?" she asked.

He paused, whipped off the towel and tossed it to her. "Wait and see."

Laughing, she grabbed the towel in midair.

He went into the living room, but returned in less than a minute, his leather jacket in his hand. She watched impatiently while he fumbled in his coat pocket. When he pulled out a tiny white box, she sucked in her breath. Oh, my God! Was that what she thought it was?

He came toward her, grinning like a cat who'd just swallowed a canary. She had to stop herself from jumping up and throwing her arms around him. Instead, she narrowed her gaze and gave him a dramatic cross look.

He sat on the edge of the bed, opened the box and removed a tiny black jeweler's case. "I went to Knoxville this afternoon and bought something for you." He held out the case.

Jazzy's hands trembled. Honest-to-God trembled. She couldn't believe how nervous she was. Or how excited. She took the case, flipped open the lid and gasped. Merciful goodness, what a rock!

"Caleb!"

"Like it?"

"Like it?" Clutching the open case in her hand, she flung her arms around his neck and hugged him. The force of her attack sent them both reeling. Caleb tumbled backward, off the bed and onto the floor. Falling with him, Jazzy landed on top of him. As they lay there laughing, their bodies entwined, Jazzy spread kisses all over his face.

"It's got to be the biggest, shiniest, most beautiful diamond ring in the world," Jazzy told him.

"Three carats, square cut," he said.

She slid off to his side, held up the box and snatched the ring from its bed. Holding it up to look at it again, she shook her head. "How on earth did you afford such an expensive—" She froze, then glared at him, her smile vanishing quickly when she realized that the only way he could have gotten the money to buy such an extravagant ring was to have asked his grandfather for it. "You didn't have to buy me something so expensive. I would have been happy with something you could have bought without going to Big Jim for the money."

Caleb sat up, then pulled her up beside him and took the ring from her. Before she realized his intent, he grabbed her left hand. She considered pulling away from him, but when she saw the determination in his eyes, she let him slip the ring onto her finger.

"Let's get something straight right now," he said. "I know you love me just for me. I've got no doubts about that. But I am Jim Upton's only heir, and someday I'll be a fucking millionaire and therefore, as my wife, you will be, too. Why shouldn't I borrow the money from Big Jim to buy the woman I love the kind of ring she deserves, the kind of ring that will make her happy?"

She stared at him and saw the truth staring back at her. She did love Caleb with all her heart. More than she'd loved Jamie? Most definitely. And in a way she'd never thought possible.

With tears clouding her vision, she lifted her left hand and held it up toward the light coming from the bathroom. When her tears fell onto her cheeks, Caleb brushed them away with his fingertips. She gazed at the ring.

"It's just a little bit gaudy." She laughed. "And it's so perfect for me."

"Then I did big?" he asked.

Jazzy lifted his arm and slid it around her shoulders, then cuddled against him. "Oh, yes, Mr. McCord, you did big."

"I made you happy?"

She gazed lovingly into his eyes. "Don't you know that you always make me happy? That just being with you makes me happy, that our making love makes me happy, that showering together and eating together and—"

He kissed her right in the middle of her grand declaration. And that made her happy, too. Life was good. Almost too good to be true.

Max Fennel eased out of bed, doing his best not to wake his wife. He'd gone to bed at eleven, but hadn't been able to

fall asleep. Ever since having lunch at Jasmine's today with
Wade Truman, he'd been wondering about the comment the
district attorney had made about Becky Olmstead. He didn't
know if Wade had even realized he'd let something confidential slip. At least, Max assumed it was confidential since not
one word of it had been in any of the news reports. The
young prostitute's murder was the main topic of conversation not only at the restaurant, but in Cherokee County, and
it was front-page news in the *Herald*. Even the local TV station had announced that a special documentary was being
prepared on Becky. Speculation was running high about another serial killer being on the loose and no one being safe,
especially not pretty young women.

Max had known Wade all his life. He'd been friends of a
sort with Wade's father, a state senator, and had once met
Wade's grandfather, who'd been a federal judge. The Truman
family, though not wealthy by MacKinnon or Upton standards, was well off and socially prominent. With his all-
American good looks—sandy brown hair and sky blue
eyes—his family's backing and using the DA's office as a
stepping stone, it was only a matter of time before young
Truman ran for governor. On more than one occasion, Farlan
had hinted at what the future held for Wade.

Being honest with himself as he slipped into his house
shoes and donned his blue silk robe, Max admitted that a
part of him was jealous of Wade Truman. After all, it hadn't
been that many years ago when he'd been the political
golden boy, with a bright future. Before he'd let his penchant
for sweet young things destroy all his hopes and dreams and
plans. One little bitch who'd gone crying to her daddy had
ended all of Max's political aspirations. Oh, Farlan had taken
care of things. He'd pulled strings and kept Max out of
prison and had paid off the fifteen-year-old's daddy, who'd
come after Max with a shotgun. So maybe his envy of
Wade's bright future colored his opinion of the man, even
elicited suspicion.

Max made his way downstairs, not turning on a light until he was in his study. As he poured whiskey into a glass, his hand shook. Damn it, he had to get control of himself. He shouldn't let what was probably an innocent comment rattle him this way. Wade Truman didn't know a damn thing about what had happened all those years ago. There was no way he could know. He'd been just a kid at the time.

Max downed the liquor—straight. He coughed and wheezed several times before tossing back another slug. He shuddered as the whiskey slid down his throat and hit his belly.

He owed everything he had to Farlan. His law degree, this fine house he lived in, the respect he had in the community. His cousin had been good to him, better than he deserved. He never wanted anyone, least of all Farlan, to know what he'd done.

Max poured another drink, sat in his weathered leather chair by the windows and drank the second glass slowly. He could hear Wade's voice in his head.

"It seems that Becky Olmstead was a looker," Wade had said earlier that day over at Jasmine's. "Big tits, bright red hair and a face like an angel. Not many men could resist that kind of temptation, especially not when it was on sale so cheap. I guess it's no secret that I've got a thing for redheads. Hell, even my ex was a redhead." That was about the time Brian and Farlan had entered the restaurant. Wade had winked at Max and added, "But I know I'm not the only man in these parts who's partial to redheads."

Max shivered. It had been an off-hand remark that meant nothing. And that was all it had been. He was worrying himself silly for nothing, losing a good night's sleep because Wade had implied— Implied what exactly? That he wasn't the only man who had a thing for redheads.

Dammit, Max Fennel, don't do this to yourself. There was no way in hell that Wade Truman could possibly know anything about Dinah.

CHAPTER 17

Jazzy's phone call woke Reve from a sound sleep. She'd been in Cherokee Pointe for five days and had spent part of each day with her sister. Odd as it seemed, that was how she had begun to think of Jasmine Talbot. The rest of the time, she'd kept busy exploring the town, its quaint shops and tourist attractions. On Tuesday she'd had lunch with Reba Upton. The minute Jazzy's name came up in their conversation, Reve had made it clear that her loyalties lay with her sister. Yesterday, she'd dined with Cherokee County's other grand dame—Veda MacKinnon. The woman's invitation came as a surprise, but she'd been so insistent on their becoming acquainted that Reve had gone as much out of curiosity as anything else. By the time lunch ended, Reve's curiosity had been satisfied. Miss Veda wanted exactly what Miss Reba wanted. To play matchmaker. Where Miss Reba had high hopes her grandson would find one redheaded twin as alluring as the other, Miss Veda was looking for a suitable wife for her son Brian.

Now Reve had a new rule—no more lunches with any woman who had an unmarried son or grandson between twenty and sixty.

Last night, after dinner together, Reve had let Jazzy and Caleb persuade her to go with them to Jazzy's Joint. She'd felt as out of place in the honky-tonk as the proverbial bull in a china shop, but she'd stayed until closing, learning about that part of Jazzy's world firsthand. What would her Chattanooga friends have thought of her if they'd seen her in the smoke-filled bar, rubbing elbows with hard-working, hard-drinking, hard-living men and women?

"Reve, are you up yet?" Jazzy asked, excitement in her voice.

Reve yawned. "Not yet. I'm still in bed." She eyed the digital clock on the nightstand. "What are you doing up this early? It's only nine-fifteen."

"Galvin just called."

"Galvin?"

"You remember—Dr. Galvin MacNair."

Reve shot straight up. "Are the DNA test results back?"

"Yep. Galvin got them first thing this morning. He said we can come right on over."

"Did he—"

"No, he didn't tell me anything. So, how long will it take you to get dressed and meet me at his office?"

"I'll need a quick shower." Reve's mind spun with a variety of thoughts, but one remained front and center. Today was D-day. "Give me fifteen minutes." Thank goodness her cabin was inside the city limits, a less than five-minute drive into the heart of town.

"Caleb's coming with me," Jazzy said. "That's okay with you, isn't it?"

"Of course it's okay with me."

"We'll know for sure in just a little while."

"Yes, we will."

"Reve?"

"What?"

"We already know, don't we? We are sisters."

"Yes, we're sisters."

"I called Aunt Sally before I called you. I told her the test results are back and I want the three of us to meet at my apartment later today."

"Did she agree to come into town and meet with us?"

"Yes, she did. And she promised that she'll tell us the whole truth."

"I hope we're ready for the whole truth," Reve said.

"If we aren't ready, we'd better get ready."

"Right. Okay, then, I'll see you in fifteen minutes."

Reve hung up the phone, jumped out of bed and stripped out of her pajamas on the way to the bathroom. As soon as she had donned a disposable plastic cap, she took a quick shower. Then she dressed hurriedly in a pair of black designer jeans and a white cable-knit sweater. After running a brush through her hair and applying lipstick and blush, she grabbed her coat, purse and car keys, then headed out the door.

The telephone rang again.

She started to ignore it, but couldn't bring herself to leave before finding out who was calling. She tossed her coat, purse and keys on the living room sofa in her dash toward the wall phone situated between the living room and kitchen area of the cabin.

She picked up the receiver. "Hello."

"Ms. Sorrell?"

"Yes."

"Griffin Powell here. I have an initial report for you. I can either fax you a copy or overnight it by FedEx, but if you'd like, I can give you the highlights over the phone right now."

Reve's stomach growled. She needed coffee and a bite of something to eat before facing so many hard, cold facts. Why had the DNA results and a preliminary report from Mr. Powell come in all at once? *Because that's the way life is,* she reminded herself.

"Give me the highlights," Reve said.

"An infant, thought to be only a few weeks old, was found in a Dumpster in Sevierville by the sanitation workers assigned to empty the Dumpster. Both men are now dead, but one man's wife remembered him telling her all about it." Griffin Powell paused as if waiting for permission to continue.

"Yes, please, go on."

"All right. The baby girl was naked, except for a diaper. She was wet, dirty and covered in ants. She'd been dumped right on top of a broken jar with some jelly still inside it, and the sugar had attracted the ants. Other than the ant bites, the child had no marks on her, except a cut on her leg where she'd hit the broken glass when tossed into the trash."

Sour bile rose from Reve's stomach. For a minute there, she thought she might throw up. She still had a tiny scar high up on her thigh and the only thing her adopted mother had ever told her was that the scar was the result of an accident when she'd been a baby. "How long had she—had I been in the Dumpster?"

"I spoke to the police department and was given access to the files on the baby. The doctor who examined her—you—believed you'd been left there between ten and twenty-four hours earlier. It was considered a miracle that you didn't die. You spent a week in the hospital. The local papers ran stories about you. They referred to you as the miracle baby and as an infant determined to live. I'll send you copies of those old newspaper clippings."

"Is that how the Sorrells found out about me, the newspaper articles?"

"In a way. The story didn't make the Chattanooga papers, but it seems that one of the Sorrell lawyers was vacationing in the mountains and just happened to pick up a local newspaper. He contacted Spencer Sorrell immediately because he knew they had decided only a few weeks earlier that they wanted to adopt a child. And even thirty years ago, Caucasian infants were at a premium."

"So you spoke to—"

"To every lawyer still alive who worked for your adopted parents at the time."

"Oh, I see. You're thorough, aren't you, Mr. Powell?"

"I do my best." He paused again, but this time didn't wait for her permission before continuing. "Using their money and power, the Sorrells took custody of you the day you were released from the hospital. But you don't need any information about your life as Lesley and Spencer Sorrell's daughter, do you? You want to know who disposed of you, who threw you into that Dumpster."

Reve's heartbeat went crazy, beating ninety-to-nothing. "Have you found out who—"

"There were no arrests made," Griffin Powell told her. "They never found the person, although they had a description of a suspicious character throwing something about the size of a baby into the Dumpster the night before you were found. The truth is, from what I've learned, the police didn't even look for the guy. Nor did they try very hard to locate your birth mother."

"What are you trying to tell me?"

"Spencer Sorrell didn't want your birth mother found. He had the clout, even out of his home territory, to have the police file the case away as unsolved."

Reve took several minutes to absorb the information. Mr. Powell waited patiently. Finally she said, "Is that it? Is that all you've come up with?"

"At this point in the investigation, yes. But I should have more within a few days. I'm trying to access records that aren't open to the public. My agents and I are greasing a few palms along the way and bypassing the proper channels, but very soon I should have a list of all the twins born anywhere within a hundred-mile radius of Sevierville and Cherokee County around the time we believe you were born, give or take a month each way."

"And once you have that list?"

"We use that list to track down the whereabouts of each set of twins and their biological mothers. If we come up with even one set of twins who are unaccounted for, then—"

"That set of missing twins might turn out to be Jazzy and me."

"And if we have a mother's name on a birth certificate, we can trace the mother's steps thirty—no, thirty-one years ago."

"It sounds too simple," Reve said.

"Something like this is never simple," Griffin told her. "Could be there are no missing twins. And if there are, we might not be able to locate the mother. If she's the one who disposed of the twins, more than likely she left the state and changed her name."

"And if the mother didn't dispose of the twins?" Strange how she could talk about such an evil act as if it had happened to someone else. But it hadn't happened to another person. It had happened to her. She'd been disposed of like unwanted trash. And what about Jazzy? Had she been thrown away, too, only somewhere other than the Dumpster in Sevierville? Maybe only Sally Talbot could answer that question.

"If the mother wasn't responsible for getting rid of her babies, then there's a chance whoever did dump the twins might have killed the mother."

Reve gasped quietly.

"That's just one theory."

"Yes, I understand. Listen, Mr. Powell, the DNA results are back and I'm on my way to meet my sister at the doctor's office."

"I don't think you need those results, do you, Ms. Sorrell?"

"Not to prove Jasmine Talbot is my sister, but Jazzy's Aunt Sally has agreed to meet with us today, once we have the undeniable proof that we're twins. I'd like for you to drive in from Knoxville and be there when we question her. It's possible she'll be able to give you some vital information that will help us discover our mother's identity and find her . . . if she's still alive."

"I'll have to rearrange my schedule, then I'll leave right away. Where do I meet y'all?"

"Jazzy's apartment is directly over Jazzy's Joint, at the end of the block on Loden Street. You can't miss the place. There's a set of outside stairs that take you straight up to the apartment."

"All right then, I'll see you in a couple of hours."

Reve hung up the phone, retraced her steps and, with purse and coat in hand, left the cabin. By noon today, she might possibly know the answers to some of the most important unanswered questions in her life.

Jazzy met Reve at the door leading into Dr. MacNair's reception room, grabbed her hands and squeezed them tightly. "Are you ready for this?"

"Yes. Are you?"

"I don't know why I'm so nervous. After all, it's like we both said—we already know the results even before Galvin tells us."

"But hearing him say it makes it an irrefutable fact."

Laughing, Jazzy let go of Reve's hands. "Would you believe I actually know what that means? I'm not stupid and I'm not illiterate. Oh, I know I don't have your college degrees or your polish and style, but I'm streetwise and I'm a self-made woman. I—"

"You're rambling, honey, that's what you're doing." Caleb came up beside Jazzy and put his arm around her waist. He smiled at Reve and said, "That's what she does when she's nervous."

Reve directed her gaze at Jazzy. "Look, I know I've been a bit of a snob ever since we first met and that I probably gave you the impression I was looking down my nose at you, but—"

"You did look down your nose at me," Jazzy said. "But who could blame you? After all, if you could have chosen a sister, it sure as hell wouldn't have been me, would it?"

"No, not when we first met, but that was before I got to know you. We're just now really becoming acquainted, and spending time with you these past few days has given me a chance to realize what a very special person you are, Jasmine Talbot. You're bright and funny and caring. You light up a room with your effervescent personality. You're a smart businesswoman who started out with nothing and has made a success of her life."

Jazzy starred at Reve, her mouth agape, a dumbfounded expression on her face.

"I believe you've rendered her speechless," Caleb said.

"Heck, this is more than I'd hoped for. I thought maybe you were warming up to me." Jazzy grinned. "But I had no idea you were beginning to like me as much as I like you. I know we're very different, but—"

"But we're twin sisters who have quite a few things in common," Reve finished for Jazzy. "The least of which is a biological mother and father."

Dr. MacNair's receptionist, Lynne Swindle, called out, "Jazzy, are you and Ms. Sorrell ready to talk to Dr. MacNair? He's waiting for y'all in his office."

Reve and Jazzy looked at each other, smiled and nodded.

"We're coming." Jazzy reached out and grabbed Caleb's hand.

When the threesome entered the doctor's small, cluttered office, he rose from behind his desk. "Have a seat." He indicated the two nondescript metal chairs in front of his desk, then glanced at Caleb and shrugged. "I'm afraid you'll have to stand. Sorry."

"No problem," Caleb replied.

Reve and Jazzy sat, side by side, their backs straight and tense. Jazzy perched on the edge of the chair while Reve crossed one ankle behind the other and placed her hands in her lap.

"I don't know how much y'all know about DNA—deoxyribonucleic acid—but it is universally accepted as the definitive means of identification. There are two methods currently in wide use, one being the RFLP technique, which is detailed and accurate, but can take anywhere from three weeks to three months to get results. Since y'all wanted quick results, the lab we sent the DNA samples to used the

PCR method, which is polymerase chain reaction, and is now used more and more by law enforcement. The whole process takes place in a single vial that contains—"

"I realize you find DNA testing fascinating, Dr. MacNair," Reve said, "but could you possibly skip over the chemistry lesson and go straight to our DNA test results?"

Galvin's ruddy face darkened, turning beet red. "Oh, certainly, Ms. Sorrell. Certainly. I apologize for—"

"Good God, Galvin, just cut to the chase will you!" Jazzy jumped to her feet. "Tell us the DNA test proved beyond any doubt that Reve and I are twin sisters."

"Uh, yes." Galvin gulped. "The PCR test results, which are seen as a series of dots—" Jazzy growled. Galvin gasped when he realized he'd been about to go into another unwanted lengthy explanation. "Yes, the test results prove that Jasmine Talbot and Reve Sorrell are identical twins."

"I knew it!" Jazzy grabbed Reve's hands and yanked her to her feet, then hugged her fiercely.

Unaccustomed to physical displays of emotion, Reve didn't respond immediately. She waited almost a whole minute before she wrapped her arms around her sister and hugged her. This was only the first step in unearthing the truth about their births. A part of Reve wished she'd never heard of Jazzy Talbot, that she'd never come to Cherokee Pointe back in the spring searching for her look-alike. But neither her life nor Jazzy's could ever return to the way it had been before. She had set things in motion out of curiosity and a burning need to know the truth. Now their lives were picking up speed and spinning out of control. DNA confirmation of their sisterhood. Sally Talbot prepared to tell them what she knew, everything she knew. And Griffin Powell on the verge of discovering their mother's identity.

All Reve could do was move forward on the tidal wave and hope the truth didn't destroy her or her sister.

CHAPTER 18

Farlan MacKinnon rose from the table, picked up his cup and saucer and carried it with him out of the dining room. Veda stood in the kitchen doorway and watched her husband leave without so much as a by-your-leave. It was as if she were invisible, as if he didn't see her at all. She wanted to scream at him, demand to know why he ignored her. But she knew. Heaven help her, she knew. Something inside Farlan had died thirty years ago, but for many years he'd been able to pretend otherwise, to put up a good front for her sake and Brian's. Not any longer.

She wasn't quite sure when he'd begun to withdraw from her. Ten years ago? Or had it been longer than that? With each passing year, her husband became more and more of a stranger to her. And there was nothing she could do about it. The old threats no longer worked. She had lost her power over him. She couldn't threaten to take Brian away from him. Brian was an adult; he'd been of legal age for over twenty years. She couldn't threaten to deny her husband sex because he was no longer interested. And although she could still threaten to commit suicide, that hollow threat had long since lost its potency. Sometimes she wondered if Farlan wouldn't be happier if she was dead.

Abra came up behind Veda and asked, "Should I clear away the breakfast dishes now, Miss Veda?"

"Yes, certainly. Mr. MacKinnon and I are finished. And both Mr. Brian and Wallace had breakfast in town this morning."

Veda laced her arms over her chest and rubbed her hands up and down her upper arms. "It's rather chilly this morning. I feel winter coming on. I hate winter. I miss being able to work in my garden."

"Yes, ma'am. Winter is worse for us when we get a bit older, isn't it, ma'am?" Abra busied herself quickly and then she, too, ignored Veda.

As she crossed the dining room, intending to go upstairs and dress for the day, Veda heard the front door burst open and a felt a gush of cool morning air. Peering out into the foyer, she caught a glimpse of Wallace as he came barreling into the house. Usually by this time of the morning, he was up on the mountain, at Genny Sloan's nursery, where he'd worked most of his adult life. He'd been employed first for Genny's grandmother, Melva Mae, and since the old witch woman's death, by Genny, who had supposedly inherited not only Melva Mae's greenhouses and mail-order business, but her spooky "gift of sight."

It wasn't that Wallace needed a job to earn a living. Farlan provided well for his brother. Always had, always would. But Wallace loved working in the greenhouses, getting his hands dirty and being useful. And he adored Genny. Almost everyone did. At least those who weren't afraid of her because of her special powers.

When Brian had become infatuated with Genny a couple of years ago, she had tried to discourage him, but he'd been adamant about his feelings. Fortunately, Genny had never reciprocated Brian's interest to any great degree and eventually married someone else.

Farlan paused at the door to his study and turned to greet his brother. "Wallace, is something wrong? Why aren't you at work?"

"I called Genny and told her I'd be late this morning," Wallace said breathlessly. "Hoot's outside in his car waiting on me. He's gotta go up on the mountain to check on some of the cabins and he's giving me a ride."

Veda waited quietly in the dining room, almost out of sight, but able to hear Farlan and Wallace's conversation.

"That's good of Hoot to give you a lift," Farlan said. "Did you forget something this morning? Is that why you've stopped back by?"

"I didn't forget nothing. I come by to tell you the news. Everybody down at the restaurant is talking about it."

"What news is that?"

Veda sincerely hoped there hadn't been another murder. Cherokee Pointe used to be such a safe little town, practically no crime at all. But lately violent crimes seemed to have made up for lost time and were escalating at an alarming rate.

"Miss Jazzy and Miss Reve got the news from Dr. MacNair. They passed that test they took," Wallace said. "They're twins all right, just like everybody thought they were."

"And this is why you came back home?" Veda walked out into the foyer. "This bit of information isn't newsworthy. You could have waited until this evening to report it."

"But everybody's talking about it," Wallace explained. "They're asking how come Sally never told nobody there was another baby." Wallace turned to Veda. "Sisters are supposed to be raised together, aren't they? Me and Farlan are brothers and we were raised together. I don't understand why—"

"For goodness sake, Wallace, who knows what goes on with the likes of Sally Talbot," Veda said. "Maybe she couldn't afford to feed and clothe two babies so she gave one away. That sort is liable to do anything."

Wallace frowned at Veda, then looked back at Farlan. "Do you think that's what happened? If Sally had told me she needed money to take care of two babies, I'd have asked you to give her some money and you would have, wouldn't you?"

Farlan set his cup and saucer on the antique walnut commode in the foyer, then grasped his brother's shoulder and softly replied, "Yes, of course I would have. Haven't I always given you anything you asked for?"

Wallace thought for a moment, mulling over Farlan's comment. A wide smile spread across his fat, wrinkled face. "Yeah, everything but that car I wanted. You told me I couldn't have a car because I didn't know how to drive."

The brothers laughed, each apparently remembering the time when Wallace had begged for a car of his own. He'd been nearly forty at the time and hadn't realized he'd need to know how to drive for a car to be of any use to him. Farlan walked his brother to the door, went out on the porch and called to Hoot Tompkins, the manger of Cherokee Cabin Rentals.

Veda wished she could have joined in their laughter, but horrid, unwanted thoughts suddenly tormented her. The harder she tried to vanquish the stupid, totally unfounded suspicions, the stronger they grew. It was all this silly talk of Jazzy Talbot and Reve Sorrell being twins. Redheaded twins. She vaguely recollected having seen Jazzy at a distance sometime in the past, but she and that young hussy certainly didn't frequent the same social circles. Perhaps, if she'd already gotten a better look at Cherokee Pointe's most notorious bad girl, she wouldn't have been so startled by Reve Sorrell's physical appearance. Of course, she'd managed to cover her surprise that Ms. Sorrell reminded Veda of another young woman, one she had tried so hard to forget ever existed. Not only did Reve have dark red hair, but she was quite lovely, with perfect features. Just like—

No! You mustn't torture yourself this way. It happened a

lifetime ago. There's no need to look back now with regrets and fears and uncertainty.

How was it that Farlan and Dodd and Maxwell all knew Jazzy Talbot and not once had any one of them ever noticed the resemblance? But was there really that strong a resemblance? Had her imagination made her see a resemblance when there was none? Imagination or guilty conscience?

She had nothing to feel guilty about, did she? She was not the one who had sinned; she had been sinned against. Dodd and Farlan were guilty, and Maxwell was, too. She had done only what she'd been forced to do, to protect herself and her son, to protect her entire family.

Suddenly Veda felt exceedingly weak. Realizing she had become unsteady on her feet, she grasped the door frame and rested her head against the smooth wooden surface.

Any resemblance was completely superficial, she thought, trying to convince herself now as she'd been trying to do since Reve Sorrell had come for lunch on Tuesday. Most red-heads look alike in various ways. Besides, there was no way Reve and Jazzy could be that woman's children. That evil woman who had nearly destroyed so many lives.

She'd been forced to accept the fact that Farlan would never forget. How could he? And poor Dodd, who had confessed to Beth Ellen and been forgiven, but who had never forgiven himself. And Maxwell, who'd been drawn into all the ugliness. If he ever told anyone what he knew, what he'd done . . .

Taking several deep breaths, Veda lifted her head.

"Are you sick?" Farlan asked as he approached her. "You look pale."

"I'm not feeling quite myself this morning," she replied.

He grasped her arm. "Perhaps you should sit down. All this talk about redheaded twins has no doubt brought back some unpleasant memories."

"You promised that we'd never speak of her."

"Did I say anything about her? Did I mention her name?"

"I suppose you and Dodd and Maxwell have talked about her from time to time, haven't you? After all, the three of you were her champions. God, what fools you men can be. She was a tramp, Farlan. A prostitute any man could have for the right price."

"Believe what you will." When Farlan glared at her, she saw undisguised hatred in his eyes. "Dodd and Max and I do not discuss her or what happened. And I do not wish to discuss it with you. Not now. Not ever."

"But you think about her, don't you? About her and—" Veda stopped herself just short of saying aloud the one thing she dared not say.

"My thoughts are my own," he told her. "Those, my dear, you don't own. You never have and never will."

With that said, he turned, walked back to his study and slammed the door behind him.

At half past one, Sally Talbot finally arrived. But not before Jazzy had called to remind her. She'd even contacted Ludie and sent her over to Sally's to encourage her aunt to keep her promise. Griffin Powell had arrived shortly before noon, and he and Caleb wound up playing several games of pool downstairs at Jazzy's Joint while they waited.

When Jazzy opened her apartment door, Sally hesitated before entering. And only after she stepped over the threshold did Jazzy and Reve realize that Ludie, who came in behind Sally, had given her old friend a gentle shove.

"Come on in and have a seat, you two," Jazzy said. She glanced at Reve. "See if anybody wants coffee while I call Caleb and let him and Mr. Powell know that she's here now."

Both old ladies declined any refreshment. They sat side by side on the sofa, solemn expressions on their faces and wary looks in their eyes. Reve couldn't help feeling sorry for them.

Better save your sympathy, she told herself. *Sally Talbot*

*may wind up being the villainess in this piece. How will you
feel if you find out she had something to do with your being
thrown in the Dumpster?*

Jazzy waited by the door until Caleb and Griffin Powell
arrived. Once everyone was assembled, Jazzy and Reve sat
facing Sally and Ludie. Mr. Powell sat in a kitchen chair that
Caleb had brought in and placed to the left of the sofa. Caleb
stood behind Jazzy's chair, his hands resting protectively on
her shoulders.

Silence filled the room.

Griffin Powell cleared his throat. "Would you like for me
to start the questioning?"

Sally glowered at him. "I ain't answering no questions for
you. I don't see why you're here. You ain't got nothing to do
with this."

"Mr. Powell is staying," Jazzy said. "You know he's a private investigator who is working for Reve."

"He's working for me and for Jazzy," Reve told Sally.
"She and I are sisters. The DNA results prove conclusively
that we are twins."

Sally breathed heavily and nodded. "I never had no idea
that there was another baby." She looked right at Reve.
"There was no way I could've known."

"We believe you, Aunt Sally," Jazzy said. "Please, tell us
what you do know. And start at the beginning, with my
mother . . . that is, with your sister, Corrine."

"It's just like I always told you—Corrine came home to
have her baby. I knew she weren't married and might not
have even known who her baby's daddy was. But she was my
sister and I loved her. We was all the family each other had
after our folks died."

"I'm not Corrine's baby, am I?" Jazzy asked.

"I know that Ludie's done told y'all Corrine's little baby
girl was born dead. Pitiful little thing. And Corrine was mighty
sick afterward and half out of her mind. I didn't have nothing to give her but some bootleg whiskey, so I kept her full

of it so she'd rest. I—I was all broke up about the baby myself. I felt like it was my fault because I'd delivered the child and—" Sally swallowed down her unshed tears.

"You wasn't to blame," Ludie said. "Them things happen. Weren't nobody's fault."

"I took me a walk in the woods to clear my head and to find me a place where I could cry without waking up Corrine." Sally ran her gaze over Jazzy. "That's when I found you. Out there in the woods. When I heard you squalling, I couldn't believe it. But there you was, this fat, pink, healthy baby girl with all that red fuzz on your head."

"You found me in the woods, up here in the mountains?" Jazzy asked.

"Yep. Somebody had stripped you down to your diaper and stuffed you in the hollow of an old tree stump. They'd sure enough put you there to die. That's what they'd done."

"Oh, God!" Jazzy gasped. Reve reached over and clasped her sister's hand.

"I took one look at you and knew you was a gift from God. He took Corrine's baby, but he gave us you. Whoever your mama was, she didn't want you. She left you out there in the woods to die. But I wanted you. I wanted you from the minute I laid eyes on you." Sally balled her hand into a fist and flopped her fist over her heart. "I knew in here that you were meant to replace Corrine's dead baby.

"So I brought you home with me and I gave you a bath and dressed you in the clothes Corrine had bought for her baby. I wrapped you up in that fancy white blanket she'd bought in Knoxville and I laid you in her arms."

"How did you explain me to your sister?" Jazzy asked.

"I told her that you was her baby girl, that she'd just dreamed her baby died. And with you lying there in her arms, why wouldn't she believe me? That night I slipped back out in the woods and buried Corrine's baby. I buried her deep and put a big stone on top of her grave so the animals couldn't get to her."

"And when Doc Webster came up the mountain to check Corrine and the baby, I was the baby he saw, the baby he examined," Jazzy said. "That's how I have a birth certificate proving Corrine Talbot was my mother."

"Do you hate me, gal? I swear I thought I was doing the right thing for you and for Corrine." Sally looked pleadingly at Jazzy. "I ain't never loved nothing or nobody as much as I love you." Tears glistened in Sally's bright blue eyes.

Jazzy released Reve's hand, stood and walked over to the sofa. She knelt in front of Sally, reached out and hugged her aunt. "I love you, you crazy old woman, you." She lifted her head and the two women gazed at each other through teary eyes. "You could have told me years ago and I would have understood."

Reve turned to Griffin Powell and asked, "Will this information help you at all in the investigation?"

He nodded. "Yes, it'll help. You two do realize that the person who separated the two infants did it for a specific reason. He—or she—not only wanted both babies to die, but he wanted to make sure that if both bodies were ever found, no one would figure out that the two abandoned infants were connected in any way. Twins could be more easily traced back to the birth mother."

"We were dumped and left for dead in two different counties," Reve said. "Jazzy in a tree stump in the woods up in the mountains here in Cherokee County and me in a Dumpster in Sevierville."

Jazzy rose to her feet and went to Reve. "That report Mr. Powell gave us says that an eyewitness claims he saw a man toss something into the Dumpster that might have been a baby. Do you think that man might have been our father?"

"Our father?" Reve had never considered that possibility. "I suppose it could have been. I've assumed it was my mother who threw me away, but it could just as easily have been my father—our father."

"I suggest that we don't jump to any conclusions," Griffin

Powell said. "That eyewitness is no longer living. And even if he was, he couldn't ID the man. He said so at the time. Medium height, build, clothing. He never got a look at the guy's face. Besides, that guy might not have been the one who threw you in the Dumpster."

"So we have nothing to go on, no real evidence of any kind," Jazzy said.

"Once we have a list of all the twins born in northeast Tennessee around the time you two were born, we'll be able to start narrowing down the info," Griffin explained. "Until then, keep one thing in mind—whoever wanted you two dead thirty years ago might still want you dead. If he ever finds out you're both alive now and looking for answers about your past, he could try to kill both of you."

"Holy shit! That thought never crossed my mind." Jazzy snorted. "There's some nut out there somewhere killing red-headed whores, and I'm probably at the top of his list. And now I find out that there's another person out there who, if he finds out he didn't kill Reve and me when we were babies, might try to do the job right this time."

"Why would anybody want to kill two innocent little babies?" Sally asked. "What sort of monster would harm a baby?"

"Someone with something to lose if he—or she—allowed the babies to live," Caleb said.

"Exactly." Griffin Powell stood and walked over to Reve. "Ms. Sorrell, if you decide that you want to pursue this investigation any further, I'll need your permission to use any and all medical information about you, including the DNA test results."

"Yes, of course. Whatever you need, I'll see to it that you get it." She glanced at Jazzy. "My sister and I definitely want to continue this investigation, don't we?"

"Damn right about that. We want to know who tried to kill us and why."

"Even if it turns out to be either your mother or your father? Or possibly both of them?" Griffin asked.

"Yes," Reve and Jazzy replied simultaneously.

"Very well. I'll head back to Knoxville and we'll proceed with the investigation."

Reve walked him to the door. They shook hands.

"I'll be in touch again as soon as I have any information," he told her.

When Reve turned around, she saw Caleb and Sally and Ludie hovering over Jazzy, each taking a turn hugging her and reassuring her. Suddenly Reve felt unwanted and unneeded. Jazzy had people who loved her, people who would die to protect her. And who did Reve have? Nobody. Not one single solitary soul. She had never felt so totally alone in her life.

"I forgot something I need to tell Mr. Powell," Reve lied. "If I go now, I can probably catch up with him." She grabbed her coat and purse, then opened the door.

"Do you want me to go with you?" Jazzy called to her.

"No. I'll—I'll phone you later."

Reve just barely made it outside, onto the open stairway, before tears welled up in her eyes. *Damn it, don't do this to yourself. What good will it do to cry? You're Reve Sorrell. You're rich and powerful and people envy you. What the hell do you have to cry about anyway?*

Clutching the handrail, Reve made her way down the stairs. She hung her shoulder bag around her neck as she struggled to put on her coat. Out of nowhere a big hand reached out to help her into her coat. She yelped in fright and jumped away from the man standing beside her. After blinking several times, her vision cleared just enough for her to see who he was. Damn, she should have known. At a moment like this when the last thing she needed was somebody to kick her while she was down, who else would cross her path?

"Sheriff Butler." She sucked back her tears.

"Are you all right?" he asked and sounded sincere.

"I'm fine, thank you. And how are you?"

He reached out and lifted the purse straps from around

her neck, then handed her the leather bag. "You've been crying."

"How astute of you."

"Usually when a person cries, there's a reason."

"Don't you have anything better to do than interrogate me? Don't you have a murder to solve?" She hooked the straps of her leather bag over her shoulder.

He grabbed her arm. Her eyes widened in alarm. "My truck is parked across the street. Why don't you ride over to the Burger Box with me and I'll buy you a late lunch. Greasy burgers and fries. And a chocolate milkshake."

"Are you trying to be nice to me?"

"Yeah, I guess I am." He seemed as surprised at the thought as she was.

"Under normal circumstances, I wouldn't accept your invitation, but . . ." But she was feeling lonely and vulnerable and was thankful for a few crumbs of kindness, even from Jacob Butler. Why him, dear God, why him? she asked and had the oddest sensation that Fate was laughing at her.

Reve glanced at Jacob's hand securely surrounding her arm. His fingers were thick and long and dark, his hand large and slightly rough. "If you'll make that a burger and onion rings, I'll accept your invitation."

"Onion rings, huh?" Jacob grinned.

The bottom dropped out of her stomach. Mercy, what a smile!

She nodded. "I love onion rings."

"Onion rings it is." He tugged on her arm. "Ordinarily my dates don't eat onions of any kind since they're looking forward to ending the date with a kiss, but since we won't be doing any kissing, you can eat all the onion rings you want."

Date? Kiss? Was he crazy? This wasn't a date. This was lunch. Nothing more.

"You're right," she told him. "We certainly won't be doing any kissing."

CHAPTER 19

The Burger Box was a remnant from the fifties, with curb service and waitresses on roller skates. The menu listed a lineup of artery-clogging, deep-fried delights and the best shakes and banana splits on earth.

Jacob parked his truck in one of the designated slots, then rolled down his window and ordered via a voice box.

"A couple of double cheeseburgers, one order of fries, one order of onion rings, a cup of coffee—" He looked at Reve and asked, "Want a chocolate shake?"

She shook her head. "I'll take coffee, too."

"Make that two coffees."

Jacob rolled up the window and turned to Reve. For the life of him, he couldn't figure out how he'd wound up in this situation. He'd been minding his own business, walking up Loden Street after dropping off some things at the cleaners. On his way back to his truck, he'd seen Ms. Sorrell scurrying downstairs from Jazzy's apartment. He'd paused to watch her, wondering why she was in such a hurry. And then he'd seen her face—she was crying.

He'd reacted instinctively and gone over to her to help her on with her coat. That had been his first mistake. His second had been actually giving a damn. To say that he and Reve disliked each other was an understatement. What had he been thinking when he'd asked her to join him for a late lunch? That was just it. He hadn't been thinking. He'd been feeling, and when a man let his feelings get in the way of common sense, it always meant trouble. He'd felt sorry for Reve. Had hated to see her hurting. Something inexplicable inside him jumped at the chance to be her white knight. And God knew, he was nobody's knight in shining armor.

"So." Jacob looked directly at Reve.

"So," she repeated.

"We're going to have lunch together."

"So we are." Her lips curved into a closed-mouth smile. "Bet you're trying to figure out how this happened, aren't you?"

"Yeah, I am," he admitted, then realized she was probably wondering the same thing. "You, too, huh?"

"I guess we were both just in the wrong place at the wrong time."

"Want to tell me why you were crying?"

"Not really."

"Everything okay between you and Jazzy?"

She eyed him quizzically, as if asking why he'd care.

"I ask because Jazzy's an old friend," he explained. "She's had a pretty rough year, and I'd hate to see her get hurt again." He sure didn't want this woman thinking he gave a damn about her. Even if he did.

"Jazzy's a very lucky lady to have so many people care about her. Caleb. Her Aunt Sally and Ludie. Genny and Dallas. And you."

He heard the sadness in her voice and noted a hint of tears in her eyes. Hell, she was on the verge of crying again. That wasn't what he'd been expecting. He'd thought that if anything, she'd rant and rave at him about how all the men in town were Jazzy's "friends."

So, what did he say to Reve now? His usual biting sarcasm wasn't appropriate. Right at the moment, she wasn't in top fighting form, and it was no fun to spar with an already wounded partner.

"Word's all over town that the DNA test results prove Jazzy and you are sisters," Jacob said. "You weren't crying about that, were you?"

Suddenly laughing, she blinked several times and released a long, slow breath. "Believe it or not, no. Jazzy and I already felt certain we were sisters. The tests results simply confirmed it."

"You might as well come clean about why you were crying. If you don't, I'll ask Jazzy and—"

"No, please, don't do that. She doesn't know. . . . Just don't say anything to her, okay?"

Before he could respond, their waitress skated over to the truck, a bright red tray in her hand. When Jacob rolled down the window, she handed him a large paper sack, which he gave to Reve, and two Styrofoam cups with lids, which he placed in the truck's cup holders. He removed his wallet from inside his suede jacket and paid the waitress, giving her a generous tip.

"Gee, thanks, Sheriff," the girl said, then skated off.

When he turned to Reve, she offered him a handful of napkins. "She must have thought we're very messy eaters."

"Honey, wait until you bite into your cheeseburger. You'll need plenty of napkins. These things are juicy and loaded with everything."

When she held out his pack of fries and then his cheeseburger, she smiled warmly. Damn, he wished she wouldn't do that. She looked a little too good to him when she smiled.

After she removed her burger and onion rings from the sack, she seemed to be at a loss as to what to do with them. She held the wrapped cheeseburger in one hand and the paper carton of rings in the other. He reached over and popped open the glove compartment creating a makeshift table for her, and his arm brushed her knees in the process. The minute he accidently touched her, she tensed, and he expected her to light into him. But instead, when he glanced at her, her smile was still in place and her cheeks were slightly flushed.

Well, I'll be damned, he thought. She had reacted to him like a woman and not a stuck-up bitch. *Don't go there, Butler. Do not think of Reve Sorrell the way you think of other women. She's off limits. She is persona non grata. Big time persona non grata.*

"Thank you," she said.

Her voice sounded different. All soft and feminine and sweet.

"Eat up," was all he could think of to say.

She nodded, then unwrapped her burger and took a huge bite. He did the same, but couldn't seem to take his eyes off her. She looked a hell of a lot like Jazzy up close, but she wore very little makeup and her eyes were dark brown. Despite their strong physical resemblance, he'd never mistake her for Jazzy. Not in a million years. And not because Jazzy was prettier. No, that wasn't it. It was because of the way he reacted to Reve. He and Jazzy had been friends forever; they'd even tried dating. But there was zero physical chemistry between them. Unfortunately, the exact opposite was true of Reve and him. Every time he was around her, she evoked a strong reaction from him. Usually he wanted to wring her neck.

But right now, that wasn't what he wanted to do to her.

"Is something wrong?" she asked.

"Huh?"

"You aren't eating."

Answer her, you idiot. "I was just thinking about how much you and Jazzy look alike and yet how different you two are."

Reve's smile disappeared. She took another bite out of her cheeseburger, then reached for her coffee.

Now would be a good time to stop talking and eat, Jacob told himself. *Finish lunch and then drive her to her cabin or*

*to Jazzy's apartment and say good-bye. You're way out of
your league with this one.*

Now why would he think that? It wasn't as if he was interested in dating Reve Sorrell. Hell, he didn't even like her.
But right this minute, he sure did want to kiss her.

They ate in relative silence, their occasional smacks and
slurps highly exaggerated in the quiet truck cab. When they
finished their meal, Jacob stuffed their garbage into the
paper sack and dumped the sack into the garbage container
he kept in his truck. When he turned to ask Reve if she was
ready to head back across town, he noticed a dab of a mus-
tard/ketchup mixture smeared on the side of her mouth.
Without thinking, he reached over and wiped off the stain
with the side of his thumb. Reve opened her mouth in a
silent gasp. His hand lingered. She stared at him, her eyes
wide and round.

He balled his hand into a clenched fist. "If you're ready,
we'd better go. I need to get back to the office."

He started the motor and backed up without waiting for
her reply. When they returned to the street and were heading
across town, he spoke to her, but kept his gaze focused
straight ahead.

"Do you want me to drop you at your cabin or back at
Jazzy's apartment?"

"If it won't be too much trouble, drop me by my cabin."

"Sure. No trouble at all."

Neither of them said a word for the seven and a half minutes it took for him to drive her to her rental cabin. When he
pulled up out front, he opened his door and jumped out without making a comment. The sooner he got rid of her, the better. For both of them. He had an uneasy feeling in the pit of
his belly that whatever was going on with his libido was happening to hers, too.

He yanked open the passenger door and held out his hand
to assist her. She put her hand in his. Heat spread through his
fingers and quickly engulfed his entire body. He practically

jerked her out of the truck so that she stumbled when her feet hit the ground. She stood there, only a couple of inches separating their bodies, and looked up at him. She was a tall woman, taller than Jazzy, but still a good seven inches shorter than he was.

"Thanks for lunch," she said. "I probably gained five pounds from the cheeseburger alone."

He could think of a good way for her to work off the calories. *Damn it, Butler, you've got to stop this.* "I like to see a woman with a healthy appetite."

She smiled again, and every instinct he had told him to run. Run like hell.

"I've got to go," he said.

"Bye." She didn't move. Neither did he.

"Yeah, bye." *Get your ass in gear, Butler.*

He backed away from her. Slowly. She stood and watched him get in his truck and close the door. When he drove away, he glanced in his rearview mirror. She was still standing there. She lifted her hand and waved. He gunned it and flew off down the street.

I can't allow the truth to be revealed. We've kept this ugly little secret for thirty years, and I intend to take it to my grave. If anyone were ever to know what happened—what really happened—my life would be ruined, my legacy worthless. Everything that has ever meant anything to me would be lost. And all because of that woman! I hated her then and I hate her now. She was evil, and her corruption destroyed everything and everyone around her.

I didn't want to get rid of those babies, but I had no choice. I couldn't allow them to live. But instead of depending on Slim to get rid of them, I should have done it myself. He swore to me that they were dead, that there was no way either of them could survive.

But he'd been wrong!

All these years, I'd thought I was safe. I believed those twin girls were dead. And all the while they were alive, one of them growing up right here in Cherokee County.

But can you be certain that Jazzy Talbot and Reve Sorrell are her babies? Just because they're beautiful, as she was beautiful, and just because they have her red hair, doesn't mean she was their mother.

Of course it does. They are thirty years old, with birthdays the same month as her twin girls. And they were both abandoned at birth, each left separately, but both left to die.

Thank God for small-town gossip. Someone had overheard Jazzy and her fiancé talking at Jasmine's, and somebody else had overheard that crazy Sally and her Indian friend talking while they were walking along the sidewalk. One person told another and then they told someone else and so on and so on. If not for busybodies spreading the news, it might have been days, even weeks, before I found out the truth. And time is of the essence. The sooner I act, the better for me and everyone else involved.

I have to kill both twins before that investigator, Griffin Powell, unearths the truth about who they are and about who their mother and father were. I will not allow her children to destroy our lives.

And I know just how I'll do it, how I'll kill them without the least bit of suspicion falling on me. It was a brilliant plan. First Jazzy. Tonight. And then Reve.

The telephone rang four times before Jazzy grabbed the receiver. Caleb had already gone over to Jazzy's Joint for the evening and she was on her way out of her office at Jasmine's, intending to join him.

She glanced at the caller ID. A cell phone number. "Hello. Jazzy Talbot here."

"Jazzy?"

"Yeah." The voice didn't sound familiar.

"I understand you're looking for your real mother."

"Who is this?"

"Someone with information."

"What kind of information?" Suspicious by nature, Jazzy immediately distrusted the caller.

"I know who your real parents are, and I'm willing to share that information with you."

"How much is this going to cost me?"

"I don't want your money."

"Then what do you want?"

"I want you to know the truth."

"Okay, so come on over here to Jasmine's right now and tell me everything you know."

Silence.

"Did you hear me?" Jazzy asked.

"I'd rather we meet somewhere. Neutral ground, so to speak. Not my place or yours."

She'd take Caleb with her, of course, and Reve, too. If this person was on the up and up, her sister should hear the truth directly from the horse's mouth, so to speak. "Okay. Name the time and the place."

"Now. As soon as you can meet me."

"Where?"

"Are you familiar with the old covered bridge about half a mile from the country club?"

"Why meet in such an out-of-the-way place?"

"Because I do not want to become involved. People know me here in town. I'll give you the information only if you come alone and if you swear you'll never tell anyone who told you about your parents."

Jazzy's gut instincts warned her against meeting this caller. After all, there was a good chance a killer with a thing for redheads was out there somewhere just waiting for a chance to grab her. On the other hand, she seriously doubted the caller was a serial killer. A phony? Someone hoping to exhort money from her? Possibly. A serial killer? Highly unlikely.

You can take your gun. And you can insist that Reve come with you. After all, if this caller was telling the truth and could ID her parents, then Reve most definitely had a right to hear the truth firsthand, just as she did.

"I'll meet you in fifteen minutes, but I won't come alone. I'll bring my sister with me."

Was that a chuckle? Jazzy wondered.

"Yes, I'll agree to that. By all means, bring Reve Sorrell with you."

The dial tone buzzed loudly.

Jazzy immediately called Reve's cabin and let the phone ring a dozen times. No answer. She tried Reve's cell number. No response. Jazzy hurried out of her office, down the hallway and out the back door. The back entrances to her two businesses were only fifteen feet apart, so it took her about a minute to go from one to the other. She entered Jazzy's Joint, bypassed her office and the restrooms and went straight into the main arena. After scanning the room and not seeing Caleb, she walked over to the bar.

"Where's Caleb?" she asked Lacy, the bartender.

"He had to drive Gus Logan home. That poor old fool was already drunk when he showed up, and he got downright nasty when I refused to serve him."

"Damn!"

"Something wrong?" Lacy asked.

"Yeah, I'm supposed to meet somebody in less than fifteen minutes, and I wanted Caleb to go with me."

"I can give him a message when he gets back and he can meet you wherever it is you're going. If you go by yourself, he'll worry, what with all the talk about some nutcase killing redheads."

"I'll bet Jacob and Dallas are wondering how that bit of confidential info got out. Nobody was supposed to know that the victims were redheads."

"You can't keep something like that under wraps for long. Stuff like that gets leaked."

"Yeah, it happens. Unfortunately. Look, I'm going to meet somebody who says they know who my real parents are. As soon as Caleb gets back, tell him to come out to the old covered bridge about half a mile from the country club."

"I don't think you should go alone. Call Reve so she can go with you."

"I tried to call her. She's not answering her phone."

"Then wait for Caleb."

Jazzy patted the inside of her coat pocket. "I'm taking my thirty-two with me, just in case. So as soon as Caleb comes back, tell him where I am. And assure him I feel certain that the person who called me is not a serial killer."

CHAPTER 20

Jazzy pulled her Jeep off to the side of the road directly in front of the old covered bridge. She'd made it there in twelve minutes flat, so she guessed she was early. She didn't see another vehicle anywhere nearby, so that had to mean the caller wasn't there yet. Of course it would be possible to park a car on the other side of the bridge, just around the curve, and be completely out of sight from this vantage point. Strumming her fingertips on the steering wheel, she waited. Impatiently.

Come on. Hurry up, will you?

The minutes ticked by slowly, each one seeming ten times longer than sixty seconds. Finally, after five minutes, she removed her phone from her jacket pocket and tried calling Reve again. First the cabin, then the cell phone. Still no response. Where the hell was Reve? Why wasn't she answering her phone?

Maybe I should call Jacob and ask him to run by and check on Reve. No, don't do that. It's a bad idea! Reve wouldn't thank me for siccing Jacob on her. Jazzy chuckled. Those two were headed for a major explosion. Genny had seen the handwriting on the wall, but it didn't take any special sixth sense abilities to figure out that that much tension between two people could be resolved in only two ways. Either they killed each other or they fucked each other.

Beginning to feel the chill in the night air, Jazzy restarted the Jeep, upped the heat and flipped on the radio. Where the hell was her mystery caller? She wasn't going to wait around half the night. And what was taking Caleb so long to get here?

She hit the keyed-in number for Jazzy's Joint, the phone at the bar.

Lacy answered on the sixth ring. "Jazzy's Joint." Lacy spoke loudly so she could hear herself over the noise from rowdy customers and shit-kicking music.

"Where's Caleb?" Jazzy asked.

"I don't know. He should have been back by now. Gus just lives over on Oakwood. Have you tried his cell phone?"

"No, but I will. I thought sure he'd be back there by now."

"Has your mystery caller showed up?" Lacy asked.

"No, not yet."

"Well, you be careful, okay?"

"I will. I will."

Jazzy hit the off button and then punched in Caleb's cell number. It rang repeatedly. No response. But just when she decided he wasn't going to answer, he did.

"Yeah, what is it?"

"Caleb?"

His voice softened. "Hi, honey. Look, I'll be there soon. I had a flat tire on my way back from Gus's house. I've just about got the tire changed."

"I'm not at Jazzy's Joint. I'm out by the country club, at the old covered bridge. When you get the tire changed, I want you to—"

"What the hell are you doing way out there?" Two seconds later, he roared into the phone, "Did you go out there by yourself?"

"Yes, I came by myself, but I'm all right. I brought my thirty-two with me. I told Lacy to tell you to meet me here, so hurry up, will you?"

"Dammit, Jazzy, why—"

"I'll explain everything when you get here."

"Listen to me—you turn around and come right back into town."

"I'll be waiting here by the old bridge. Hurry." She hung up on him. He might call back, but she doubted he'd waste his time. He knew her well enough to realize that if he called back, she wouldn't answer. His time would be better spent fixing that tire.

Five minutes passed, then ten. Jazzy turned off the radio, killed the motor and opened the driver's door. As she emerged from her Jeep, she patted her breast pocket to reassure herself that the thirty-two was still in place. She doubted seriously that she'd need a gun, but if she did, it would take only a matter of a few seconds to put her hands on the weapon.

Jazzy closed the door and stood by the hood for several minutes. This was ridiculous. Why call her and ask to met her and then not show up? Had the call been nothing more than a hoax? Someone's idea of a practical joke? She pressed the tab on her lighted digital wristwatch. Nine-twenty. She'd wait ten more minutes and then she was out of there.

Submerged up to her shoulders in the soothing warm water of the hot tub on the screened porch of her cabin, Reve lifted an iced glass of Tennessee Tea and sipped leisurely on the delicious brew. She'd found the four-pack of small bottles in the guest basket, which had been filled with a variety of speciality items. The basket was a gift Jazzy had left at the cabin before her arrival. She'd never tried this drink before—a combination of Jack Daniels and sweet tea—but found she really liked the taste. Of course she'd always had a weakness for anything sweet.

Jacob Butler wasn't sweet. He was tough and surly and—

Now, how had her mind made that colossal jump from Tennessee Tea to Jacob Butler?

It could be because she couldn't seem to get him out of her thoughts.

Stop it, Reve. You're obsessing about that man again.

Ever since he'd dropped her off at her cabin earlier today, she'd done everything possible to get him off her mind. She'd called Jazzy to beg off supper tonight, then she'd placed a call home to speak to her housekeeper and even phoned Paul Welby again, although that call had been totally unnecessary. Paul was like a futuristic robot—efficient, brilliant and unemotional. She had inherited him from her mother. Lesley Sorrell had hired him as her personal assistant when he was fresh out of college. Vanderbilt. By the time Lesley passed away, Paul was earning a six-figure salary. But only after he became Reve's assistant had she learned that he was worth every cent.

Watching TV and reading hadn't captured her attention for very long, nor had preparing her evening meal. Her mind kept wandering off in one particular direction. An unwanted direction. She had replayed the forty-five minutes she'd spent with Jacob over and over again in her mind. From the moment he had startled her by helping her on with her coat until he'd helped her down out of his truck when he dropped her off at the cabin, she had seen another side of a man she thought she hated. Today, he'd been kind to her. Not once had he ridiculed her or tried to provoke her. He had acted as if he actually liked her.

Was that possible? Could she and Jacob ever be friends? After the way their relationship had started—

Wait just a darn minute! You do not have a relationship with Jacob. He's Jazzy's friend, not yours. Okay, so he treated you as if he thought you were human this afternoon, that doesn't mean he likes you or that he wants to be friends.

Reve took several more sips of her Tennessee Tea, then set the glass on the rim of the hot tub and scooted down until only her head protruded above the water. She'd been out here nearly thirty minutes, hoping the liquor and soak would relax her so she could sleep tonight. Sleep without dreaming about anything unpleasant. Like Jacob Butler.

Admit it, you're afraid you'll have another erotic dream about the man. You're accustomed to being in total control of your life, of everything and everyone in your world. And you hate having no control over Sheriff Butler or over the way he makes you feel.

Reve groaned, then forced herself to get out of the hot tub. If she stayed in here much longer, she'd turn into a prune. Either that or go to sleep and drown. The moment she emerged from the tub, the cool night air hit her, sending a shuddering chill through her body. She grabbed the huge towel off the hook on the back wall and dried herself quickly, then lifted her robe from the nearby rocking chair and put it on. When she entered the cabin, heavenly warm air encompassed her. She closed her eyes and sighed. Then it happened. She could almost feel a pair of strong arms surround her. Jacob's strong arms. Her eyes flew open. She was alone in her cabin. Damn her vivid imagination!

Jazzy walked down the road and onto the covered bridge. Maybe the caller had meant for her to come across the bridge and park on the other side. Had she misunderstood the instructions? When she was about a third of the way across the bridge, she thought she heard a sound from behind her. Footsteps?

Okay, run back to the Jeep, jump in and get the hell out of here.

She shouldn't panic. Not yet.

There, she heard the noise again. Definitely footsteps behind her. Putting her hand in her pocket so that she could whip out the thirty-two, if needed, she started to whirl around, but before she did, something hit her on the head. Something hard and heavy. Excruciating pain shot through her head. She dropped to her knees.

What the hell?

"Slut," someone said. "You're a whore just like your mother!"

Despite the debilitating pain pounding in her head and radiating through her body, Jazzy managed to jerk the gun from her pocket. But before she could face her attacker, another hard blow came down on her head. She saw stars—literally saw stars. The thirty-two dropped from her hand as an odd weakness possessed her. And then everything went pitch black.

Farlan hated riding in Brian's Porsche. He felt like a mackerel stuffed into a sardine can whenever he rode in any small sports car. But he'd asked Brian to pick him up at the country club this evening in the hope that they could have a father-son talk. Farlan had come to the club with Dodd earlier with the express purpose of being without his car so that he could use it as an excuse to trap Brian into this meeting. When he'd finally caught up with his son, reaching him on his cell phone, Brian had sounded peculiar, as if he was upset that his father had disturbed him. Farlan wished he understood his son better, wished they had a better relationship. But Brian was his mother's son. Temperamental. High-strung. Self-centered. Emotionally needy.

When they left the country club, Farlan had suggested they take the back way home, a longer route that took them over the old covered bridge and around a winding two-lane road through a densely wooded area the MacKinnon family owned. Farlan wanted the ten extra minutes it would take them to go home by this route, so that he could broach a subject that had been bothering him since going over the latest report from his accountants.

Brian had embezzled money from the family business in the past. Not huge sums, so Farlan had turned a blind eye and personally made up the losses. But recently, Brian had stolen over a quarter of a million dollars and hadn't covered his tracks very well, almost as if he wasn't concerned about being caught. What bothered Farlan was why his son, who drew a generous yearly salary, felt the need to take money from the business, to commit a criminal act. Didn't he know that all he had to do was come to Farlan and ask for the money?

"I hate driving across that damn old bridge," Brian said. "I always have the feeling it's going to collapse out from under me."

"That bridge is as sturdy as the day it was built," Farlan replied. "I personally see to it that the county keeps it up. Your grandfather was the man responsible for having that bridge remodeled back in the sixties. At one time the sides were covered, too, not partially open the way they are now."

Brian didn't respond. His son had never been interested in family history, let alone Cherokee County history.

Farlan tried to think of the best way to approach the subject of Brain embezzling funds from MacKinnon Media, but before he came up with a suitable idea, he noticed a vehicle pulled off to the side of the road.

"Is that somebody with car trouble?" Farlan questioned aloud.

Brian eased his sleek Porsche to a stop in the middle of the road, directly in front of the old covered bridge. "I don't see anybody. Looks like the car is empty."

"Do you recognize the vehicle. It's a Jeep, isn't it?"

"Yes, it's a Jeep. As a matter of fact, it looks just like Jazzy Talbot's red Jeep."

"Maybe we should make sure everything is okay before we go on."

"I don't feel like playing Good Samaritan tonight."

"Humor me," Farlan said. "Go see if there's a problem."

Brian grumbled under his breath when he got out of the Porsche. Farlan watched his son as he walked over to the

Jeep, circled the vehicle and then peered into the closed window on the driver's side.

He called back to Farlan. "It's empty. No sign of anybody. But I'm sure this is Jazzy's car." Standing at the back of the Jeep, he pointed to the car tag. "That's her personalized tag. Jazzy One."

An uneasy feeling settled in the pit of Farlan's stomach. He didn't know Jazzy Talbot, but he'd heard all about her. She'd been front page news only a few months ago when she'd been arrested for murdering her former lover, Jamie Upton. In every newspaper photo printed in the Herald, she'd been holding her hand across her face; and he hadn't bothered watching any of the TV coverage. Of course, he'd seen her at a distance from time to time, either in town or at her restaurant. Even once or twice in Jazzy's Joint. A pretty girl, as he recalled.

"I think we should look around to see if she's sick or hurt." Farlan undid the glove compartment, pulled out a couple of flashlights and opened the car door. He got out and rounded the Porsche's hood.

Brian grunted. "She probably came out here to meet some man and they're in his car fucking their brains out."

"Humor me again," Farlan said. "I can't say exactly why, but I think the woman's in trouble. Let's just look around and make sure. You take the right side of the road, and I'll take the left. We'll cross the bridge and then backtrack. If we don't find anything, we'll call the police and let them find out why she abandoned her Jeep."

"I think we should call the police now and just go on home."

Disregarding his son's comment, Farlan walked up the road. Brian huffed loudly, then followed. Keeping to the edge of the bridge, Farlan ran his flashlight down into the murky water below. A series of large boulders rested directly underneath the bridge. These huge rocks, formations that had been rounded and smoothed by eons of flowing water, were scattered throughout the shallow areas of the creek.

"See anything?" Farlan asked.

"Not a damn thing."

When he was about a third of the way across the bridge, his foot hit something. Glancing down, he saw what looked like a small handgun. *Don't touch it,* he told himself.

"What's the matter?" Brian asked.

"There's a gun on the bridge." Farlan toed it with the tip of his shoe. "Right there."

"Whatever you do, don't touch the damn thing."

"Hell, boy, I've got better sense than to do something that stupid." Farlan moved his flashlight over the bridge railing, scanning back and forth as far as he could see. Suddenly, he noticed something red smeared across the railing several feet down from where he stood. With Brian right behind him, he made his way to the spot, then reached out toward the red stain. Brian caught his hand only seconds before he touched the still damp liquid.

"It's blood," Farlan said.

"Yes, I believe it is."

Farlan shot the flashlight over the bridge, right below where the railing bore the bloody marks. Good God! He blinked several times, wondering if he was actually seeing part of a body on top of one of the boulders. He refocused and looked again. It was no hallucination. She was real. The lower half of her body lay submerged in the water, while the upper half lay sprawled on the boulder.

"Brian, I think I've found her."

Brian rushed to Farlan's side and looked over the rail.

"Damn!"

"Is that Jazzy Talbot?" Farlan asked.

"I'm not sure, but it's definitely a woman's body." He shined his flashlight on the spot where Farlan had his flashlight focused. "She's a redhead, so since that's Jazzy's Jeep back there, I'd say the odds are that—"

"Lord, do you suppose the man who killed those two prostitutes, killed Jazzy? The rumor is that both that Olmstead girl and the one found up around Loudon Dam were redheads."

"This can't have anything to do with those murders," Brian said rather emphatically, then quickly added, "At least I doubt it."

"I'd better call the police." Farlan shook his head. "Poor girl."

"Wait!" Brian grabbed Farlan's arm. "Look—did she just move? I think she's still breathing."

"What?" Farlan narrowed his gaze and peered over the wooden railing. Sure enough, the woman moved, ever so slightly, as if struggling to breathe.

"You call the police and tell them to send an ambulance," Brian said. "I'll go down there and get her out of that cold water. If she's been down there for a while, hypothermia could have already set in. Besides, her body could wash loose from the boulder at any time and be swept away down the creek."

Farlan patted Brian on the back. "You go on, son, and see if you can help her. I'll call 911 for the police and an ambulance."

Caleb brought his T-Bird to a screeching halt behind the Porsche blocking the road. Parked just off the road in the grass, Jazzy's red Jeep glistened in the moonlight like fresh blood. Off in the distance he heard the wail of sirens. His heartbeat went wild. Adrenaline pumped through his body at an alarming rate. Even before he jumped out of his car, he saw Farlan MacKinnon pacing back and forth on the old covered bridge.

Where's Jazzy? His mind screamed. *Where's my Jazzy!*

"What the hell's going on here?" Caleb ran toward Farlan MacKinnon.

The old man, his face pale, his eyes round with shock,

whirled around and stared at Caleb. "He's gone down to get her."

"Who's gone down where to get who?" Caleb asked as he ran toward MacKinnon. "Answer me, damn it!"

"We saw her Jeep, and I got this crazy notion something was wrong," the old man rattled. "I told him we'd better check and see if something had happened to her."

Caleb grabbed MacKinnon by the lapels of his overcoat and shook him several times. "Is it Jazzy? Has something happened to her?"

"Jazzy? Yes, Jazzy Talbot. I don't know the girl well. I've seen her around—"

Caleb shook the old man again. "Where is she? What happened to her? Who's gone to get her?"

"She was down in the creek," MacKinnon replied. "At first we thought she was dead, but then we saw her move. She was just barely breathing. He went down to get her, to see if she's still alive. I—I called 911."

Caleb released his firm hold on MacKinnon's lapels and turned to search for Jazzy and for whomever MacKinnon had sent to help her. The sirens grew louder. Closer.

Whatever's happened, Jazzy, honey, hang in there.

Suddenly, coming from the other side of the bridge, a man appeared. Caleb felt as if there were lead weights on his ankles as he moved forward, trying to gain a better look at the dark figure moving toward him. Instinctively, he reached out and grabbed the flashlight from MacKinnon's hand and held it up to spotlight the figure moving steadily toward them.

"Give me a hand, will you?" the man called.

Caleb realized two things simultaneously. The man was Brian MacKinnon. And he was holding a wet, bloody body in his arms. Jazzy's body!

CHAPTER 21

Reve sat beside Jacob in the cab of his truck as he raced along the road from her cabin to County General Hospital, the siren blasting and the blue light atop the truck flashing. The minute Dallas had called him and told him about Jazzy, he'd come straight to Reve.

"I didn't think this was something you needed to hear over the phone," he'd told her as he stood at her front door. "Dallas just called me. He and Genny are on their way to the hospital. Jazzy's been hurt. Hurt real bad. They don't know if she's going to make it."

Reve had grabbed her coat and purse, and with Jacob's arm around her for support, she'd hurried with him to his truck. When she'd stumbled in her attempt to climb into the cab, he had gripped her by the waist, hoisted her up off the ground and placed her on the seat.

"Jacob?"

"Huh?" He kept his eyes on the road.

"Did Dallas say what happened?"

"Apparently somebody called Jazzy and told her they had information about her birth parents and set up a meeting out by the old covered bridge near the country club."

"Tell me she didn't go out there alone."

"Hell, yes. You know Jazzy. Bull-headed and determined." Jacob swallowed hard.

Without thinking, acting purely on instinct when she realized how worried Jacob was, Reve reached over and squeezed his arm. He tensed.

"She's tough," he said. "She'll make it."

"Do they know exactly what happened to her and how it happened?"

"Dallas knew only what the officers who were at the site told him. It appears someone knocked Jazzy in the head hard enough to render her unconscious and then threw her off the bridge and into the creek. She landed halfway in the creek and partly on the rocks below."

Reve's hand rose from Jacob's arm and flew up to cover her mouth. "Oh, dear God." How could this have happened? What had prompted Jazzy to take such a risk? "Caleb?" She suddenly wondered about Jazzy's fiancé. "Does he know?"

"He was on his way there to meet her when it happened. He got there a few minutes before the police and the ambulance."

"Who would possibly want to hurt Jazzy?" The question was no sooner uttered than Reve remembered that Jacob and Dallas had warned them that a possible serial killer was on the loose in northeast Tennessee. A man who was murdering redheads. "You don't think the man who killed those prostitutes tried to kill Jazzy, do you?"

"I have no idea. I don't know all the facts yet. The only two things Jazzy's attack has in common with the two murder cases are the facts that Jazzy is a redhead and her body was thrown into the creek. Other than that, there don't seem to be any similarities."

"Does that mean you've ruled out—"

"It means I don't know."

"But there could be a connection to the murders of those two redheaded prostitutes, couldn't there?"

Jacob grunted. "I didn't ask Dallas what he thought, but I will. And I figure he'll agree with me. I'd say if there is a connection, we're probably dealing with a copycat killer."

"What makes you think that?"

"Look, Reve, I know you're as confused and concerned as I am, but asking me a bunch of questions I don't know the answers to isn't helping anybody, least of all Jazzy."

Reve felt as if he'd slapped her. "I—I'm sorry. I didn't mean to . . ." Her voice trailed off as she struggled not to cry.

He cut his eyes toward her quickly, then refocused immediately on the road. "No, I'm the one who's sorry. I didn't mean to bite your head off that way."

"We're both worried about Jazzy."

"Yeah."

Neither of them said another word until Jacob parked at the ER entrance. By the time he came around to the passenger's side, Reve had opened the door and was getting out by herself. He grasped her around the waist, lifted her down and set her on her feet, then took her hand in his. Together, their long-legged strides in unison, they rushed toward the hospital. Once they reached the waiting area, Jacob released her hand.

Dallas Sloan, who hovered over Genny as she paced restlessly back and forth, noticed them and threw up his hand to motion them over.

Jacob punched Reve gently in the center of her back, urging her into movement. When they walked over to the other couple, Reve saw Sally and Ludie sitting side by side in the corner. Lacy Fallon, the bartender at Jazzy's Joint and one of Jazzy's friends, stood by the bank of telephones along the back wall. She was talking to someone. Reve figured she was calling other friends who'd want to know what had happened to Jazzy.

"Any word?" Jacob asked Dallas.

"We're waiting to hear something. Caleb's back there. They tried to make him come out here with us, but he refused," Dallas said. "When the receptionist threatened to call security, I stepped in and told her that only if Caleb caused a problem would anyone forcibly remove him. Caleb swore he'd stay out of the way."

"You did the right thing."

"Hell, all I could think about was how I felt when Genny got shot. I should have done what Caleb did and demanded to stay with her as long as I could."

The ER waiting area was crowded, filled with an assortment of people, none of whom Reve knew, other than Jazzy's friends. As she surveyed the room, two men entered, each carrying a cardboard caddy of Styrofoam cups. She recognized the younger man as Brian MacKinnon, someone Jazzy intensely disliked. Noting the vague resemblance between Brian and the older man, she assumed he must be Brian's father, Farlan MacKinnon.

The two men approached and held out their cardboard caddies.

"Here's coffee for everyone," the elder MacKinnon said.

"Thank you." Genny stood and offered Mr. MacKinnon a gracious smile, then she turned to Brian. "How can we ever repay you for rescuing Jazzy? You might have saved her life."

Brian flushed. "I didn't do anything. Not really."

"Any word?" Farlan asked.

"Not yet." Genny lifted a cup from the caddy. She spread her glance around to the others, her look inviting them to accept the coffee that was being offered.

Dallas lifted a cup and so did Reve. Jacob declined.

"Go see if Sally and her friend want coffee," Farlan told his son, who immediately walked over to the two old ladies.

"We won't get in the way," Farlan said. "I told Brian I wanted to stay until we knew something. It was quite a shock finding her the way we did. Poor little thing."

"You and Brian found her?" Reve asked.

Farlan MacKinnon turned to Reve, his mouth open to

speak, but suddenly he went dead still and stared at Reve. For a minute there, she thought the old man was going to faint.

"Who are you?" he asked.

"I'm Reve Sorrell," she replied. "I'm Jazzy Talbot's—"

"Twin sister," he finished for her.

His hands shook so badly that Genny took the cardboard caddy from him and placed it in a nearby chair. "Are you all right, Mr. MacKinnon? Do you need to sit down?"

He kept staring at Reve. "Identical twins. Redheaded identical twins. How old are you, Ms. Sorrell?"

"I'm thirty."

"Yes, you would be."

Brian came up to his father and put his hand under the old man's elbow. "Come on over here and sit down. And just as soon as we get word on Jazzy, I'm taking you home."

Farlan MacKinnon allowed his son to escort him across the room to where a couple of seats remained empty. But once seated, he looked back across the room at Reve, seeming unable to take his eyes off her. *He sure is acting odd,* she thought. But then, he was probably partly in shock after what happened.

"Are you telling me that Brian MacKinnon rescued Jazzy?" Jacob asked.

"It seems he and old man MacKinnon were on their way home from the country club when they spotted Jazzy's Jeep parked on the side of the road," Dallas said. "They stopped to investigate, and Mr. Farlan saw Jazzy's body in the creek. Brian went down and got her. He was bringing her up out of the creek when Caleb arrived."

Jacob snorted. "I can see the headlines in tomorrow's Cherokee Pointe Herald. 'Brian MacKinnon, Hero!' is what it'll say."

"I take it that you don't like Brian MacKinnon," Reve said.

"He's a pompous jackass who throws his daddy's money around and thinks that because he's a MacKinnon he can do whatever the hell he pleases." Jacob shot a disapproving look in Brian's direction. "Be forewarned, Ms. Sorrell, that despite his prestigious pedigree, Brian MacKinnon is not a very nice man."

"Keep your voice down." Genny whispered the warning. "And despite what you think of him, Brian did try to help Jazzy tonight and we mustn't forget that fact."

"Yeah, yeah. We're all very grateful," Jacob said, his voice a low growl. "I just wanted to make sure Reve understood that just because MacKinnon is on a social level with her kind, he's no gentleman."

Reve stood there staring at Jacob, uncertain how to reply or if she should bother to comment at all on what he'd said. But before she could decide, Caleb came hurtling through the door leading to the private cubicles inside the heart of the emergency room. He rushed straight to Reve and Genny.

"They're taking her up to surgery. She sustained some internal injuries from the fall and they're certain she has some internal bleeding," Caleb said. "But—" He swallowed. "It's more than just her body. The son of a bitch who hit her cracked her skull. Dr. Meadows ordered an emergency CT scan. He said that there's evidence of bleeding from torn veins." Caleb's voice trembled. Tears glistened in his eyes. "He said something about a growing subdural hematoma." Caleb sucked in a deep breath. "That's a blood clot. Bottom line—if they don't do surgery immediately, she'll die. He's called in a neurological surgeon."

Dallas curled his arm around Genny's waist and pulled her close. She rested her head on his chest and wrapped her arms around him. Jacob clamped his big hand down on Reve's shoulder. She looked up at him and saw her own fears reflected in his eyes.

Reve walked over and put her arms around Caleb. When he hugged her for dear life, she stroked his back as tears streamed down her face.

"She's going to make it," Caleb said.

"Yes, of course she is," Reve replied, swallowing her tears.

"And we're going to find the bastard who tried to kill her." Caleb spoke through clenched teeth, anger evident in his voice. When he pulled away from Reve, there was an expression of pure rage on his face. "And when we do—"

"You let us take care of finding the person who did this to Jazzy," Dallas said.

Caleb looked at Reve. "You probably aren't safe either. He might come after you next."

Startled by Caleb's dire warning, Reve gasped. Undoubtedly Caleb believed Jazzy had been the serial killer's latest victim.

Jacob draped his arm around Reve's shoulders. "I'll take care of Reve."

Instinctively, desperately needing comfort and longing for strong arms to hold her, Reve laid her head on Jacob's shoulder.

Still resting against Dallas, Genny turned and stared at Jacob. The two exchanged rather odd looks that made Reve curious about what they had silently said to each other.

"Yeah, I know I need to let the law handle this," Caleb said to Dallas. "But you've got to understand how I feel."

"We all understand," Dallas replied. Then, after a slight hesitation, he said point-blank, "I hate to ask this, but we need to know—did Dr. Meadows say if there was any evidence of sexual assault?"

A collective hush settled over Jazzy's friends and family.

"No." Caleb sighed heavily. "I asked. He said no, there was no sign of sexual assault."

Dallas nodded.

"Surgery could take hours," Caleb told the others. "They said we can wait upstairs and the surgeon, a Dr. Behel, will come out and talk to us . . . afterward."

"Do you think you can look out for the ladies while we're gone?" Dallas glanced from Reve to Genny and then over to

Sally and Ludie. "I need Jacob and his department to work with us on this case. I want him to go with me out to the crime scene so we can take a look at things ourselves."

Reve realized that by putting Caleb in charge of their care, Dallas was giving Caleb something to think about other than the very real possibility that the woman he loved was going to die. Just the thought that she could lose her sister before they had a chance to really become sisters hurt Reve in a way nothing else ever had. It was at that moment she realized she loved Jasmine. And more than anything on earth, she wanted her to live.

I did what I had to do. Jazzy had to die. It was easier than I thought it would be to kill her. Two hard blows to the back of her head was all it took. She dropped instantly after the second blow. Although she was slender, it wasn't easy lifting her up and over the railing. And I hadn't realized there would be so much blood. All over the hammer I used to kill her. All over my gloves. And it even splattered across my coat and on my shoes.

I burned everything as soon as I returned home. Even my underwear. But the metal hammer wouldn't burn, so I hid it. I removed it from the fireplace and once it cooled, I wrapped it in an old pillowcase and took it up to the attic. It's there now, hidden away at the bottom of an old trunk, safely tucked away where no one will ever find it.

I wonder how long it will be before her body is discovered? Days? Weeks? Of course there will be a search for her once it's discovered that she's missing, so they could find her by morning, especially if they bring out Sally Talbot's bloodhounds.

Oh, God! What if—No, no, I didn't leave anything behind with my smell on it. But what if they're able to pick up a scent simply out of the air? I hadn't thought of that. Just how long did a human's scent remain in the air? Surely not very long.

I can't worry about it now. Besides, no one would ever believe me capable of such a horrendous crime.

Should I act again quickly? Or should I wait? With Jazzy dead, that leaves only her twin. But what if they suspect that Reve will be the killer's next victim? They'll be watching her, guarding her day and night.

I'll have to wait. The perfect opportunity will present itself. And soon. I have to wait for the right moment. But I dare not wait too long. I have to put a stop to the investigation into the past before they discover the truth. I can't let that happen. If Slim had done his job thirty years ago, I wouldn't be in this situation now. If he'd just killed those damn babies as I'd told him to do . . . Her babies. Those beautiful little redheaded twins.

When they arrived at the crime scene, Jacob and Dallas found what appeared at first glance to be an unruly crowd and mass confusion. Jacob parked his truck on the side of the road behind three black-and-white cruisers. After Dallas and he emerged from the truck, they hurried up the road, only to be bombarded by a small horde of TV and newspaper reporters. They kept walking, forcing the ones spouting questions at them to follow along.

"Is this the work of a serial killer?"

"Was Jazzy Talbot attacked because she's a redheaded whore?"

"What's Jazzy's condition? Is she going to live?"

"If y'all expected her to be the next victim, why wasn't she better protected?"

The news camera zoomed in, getting a closeup of their faces when the cameraman jumped around in front of them. Within seconds the reporters formed a circle, effectively surrounding them. Jacob wanted to smash the camera and knock the cameraman's teeth down his throat. But he was already notorious for his bad temper, so he did his level best to keep it under control tonight.

"No comment," Dallas said.

"Can't you tell us whether Jazzy is going to make it or not?" a female reporter for the *Herald* asked.

"Contact the hospital for an update on Ms. Talbot's condition," Dallas told her, then gently shoved her out of the way, making an escape route for Jacob and him.

Jacob saw Jazzy's red Jeep up ahead, just off the road, parked in the grass. A tight knot formed in his stomach. If only Jazzy had waited for Caleb before coming out here to meet some mysterious caller. Yeah, hindsight was twenty-twenty, and the world was filled with people asking themselves "What if?" But it wasn't in Jazzy's nature to be cautious. Even as a kid she'd been bold and fearless. And that meant she'd often leaped before looking and gotten herself into all kinds of trouble.

Noticing one of his deputies, Moody Ryan, standing guard over the Jeep, he threw up his hand and waved. Moody waved back.

When they reached the corded-off area, they found two-thirds of the police force and half of Jacob's deputies keeping the crime scene protected from reporters and curiosity seekers. He sure as hell hoped this many officers didn't mean that by their numbers alone they had compromised the scene. All it took was one wrong move to screw up the evidence. And with this many people milling around on the bridge, putting out dozens of different scents, there was no point in bringing in Sally's bloodhounds.

Bobby Joe Harte met them when they approached the bridge "How's Jazzy?" he asked.

"In surgery," Jacob replied.

"Lieutenant Glenn put me in charge of crowd control," Bobby Joe said. "I called in as many deputies as I could on short notice, and we're manning the parameter. Luckily, we got in place before that bunch showed up." He nodded toward the clamoring reporters kept at bay only by the presence of the deputies. "The crowd's been getting bigger by the minute. More and more folks are hearing about what happened and showing up. But I think we can handle things."

"Where's Glenn?" Dallas asked.

"He's on the other side of the bridge, overseeing the investigation. He's got Burt and Dwayne and Earl collecting evidence."

"Who were the first officers on the scene?" Dallas gazed out across the bridge and surrounding area, apparently taking note of his personnel working the site.

"Hendrix and Kirk," Bobby Joe replied.

"Hm—mm. Kirk's a rookie, but Hendrix has been around long enough to know the proper procedure."

Jacob followed Dallas as he headed across the bridge. He'd learned that the first two rules you follow at a crime scene are don't touch anything and write everything down. Anything taken away or added to a scene could mean the difference between solving a crime and a perpetrator getting away scot free.

Tommy Glenn, a heavyset, bearded guy in his early thirties, had been with the Cherokee Pointe police department since he was nineteen. He was a seasoned professional, a small-town-cop pro. When Glenn saw Dallas and Jacob heading his way, he came toward them, a grim look on his face.

"Chief." Glenn nodded to Dallas. "Sheriff." He looked at Jacob. "How's Jazzy?"

"In surgery," Jacob said. "Fighting for her life."

"Have we got anything here?" Dallas motioned with a subtle move of his right hand.

"Nothing was touched before Earl got here. Of course, he called in Burt and Dwayne. They're collecting evidence now. Blood from the bridge railing and the rocks below appear at first glance to be about it. But we've got some bloody shoe prints, too. And tire tracks, although it'll be just about impossible to prove the tracks belong to our perpetrator since there's traffic along this road all the time, but we photographed them and I think we should make casts."

"I want every scrap of possible evidence documented and no stone left unturned," Dallas told Glenn. "And be sure to keep accurate records and see to it that every tidbit of evidence is clearly marked."

"Yes, sir." Glenn nearly saluted before he turned and motioned to one of the uniformed officers assisting the men in charge of collecting evidence. "Bring the gun over here."

"Gun?" Dallas and Jacob said simultaneously.

"We found a Beretta Tomcat pistol on the bridge not far from where the railing is smeared with blood," Glenn said.

The officer brought the gun, sealed in a plastic bag and appropriately tagged, and handed it to the lieutenant. Glenn held up the bag.

"Polished blue finish," Jacob said. "That's Jazzy's gun or one just like it. I was with her when she bought it."

"Was it fired tonight?" Dallas asked.

"Nope. It still has a full seven-shot magazine in it."

"That tells us that whoever hit her probably came up behind her quickly and got in at least the first blow before Jazzy knew what was happening," Jacob surmised.

"Any sign of the weapon her attacker used?" Dallas asked.

"Not so far," Glenn said. "But we're going to scour every inch of the bridge, as well as the creek and ground within sight, then we'll span out and search the woods."

"I'll let you get back to work." Dallas cordially dismissed Glenn, who immediately returned to his duties.

By the differential way Glenn acted toward Dallas, it was obvious he admired and respected the chief of police. It said a lot about the kind of man Tommy Glenn was because everybody knew he'd badly wanted the job Dallas had been given.

"What are the odds we'll find anything that will help us?" Jacob asked.

"You never know. Criminals make mistakes all the time, especially amateurs."

"You believe whoever tried to kill Jazzy is an amateur?"

"Either that or he's somebody who wants us to think he is. I suspect this isn't the work of the guy who killed Becky Olmstead, Kat Baker and all those other redheads over the past few years. The MO isn't identical."

"Do you think we have a copycat killer on our hands?"

"Possibly. The public knows that a couple of prostitutes were murdered and their corpses dumped in a body of water. The Tennessee River and Douglas Lake. And word leaked out that both women were redheads."

"Those are the only two things about Jazzy's attack that are the same as the two murders."

"She was hit over the head, not strangled," Dallas said. "And she wasn't raped."

"What if it wasn't the serial killer or a copycat killer?"

Dallas cocked his head to one side and gave Jacob an inquisitive look. "Do you have another theory?"

"I know we can't completely rule out the serial killer, and I'm not saying it isn't a copycat, but what if the person who attacked Jazzy had a personal reason for wanting her dead?"

"Like what?" Dallas smiled like a proud papa whose son had just become a man.

"She and Reve have hired the top private investigation firm in Tennessee to search for their birth parents. What if somebody in Cherokee County doesn't want the twins to learn the truth? What if whoever tried to kill them when they were babies is still around?"

"If that's the case, then neither Jazzy nor Reve will be safe until the truth is revealed."

CHAPTER 22

Five days after her surgery, Jazzy remained in a coma. Everything possible was being done for her. Reve had called in the most renowned specialists, sparing no expense to fly in the leading neurologists. Every available test had been done, except those the doctors deemed either unnecessary or too risky at this point. An MRI and a CT Scan, which looks at the structure of the brain, were followed by other diagnostic testing, most of which Reve couldn't remember. The local neurologist, Dr. Behel, and his colleague from Vanderbilt, Dr. Alfred Cornelius, had agreed not to run a SPECT Scan, despite the fact the results of both the MRI and the CT Scan were normal, and yet Jazzy had not awakened. In patients of reproductive age, the SPECT Scan procedure was used judiciously.

Dr. Cornelius had said, "If Ms. Talbot's condition doesn't change in the next few weeks, I suggest moving her to Nashville, to Vanderbilt, where we can run a PET Scan, and if we feel it necessary at that time, we'll discuss running the SPECT Scan."

Although Reve hadn't lived at the hospital 24/7, as Caleb had, even when she wasn't there, she got little sleep or rest.

She had remained at the hospital for the first thirty-six hours, as had Genny; then Dallas had driven them to Genny's home in the mountains and placed an officer outside to guard them. She had stayed with Genny a couple of days, the two making the trip to the hospital together daily. But yesterday morning, Lacy Fallon had phoned her and asked what should be done about managing both Jazzy's Joint and Jasmine's. It seemed that Jazzy, being a bit of a control freak, hadn't trained anyone to take over in case of an emergency. Even though both establishments were continuing business as usual, if someone didn't take charge soon, both would have to close. So Reve had moved into Jazzy's upstairs apartment and, using her basic business skills, took over the reins of her sister's two establishments. After all, there was little she could do for Jazzy just sitting in the ICU waiting room, but by taking charge of her sister's business affairs, she'd be doing something useful.

The policeman who'd parked outside the apartment last night had been replaced by a sheriff's deputy this morning. Moody Ryan had followed her to the hospital and come up on the elevator with her.

"I'm going to be here for at least an hour." Reve stopped outside the waiting room and turned to the young deputy. "Why don't you go down to the cafeteria and eat breakfast?"

"I had breakfast before I came on duty, ma'am."

"Then go get a cup of coffee."

"Ma'am, I'll stay out of your way. You won't even know I'm here. But my orders are to keep you under constant surveillance."

"And those orders came from?"

Moody's lips twitched. "Sheriff Butler."

"I sincerely hope Sheriff Butler doesn't expect you to go to the ladies' room with me."

Moody blushed. "No, ma'am, I'm sure he doesn't."

Giving up on trying to escape her shadow, Reve opened the door and entered the small ICU waiting room. Moody

Ryan came in behind her. On the solitary sofa nestled against
the back wall, Caleb lay curled up in an awkward position, a
hospital-issue blanket wrapped around him from armpits
down to the top of his booted feet. The poor guy looked like
hell. He'd been cleaning up in the bathroom, but he hadn't
shaved and the brown stubble on his face was turning into a
beard. If she'd ever seen a guy madly in love, that guy was
Caleb McCord. If, God forbid, Jazzy didn't make it, Reve
didn't think Caleb would either.

She turned to Moody. "Look, if I promise not to leave this
room, would you go to the snack bar and get a cup of fresh
coffee and a sausage biscuit?"

Moody stared at her questioningly.

"I'm sure Caleb hasn't had a bite to eat since sometime
yesterday. I want him to have breakfast, but I see no point in
both you and I going to the snack bar."

"Yeah, I guess it would be okay for me leave you, if you
promise to stay right here with Caleb."

Just as Moody headed out of the waiting room, Caleb
roused and gazed bleary-eyed at Reve. He threw up a hand
and waved.

"Morning," she said.

He kicked off the blanket, sat up and stretched. "What
time is it?"

"A little after eight. I sent Moody down to the snack bar
to get you something to eat."

Caleb rubbed the back of his neck. "They don't make
these couches for sleeping."

"You really should go home, take a shower and sleep in
your own bed for a few hours."

Caleb stood, picked up the blanket, folded it unevenly and
laid it across the arm of the sofa. "I'm not leaving this hospital until Jazzy comes out of that damn coma."

"That could be weeks," Reve reminded him.

"Don't waste your breath. I'm not going anywhere until
she opens her eyes and looks at me."

Reve nodded, then went over and hugged him. "You keep your vigil here at the hospital, and I'll make sure her business interests are taken care of. When she recovers, I'll turn things back over to her in tip-top shape."

Caleb eased back and took Reve's hands in his. "She's going to come out of the coma and recover completely."

Caleb had stated his hopes confidently. Too confidently? No. They shouldn't expect the worst. They should remain cautiously optimistic. Hadn't Dr. Cornelius told them that using the standard Glasgow Coma Scale, which estimated a patient's chances of living and recovering by assigning numbers ranging from three to fifteen, Jazzy had a chance for a full recovery? The higher the number, the better the odds. Jazzy's case was a ten, and a ten was on the high end of the mid-range.

"With patients scoring eight to ten, twenty-seven percent will die," the doctor had explained frankly. "But the good news is that sixty-eight percent will have a good recovery, with moderate disabilities."

"You're absolutely right," Reve said to Caleb. "Jazzy's a fighter. She'll wake up any time now, and when she does, she'll do whatever it takes to recover. And we'll be here to help her. If she needs her own personal physical therapist, I'll hire the best. She may not be ready for that Christmas wedding y'all planned, but—"

"Then maybe a New Year's wedding," a female voice said.

Reve and Caleb looked around to see who'd spoken. There stood Miss Reba and Big Jim. She carried a small overnight case, and he held a garment bag.

"Any change in Jazzy's condition?" Big Jim asked.

"No change," Caleb replied.

Reve noted a genuinely sad expression on Jim Upton's face. A strong, handsome face, she thought, especially for a man of seventy-five. Although handsome in his own right, Caleb didn't resemble his grandfather and wasn't quite as tall. But there was a strong hint of Miss Reba's beauty in her grandson's attractive features.

"We've brought some toiletries and a change of clothes." Reba marched into the waiting area. Though a petite woman, her presence filled the entire space. "And your grandfather has arranged for you a room on this floor, directly down the hall." She kissed Caleb's cheek. "Now you run along with Jim and get freshened up, then go down to the cafeteria for breakfast. I'll stay here with Reve until you return."

"I can't—"

Big Jim grabbed Caleb's arm. "Nobody's asking you to leave the hospital, son. But if you don't take better care of yourself, you're not going to be able to help Jazzy when she comes out of that coma."

"I don't know how your grandfather managed to commandeer a hospital room for you," Reve said, her eyes wide in astonishment, "but you should take advantage of this opportunity. If Jazzy sees you looking like this, she won't know you."

"How did you get them to give me a room here?" Caleb asked.

"The Uptons are major contributors to every charity in Cherokee County. Everybody knows how generous we can be," Jim replied. "I just called in a few favors."

"And twisted a few arms," Reba added, then winked at her grandson as she handed him the overnight case.

"Okay, I'll take a shower and change clothes," Caleb said. "But Reve's already sent Moody Ryan to the snack bar for something to eat so I won't need to go to the cafeteria."

Jim put his arm around his grandson's shoulders and guided him out of the room. Once alone with Reve, Miss Reba turned to her and smiled.

"How are you, my dear?"

"I'm doing okay."

"You're keeping tabs on Jazzy's business concerns, I hear."

"Yes, ma'am."

"If there's anything you need from Jim or me—"

"I'd like to ask you something, and I'd appreciate a completely honest answer."

The fact that Miss Reba had come to the hospital every day and had encouraged Caleb's hopes that Jazzy would live and recover completely hadn't escaped Reve's notice. Whether Miss Reba's sentiments were sincere was another matter entirely.

"Let's sit down." Reba indicated the sofa.

When Reba sat, Reve moved Caleb's blanket to a nearby chair and joined his grandmother. She faced the woman and from her expression suspected Miss Reba knew what she intended to ask.

"You've been wonderfully caring and supportive of Caleb these past five days," Reve said. "No grandson could ask for a more loving, concerned grandmother."

"And you want to know if those feelings of care and support extend to his fiancée."

"Yes, I do. Because when Jazzy comes out of the coma—"

"You mean if she comes out of the coma."

"Is that what you're hoping for? You hope she—"

"What I want does not matter," Miss Reba said. "But to answer your question—no, I don't want Jazzy to die or remain in a coma. Am I thrilled that she's going to one day be my grandson's wife? No. Have I accepted the inevitable? Yes."

"And what does that mean exactly?"

"You've become very fond of Jazzy in a relatively short period of time, and I believe it's not simply because she's your biological sister, is it?"

"Jazzy is not what she seems to be," Reve said. "She puts up that bad-girl front, even does things to perpetuate her reputation. But Jazzy isn't bad. She has a big heart, a good heart. And believe this, Miss Reba, if you don't believe anything else about her—she loves Caleb."

"Yes, I think she does. I know he worships her. And that's

the reason that as soon as Jazzy is well enough, I intend to give Caleb and her the biggest, fanciest wedding Cherokee County has ever seen."

"I'm surprised. Pleasantly surprised." Reve believed that Miss Reba meant exactly what she'd said.

"Well, my dear, you see, I've learned from my mistakes. I will never do anything to jeopardize my relationship with Caleb, and if that means welcoming Jazzy Talbot into our family with open arms, then that's what I intend to do."

Dallas removed the faxed documents the moment they came out of the machine, scanned them quickly and then handed them to Jacob. The two men had been holed up in Dallas's office since six that morning and it was now nearly noon. Despite as thorough an investigation as their combined forensics teams could do, the end results were that whoever had attacked Jazzy was still on the loose and they were no closer to solving the mystery of Jeremy Timmons's murder than they were the night Amber Chaney found his body.

Dallas had arranged to send the evidence collected in each case to his old FBI friend Chet in Knoxville, who would use the Tennessee Bureau of Investigation's more sophisticated equipment to examine everything. And Dallas had contacted a former colleague, Teri Nash, now engaged to FBI profiler Linc Hughes, and asked for her help in collecting data on any similar murders in and around northeast Tennessee in the past quarter century. The faxes in Jacob's hands were the results of Teri's week-long search.

"You know what this means, don't you?" Jacob said.

"It means somebody has been getting away with murder for the past twenty-five years. And not just one or two murders, but over twenty murders, possibly more."

"He could have killed other women whose bodies were never found." Holding the papers tightly in his right hand, Jacob slapped the faxed documents against his left palm.

"It's got to be the same guy. It's the exact same MO. All the victims were redheads. Either prostitutes or reputed to be bad girls. They were all raped, strangled with a black braided ribbon—left around their necks—and their naked bodies dumped in either a river or a lake or a creek."

"When I spoke to Teri, she said that with the evidence she's compiled, the Bureau will definitely want to become involved, but she's giving us twenty-four hours to get our act together before she reports what she's found."

"Did she get Linc to come up with a profile of this killer?"

"Yeah. And Linc says our guy is definitely the organized type," Dallas said. "High IQ, possibly college educated. Could have been a mama's boy or at least the family favorite. And there's a good chance he suffered some type of either physical or mental abuse as a child. And Terry said that Linc suspects some traumatic experience involving a red-haired woman was the catalyst that brought out his killer instincts. In Linc's opinion, this guy is probably a psychopath."

Jacob studied the facts in the documents he held, then shook his head. "Some of these murders were a year or two apart, then less than a year and most recently, about every six or seven months. Until Becky Olmstead. It had been less than a week since he'd killed Kat Baker when he murdered Becky."

"Which means he will probably kill again soon."

"I just hope to hell it isn't in Cherokee County."

"Whether it is or not, we're involved now. We're all looking for the same guy."

"Becky Olmstead's murder case doesn't belong to us," Jacob said. "And since we're pretty sure Timmons's murder and Becky's are connected, you're right—we're looking for the same person that Sheriff Floyd is. If one case is solved—"

"Not only will they both be solved, but a string of murder cases that goes back at least twenty-five years gets solved, too."

"It might be simpler if Jazzy's attacker turned out to be our serial killer. If that were the case, we'd be looking for one man, not two."

Dallas nodded. "I'm hoping that when Jazzy comes out of the coma, she'll be able to tell us who attacked her."

"And her attacker has got to know he's safe only as long as she remains in that coma."

Reve had stayed at County General long enough to see Jazzy during the nine o'clock ICU visitation time. She'd sat beside her sister, held her hand and talked to her.

"I promise I won't screw things up too badly at Jazzy's Joint before you return," Reve had said. "I don't have a problem overseeing Jasmine's, but so far, I've stayed strictly in the background at Jazzy's Joint. You know what a snob I am. We rich-bitch types hate smoky honky-tonks and sweaty men."

For the past half hour, she'd been trying to concentrate on a stack of unpaid bills piled on Jazzy's desk in her office at the back of Jasmine's, but her mind kept wandering to her sister. She could think of little else. Both Jacob and Dallas had convinced her that Jazzy wasn't a victim of the unknown serial killer.

"If it wasn't the serial killer, then who?" she had asked. "Who would want to harm Jazzy?"

"The same person who thought he'd killed both of you thirty years ago," Dallas had replied.

That was the reason she had agreed to allow Jacob and Dallas to rotate watchdogs for her. And that was one of the reasons she didn't sleep well at night and wasn't functioning normally. Not only did she have to be concerned with Jazzy's recovery, but she had to worry about someone from their past trying again to kill Jazzy or possibly making an attempt on her life as well.

When her cell phone ran, Reve jumped as if she'd been shot. *Get a grip!* She snapped open her leather clutch purse and removed her phone. The number shown on the caller ID was one she instantly recognized. The Powell Private Security and Investigation Agency.

She flipped open her phone. "Hello, this is Reve Sorrell."

"Ms. Sorrell, it's Griffin Powell. I have some important information for you."

Reve's heartbeat quickened. "Have you found out who tried to kill Jazzy and me when we were infants?"

"No, ma'am, that I don't know yet. But it's only a matter of time. You see, I've narrowed down the field of women who could possibly be your mother."

"And?"

"And I think I know who your mother was. I'm holding in my hand a copy of what I believe is your birth certificate."

CHAPTER 23

Reve met Griffin Powell at a restaurant in Sevierville at four-forty-five. They ordered coffee and dessert. One of Dallas's men had followed her there and sat several tables over, being as discreet as possible. She hadn't told anyone why she was meeting with Griffin. After all, until she saw the evidence he possessed, she couldn't be sure she had anything to tell. And even if it turned out that he'd discovered the identity of her mother, Jazzy was the first person—the only person—with whom she wanted to share the news.

Shoving aside the apple pie he'd ordered, Griffin laid his briefcase on the table, flipped it open and pulled out a file folder. Reve's heartbeat accelerated alarmingly. Griffin slipped two documents from the folder and held them out to Reve. She hesitated.

"These are copies of what I believe to be your and Jazzy's birth certificates," he said.

She took the documents from him and scanned first one and then the other. Mary Leanne Collins had been born five minutes before her identical twin sister Martha Deanne Collins. Mary Leanne had weighed six pounds even. Martha Deanne had weighed five pounds four ounces.

Mother's name: Mary Dinah Collins.

Father's name: Unknown.

Mother marital status: single.

Mother's age: twenty.

Mother's address: 1803 Hyatt Street, Apt. 2-B, Sevierville, Tennessee.

Reve drew in a deep breath and released it slowly as she laid the two birth certificates on the table and looked right at Griffin.

"Why do you think these twins are Jazzy and me?" she asked.

"Because every other set of twins born anywhere in the state of Tennessee within six months of your approximate date of birth, before and after, is accounted for. Mary and Martha Collins seem to have disappeared off the face of the earth."

"What about Mary Dinah Collins?"

"She disappeared the same day as her four-week-old daughters."

"Four weeks old?" She and Jazzy hadn't been abandoned at birth. Their mother had kept them for four weeks.

"I've managed to track down a couple of neighbors who lived in the same apartment building as Dinah Collins," Griffin said. "Both told me that she went by the name Dinah. And they both agreed that she was a very sweet, quiet young woman who kept to herself and didn't bother anyone. But . . ." He paused as if trying to come up with just the right words before continuing. "They knew she was pregnant and un-married. She did have a frequent visitor, and they thought perhaps the man was her father."

"Her father? Are you saying we have a grandfather—"

"Or a father old enough to be your grandfather."

"Oh, great. Some guy old enough to be Dinah's father got her pregnant, didn't or couldn't marry her and then . . . what?"

"I'm searching for Dinah Collins, but so far it appears she was here in Sevierville one day and gone the next. She'd told

her neighbors she was taking her babies and moving out of
state, probably to Atlanta." He held up a restraining hand.
"Before you ask, yes, I already have agents in Atlanta searching for any clue to Dinah's whereabouts."

"Is there any other reason than the fact that Dinah and her
twins disappeared that you think she might be our mother?"
Reve needed more; she needed substantial proof of some
kind.

"Dinah Collins was a pretty little redhead. Auburn-red
hair. About the color of yours."

"How do you—" Griffin removed a photograph from the
file folder.

She reached out and grabbed it, her hand trembling. Gar-
nering her courage, she looked at the color snapshot of the
young woman. Oh, yes, Dinah was indeed a pretty little redhead. No taller than five-four, with an hourglass figure that
reminded Reve of Jazzy's build and perfect facial features
that strongly resembled both her own and Jazzy's.

This *was* her mother. Reve knew it as surely as she knew
the sun would rise in the east tomorrow morning.

Mary Dinah Collins.

Hello, Mother. Who were you? What happened to you?

"From what her neighbors said, I don't think Dinah Collins
was the type who would have tried to kill her babies," Griffin
told her. "One of the neighbors, a Mrs. Burton, said that
Dinah adored her twins, that she was a good little mother."

"Then you think someone stole us from her and left us for
dead. Who and why?"

"Possibly your father, who was probably a married man."

"I suppose it's not quite as horrible to believe your father
left you for dead as it is to think your mother did."

"There are other possibilities," Griffin said.

"Okay, give me your take on what happened. You're the
one with experience in these matters."

"All right. Let's say you and Jazzy were kidnapped, then
why didn't Dinah contact the police to report her babies

missing? She'd have been hysterical, wouldn't she? She'd have done anything to have found her baby girls."

"Oh, God! You think whoever left me in that Dumpster and Jazzy in that tree stump in the mountains killed our mother, don't you?"

Griffin didn't say anything for several seconds, then nodded. "I don't think we'll find Dinah Collins alive."

"Not unless she's the one who left us for dead."

"I'll keep up the search for Dinah," Griffin said. "And I'll do what I can to track down anyone else who might have known her. Old Mrs. Burton said Dinah had lived in the apartment on Hyatt Street for about a year and a half, but she never mentioned where she'd come from or who her people were."

"And this older gentleman was her only visitor?"

"No, not her only visitor, but her most frequent one. He came to see her weekly."

"So, what do you make of that? Looks like Dinah was some rich old man's mistress, doesn't it?"

"Do you want me to go any further with this investigation?" he asked. "Do you really want to know who your father was?"

"Oh, yes, I want to know who the son of a bitch was," Reve said emphatically. "And if he's still alive, I want to look him in the face and spit in his eye."

"It's your money, Ms. Sorrell." Griffin Powell stood. "I'll be in touch when I have more information."

Reve sat alone for several minutes, allowing her mind and her emotions to absorb this mind-boggling news. If only she could tell Jazzy, share this all-important revelation with her.

Jazzy, please, please come out of that damn coma soon. I need you. I need my sister.

Shelly Bonner hated nights alone. She didn't like the dark, always slept with a nightlight on and when Ronnie Gene was on a run, halfway across the country in that eighteen-wheeler of his, she usually made a point of finding her a man to keep her from getting lonely. More often than not, she knew her lover—his name, where he lived, whether or not he was married. She'd even screwed around with a few of Ronnie Gene's buddies, but found out right quick what a mistake that was. These days she usually picked up a guy in Jazzy's Joint or across the county line at either Barney's or the Smoky Mountain Roadhouse. Tonight she'd run into this fellow at Barney's and knew right away that he looked familiar. He'd called himself Harry, but she figured that wasn't his real name. Who he really was hadn't come to her—not yet. But she figured that by morning, she would have remembered where she'd seen him before tonight.

He was older than her usual pickup and definitely a cut above the rough, rugged rednecks she preferred. But this guy had come on all sweet and attentive, telling her right off how pretty she was and how much he loved her long hair. She'd been a dishwater blonde most of her life, but recently she'd started streaking her shoulder-length hair with red highlights, making it a dark strawberry blonde.

When she'd made it clear to this guy that she was interested in more than him buying her a drink, he'd told her, "Meet me outside in about five minutes, and don't tell anyone you're hooking up with me."

"You're married, aren't you?"

"Yeah. And I don't want my wife to—"

"I'll be out in five minutes to get in my car. Why don't you follow me home? That way nobody here will know we're leaving together."

When he'd smiled at her, she'd thought the guy had a really nice smile. A kind, gentle smile. She was usually a pretty good judge of character, and her guess was that old Harry was a real gentleman, somebody with a good job and lots of money. Being with a man like that would be a new experience for her, and she kind of liked the idea.

Harry had parked his car down the street, almost a block away, and walked to her house. She'd been a bit disappointed in the car he drove. Nothing special. No Lincoln or Corvette. Just a dark sedan of some kind. A late-model Chevy, she thought. Maybe the guy wasn't so rich after all. Despite the chill in the air, she'd waited for him on her front stoop after she unlocked the door to the house she and Ronnie Gene rented on Crenshaw Avenue. The place wasn't nothing fancy, but it beat the shack they'd lived in when they first got married eight years ago.

"Come on in." Shelly opened the door, entered the twelve-by-twelve living room and flipped on the light switch.

Harry came in behind her, then closed the door and locked it. He glanced around for a couple of seconds, then came up behind her and slipped his arm around her waist. She leaned back into him and was surprised when her hips encountered his erection. The guy was stiff as a poker. He'd probably want to jump in the sack right away, which was okay by her, just as long as she could persuade him to stay at least part of the night.

"I don't like guys who don't hang around for a while afterward," she told him as she turned slowly and lifted her arms up and around his neck.

"I've got all night."

"Your wife's not expecting you home?" Shelly rubbed herself against him, pressing her mound against his sex.

He shook his head. "Not tonight."

"You want something else to drink first? I got a bottle of rotgut in the kitchen cabinet and a six-pack of beer in the fridge."

"I'm fine," he replied. "Maybe later. After . . ."

"Yeah, after." She grabbed his hand and tugged. "My bedroom's this way."

He followed her like an obedient puppy, out of the living room, down the small, narrow hall and into the bedroom she shared with Ronnie Gene when he wasn't on the road.

"Don't look at the mess," she said. "I never bother making the bed."

Not only did she never bother making the bed, she seldom did a lick of housework of any kind. Once in a blue moon, she'd pick up a little, and she did change the sheets once a month. Ronnie Gene was always complaining that they lived in a pigsty.

"A pigsty's good enough for a hog like you," she'd told him.

He'd backhanded her, sent her flying halfway across the room. He'd never hit her before, except a couple of times when he'd been drinking. She'd given him fair warning that if he ever struck her again, she'd leave him. That had been a year ago, and he'd been on good behavior ever since.

Shelly picked up the clothes strewn across the foot of the bed, tossed them on top of the dresser and then turned to Harry. "I like to leave at least one light on. Is that okay with you?"

"That's fine with me. I'll enjoy looking at you."

Oh, this guy was going to be fun. She decided right then to give him a seductive strip tease. Nothing too slow, since he was already primed and ready, but just slow enough to get him really worked up.

"Why don't you sit on the bed while I get undressed, then I'll help you take off your clothes."

He sat on the bed, anticipation bright in his eyes.

She removed her sweater first and tossed it onto the floor. Then she stripped out of her blouse and jeans. He sucked in a deep breath when she stood before him in nothing but her bra and panties. Butt floss panties. While he stared at her, his mouth open and his hands balled into tight fists set atop his knees, she leaned over and kissed him. He grabbed her around the waist and toppled her over onto the bed. Hovering over her, he slid his hand into his jacket pocket and pulled out a condom. Before she had a chance to protest, he tore off her panties, unzipped his slacks and freed his jutting penis.

"You want it pretty bad, huh?" she said.

He sheathed his dick, which she got a quick glimpse of before he rammed it into her. Not very impressive. A bit on the small side. But Lordy, Lordy, what the guy lacked in size, he made up for in action. He was humping her like there was no tomorrow, like a green kid with his first woman. She wanted to tell him to slow down, to take it easy, but the poor guy was in a frenzy, so she started caressing him, kissing him and whispering sweet nothings in his ear. He seemed to like her touching him and slowed down just a little, but not soon enough to stem the tide of his release.

"Oh, God!" he cried out just as he ejaculated.

While relief shuddered through him, he opened his eyes and looked down at her, then smiled. "I had a feeling it was you. Now I know for sure."

"Huh? What are you talking about?" She thought she recognized this guy, so maybe it was possible they'd known each other years ago. Not high school, though. The guy was a lot older than she was.

"You like to play games with me, don't you, Dinah?"

"Dinah? My name's Shelly."

"Yes, I know, I know. You can call yourself whatever you like, but we both know who you really are." He reached between them and cupped her mound. "Deep down inside you're Dinah. My Dinah."

Was this guy nuts or what? He hadn't had that much to drink over at Barney's, so he couldn't be drunk. "Are you on drugs?"

"I'm high," he said. "High on you, Dinah."

"Jeez, I'm not—"

He cut off her denial by kissing her, ramming his tongue halfway down her throat. When she felt his hands on her shoulders, pressing her into the bed, holding her down, a trickle of panic jittered in her belly. But as quickly as he'd restricted her, he jumped up and off her.

"Where's your bathroom?" he asked.

"Down the hall. First door on the left."

"Why don't you crawl under the covers and wait for me," he suggested. "I'll wash up and be right back."

She halfway wished he would leave. The guy had spooked her when he'd called her Dinah. But what did she care what he called her? It wasn't as if she'd ever see him again after tonight. Besides, the part of her that was afraid of the dark wanted him to stay so she wouldn't be alone all night. "Are you going to stay?"

"Of course I'm going to stay. I wouldn't leave now, not when we've only just begun to play our little game."

Jacob finished off the piece of chocolate pie he'd ordered for dessert. Lately he'd been skipping meals, working overtime and losing sleep. It bothered him more than he'd let on to anybody other than Dallas that he hadn't been able to come up with any suspects in Jazzy's attempted murder case. He was beginning to feel like a total failure as a lawman.

"More coffee?" Tiffany Reid asked as she stood by his table, coffee pot in hand.

"Yeah, thanks."

"Anything new on finding Jazzy's attacker?"

"If there was something new, I'd tell you," Jacob snapped angrily at Tiffany, then regretted he'd taken his frustration out on her. "Sorry. Didn't mean to bite your head off."

"It's okay. Really. We're all worried about her, you know. She's special to a lot of people." Tiffany nodded toward the corner booth at the back where Reve Sorrell sat nibbling on a salad. "Especially her. She calls the hospital ten times a day."

He looked back toward Reve, who didn't even notice him. Although she was eating a bite now and again, she didn't seem totally conscious of what she was doing, as if she was simply eating out of habit.

"Yeah, I guess it's pretty rough on Ms. Sorrell." Ever since the night of Jazzy's attack, Jacob had seen a different side of Reve, a side he liked. It was apparent to everyone that she genuinely cared about her sister. Hadn't she called in specialists from across the country, at her own expense, to help Jazzy? Hadn't she taken over the reins at Jazzy's restaurant and bar so neither place would have to close down?

Tiffany poured Jacob's cup to the brim, then smiled at him and walked on to another customer. He took a sip of the hot liquid, then put down his cup. After scooting out of his booth and standing, he picked up the cup and walked back toward the booth where Reve sat. When he stopped directly beside her, she glanced up at him.

"Evening," he said.

She nodded.

"Mind if I join you?" he asked.

"Please, sit down." She indicated for him to join her with a wave of her hand.

He sat, placed his cup on the table and looked at Reve. "Are you all right?"

"Yes, I'm fine. Why shouldn't I be? After all, I have protection around the clock, don't I? One of your deputies or one of Dallas's men keeps an eye on me day and night."

"I wasn't referring to your safety. I know we're keeping close tabs on you. I was talking about how you're handling everything else. Jazzy still being in a coma. A serial killer on the loose and Jazzy's attacker still at large."

"I'm worried. I'm nervous. And I keep wondering what will happen next."

"You have to hang on to the hope that Jazzy will come out of the coma soon. She's tough. If anyone can lick this thing, she can."

Reve nodded, then studied him closely, her gaze traveling over him as if he were a bug under a microscope. "Tell me something—why is that, if you love her and she loves you, you two never did—?"

"There's love and then there's love," Jacob replied, feeling a mite uncomfortable discussing feelings with Reve Sorrell. This woman evoked all kinds of unwanted feelings in him. Not that he'd ever admit it to her, of course. Most people figured Jacob Butler was a big, tough, unemotional kind of man. He wanted to maintain that image. "Jazzy and I love each other like friends, almost like brother and sister."

"But you did date each other, didn't you?"

"Yeah, we gave dating a try." Jacob chuckled. "We even kissed a time or two."

"And?"

"Why so curious?"

"I'm not. And I apologize. I suppose I'm simply trying to make conversation. After all, it's not as if you and I have anything in common to discuss, other than Jazzy and Genny and Dallas. Right?"

He had the oddest notion that by that particular comment, she'd been deliberately trying to insult him, and he couldn't help wondering why. Why now, tonight? Why now, when since the day they'd shared a meal at the Burger Box, they hadn't traded so much as one insult?

"Oh, I suppose we could find some things to discuss," he told her. "There's the weather. Nice, safe subject. And there's world events. Or even local events—murder and mayhem. Or is that too personal, considering you could easily be on either killer's hit list?"

Tensing, her gaze narrowing, she glared at him. "We could discuss why you haven't apprehended either killer."

His comment had been aimed to counter her snooty remark, but he should have remembered that with Reve, she gave as good as she got. "You know how to hit below the belt, don't you, Ms. Sorrell?"

"What's wrong, Sheriff, did I hit a sore spot?"

"You know you did. You aimed and fired a direct hit. But that was your intention all along, wasn't it? For some reason, you want to put up a barrier between us again." He reached over and grabbed her hand. Her gaze collided with his. "Have I got you running scared?"

"Let me go." She tugged on her hand. He held fast. With her gaze firing darts into him, she snarled. "I'm not the one running scared."

"Are you implying—?

"If the shoe fits—"

"I thought we'd called a truce. What happened? Did you get to liking me a little too much?"

"What a stupid thing to say."

He turned her hand over in his, clasped her fingers and caressed her palm with the pad of his thumb. "What bothers you the most, the fact that you're attracted to a quarter-breed roughneck or the fact that despite your recent friendly overtures, I haven't come knocking on your door?"

Her mouth gaped open, as if she couldn't believe he'd said such a thing to her.

"Better close your mouth, honey. You'll catch flies if you leave it that way."

"You are without a doubt the most infuriating man I've ever met." She clenched her teeth. "You have an ego the size of the Smoky Mountains. I am not attracted to you. And I have not been waiting, with bated breath, for you to come knocking on my door."

"If you say so."

"I say so!"

"Then if I showed up on your doorstep later tonight, you'd send me away. Right?"

She stared at him in total disbelief, but he caught a glimmer of another emotion. Anticipation, maybe? He should be shot for deliberately aggravating her, especially now, but God forgive him, he couldn't stop himself. It was either make her mad or drag her out of the restaurant and into the nearest dark corner where he could fuck her.

He'd lay odds that although Ms. Sorrell had probably been

made love to by several wealthy, cultured gentlemen, she'd never been fucked by a quarter-breed, ex-Navy SEAL hellion.

"You're deliberately being insulting," Reve told him.

"How did I insult you?"

"By implying that I want something . . . something intimate with you."

"What do you mean by intimate?" he teased.

She flushed. "You know exactly what I mean."

"If you're talking about fucking, then just come right out and say so."

"You're infuriating, insufferable, crude, rude and—"

"And you want me anyway."

Exasperated, Reve gasped. "I do not want you."

He chuckled. She fumed.

"What if I told you that I want you?" he asked.

Her eyes widened.

Suddenly Jacob's cell phone rang.

Damn! Just when their conversation was getting interesting.

"Hold that thought, will you, honey," he told her as he retrieved his phone and flipped it open. "Sheriff Butler here."

"Jacob, it's Dallas."

"What's wrong?"

"Genny's had another vision. She's seen another murder. A strawberry blonde this time. Young. Pretty. He drugged her, raped her and then strangled her."

"Has this already happened? Or do we have a shot at saving this woman?"

"Don't know. Genny's pretty shook up. She's in the bathroom vomiting. I don't want to leave her for long, but she insisted I call you. She thinks she recognized the area where he either has or will dump the body."

"Where?"

"She thinks it's somewhere in or around Tayanita Springs, right here in Cherokee County."

"Tayanita Springs feeds into several creeks. Does she have any idea—"

"That's as specific as it gets. And I'm not going to let her go under again."

"Yeah, I understand. You take care of Genny. I'll get somebody out to Tayanita Springs right away," Jacob said. "Maybe we'll luck out and catch this guy in the act."

The minute he returned his phone to the belt holder, Reve grabbed his arm. "What's wrong? Is Genny all right?"

"She will be, if she'll let Dallas take care of her. She had another vision, saw another murder."

"Who?"

"She didn't recognize the woman. Another redhead." Jacob picked up his cup and downed several swigs of the warm coffee. "Look, Reve, I've got to go. Tim Willingham is coming by in about an hour to take over. He'll see you home and keep watch on Jazzy's apartment tonight."

"Where are you going?" She squeezed his arm.

"To see if we can stop a murder before it happens—or at the very least catch a killer before he gets away."

Reve released his arm, but stood when he did. She looked at him with concern in her big, brown eyes. He wanted to kiss the breath out of her. Heaven help them both.

"Please, be careful," she said softly, almost as if she didn't want him to hear her.

"Worried about me, honey?"

"You don't make it easy for me to be nice to you."

"Is that what you've been doing—being nice to me?"

"I try, but you—"

He tapped his index finger over her lips, then let his finger settle there for a couple of seconds. "Soon, Miss Reve, very soon, you and I are going to have to come to terms with this hot, nasty, gut-twisting thing that's driving us both crazy."

She didn't say a word when he removed his finger from her lips. She simply stood there staring at him. He turned and walked away, stopping to pick up his suede jacket and Stetson on his way out of the restaurant.

CHAPTER 24

The whole county was in an uproar over the most recent murder. Shelly Bonner's body didn't show up for two days after Genny's latest vision. Jacob's and Dallas's combined forces had gone over every tributary of Tayanita Springs, but since the springs, high up in the mountain, fed several creeks that meandered through the county, it had taken them a good forty-eight hours to locate a body. The assumption was that although the body had been dumped into Tayanita Springs, the force of the downhill flow had swept it downstream pretty quickly. Two FBI agents out of Knoxville had shown up yesterday afternoon, only hours after the body had been fished out of Camden Creek. And MacKinnon Media had been playing up the local authorities' ineptitude, all but calling Jacob a backwoods buffoon. Dallas hadn't fared much better in the press, but he managed to keep a cooler head than Jacob.

With continuous phone calls, citizens storming the courthouse and the local and state media camping out on their doorsteps, Jacob had finally escaped to his office, closing the door and warning his deputies to keep everybody out. If he heard one more derogatory comment, he'd wind up knocking out somebody's lights. He knew himself, knew what a short fuse he had. He could control his temper—up to a point. Once pure rage took over, he was lost. Only the discipline he'd learned in the Navy, during SEAL training, saved him from himself.

Shutting out the world this way would give him time to settle down, to regain his composure. A few minutes ago, he'd come mighty close to telling a reporter where he could stick his damn microphone.

Sitting behind his desk, Jacob closed his eyes and took a deep breath. He needed a few minutes of peace and quiet. Someone knocked on the closed door.

"Shit!" Jacob wanted to shout, "Go away and leave me the hell alone."

Opening his eyes and focusing on the closed door, he called, "Yeah, who—"

"It's Dallas. I'm with Special Agents Cox and Hudson."

Jacob blew out an aggravated breath. "Come on in."

He stood just as the door opened. The two FBI men came in first. One young, slender and blond, the other middle-aged, stocky and balding. Dallas entered last and closed the door.

"Jacob, this is Steve Cox," Dallas introduced the older man first. They shook hands. "And this is Josh Hudson." The young, pretty-boy agent nodded brusquely.

"Have a seat," Jacob said. "If anybody wants coffee—"

"We're fine," Hudson said. "No coffee."

Yeah, sure, no coffee. Jacob had made the offer simply to show good manners. From time to time he did remember his manners, the ones Granny had done her best to instill in him. But apparently this fancy-pants agent wasn't into good manners or even civility.

"I know this is your case, Sheriff," Agent Cox said as he sat in one of the two chairs in front of Jacob's desk. "And we don't want to step on any toes, but since it's obvious we're dealing with a serial killer—"

"Which y'all wouldn't have known if Jacob and I hadn't put together the puzzle pieces," Dallas reminded them.

"Agreed," Cox said. "And our goal is to work with local law enforcement in every county where this killer has struck, but since his two most recent victims were Cherokee County women, we're going to start here."

"We expect your complete cooperation." Still standing, Hudson glanced from Dallas to Jacob. "Y'all need to understand that we're in charge now. We make the decisions. We call the shots." When neither Jacob nor Dallas replied, Hudson continued, going one step too far, "I'd think you would be grateful for our help, considering how ill equipped you are to solve a case like this and how badly you've handled things up to now."

Jacob growled, his basic instincts telling him to rip out Hudson's throat. When he took a step out from behind his desk and toward Hudson, Dallas intervened, blocking Jacob's path.

Dallas grinned at Hudson "Look, you cocky little son of a bitch—"

"Apologize," Agent Cox told his young associate.

"What?" Hudson's eyes widened in indignation.

Jacob smiled as he gained control over his desire to do bodily harm to the young agent. He nudged Dallas aside, but didn't move any closer to Hudson. Instead, he stabbed the guy with his deadly glare. Hudson's face turned red.

"You heard the man," Jacob said. "You owe us an apology, and I'm waiting to hear it."

Hudson took a really good look at Jacob then and apparently realized he was in deep shit. All the way up to his eyeballs. Hudson swallowed hard, choking on his own smart-ass attitude.

"I—I apologize," he said reluctantly.

"There, that's settled," Cox said. "Now, let's get down to work." He looked at Hudson. "Sit down, boy, and try to keep your foot out of your mouth."

Hudson sat. Dallas perched on the edge of Jacob's desk, while Jacob returned to his swivel chair behind the desk.

"We know Shelly Bonner's murder fits the MO of our serial killer," Jacob said. "And we just might have gotten a break in this one. It seems he killed her at her house and left behind some evidence. A few hairs in her bed that aren't hers or her husband's and some semen on the commode seat. It's not much, but it's more than we've had before now."

"This Bonner woman was known for picking up guys in bars," Cox said. "According to people who knew her, she often had a different guy in her bed every night her husband was out of town."

"Which means the hairs and the semen might not belong to our perp," Hudson said.

"But they could," Dallas told him. "Besides the DNA evidence, we've got a couple of eyewitnesses who saw Shelly at Barney's the night she was murdered. They said she left the bar alone, but that she'd been cozying up to some guy who looked out of place in the roadhouse. An upper-class kind of guy. He left about five minutes before Shelly did."

"They could have easily met up outside in the parking lot and gone from there to her house," Cox said.

"What about the guy's car?" Hudson asked.

"Nobody at the bar saw the car," Jacob replied. "But one of Shelly's neighbors, who claims she's an insomniac, said she saw a dark sedan pulling out of Shelly's driveway around midnight the night she was murdered."

"Did they see the guy driving the car?" Cox asked. "Could they tell if Shelly Bonner was with this guy when he left?"

"No to both questions," Dallas said.

"What are the odds this guy is a local?" Cox looked to Jacob. "The other twenty-odd murders during the past twenty-five years have been spread out over northeast Tennessee and southwest North Carolina. These two recent murders are the first in Cherokee County. I find that rather odd since he's killed more than once in every surrounding county."

"He killed once every couple of years in the beginning, at what we assume was the beginning. Then every eighteen months and eventually every year. But recently it's been every six to eight months and now the last three murders have all occurred in a two-week time span."

"He's accelerating his kills," Cox said. "And he's taking risks he hasn't taken before. He's killing in his home territory, if our guess is right. And if he left hairs in Shelley Bonner's bed and semen on her commode seat, then he's getting careless."

"Maybe he thinks he's safe," Dallas said. "If he's some well-to-do man with an unquestionable reputation, then he could have convinced himself that he'd be impervious, that there's no way we can discover his identity."

"He's been getting away with murder for twenty-five years," Cox reminded them. "I'd say he has good reason to be self-confident."

"If he's been killing for twenty-five years, then he's not young," Hudson said. "I thought the typical serial killer was between the ages of—"

"We're not dealing with a typical killer," Jacob said.

"This man was probably young, maybe as young as eighteen or nineteen, when he made his first kill," Dallas said. "Or he could have been older, late twenties or early thirties. The only thing we know—or at least suspect—is that something traumatic happened to him with some redhead, who was probably his first victim."

"Then our guy could be anywhere between forty-five and sixty-five." Hudson looked to Cox. "What's the chance of our getting a profile worked up on this killer?"

Dallas chuckled. Hudson glared at him.

"You find that amusing, Chief Sloan?" Hudson asked.

"Linc Hughes, one of the Bureau's top profilers, has already—"

Hudson jumped to his feet. "How the hell did you—"

"Sit down and shut up," Jacob said calmly, a threat in every word. He turned to Cox. "You'd better rein in pretty boy here or send him back to Knoxville."

Cox gave Hudson a warning glare. "Why don't you go out to the vending machines down the hall and get yourself a Coke?"

Red-faced and fuming, but smart enough to keep his mouth shut, Hudson nodded, then turned around and walked out of Jacob's office.

"Sorry about that," Cox said. "Hudson is a cocky little prick, but he graduated top in his class. He's book smart and common sense stupid. He thinks he knows everything."

"And he doesn't know a damn thing." Dallas eyed the closed door. "If you can, send him back to Knoxville. If you don't, sooner or later he's going to piss off Sheriff Butler and if those two tangle, Hudson's going to wish he'd never been born."

Cox eyed Jacob, who smiled at the FBI agent. "I'll see what I can do."

He hadn't meant to kill her in her own bed, but once he'd realized she was Dinah, he'd gone mad and been unable to control himself. He'd lain beside her for several hours, waiting until she was asleep before he went up the block to his car and drove it into her driveway. He'd put the knock-out drops in the glove compartment, along with the black braided ribbon. Always be prepared was his motto. After removing the bottle and ribbon from the glove compartment of the rental car and putting them in his coat pocket, he'd reentered her house.

It had taken several minutes for him to find the bottle of cheap whiskey she'd told him about earlier. He'd poured the liquor into two glasses, doctoring her drink before returning to the bedroom. She'd been a bit grumpy when he woke her, but after he kissed her and flattered her with a few well-chosen compliments, she'd taken the glass of whiskey from him and they'd sat in the middle of her bed drinking and talking. It hadn't taken long for her to pass out, and as soon as she did, he'd gotten so excited that he nearly came before he entered her. But he took the time to wrap the black braided ribbon around her neck, as he always did. And he'd touched her, stroked her, his power and pleasure growing stronger with each passing moment.

Two hard lunges and he'd lost it, spewing into the condom. Why was it that with Dinah he couldn't make it last? But what did it matter? Sex was only the preliminary to his real satisfaction, to the total fulfillment he found only when he killed Dinah.

Even now, days later, he could still feel his fingers tightening the ribbon around her neck, cutting off her air, killing her once again. Just the memory of it aroused him, made him hungry to reenact their little game. Now that he'd realized she could come back to him without any long delays, he was eager to rush out and find her again.

Jazzy Talbot. Dinah had intended to use Jazzy's body, but when Jazzy had been viciously attacked, Dinah had left her and sought another body.

How dare some fool try to copy his actions. How dare they try to make the police think Jazzy's attack had been the work of the man the FBI was now referring to as the Redhead Killer. Jazzy was supposed to have been his. Dinah had chosen her. She had simply been waiting on him. He should have been the who killed Jazzy, not some copycat murderer who'd botched the job.

Who the hell had dared to mimic him? If he ever found out, he'd make them pay. Didn't they know he had a unique relationship with Dinah, that only he was allowed to kill her? It was their special game. Just his and hers. In death Dinah belonged to him in a way she never had in life.

She would come back to him again. And soon. Perhaps Jazzy would awaken from her coma so that Dinah could use her body. Or maybe she'd choose Jazzy's twin, although if she did, it would be the first time she'd chosen a woman who wasn't a slut like her. But since other things were changing—

she was returning quickly now and tempting him to be reck-less—why not the type of woman she chose to possess, why not a decent woman, one whose purity might bring him more pleasure than he'd ever known?

Veda stood outside the closed door of Farlan's study and listened, fearing what she would hear. Her husband hadn't been himself since the night Jazzy Talbot had been attacked.

At first she hadn't understood why he'd been so over-wrought when Brian brought him home early the following morning. Farlan had babbled to Brian and her, what he'd said not making much sense. And then after Brian had gone to bed, Farlan had turned to her and said something that had chilled her to the bone.

"She took the twins and left town," Farlan had said. "That's what she told Dodd she was going to do. I sent her the money to take care of her and the babies. Max took the cash—ten thousand dollars—to her apartment in Sevierville and gave her the checkbook for the account I set up for her with the understanding I'd deposit ten thousand every month."

"Yes, I—I remember your telling me what you intended to do."

"She took the ten thousand and then drew from the ac-count for a few years, but suddenly she stopped withdrawing the money each month as she'd been doing."

"Perhaps she found someone else to support her and the children," Veda had said, knowing it was a lie. Knowing Dinah had never seen a dime of that money.

"Or maybe she never got the money—any of it. Or if she did . . ." He'd let his words trail off into silence. "I saw Reve Sorrell tonight. You've seen her. The day you had her here for lunch. You know who she looks like, don't you?"

"No, Farlan, don't think that. It's just your mind playing tricks on you because she has the same color hair."

He'd grabbed her shoulders and shook her. "Reve Sorrell

looks enough like Dinah to be her daughter. I think she is her daughter. And if she is, that means Reve Sorrel and Jazzy Talbot are Dinah's twin babies."

"No, you're wrong. Those babies are—"

"They're what?"

"They're hundreds of miles away from here, grown up and married and living happy lives, just as Dinah is." If only that was true. If only . . .

Farlan had quieted down then and gone to bed, but he'd been restless and moody ever since that night. She thought she'd managed to control his irrational thoughts, but tonight when he'd called for Max and Dodd to come to the house, she'd known what he was going to do. And there hadn't been anything she could do to stop him.

But what bothered her most was the fact that Farlan had included Brian in this meeting. Brian had nothing to do with those old men's sins. He'd been a boy of twelve when Dinah had wreaked havoc in their lives, nearly destroying two marriages and putting six people through pure hell. Her son had been an innocent boy.

Without any warning, the door to Farlan's study opened and he glared down at her. "Come on in. No sense your standing out there listening through the keyhole."

"Whatever you intend to do tonight, please, don't do it," Veda said.

He grabbed her arm and dragged her into his study. "Have a seat, my dear."

She sat in the nearest chair as quickly as she could. The look in Farlan's eyes frightened her. She glanced around the room. Dodd stood by the fireplace, his face as pale as a ghost. Max sat on the sofa nervously twiddling his thumbs. Brian, sitting behind his father's desk, looked right at her and lifted his brows in an inquisitive manner, as if asking, "What's going on?"

"Brian, everyone else here knows what I'm going to tell you, and everyone played a part in this ungodly story." Farlan paced across the room, then turned and stared down at the floor for several seconds before facing his son.

No one said a word. Veda could actually hear her own heart beating over the tick-tock of the antique mantel clock.

"Thirty-two years ago, I went to Knoxville with Dodd for a boys' night out," Farlan said. "For quite some time, Dodd had been making frequent trips to visit a certain young woman."

"God, Farlan, why bring this up now?" Dodd asked.

"Dodd's right," Veda said. "The past is the past. What earthly good will it do any of us for you to bare your soul to Brian? Didn't we all do what we did back then to protect him from the truth?"

Farlan nailed her with a furious glance. "Is protecting our son the reason you tried to commit suicide, the reason you threatened to try again if I didn't do exactly as you said?"

Veda clenched her teeth.

"I don't understand what's going on," Max said. "Is this about . . . about Dinah?"

Veda gasped. She hated the sound of the woman's name.

"Only indirectly," Farlan said. "It's about Dinah's twin daughters."

"Who the hell is Dinah?" Brian asked.

"She was a Knoxville prostitute that I first met when she was barely eighteen," Dodd said. "Dinah was the prettiest thing I'd ever seen. Your Aunt Beth Ann and I were having marital problems. No real excuse, I know, but . . . That's neither here nor there. I fell under Dinah's spell, thought I was in love with her."

"And this woman had twins?" Brian asked. "Were they your children, Uncle Dodd?"

No matter how hard she tried, Reve couldn't make herself feel entirely comfortable at Jazzy's Joint. There hadn't been any real trouble since she'd taken over control of the establishment, due in part to the bouncer she'd hired. A real tough-looking guy named Brownie, someone her assistant Paul Welby had found for her on very short notice and assured her came highly recommended.

Tonight she was as antsy as the proverbial whore in church—more due to the conversation she'd had with Griffin Powell a few days ago than her discomfort at being out front here at Jazzy's Joint. She'd hoped Griffin would call with news about Dinah Collins. Deep inside her was the insane hope that the woman was still alive and had had nothing to do with trying to kill her babies, that she'd be thrilled they were alive and would want to meet them.

And just what were the odds of that happening? Slim to none. Griffin was probably right. Dinah Collins was dead.

"Want a Coke?" Lacy Fallon asked when Reve walked up to the bar.

"A Coke's fine," she said. "In a bottle, please."

Lacy retrieved the drink from the mini-fridge under the bar, snapped off the lid with a bottle opener and handed Reve the icy Coke.

"Are you all right?" Lacy asked.

"Yes, why do you ask?"

"No reason really. It's just you seem to be a million miles away tonight. Worrying about Jazzy?"

Reve nodded. "She's got to come out of that coma soon."

"She will. I know Jazzy. She's too tough to let getting her head cracked open keep her down for long."

"Oh, God, Lacy, why did this have to happen? I was just beginning to know Jazzy, starting to like her . . ."

Lacy looked beyond Reve, her gaze focused on the front door that had just opened and let in a cool puff of night air. "Here comes trouble."

Reve turned in time to see Jacob Butler enter. Now why had Lacy said— Before she finished the thought, Reve saw a curvy little blonde in a pair of skin-tight jeans and a slinky cut-off silk top all but attack Jacob the minute he set foot in Jazzy's Joint.

"Who is she?" Reve asked.

"Mindy Harper. She's one of Jacob's old girlfriends. She's newly divorced and just moved back to Cherokee Pointe. She was asking about him less than half an hour ago."

"Why is she trouble?"

"She's not trouble, except for Jacob. That gal's got an agenda, if you know what I mean. She intends to rope, hog-tie and brand our sheriff. She all but told me so."

Reve shrugged, doing her best to act as if she didn't care. "It's really none of our business, is it?" Reve watched as Mindy practically dragged Jacob onto the dance floor and wrapped herself around him like a cheap coat. A tight-fitting cheap coat.

"If you could see the look on your face, Reve Sorrell, you'd know why nobody would believe what you just said." Lacy nodded toward the twosome on the dance floor. "Jacob's having a pretty difficult time right now, what with three un-solved murder cases and Jazzy's attacker still running free. Don't forget that Jacob's just a man, with a man's weak-nesses and a man's needs. Mindy will stroke his ego, offer him comfort and understanding and then drag him out of here to the nearest bed, unless you do something to stop her."

"Me?" Reve squeaked the question.

"Yes, you, missy."

"And what could I do to prevent Jacob from—" Reve huffed. "I don't give a damn what Jacob does or who he does it with."

Liar, liar, pants on fire.

"Now's your chance," Lacy said. "Hoot Tompkins just cut in. Go save Jacob while you can."

"I'll do no such thing."

"Doesn't look as if you'll have to." Lacy grinned. "He's coming this way." She leaned over and grabbed Reve's arm. "If he asks you to dance, don't say no. The guy needs rescu-ing, and you're the one gal who can do it."

"Evening, ladies," Jacob said as he approached the bar.

"Evening, sheriff," Lacy replied. "Want something to drink?"

"A Coke is fine."

Lacy handed him a bottled Coke, then said, "Reve was just saying how she sure would like to dance, that seeing folks having so much fun, she wished she could kick up her heels a bit. It would do her a world of good."

Reve gasped silently, but when Jacob turned to her, she forced a smile.

He held out his hand. "Care to dance?"

"I—uh—" She looked at Lacy, who nodded and mouthed the word yes. "Yes, I'd like to dance."

He kept his hand in the middle of her back as they walked onto the dance floor. Feeling more awkward than she'd felt at her first formal dance when she was fifteen, Reve sucked in a big breath and went right into Jacob's open arms. He kept a couple of inches between their bodies. Thank God!

The jukebox played an old Patsy Cline number, something titled "He Called Me Baby." The words wove themselves around her, creating images in her mind, thoughts of lying in bed with Jacob and having him call her baby. All night long.

Somehow before she realized it was happening, she was pressed close to Jacob, her body melded with his, her head on his shoulder, his lips in her hair. He moved her slowly around the dance floor, his embrace strong and protective. She'd been afraid it would feel like this in his arms, afraid she'd love having him hold her this way.

The song ended, but Jacob didn't release her, not until Mindy grabbed his arm. He turned to the other woman, one arm still around Reve's waist.

"Hey, big boy, did you forget about me?"

"Nobody ever forgets about you, Mindy."

"Who's she?" Mindy asked.

"This is Reve Sorrell, Jazzy's sister."

Mindy looked Reve over, from head to toe. "I didn't know Jazzy had a sister."

Reve pulled away from Jacob. "If you two will excuse me, I'll—"

Jacob grabbed her wrist. "Don't run off."

"Hey, what's this? You're with me tonight, Jacob," Mindy said, then glowered at Reve. "Get lost, sister. I was here first."

Reve hated this type of scene. It was so white trash, so totally beneath her.

"He's all yours." Reve jerked free and all but ran toward the bar.

When she paused at the bar, her pulse fast, her nerves unsettled, Lacy looked over Reve's shoulder and said, "He's not coming after you. What happened?"

"Mindy laid a claim on Jacob, in no uncertain terms."

"And you let her get away with that?"

"I do not lower myself to squabble over a man with some trashy bleached blonde in a honky-tonk," Reve said.

"Jacob isn't just any man."

"Give me a drink."

"Another Coke?"

"Brandy."

Lacy arched an eyebrow, but hurriedly poured the liquor Reve had requested.

Reve drank the brandy quickly. Too quickly. It burned a path down her throat and hit her belly like a hot potato. She gagged, then coughed several times.

"I'm getting out of here," Reve said. "If anything comes up tonight that you can't handle, I'll be upstairs in Jazzy's apartment."

"Running away won't solve anything," Lacy said. "You'll just spend a sleepless night wondering if Jacob's bonking Mindy."

Reve growled. "Good night, Lacy."

If she didn't get out of here—and fast—she might do something to embarrass herself, something she'd probably regret.

Without looking back, Reve flung open the front door. A

zip of lightning pierced the black night sky. Her heartbeat pounded in her ears as she ran out of Jazzy's Joint, her only thought to get away from Jacob. Crackling thunder exploded in the distance. Light raindrops dappled her hair and face. By the time she reached the outside stairs leading to Jazzy's apartment, the cold rain was coming down in a heavy torrent, soaking through her pullover cashmere sweater, making her regret leaving her jacket behind in her haste to escape. She patted the right side pocket of her wool slacks and sighed with relief when she felt the door key she'd slipped in there earlier this evening.

The words to the old Patsy Cline song once again playing on the jukebox downstairs echoed in her head. More unwanted images appeared in her mind. Thoughts and feelings inspired by a man she wished she'd never met. Images of moss-green eyes peering into her, through her, reaching her very soul. Images of a thin-lipped, wide mouth curving into a mocking smile.

She hated him! Hated him for making her feel things she'd never felt. Hated him for releasing her most basic, most primitive emotions. Hated him for making her doubt herself, for weakening her strong resolve to always be in control. He seemed to derive a great deal of pleasure from tormenting her, as if he knew that one piercing look from him made her go weak in the knees. She'd done her best to hide her overwhelming physical attraction to him. Ever since returning to Cherokee Pointe, she had fought an internal battle against her own deep-seated desire for a man totally wrong for her.

For pity's sake, she didn't like him and he didn't like her. They despised each other, didn't they?

Reve stood outside Jazzy's apartment, the rain drenching her, and fumbled in her pants pocket for the door key. Her hand trembled as she tried to insert the key in the lock. Damn, what was wrong with her? What difference did it make that Jacob Butler was down there in Jazzy's Joint dancing with some floozy? Touching her with those big, hard hands of his. Nuzzling her ear. Whispering sweet nothings.

She dropped the key. It hit the floor and bounced off the stoop onto the first step. Tears clouded her vision.

Get hold of yourself! You're acting like an idiot. You don't want his hands on you, touching, caressing. You don't want him. You don't, don't, don't . . .

From down below, she could still hear music wafting up from Jazzy's Joint. It was that same damn Patsy Cline song playing on the old jukebox. Again. Had Jacob punched in the number one more time? Probably. He must really like that song. Either that or he'd realized the words to that particular song had really gotten to her. It was so like Jacob to taunt her. She felt as if that was all he'd been doing since the first moment they met.

I hope when he takes that bleached blond bitch home tonight, he can't get it up. I hope she laughs in his face.

Yeah, like that would ever happen. She'd bet all her millions that he'd never had a problem getting it up. Not that big, savage stud. Her body tightened at the thought of Jacob's erection. Once again images flashed through her mind. Jacob, naked, aroused, coming toward her.

Another streak of lightning illuminated the night sky, and a boom of thunder warned that the storm was intensifying, coming closer. Reve swallowed hard, then bent over to pick up the house key. But just as she reached for the small key lying on the wet step, a large, dark hand shot out and grabbed the key. Every nerve in Reve's body screamed. She lifted her gaze and looked into a pair of slanted green eyes. Jacob Butler's eyes.

"You shouldn't be standing out here in the rain," he told her. "You're getting all wet."

When he stood to his full six-five height and reached out to wipe the raindrops from her cheek, Reve shivered and backed away from him. Her hips pressed against the railing that surrounded the outer edges of the stoop.

Say something, she told herself. *Don't just stand here staring at him like an idiot, trembling like a frightened virgin on the verge of being sacrificed.* But her mind went blank. Her throat tightened.

He reached around her, his arm brushing her side, and inserted the key in the lock, turned the doorknob and opened the door. When she didn't move—couldn't move—he grasped her arm just above her elbow and pulled her to him. Her body stopped just short of touching his, a hairbreadth between them. His mouth twitched in an almost smile.

"Get inside," he told her, his voice a low, deep rumble.

She jerked away from him and rushed into the apartment, her wet feet making moist tracks on the floor.

Please, dear God, make him go away.

"You should get out of those wet clothes." He came up behind her, but didn't touch her.

Nervous, on the verge of hyperventilating, Reve gasped for air. If he touched her, she would die. But on the other hand, if he didn't touch her, she would die.

CHAPTER 25

"Please, let's not do this." Veda looked from Farlan to Dodd and then to Max. "Didn't we all suffer enough thirty years ago? Do we have to open old wounds?"

"I agree." Dodd looked imploringly at Farlan. "I can't understand why you'd—"

"Because I believe that Jazzy Talbot and Reve Sorrell are Dinah's twins," Farlan said. "When I met Reve Sorrell at the hospital the night Jazzy was attacked, I knew then that she was Dinah's daughter. The resemblance is remarkable."

A deadly hush fell over the room. Max's eyes widened, his expression a combination of shock and fear. Dodd shook his head, denial written plainly on his face.

"I've told Farlan that it's his imagination," Veda said. "There might be some vague similarities, but that's all. Dinah moved away and took her babies with her thirty years ago. There's no way—"

"Good God, are you telling me that Jazzy Talbot is my cousin?" Brian asked. "How is that possible? She's Sally Talbot's niece. She's lived here in Cherokee County all her life. If she was Uncle Dodd's child, wouldn't he have known?

And what about Max? If he knew this Dinah person, wouldn't he have seen the resemblance before now?"

"I never made the connection." Max wrung his hands nervously. "I had no idea Jazzy was a twin. If I had known, I might have seen something, but—" he looked directly at Farlan. "What are you going to do about—I mean, if they are Dinah's twins, will you—?"

"What's the big deal?" Brian asked. "So Uncle Dodd fathered a set of twins thirty years ago. Either he acknowledges them as his children or he doesn't. It's not like the truth is going to hurt anybody."

Brian's calm, indifferent attitude amazed Veda. Knowing how detrimental the complete truth could be to him, Veda thanked God that he was unaware of those past events, that he'd been spared the memories that haunted her.

"You're assuming the twins were mine," Dodd said.

"Yes, I—" Brian stared quizzically at his uncle. "Are you saying they weren't your children?" When Dodd didn't reply, Brian looked to his father. "Who—?"

"The twins were—are—my daughters," Farlan confessed.

"Damn!" Brian turned to his mother. "And you knew?"

Veda didn't think she could bear another moment of this insanity. Everything she'd done, she'd done to protect her son, but if Farlan insisted on taking this revelation to its logical conclusion, how would the outcome affect Brian? He had always been Farlan's only child, the heir to the MacKinnon fortune, but if Farlan proclaimed Reve and Jazzy as his children, what would happen? Thirty years ago that damn Dinah had done enough to hurt her family, to put Brian's future in jeopardy. She had to find a way to end this nightmare before it went any further.

"Your mother and I came to an agreement," Farlan told Brian. "When I explained to Dinah that I could never marry her, could never leave Veda and you, she agreed that the best thing for her to do was take the twins and move away. And that's what she did. Or at least that's what I thought she did."

Farlan zeroed in on Max. "You took her ten thousand in cash. And she drew on the account I set up for her for several years. Isn't that right?"

Sheer terror in his eyes, Max looked away and stared at the floor.

"Answer me, damn it," Farlan said. "That's right, isn't it? I entrusted you to handle the matter for me, as my lawyer and a member of my family."

"I—I took the money to her apartment, just as you'd instructed me to do," Max replied. "But she wasn't there. She and the babies were gone. She'd already moved away. I asked some of the neighbors, and nobody had any idea where she'd gone. She hadn't left a forwarding address or anything."

Rage burned in Farlan's eyes. Veda cringed. Oh, God, she had never dreamed this day would come—the day that Farlan would find out that Max had stolen hundreds of thousands of dollars from him, that Dinah and her twins had never seen a dime of the money he'd intended for them. Of course, she had known the truth all these years, but she'd kept Max's dirty little secret because it had been to her advantage to do so. If Farlan had known Dinah and those babies had simply disappeared, he would have hired a private detective to find them.

"I'm sorry." Max still couldn't bring himself to look Farlan in the eyes. "You know how I was always short on money back then. When I couldn't find Dinah, I thought what harm would it do for me to keep the money. I'd just intended to keep the ten thousand, but then when she never did show up asking for the money, I—I decided to forge her signature and withdraw the money you put into her account each month."

"Are you telling me that Dinah and my daughters never received the money?" Farlan's features were contorted with rage, his hands tightened into huge fists. "Why did you suddenly stop withdrawing money from the account? You told me that there was no need to keep depositing money into the account because Dinah hadn't withdrawn anything from the account in quite some time. But it was a lie. All lies!"

"I don't know why I did it. And I stopped because . . . well, I guess I got scared. And I started feeling really guilty. After all, Farlan, you've always been good to me, helped me and—"

"What do you know about Dinah's disappearance? About the fact that those babies were abandoned?" Farlan charged Max, grabbed his coat lapels and shook him. "Answer me, damn you! I trusted you to help me take care of Dinah and my daughters."

Dodd interceded, grabbing Farlan by the arm and jerking him away from Max. "None of that matters, now, does it? If Jazzy Talbot and Reve Sorrell are Dinah's twins, then I'd say that they are what matters now. Everything else is unimportant. You can deal with Max later, once this current crisis has been handled."

Farlan nodded. "You're right. I have to find out for sure if they're my daughters. I think I should go to Jacob Butler and tell him everything."

"No!" Veda screamed. Had her husband lost his mind?

"I agree with Veda," Max said. "What will going to the sheriff accomplish?"

Farlan speared Max with his gaze. "You, Maxwell, don't have a say in this matter. You'll be lucky if I don't bring you up on charges."

"Farlan, you wouldn't," Veda said. "Max is family. We protect family."

"Jazzy and Reve may well be family, too. Someone tried to kill Jazzy," Farlan said. "And there's a possibility that it wasn't the serial killer. That means—"

"Of course it was the serial killer," Veda said. "She's a redheaded slut who got dumped in the creek, just like those other women."

"Don't ever call my daughter a slut again," Farlan told his wife. "Do you understand?"

Oh, yes, she understood. Farlan would defend and protect Dinah's children, just as he had tried to take care of her. And he would love those girls, just as he'd loved Dinah.

"She's not your daughter," Veda replied in a voice far calmer than she felt. Inside, she was a mass of jittery nerves. "But even if she is, she's still a slut. Just like Dinah."

"Dinah was the sweetest, most loving young woman I've ever known." Farlan focused all his attention on Veda. "She knew how to love." He swallowed the emotions lodged in his throat. "She loved me."

"She loved your money, you damn fool!" Veda stood to face her husband.

"No, you're wrong. A man knows when a woman loves him. Dinah loved me. You're the one who loves my money. You've been obsessed with being Mrs. Farlan MacKinnon all our married life. Your one thought has been to retain your position as my wife, to keep your hands on my money."

"For Brian! Not for myself. He's your son."

"And Dinah's twins are my daughters."

"You say that as if you're proud of the fact that you fathered some trashy whore's two bastard children."

When Farlan lifted his hand to strike Veda, Brian stepped between them. Farlan's arm froze in midair.

"Don't," Brian said calmly. "You don't want to hit Mother."

Veda could not stem the tide of tears cascading down her cheeks. How was it possible that the pain was as fresh and raw this very moment as it had been all those years ago when she'd discovered that not only had her husband been unfaithful, but that he had fathered his mistress's babies?

Farlan stared at Brian, his eyes glazed. He lowered his arm.

"And you don't want to go to Sheriff Butler," Brian said. "What would that accomplish? If something happened to Dinah and her twins years ago, you know nothing about it. None of us do. So how would making some personal confession to the sheriff do you or anyone else any good?"

"I want proof that those girls are mine," Farlan said. "And if somebody hurt Dinah . . . If somebody tried to hurt those babies . . ."

"I suggest that if you're hell-bent on revealing the truth, you should contact Griffin Powell," Dodd said. "Reve Sorrell hired him to investigate her past, didn't she? Speak to Mr. Powell, tell him whatever you need to tell him to see if he will reveal what he knows."

"He'll go straight to Reve Sorrell with whatever you tell him," Veda said.

"Probably." Dodd looked at her with sadness and sympathy in his eyes. "But if Reve and Jazzy are Dinah's daughters, it's only a matter of time before Mr. Powell finds out and once he does, then everyone will know."

"They won't know that Farlan is their father, not unless he makes some foolish confession." Veda hated the desperation in her voice, but God help her, she was desperate. Desperate to save Brian's inheritance, desperate to save her marriage, and desperate to keep the truth buried in the past.

"I suggest that we all sleep on this tonight," Brian said. "And tomorrow, when everyone's emotions have settled down a bit, then Father can decide what he wants to do."

"I agree." Dodd patted Brian on the back. "That's a sensible suggestion."

"Yeah, yeah, sure," Max said. "Sounds right to me."

"Mother?" Brian slipped his arm around Veda's shoulders.

Her precious son. Always loyal to her.

"Of course, whatever Farlan decides to do, we will support him." What choice did she have? She hadn't come this far, kept so many deadly secrets, to lose everything now. But she knew exactly what she had to do, no matter what Farlan decided. And she had to do it soon. Very soon.

Touch me, her mind screamed. *Dear God, touch me.* She was wound so tightly, her body so hungry for him, that she feared she would climax the moment he put his hands on her.

How had this happened? How had cool, calm and in-control Reve Sorrell become nothing more than a woman in heat? Not in her entire life had she ever wanted anything as desperately as she wanted Jacob Butler. Her few sexual experiences had been with men her social equal, men with whom she shared a long-standing personal relationship. The sex had been good—wasn't sex always good?—but right at this moment she couldn't remember what those other men looked like. Hell, she couldn't even remember their names.

Jacob Butler's presence filled her whole world. Every centimeter. Leaving no room for anything or anyone else. And that was what she had feared most—allowing him to dominate her. He was a man accustomed to taking what he wanted, to consuming all he needed, and doing it with a passion that Reve had never experienced.

When he inched closer to her, she felt the heat of his big body behind her, his chest almost touching her back. She shivered, more from fear than the damp coolness of her wet body. Standing perfectly still, holding her breath, she waited.

He touched her. Trembling from head to toe, she sighed loudly. Warmth spread through her, from where his arms circled her waist and his big hands clutched the edge of her sweater to her entire body. Every muscle. Every nerve. Every inch of flesh. Whether she leaned back against him or he pulled her, she didn't know. Didn't care. He surrounded her, encompassed her. Allowing her head to fall backward onto his chest, she closed her eyes and savored the moment. He lowered his mouth just enough to kiss her temple, then moved on to nuzzle her ear.

"Let's get you out of these wet clothes . . . baby."

Baby! Dear Lord, he'd called her baby.

Her femininity clenched and unclenched. Tingles of pure sexual desire set her on fire. Hot. Burning hot. His touch was electric.

And when he eased the edge of her sweater up over her belly, she didn't protest; instead she lifted her arms and allowed him to pull it over her head and off. Feeling as if she'd been drugged, she rubbed herself against him as he undid the snap of her bra and eased the straps down her shoulders. She quivered, high on passion, her flesh super-sensitive. He kissed first one shoulder and then the other, just before he removed her bra completely and tossed it aside. His huge, rough hands cupped her breasts, lifting them as if he were weighing them. Her breasts filled his palms to overflowing.

He scraped his thumbs over her nipples and elicited a cry of pure pleasure-pain from her lips. While she writhed against him, wild with need, he kissed her neck, then licked a path downward to her shoulder as he continued tormenting her nipples.

Acting entirely on instinct, she turned in his arms and reached for the buttons on his shirt, wanting—needing—to touch his bare skin. When her hands trembled so badly that she couldn't undo the first button, he grabbed her hands and eased them up and under his shirt, flat against his chest. Then he undid the buttons and tossed his shirt aside. The moment his shirt hit the floor, he grasped her by the waist and hauled her up against him. Naked breasts to naked chest.

She loved the feel of him, of that smooth, hard chest, that taut flesh. He exuded an aura of strength and pure masculine power unlike anything she'd known. He was, as his ancestors eons ago, a primitive male, now in his prime. And she had never felt more like a woman, as if she ruled the world, as if she could control this man with a look . . . a touch . . . a word.

Lifting her hand to drape his neck, she brought her gaze up to meet his and saw the depth of his desire.

"Jacob." His name came softly, like a whisper. Almost like a prayer.

He kissed her then, kissed her the way he had in her dreams, with a primeval force that shook her to the very core of her being. Overwhelming in intensity, consuming her totally, his mouth took hers, but the moment she responded, opening her mouth freely for his invasion, his entire demeanor gentled. The tenderness that followed the brutal storm conquered her completely. She was his. Heart, mind and body. And she understood, without any doubts, that for this night, he belonged to her and her alone.

They kissed until she went weak in the knees and gasped for air. She couldn't get enough of him, couldn't get as close as she wanted. Only by joining her body to his could she reach the level of intimacy she craved.

When he cupped her buttocks and lifted her up and into his erection, she tossed back her head and keened, the sound one of complete surrender. Surrender not only to him, but to herself, her own human needs. His mouth came down to one breast, his tongue flicking back and forth over the nipple. She grasped his shoulders to steady herself and nearly came unraveled when he suckled her.

He lifted his head. She eased her palms down his arms and captured his hands in hers. "Make love to me." The plea came from deep within her, emerging from the center of her soul.

"All night long," he said, then swooped her up into his arms.

Startled by the suddenness of his actions, she gasped, then threw her arm around his neck and nuzzled her head against his shoulder. He carried her into the bedroom, placed her on the edge of the bed and knelt in front of her. Without asking her permission, he removed her shoes and knee highs, then undid the button on her slacks, unzipped them and tugged them over her hips and off. She sat before him, shivering with anticipation, longing for him to hurry and finish the job and yet at the same time wanting to savor these moments, to make them last forever.

His next move surprised her. Instead of removing her panties, he stood and divested himself of his pants and boxer shorts. Standing over her, a man of hard muscle and bronze flesh, he allowed her to study him, to caress him with her gaze. He was the most beautiful man she'd ever seen. Not beautiful in any traditional way. His features were harsh, as if chiseled from stone and his body was the same. Everything about him evoked power. Especially his large, jutting penis. Her hand trembled uncontrollably as she reached out to touch him. First his chest. His tiny male nipples went pebble hard when she teased them. As he waited, allowing her unparalleled pleasure, he stood as still as a statue. She skimmed her open palms over his flat belly, down his slender hips and over his long, sinewy thighs. She deliberately avoided touching his sex, but whenever her fingertips got close, his penis jerked, almost as if it was begging for her touch.

After withdrawing her hands from his body, she eased to her feet and took off her panties. They were equals now. Both completely naked. Both thoroughly aroused.

He placed his open hand over her mound and squeezed. Tension tightened inside her, damn near close to the breaking point.

"You're almost ready," he said, his words low and deep.

"I am ready. Oh, God, I'm ready."

She held out her arms to him.

He toppled her into the bed sideways and came down over her. He kissed her mouth, but not long enough or thoroughly enough before his lips and tongue explored her from head to toe. And then, as he worked his way back up her body, he spread her thighs apart and petted her. Before she realized his intent, his mouth had replaced his hand, his tongue pressing and probing. Licking and sucking. Driving her wild. Within seconds she came, gushing with completion, crying out as her body shook with release.

Suddenly Jacob was gone, depriving her of his heat and strength. Weak and trembling from her orgasm and unable to do more than lift her head, she turned to seek him and found him removing a foil packet from his discarded pants. She watched in fascination as he sheathed his wet, rock-hard penis with the condom. With the aftershocks of her orgasm tingling through her, she opened her arms and her body to him when he returned to her. He lifted her hips in his big hands and thrust deep and hard, taking her with one swift lunge that united their bodies, making them one. No words were necessary. Anything either could have said would have been redundant. Their bodies spoke in a language all their own and were saying everything that needed to be said.

The feel of him inside her was ecstasy. There was no other way to describe it. Before he'd entered her, she had been empty. And now she was complete, her body made for his and his for hers. The fit was perfect. For several minutes he went about their lovemaking slowly, his movements gentle and coaxing. But when she responded, urging him into action, telling him without words that she wanted all he could give, that she could take everything he had, Jacob gave himself over completely to the animal inside him. He pumped into her with savage force and she loved it. She loved him. Loved the feel of him, the taste of him.

His long back hair fell to his shoulders and feathered over her upper body. They mated wildly, Reve discovering that when it came to this man, she was no lady. She had never known it could be like this. And she wanted more. She wanted it all. Everything!

Only seconds before she realized that Jacob was on the verge of climaxing, she felt her own body building to a second orgasm. As he hammered into her, she clung to him for dear life, knowing that his hunger for fulfillment would appease her own desire as well.

He came, like a raging bull, grunting and snorting, his whole body shaking with the force of his release. When he was spent, Reve came a second time, this climax more earthshattering than the first. He collapsed on top of her, then eased off to her side and wrapped her in his arms. She hugged him and kissed him and repeated his name over and over again.

He caressed her naked hip and nuzzled her neck as he growled, "Baby, baby . . ."

She never thought one word could sound so sweet. And she'd never dreamed that a man could ever make her feel this good.

CHAPTER 26

If it was true, if Reve Sorrell and Jazzy Talbot were Dinah's daughters, then what would he do? Recently the thought had crossed his mind that they might be Dinah's twins, but he'd dismissed the notion because he'd believed those babies had been disposed of shortly after he'd killed Dinah for the first time. Now he wasn't so sure. What if Slim hadn't done as he'd been told? What if everything he thought was the truth was really a lie? He had to find out, had to be sure.

This was all Dinah's fault. If only she had loved him and not the great Farlan MacKinnon, she'd still be alive. And she would be his. They would be together now. They would be happy.

After undressing, he walked into the shower, savoring the feel of the warm water peppering his body. Why had he never paid closer attention to Jazzy Talbot? He didn't think he'd ever actually taken a good look at her face. Oh, he'd ogled her dynamite body, just like all the other men in Cherokee County, but he'd seldom looked farther than her big boobs and her long, slim legs. Dinah had had a great figure, too, only she'd been a much smaller woman than either Jazzy or Reve Sorrell.

But then, with a father the size of Farlan MacKinnon, it was no surprise that those women possessed more Amazonian proportions.

He chuckled as he soaped his body with the imported hand-milled soap he preferred. Just to think that, all these years, the closest thing to Dinah might have been right here in his own hometown, right under his nose. Had Dinah deliberately led him away from Cherokee Pointe time and again, led him away from her precious daughter?

"You didn't want me to kill her, did you, my darling? That's why you chose all those other women."

His hand lingered lovingly over his penis, lathering and rinsing, then discarding the soap. He touched himself as he thought about Dinah.

If the truth about Farlan having fathered Dinah's babies came out—and it seemed inevitable that it would—how would it affect him? Would the authorities put everyone associated with Farlan, all the members of his family, under a microscope and examine their lives? He couldn't risk anyone poking his nose too closely into his personal business. He'd been careful, but he wasn't perfect. There had been times when he'd made mistakes.

"Dinah, Dinah, why did you force me to kill you?"

His hand circled his erection. He sighed as he thought about that day when he'd forced himself on her. She'd tried to fight him, but she'd still been weak from having given birth to twins. Besides, she'd been a small, slender woman and easily subdued after he'd hit her a couple of times.

His mind filled with Dinah, thoughts of fucking her and killing her exciting him more and more, he came suddenly. He could feel his hands twisting the black braided ribbon around her neck, choking the life out of her. He should have known that very first time that once would never be enough. She wasn't the kind of woman who'd stay dead. And apparently her two little redheaded mongrels were just like her—

they wouldn't stay dead either. But he could kill them, just as he'd killed Dinah. And if necessary, he could kill them over and over again.

As he washed the cum from his hand and penis, he considered his options. Both Jazzy and Reve had to die. And die at his hands, not the victims of some copycat killer with delusions of grandeur. Jazzy was in the hospital, still in a coma. Helpless. But she was surrounded by people twenty-four hours a day, he reminded himself. *Wait. Wait to see if she recovers. She might never come out of that coma. There's even a chance she could still die.*

But he didn't want her to die. Not yet. She should be his victim. Jazzy and Reve should be his prey. He would kill each of them, just as he'd killed Dinah. He'd take them away from Farlan as he'd taken their mother away from him.

After he killed them, would Jazzy and Reve come back again and again, just as Dinah did? How odd would that be? Three redheads coming back from the dead to haunt him, to entice him, to give him a pleasure almost beyond bearing.

He had to be very careful not to draw attention to himself in any way. But he had to get rid of Dinah's daughters. Wouldn't it be true justice if he could somehow frame Farlan MacKinnon for their murders?

Farlan had to call in several favors in order to get Griffin Powell's home telephone number. He was determined to speak to the renowned private investigator who was probing into Reve Sorrell's past. And he intended to speak to the man tonight. After all these years of wondering about Dinah and the babies, of telling himself that they were all three well and happy, he now suspected a horrible truth. Something terrible had happened to Dinah, and someone had taken the twins away from her and left them for dead. Apparently, everyone in Cherokee County knew part of the truth about Jazzy and

Reve's infancy. But what they didn't know, what no one would ever suspect, was that he was their father.

He'd never forget the first time he saw Dinah. Prettiest little thing on earth. But he'd known she was a prostitute, a teenage prostitute who'd been servicing Dodd for months. Dodd had thought he was in love with the girl, had been totally infatuated with her. But his brother-in-law had begun feeling guilty and had wanted to find a way to end their relationship. That was why he'd taken Farlan along that night, to help keep his courage bolstered so he could end things with Dinah.

With Farlan backing him, Dodd had said good-bye to Dinah that night and walked away, intending to never come back. For days afterward, Farlan hadn't been able to get the girl out of his mind. Finally, two weeks later, he'd gone into Knoxville to see her. He'd wound up paying for her services for the entire night. After that, he'd made weekly trips to see her. Then, when he fell in love with her and asked her to get out of the business and belong to him exclusively, she admitted Dodd was still coming to see her.

"Do you love Dodd?" he'd asked.

"No, of course I don't. I'm fond of him. He's a kind, dear man, but I don't love any of my customers. Screwing guys is what I do for a living."

Farlan had grabbed her and shook her. "What about me? Is that all I am to you—just another customer?"

Tears had flooded her eyes as she shook her head. "It's different with you. You know it is. I think I fell for you that first night. Oh, damn it, Farlan, I'm crazy in love with you."

He'd taken her with him that very night and they'd stayed together in a motel in Sevierville. The next day, he'd called Max, fresh out of law school, and had him look for a place for her to live. He'd found her a nice apartment on Hyatt Street and took out a year's lease, paid for in cash. After that, Farlan got away from Cherokee Pointe as often as possible to be with her. And he had assigned Max to look after all of Dinah's financial needs.

Max. The little weasel. He'd trusted him to take care of Dinah, especially there at the end when she'd planned to take the babies and leave town.

"Farlan?" Veda called from the doorway.

He glanced at her and frowned. "Go away. Leave me alone."

"Please, we need to talk."

"We have nothing to talk about."

"Yes, we do. We have to talk about Brian." She came into the room, but hesitated several feet away from him.

"Brian is a grown man. He doesn't need you to protect him."

"If you're thinking of doing something foolish—of proclaiming those women as your daughters—then I most certainly have to protect my son. Our son. And you know Brian is yours. With those twins, you never could have been certain they were yours. For all you know, they could have been Dodd's or Max's or God knows who else could have fathered them. Dinah was a prostitute. She slept with men for money. She used you, Farlan. She never loved you."

He slapped Veda. Struck her across the mouth, the force of his blow cutting her lip and making it bleed. She cried out, then drew up into a fat ball, her blue eyes wide with fear and shock. He'd never laid a hand on her in all the years they'd been married. The fact that he'd struck her tonight shamed him.

"I'm sorry, Veda. I never meant to hit you. I never meant to hurt you. Not ever."

She lifted her head and looked at him, tears swimming in her eyes. "You want Reve Sorrell and Jazzy Talbot to be Dinah's twins, don't you? If Dinah could walk through the door right now, you'd take her back, wouldn't you?"

"Don't do this to yourself," Farlan said.

"I won't give you up," she told him. "And I won't allow you to take anything away from Brian."

"Go to bed, Veda. Leave me alone. We can talk again in the morning, after we've both had time to think things through more thoroughly." When he reached out to touch her, she cringed and withdrew from him. He nodded understanding, knowing she couldn't bear his touch now, not even a gentle one. "I'd never do anything to hurt Brian. You, of all people, must know to what lengths I'd go to protect him. I gave up the woman I loved and my two daughters so that Brian wouldn't have to lose his mother when he was just a boy. You were so crazy back then that you'd have actually killed yourself. You weren't thinking of our son when you tried to commit suicide, only of yourself."

Straightening her back, squaring her shoulders and tilting her chin, Veda glared at him, then turned and walked out of his study. He sighed heavily the moment she left, thankful to be alone again. Not hesitating, he picked up the phone on his desk and dialed Griffin Powell's private number.

"Powell residence," a masculine voice answered on the third ring. A butler? A personal assistant?

"I'd like to speak to Griffin Powell. It's urgent business."

"Who may I say is calling?"

"Farlan MacKinnon, of MacKinnon Media."

"Yes, sir. Please wait just a moment."

Farlan waited. And waited. He watched the clock on his desk. One minute. Two. Three. He wasn't accustomed to being kept waiting. Four minutes.

"Mr. MacKinnon, this is Griffin Powell. How may I help you?"

"I know that you're investigating the background of Reve Sorrell and Jazzy Talbot, that you're trying to locate their birth mother."

"I would ask how you came by this information," Powell said. "But I suppose everyone in Cherokee County knows about the twins' search for their biological parents."

"I may have information that can help you discover their identity."

"Is that right? And just what information would that be?"

"There was a young woman named Dinah Collins who gave birth to twin daughters thirty years ago. I have reason to believe Dinah is Reve and Jazzy's birth mother."

"What reason do you have to believe this, Mr. MacKinnon?"

"Because I saw Reve Sorrell for the first time recently. And I knew Dinah Collins. Ms. Sorrell is a taller, larger woman than Dinah, but her facial features are almost identical, and her hair is the exact shade of auburn red."

"How well did you know Dinah Collins?" Powell asked, and Farlan caught a hint of something odd in the man's voice.

"You already know that Reve and Jazzy are Dinah's daughters, don't you?"

"I know more than that," Powell said. "I've narrowed the identity of their father down to three men. Only three men were known to have visited Dinah Collins at her apartment on Hyatt Street in Sevierville in the year before she gave birth to twin daughters. Judge Dodd Keefer, Maxwell Fennel and—"

"Me."

"I plan to contact Ms. Sorrell in the morning with this information. Is it possible you could narrow down the field even more so that I can give her only one name—her biological father's name?"

"Tell her that Farlan MacKinnon is her father. And tell her that I want to see her, talk to her, explain to her why . . ." Farlan choked on unshed tears. How could he ever make his daughter understand why he had abandoned her and her twin? How could he ever prove to her that he not only had loved their mother, but that he had loved them?

"Knowing Ms. Sorrell, I'm sure she'll ask for a DNA test."

"I'll agree to a DNA test. And the sooner the better."

"Mr. MacKinnon, out of curiosity, what is your blood type?"

"My blood type?"

"Yes, Dinah Collins was O-negative."

"I'm AB-negative," Farlan said. "Why?"

"Reve Sorrell and Jazzy Talbot are AB-negative."

Farlan gasped for air. They *were* Dinah's babies. His and Dinah's twins. "Please, tell Reve that I . . . I want to see her."

Jacob awoke slowly, languidly. The bedside lamp was still on, casting a forty-watt glow over the room. When he stretched, the covers slid off his shoulders and down to mid-chest. He turned over on his side and stared at the woman sleeping beside him. She looked like Jazzy. Same features—nose, mouth, chin. Same long neck. But he'd never gotten a hard-on just being near Jazzy. The two women might be identical twins, but when he looked at Reve, all he saw was Reve, despite her striking physical resemblance to her sister.

He wanted to touch her. Lying there so peacefully, her long hair tousled, her face void of makeup, her body warm and inviting, she posed an irresistible temptation. Having her once hadn't been enough. He wanted her again. Wanted her right now. And he'd probably want her again in the morning.

Reve Sorrell might be a refined lady outside the bedroom, but naked and aroused, she was a hellcat. Every step of the way, every touch, every kiss, every passionate exchange, she'd given as good as she got.

He'd wanted her more than he'd ever wanted another woman. And his gut instincts told him that she'd wanted him just as badly. They'd gone at each other like a pair of wild animals. This time he wanted to go slower, easier, make it last longer.

Jacob tugged the covers off her left shoulder, then kissed the smattering of tiny freckles that dotted her flesh there. She sighed. He slid his hand beneath the cover and cupped one large breast. She sighed again. When he teased her nipple, she wriggled and groaned.

He grinned, then yanked the covers off her completely. While she was awakening, he cupped her mound and lowered his head to one breast. She gasped. He slipped two fingers between her moist feminine lips and inserted them inside her.

"Jacob." His name came out whisper soft and sultry.

"Yeah, baby?"

She turned into him, a sexy smile on her face. "Let's make love again."

He laughed. "Lady, there's nothing in this world I'd rather do."

When he took her into his arms, she slid one leg over his and burrowed against him as he sought her mouth. The kiss began sweet and tender, but within seconds turned hot and wild. He kicked the bunched covers to the foot of the bed. Still kissing him, her hands raking over him frantically, she crawled on top of him and settled her thighs on either side of his hips.

"You want to ride me, baby?" he asked.

"Oh, I'm going to ride you, Sheriff Butler. I'm going to ride you hard and fast." She rose up enough to center her body perfectly over his, her intention apparently to ease herself down over his erection.

Before she could take charge, he grabbed her buttocks, then thrust up and into her. Gasping when he took her completely, she tossed back her head and keened softly.

"You wanted it, you got it," he told her, doing his best not to move once he was buried to the hilt inside her. God, she was hot and wet and tight. If he moved at all right now, he was liable to come.

Leaning forward, positioning herself so that her hands splayed out on either side of his head and her tits hung over his mouth, Reve began rocking back and forth, then up and down. She was killing him. It was all he could do to slow the inevitable, but he couldn't wait much longer. While he caressed her hips, loving the feel of her soft, supple skin, he lifted his head and opened his mouth to capture one tight, begging nipple. He gave each breast equal attention, alternating back and forth. When she increased the tempo, he suckled one breast and tormented the other with his fingertips. He had to bring her to the breaking point where he was heading right now, and hanging on only by a thread. And he had to do it fast.

He'd wanted to make this second time last longer, but God Almighty, it wasn't possible. He was on the verge of losing it. And if she didn't come any minute now, he wouldn't be able to wait for her. Reve Sorrell turned him inside out and every which way but loose.

He felt her tightening around him, knew her body was swelling as it gushed with moisture. She took complete charge, seeking and finding what she wanted, taking her own pleasure. She whimpered and shook, then cried out when her climax hit. That was all he could take, the final blow that sent him toppling over the edge. When he came, his ears rang and he thought the top of his head would blow off.

While he groaned and jetted into her, he suddenly realized he hadn't used any protection. Damn, he'd never done anything that stupid. But then he'd never lost his head over a woman the way he had Reve. She was such bad news for him. But right this minute, he didn't give a damn. He felt too good. Had enjoyed loving her far too much to have any regrets. Time enough for recriminations in the morning.

She lay on top of him, sprawled out as if they were permanently attached. Using his foot, he drew the edge of the covers up far enough in the bed to manage to grab them and drag them up and over Reve.

"I'm too heavy," she said. "I should—"

He wrapped his arms around her and held tightly. "Baby, don't you dare move. You stay right where you are."

Sighing, curling herself around him, she kissed his neck, his ear and then sought his mouth. With her lips almost on his, she said, "We're going to do this again later, aren't we?"

"You bet your sweet ass we are. I haven't had nearly enough of you."

"I feel the same way."

"Then you'd better go to sleep and get a little rest so you'll be ready for the next time."

Smiling dreamily, she settled on top of him. He'd never known a sweeter weight against his body. As far as he was concerned, they could stay like this from now on. He laid his hand possessively over her butt, then closed his eyes.

When the telephone rang, Jacob woke with a start, not realizing at first that he'd fallen off to sleep. In his effort to reach the phone, he toppled Reve off him and onto the bed. By the time he managed to grab the receiver, Reve was wide awake.

"Yeah?" Jacob said.

"Who's this?" a male voice asked.

"Who's this?" Jacob countered.

"Jacob, is that you?"

He suddenly recognized the voice. "Yeah, Caleb, it's me."

"Keeping Reve company?" Caleb chuckled.

"What's up? Why are you calling? Has something happened to Jazzy?"

Reve sat straight up and grabbed Jacob's arm. "What's wrong?"

"Yeah, something's happened all right," Caleb said. "Jazzy woke up about five minutes ago. She woke up, looked right at me and smiled. The nurses are in there with her now, and they've called Dr. Behel and Dr. Cornelius."

Emotion knotted in Jacob's chest. A lot of prayers had been answered, including his. "I'll bring Reve right on over there." After hanging up the phone, he turned and grabbed Reve by the shoulders. She stared at him, hope and fear in her eyes. "Jazzy's come out of the coma. She looked at Caleb and smiled."

Reve threw her arms around Jacob and hugged him as

tears streamed down her cheeks. "This is the best possible news. Jazzy's awake. She's really going to be all right, isn't she?"

Jacob pulled back, cupped Reve's face in his hands and kissed her. "Yeah, baby, Jazzy's going to be all right."

CHAPTER 27

Reve was glad to have a big, strong man at her side, someone who so obviously had appointed himself her protector. In the past she'd never felt the need for a man to complete her life. Perhaps that was because she'd never met a man who was her match or, in the case of this man, more than her match. Jacob wasn't her social or financial equal by any means, but that really didn't seem to matter. At least not to her. Odd how she'd always believed it did matter, that those would be the defining factors in choosing a mate.

"You okay, Reve?" Jacob asked, his arm tightly surrounding her shoulders as they rode up on the elevator at County General.

She nodded, then looked at him and smiled. "I'm more than okay and for more than one reason."

When he hugged her to him, she closed her arms around his waist and laid her head on his chest. He kissed the top of her head.

"I can't wait to see Jazzy," Reve said, her lips grazing the soft, supple suede of his jacket. "I'm so thankful she's come out of the coma."

Before Jacob had time to do more than hug her again, the

elevator doors opened. Reve turned, grasped his hand and together they made their way past the nurses' station and directly to the ICU area. They found Caleb pacing the floor in the hallway. When he saw them, he smiled broadly and hurried toward them. He grabbed Reve, lifted her off her feet and swung her around. She laughed and hugged him after he set her back on her feet, happily sharing his exuberance.

"She's awake," Caleb said. "She opened those big brown eyes and smiled at me. And she said my name." Caleb swallowed hard.

"Can I go in to see her?" Reve asked.

"Soon," Caleb replied. "Dr. Cornelius just got here and he's in there with her now, examining her."

Reve covered her mouth with her hand and sucked back the tears threatening to overflow. Jacob came up behind her, slid his arm around her waist and drew her to his side.

"This is what we've all been praying for," Jacob said.

"Yeah, it is." Caleb turned from them, overcome with emotion.

Reve lifted her hand to reach out and touch his back, but Jacob caught her wrist. She looked at him, questioning his action. He shook his head, and strangely enough, she understood the verbal translation of his action. As a man, he understood that Caleb didn't want anyone to see him crying and wouldn't appreciate her trying to comfort him.

They had to wait less than twenty minutes, but it had begun to feel like twenty years by the time Dr. Cornelius emerged from the intensive care unit. Just as the doctor walked toward Reve, the rest of Jazzy's family—Genny, Dallas, Sally and Ludie—came rushing down the hall.

"Jazzy is going to be all right." Genny's words were a firm statement, a prediction Reve believed in wholeheartedly.

"Jazzy is doing remarkably well, considering the seriousness of her injuries and the length of time she remained in a coma," Dr. Cornelius said. "She's a fighter."

"We knew that," Reve said. "Will she recover fully? Is there any permanent damage?"

Standing directly behind her in a possessive, protective stance, Jacob kept his hand on Reve's shoulder.

"There's no way to tell at this stage if Jazzy will have a complete recovery, but I believe there's a good chance she will." Dr. Cornelius glanced from Reve to Caleb. "Her mind isn't quite clear, but she knows who she is and her recognizing Mr. McCord immediately is a good sign. However, she didn't know where she was. When I explained she was in the hospital, she asked why. She has no memory of the night she was attacked. As a matter of fact, she has partial amnesia, but that's only temporary. She should regain her memory within a few weeks. However, she may never remember the exact details of her attack."

"Is this temporary amnesia the only problem she has to overcome?" Caleb asked.

Dr. Cornelius frowned. "At present, Jazzy is showing some mild, partial paralysis in her legs and arms, but this, too, should be only temporary. And she has a minor problem with her speech. But with extensive physical therapy—"

"Damn!" Caleb turned and walked off.

"Whatever Jazzy needs to help her recover, she'll get it," Reve said. "I don't care where we have to take her or how much it costs, I want the best for my sister." Tears choked Reve.

Jacob tightened his grip on her shoulder.

"May we see Jazzy?" Genny asked.

"Yes, of course," the doctor replied. "Two at a time and only for a few minutes."

"We understand," Genny said, then looked to Reve. "You and Jacob go in first."

"Are you sure?" Reve asked. "After all, you're her best friend."

"And you're her sister." Genny reached out and hugged Reve.

Reve looked to Sally Talbot. The old woman nodded. "Genny's right. You go in first."

"What about Caleb?" Reve asked.

Dallas glanced in Caleb's direction. He stood alone at the end of the hall, his back to them, his shoulders hunched. "I'll go talk to Caleb. He'll be all right."

Jacob took Reve's hand and together they entered Jazzy's ICU cubicle. Although still pale, still connected to numerous wires and tubes, Jazzy smiled as her gaze focused on Reve. An odd sensation hit Reve in the pit of her belly. Without make-up, without her green tinted contacts and with the bright red rinse on her hair beginning to fade, Jazzy looked more like Reve than ever. Truly identical twins.

"Reve." Jazzy's voice was very weak and slightly hoarse from lack of use.

Reve rushed to her sister, grasped her hand and leaned over to kiss her. "It's about time you woke up. You gave us all a really bad scare."

"Sorry." Jazzy mouthed the word.

"You're going to be just fine. Dr. Cornelius said so, and he should know. He's the best in the business."

Jazzy nodded. "You . . . you made sure . . . of that."

Reve laughed.

"You got that damn straight," Jacob said as he came up behind Reve. "Your sister has made sure you received the best care possible."

Jazzy frowned. "Watch her."

"Watch who?" Reve asked.

Jacob put his arm around Reve. "You want me to watch out for Reve? You want me to keep her safe?"

Jazzy nodded. "Yes. Danger."

"Dr. Cornelius told you what happened, why you're in the hospital," Reve said.

Jazzy nodded again. "Attacked. Head."

Reve squeezed her sister's hand. "You rest now. Jacob and

I are going to leave so Genny and Dallas and your aunt Sally and Ludie can come in to see you."

"Caleb?"

"He's still here. He hasn't left the hospital since you were brought in."

"Loves me."

"Oh, yes, ma'am, he surely does." In that one split second Reve envied her sister greatly. Not for the first time she wondered what it would feel like to have a man love her the way Caleb loved Jazzy. If only . . . *Don't you dare go there, Reve Sorrell,* she warned herself. *Just because you shared the most incredible night of sex in your life with Jacob Butler does not mean he loves you. The "L" word was never mentioned. By either of you.*

Griffin Powell arrived in Cherokee Pointe around ten-thirty and met with Reve in Jazzy's office at Jasmine's. Jacob had offered to be with her when she met with Griffin, but she'd assured him she could handle things without him. He'd kissed her and left without another word. They hadn't talked about last night, hadn't scrutinized their actions or tried to explain to each other that it had just been sex and nothing more. Nor had either of them declared undying love for the other.

"As of yesterday evening, our investigation into Dinah Collins's life led us to three men," Griffin said. "It seems that while she lived on Hyatt Street in Sevierville, Dinah had only three frequent male visitors. One man came to see her every week, occasionally more often. Another man came once a month. And a third visited her several times."

"Do you know who those three men were?" Reve asked.

Griffin nodded. "Maxwell Fennel, a well-known lawyer here in Cherokee Pointe; Dodd Keefer, a highly respected circuit court judge here in Cherokee County; and Farlan MacKinnon, who owns MacKinnon Media and lives here in Cherokee Pointe."

Reve's stomach muscles tightened. A queasy unease churned inside her. "Do you believe that one of those three men is our father?"

"Yes."

"How do we find out which one?"

When Griffin hesitated, Reve could tell he had more information, but for some reason seemed reluctant to share it with her.

"What is it?" she asked. "Whatever it is, just tell me. I can handle it."

"Last night Farlan MacKinnon telephoned me. It seems that he met you recently and realized how much you resembled Dinah Collins, a woman who was once his mistress."

"My mother was Farlan MacKinnon's mistress?"

"Yes, and he claims that he is the father of her twin daughters."

For a moment, Reve couldn't breathe; then she sucked in huge gulps of air.

"Are you all right?" Griffin asked.

"I'm fine." She wasn't, but she would be. "Did Mr. MacKinnon offer any explanation about what happened to my mother and how Jazzy and I wound up abandoned and left for dead when we were infants?"

"No, but he does want to meet you. He told me that he wants to explain things to you himself."

"How the hell can he explain?"

"I don't know, but if you're willing to meet with him, all I have to do is telephone him right now and my guess is that he'll come straight here."

Did she want to do this now? Was she strong enough to face this man who claimed to be her father—Jazzy's father—and listen to his explanations?

"Call him. Tell him I'll see him. Today."

* * *

"The only way this might work is if we tell no one," Dallas said. "Not Genny or Reve. And certainly not Caleb."

"I suppose all that matters is that Jazzy has agreed," Jacob said, "but God help me, I don't feel right about this. It's almost as if we're taking advantage of Jazzy, considering her condition. And when Caleb finds out, he's liable to kill us both."

"He'll be pissed as hell, but if we capture Jazzy's attacker, he might let us live."

"Logic says our plan will work, that it's the best way to trap a killer, but because I love Jazzy, I'm concerned that something could go wrong and she'll get hurt."

"We're going to keep close watch over her, twenty-four/ seven," Dallas said. "My guess is that once the word is out that Jazzy has regained consciousness and it's only a matter of time before she names her attacker, we'll see some action. Possibly tonight."

"Not if this guy's smart. He won't fall into our trap. We could be putting Jazzy's life in danger for no good reason."

"He's a copycat would-be killer, not an original thinker. My experience tells me that he'll panic when he thinks Jazzy is on the verge of identifying him. He'll take some big risks to try to shut her up."

"Once we put the word out about Jazzy, Caleb's going to start questioning how it happened, how word leaked out. He's a former cop," Jacob reminded Dallas. "It won't take him long to figure out what we're doing, and when he does figure it out—"

"If we're lucky, Jazzy's attacker will act before Caleb finds out what we've done. The main thing is not to forget that unless we want to fake Jazzy's death, which would be a pretty drastic measure, once word leaks out that she's no longer in a coma—and word will leak out whether we do it or not— her attacker will try again. It's much safer for Jazzy if we make sure he comes to us when we're expecting him."

"I say we both stay at the hospital tonight and not leave this to anyone else."

"And if he doesn't strike tonight, you and I can take shifts until he shows."

"How do we explain this to Genny and Reve? And Caleb's sure to wonder what's up."

"We can be honest, up to a point," Dallas said. "We'll tell them that we're beefing up security because we're afraid word might leak out that Jazzy's conscious. Nobody will have to know that we're putting the word out ourselves and embellishing the truth a bit."

"Heaven help us if anything goes wrong," Jacob said. "Or if Genny senses what we're up to."

Reve wasn't sure how she'd feel when she saw Farlan MacKinnon again. She only vaguely remembered him from the night at the ER, the night when his son Brian had rescued Jazzy. Try as she might, all she could recall was that he was a big, tall man with thinning white hair and brown eyes. An old man. Was he seventy? Probably.

Dinah Collins had been twenty when she gave birth to twins. If Farlan MacKinnon was now seventy or seventy-five, then he'd have been forty or forty-five when . . .

You don't know that he's your father, she reminded herself. *Just because he says he is doesn't make it so. But what would he have to gain by making such a monumental confession?*

When Reve heard a firm knock on the closed office door, she tensed. "Yes?"

"Reve, it's Griffin Powell. I have Mr. MacKinnon with me. May we come in?"

"Yes, come in. Please." Reve stood, steeling her nerves to face whatever might happen.

Griffin Powell came into the office first, then Farlan Mac-Kinnon, who stood shoulder-to-shoulder with Griffin, the two men approximately the same height. About six-four. She studied the man who claimed to be her father. He was a rather good-looking old man, his shoulders wide, his back straight. He was staring at her as if he was seeing a ghost.

"You look so much like your mother," Farlan said. "Except you're tall. Like me."

His words hit her like a sledgehammer. "I don't know what you expect me to say. I don't know how to respond."

"It's all right. I understand. This has been quite a shock for you." He looked at her through a mist of tears overlaying his dark, whiskey-brown eyes. Eyes the exact color of hers and Jazzy's.

Reve clasped the back of the chair with white-knuckled fierceness. "Won't y'all sit down?" Ever mindful of her manners, Reve acted purely on a lifetime of training.

"Why don't you sit down, Mr. MacKinnon?" Griffin suggested.

After Farlan MacKinnon sat in one of the empty office chairs, Griffin took the other one. Reve sat down behind Jazzy's desk.

"How is Jazzy?" Mr. MacKinnon asked.

"She's still alive." *Do you care?* Reve wanted to scream. *Do you really care whether either of us is all right? If you'd cared about us thirty years ago, you would have protected us.*

"You're angry," he said, and when she opened her mouth to reply, a biting comment on the tip of her tongue, he held up a restraining hand. "You have every right to be. I failed you and your sister. I failed your mother."

"Why should I believe that you're my father?" Reve asked, unable to keep the bitterness out of her voice.

"I'm willing to undergo a DNA test."

"I see."

"You have Dinah's beautiful features," Farlan MacKinnon said. "I assume you and Jazzy look just alike. I—I've never seen her, you know, except at a distance. I never paid much attention to her, never dreamed she was my daughter."

"I've seen Dinah Collins's picture," Reve said. "I know that Jazzy and I look a lot like her."

"You do, except she was a little thing, about five-three and very delicate. You got your height and size from me."

"Tell me about her. Tell me about the two of you." *Do I really want to hear this, even if every word is the truth?*

"I'm going to be as truthful as I know how to be." He paused as if it hurt him to say more. "Some of the things I'm going to tell you about your mother will bother you, but you must remember that she had a kind and loving heart. She was not a bad person."

Reve tensed. Was she prepared to hear awful things about her birth mother? "Go on."

"I met Dinah when she was seventeen, almost eighteen. She was a prostitute in Knoxville."

Reve gasped. Emotion flooded her senses. It was all she could do to keep herself from bursting into tears. Her mother had been a prostitute? How was that possible?

"I didn't find out about her background, about her life before she wound up in Knoxville, until much later. When I took her away from Knoxville, away from the terrible life she'd been living and—"

"And made a teenage girl your mistress," Reve finished for him.

He hung his head in shame, as well he should have. When he lifted his head, his gaze met hers and locked. "I take full blame for everything that happened. But there's something you should know. I loved Dinah. And she loved me."

Oh, God, why had he told her that? Didn't he realize that whether it was true or not, she would want to believe it?

"Dinah had run away from home when she was thirteen. Her mother was an alcoholic, and her father deserted them when Dinah was just a toddler. She lived with her aunt and uncle on and off from the time she was seven. Her mother's sister and her husband.

"The uncle began sexually abusing Dinah when she was ten." Farlan became very quiet. A lone tear trickled down his left cheek. "When she was thirteen, she found out she was pregnant and when she told her aunt, the woman blamed her."

"Oh, God." Reve jumped up and flew across the room, flung open the door and rushed down the hall to the bathroom.

She had just barely made it inside one of the stalls when she retched and threw up. She wiped her mouth with toilet tissue, then took several deep breaths before going to one of the sinks and washing out her mouth. After dampening her face with a moist paper towel, she washed and dried her hands, then squared her shoulders and went back to Jazzy's office. Both Griffin and Farlan were standing.

"Are you all right?" Farlan asked. "I'm sorry—"

"Don't apologize for telling me the truth. If you can't do anything else for me, you can be honest with me." When Jazzy sat back behind the desk, she looked right at Farlan. "What happened to her and to her baby?"

"She ran away and wound up in Knoxville, on the streets, a thirteen-year-old kid who was four months pregnant." Farlan rubbed his big, age-spotted hands up and down his thighs. "She got hooked up with a rough bunch, and within a week she was turning tricks. She told me she hated it, hated all those men touching her. And I hated it for her."

"What happened to her baby?"

"The baby died. She was born prematurely. Dinah was only about six months along. After that, she grew up fast and learned to take care of herself. When I met her, she was a sassy, street-smart hooker. She'd closed off her feelings completely. Until we fell in love. Neither of us meant for it to happen. And I know it surprised her that she could actually love somebody, least of all a man old enough to be her father."

Reve glanced at Griffin. "You said that two other men continued to see Dinah after she moved to Sevierville, right?"

"That's correct," Griffin replied.

"Maxwell Fennel was my cousin and fresh out of law school," Farlan explained. "I hired him to take charge of Dinah's finances, to see to it that she had anything she wanted. That's why Max visited her on a monthly basis."

"And the other man was Judge Dodd Keefer," Reve said.

"Dodd is my brother-in-law. I met Dinah through him. He'd been one of Dinah's regular customers, and he fell in love with her. But he wanted to end things because the guilt nearly destroyed him. Dodd is an honorable man and he truly loved his wife. He confessed his sins to his wife and she forgave him, but for quite some time after he was no longer Dinah's lover, he visited her. He couldn't quite let go. Not until he learned she was pregnant with my baby."

"I take it that you were married and had no intention of divorcing your wife," Reve said. "Why didn't you just arrange for Dinah to have an abortion?"

"Neither of us wanted that. She wanted to have my child—my children. And I asked my wife for a divorce."

"You did?" Reve couldn't believe what he'd told her.

"Yes, I did. But my wife, who was and still is mentally unbalanced, refused to give me a divorce. She even tried to kill herself, and when she survived the attempt, she swore she'd try again if I left her. We had a twelve-year-old son. How could I have taken the chance that his mother would kill herself?"

"So you made a choice between your wife and son and your mistress and twin daughters?" The rage boiling inside her surprised Reve. She'd wanted to know the truth, but now she hated the truth. She hated this man's wife and son. And she hated him.

"Dinah understood," Farlan said. "She's actually the one who made what she believed was the right decision for us. She made plans to move to Atlanta and take our babies with her. And I arranged through Maxwell to care of her and our children financially."

"How noble of you!"

"I don't blame you for being angry. I don't blame you for hating me."

"Obviously Dinah didn't take her twins and move to Atlanta," Reve said. "Do you want to tell me what went wrong? What happened? How did Jazzy wind up being stuck in a tree stump and left for dead? How did I wind up being thrown in a Dumpster, like a piece of trash?"

Farlan shook his head. "I don't know. I swear, I don't know." Tears welled up in his eyes. "All these years, I believed the three of you were safe and happy and—"

"But not once"—Reve spoke through clenched teeth— "not once in thirty years did you ever make sure, did you? You just sent us packing and forgot about us."

"No!" Farlan jumped to his feet. "Not one day of my life has passed that I didn't think about Dinah, about our two little girls and wonder—"

Reve looked at her father—and she knew in her heart that this man was her father, just as she'd known Jazzy was her sister—and almost felt sorry for him. Almost.

"Do you know of anyone who might have hated my mother enough to harm her?" Reve asked. "Who would have wanted to see Jazzy and me dead?"

Farlan's face went chalk white. "Oh, God. No. No."

"Who?" Reve demanded, but Farlan simply sat back down, buried his face in his hands and wept.

CHAPTER 28

He watched from across the street when Farlan Mac-Kinnon left Jasmine's with Griffin Powell. Reve Sorrell stood in the doorway of the restaurant and shook hands with the private investigator, then turned to Farlan. They just looked at each other and he could tell, even from this distance, that the old man wanted to put his arms around his daughter and hug her. But he didn't. He couldn't see Reve's face so he couldn't be sure about her feelings. He'd hoped she would hate Farlan and tell him to go to hell. Apparently that hadn't happened. But she wasn't exactly kissing her daddy good-bye, so maybe all wasn't lost.

But what did it matter? He was going to kill Reve, just as he'd killed Dinah. And then he would kill Jazzy and finish off the unholy trinity. Mother and both daughters. He'd heard Jazzy had come out of her coma and was on the verge of remembering the face of her attacker. Good. Whoever the idiot was who had presumed to copy him, the man deserved to be caught.

Sheriff Butler and Chief Sloan kept close watch over Reve, day and night, but that little problem wouldn't defeat him. It was simply a matter of eliminating the guard and finding

Reve unawares. After all, how difficult could it be to outsmart one of these yokel lawmen?

He chuckled to himself as he studied Reve Sorrell. *You're mine. Perhaps tonight. After all, I don't dare wait much longer. Dinah will seek me out again soon and tempt me to play our little game. Before that happens, I have to concentrate on riding myself of her two daughters. Reve first and then Jazzy.*

And he knew just how he'd kill them. The same way he'd killed Dinah. He would strangle them with a black ribbon. But before he killed Reve, he would make love to her, as he'd made love to her mother. Just the thought of touching her, of thrusting into her, aroused him unbearably. No, he couldn't wait much longer.

"I'm going to kill your babies," he whispered. "Do you hear me, Dinah? I'm going to take them away from Farlan just as I took you away from him."

The only way they had been able to convince Caleb to go home and get a good night's rest was by Jacob agreeing to stay at the hospital and keep watch over Jazzy. Reve had dropped Caleb off at his cabin and then driven back into town. She'd been hearing murmurs all day long, gossip about Jazzy. When she'd told Jacob that somehow word had leaked out that Jazzy had regained consciousness and would soon be able to identify her attacker, he'd made her promise not to mention it to Caleb.

"If he knows Jazzy's attacker might hear about her recovery, Caleb will never leave her side," Jacob had said. "The guy is one of the walking wounded. If he doesn't get some rest soon, he'll collapse and wind up in the hospital himself."

Reve had agreed, so she'd kept quiet, especially after Jacob told her that both he and Dallas were staying at the hospital tonight.

"I promise you that we won't let anything happen to Jazzy," he'd sworn to her.

After she parked her Jag at the back of Jazzy's Joint, she wondered if she should run by both the restaurant and the bar tonight and check on things. But she was tired and sleepy. She hadn't gotten much rest last night. Remembering how she'd spent those hours, she smiled. There was nothing she'd like better than to lie in Jacob's arms all night again tonight.

He'd pulled her aside and kissed her before she left the hospital. "I'd rather be spending the night with you tonight."

"Yes, I'd like that, too," she'd told him.

"One of Dallas's men, Officer Graves, will follow you home and be outside Jazzy's apartment all night tonight." Jacob had cupped her face with both hands. "I'll come by first thing in the morning."

Sighing, her mind fast-forwarding to morning and the possibility that she and Jacob would make love again, Reve waved good night to Officer Graves, a dark-haired young man in his mid-twenties. He'd parked the black-and-white police vehicle on the side of the street, directly below the staircase that led up to Jazzy's apartment. When she waved at him, he waved back and smiled.

Once inside the apartment, she flipped on the overhead light in the living room and tossed her purse and keys on the closest chair, then made her way straight to the bedroom. Glancing at the clock on the nightstand, she couldn't believe it was only seven-forty-five. She kicked off her shoes and undressed, dumping her clothes on the bed. Getting used to picking up after herself when she'd spent a lifetime being waited on by servants hadn't come easy to Reve. Occasionally she forgot that no one would come along behind her and clean up after her. Oh, well, she'd gather up everything later.

Once completely naked, she headed for the bathroom. Tonight she wanted a tub bath. She wanted to soak in some scented hot water—maybe some bubble bath—for a good twenty minutes and think about everything that had happened. Everything from becoming lovers with a man she thought she despised to meeting the man she believed was her father.

And she wanted to celebrate in her own quiet, private way, the fact that her sister had come out of a coma and was not only going to live, but had a good chance of fully recovering.

Moments later, after pinning her hair atop her head, Reve settled into the foamy bathwater and closed her eyes. She tried to concentrate on the positive, on Jazzy's recovery and her relationship with Jacob—whatever that relationship was— but all she could think about was Farlan MacKinnon and Dinah Collins. Her parents.

When Farlan had sworn to her that for all these years he'd thought Dinah and her twins were alive and well and living happily in Atlanta, she'd believed him. She couldn't easily forgive him, but she did believe him. He wasn't totally blameless, but he hadn't deliberately harmed either Dinah or her babies. Reve felt certain that the man really had loved Dinah.

Perhaps he's paid for his sins, she thought. After all, he had spent a lifetime with a crazy woman he didn't love. And their only child was Brian MacKinnon, a not-so-nice man whom Jazzy disliked intensely.

Oh, Lord, what would Jazzy say when she found out that Brian was their half-brother?

I haven't seen anyone I know since arriving at the hospital and the few people I've seen paid little attention to me. Why should they? I dressed very discreetly and have done nothing to draw attention to myself. As far as anyone knows, I'm simply here to visit a sick friend. And if by some horrific chance I actually do run into anyone who recognizes me, I have a very good excuse. A sweet old lady from church had been admitted to the hospital only yesterday, so wasn't it a good Christian's duty to visit the sick?

I wonder if there will be guards outside Jazzy's door. When I called earlier, from a pay phone downtown, I was told she'd been put in a private room. Room # 310. I had so hoped the

*bitch would die, but I should have known that if she had sur-
vived being abandoned in the woods as an infant, she might
survive being hit in the head with a hammer—twice.*

*There's the nurses' station up ahead. I must keep my head
down and not look directly at anyone. If somebody approaches
me, I'll pretend I'm lost. Keep walking. Don't slow down.*

*I just passed Room 304. Jazzy Talbot is only three doors
down.*

*Uh-oh, there's a nurse talking to some man. Is he a plain-
clothes policeman? No, no, he's not. He's thanking the nurse
and coming this way. He just passed me without even glancing my way. And the nurse returned to Room 305.*

*I can breath a sigh of relief. There's Room 310. Not a
guard in sight. But there could be one inside. Yes, there could
be, but I won't know until I check. And if there is a guard in
Jazzy's room, what then? I'll apologize for being in the wrong
room, then I'll leave and figure out another way to get to
Jazzy before she remembers anything about the night I attacked her.*

She never saw my face.

Are you sure?

I'm certain. At least, I'm almost certain.

Almost isn't good enough.

That's one of the reasons she has to die.

*Don't be afraid. Walk right on into the room as if you be-
longed there.*

*There's Jazzy lying on the narrow hospital bed, her short
red hair bright against the white pillow. Go over and take a
really good look at her. See if she looks as much like Dinah
as Reve does. Take a good hard look at Farlan's other bastard daughter.*

*Oh, she's a pretty thing. Every bit as pretty as Dinah and
the spitting image of her twin sister.*

*If only Slim had killed those babies, I wouldn't have to be
here now, forced to murder another human being. I hate the*

thought of killing her now, just as much as I did the night I hit her in the head with the hammer and threw her off the bridge.

Look around, check in the bathroom, make sure you and Jazzy are all alone.

Ah, yes, we're alone. Just the two of us.

It will be so easy. All I have to do is simply pick up the extra pillow lying in the chair there and cover her face. Yes, that's all there is to it. I'll hold the pillow over her face until she stops breathing. Then I'll put the pillow back in the chair and walk out of here as if nothing happened.

I can do it. I have to do it.

The pillow was fluffy and soft, the case lightly starched. Jazzy hadn't opened her eyes, hadn't moved. No doubt she was drugged. Good. That way she wouldn't put up a fight.

Lower the pillow. Down. Down. That's it. Cover her face completely. Hold the pillow down tightly.

No, no, Jazzy was supposed to be asleep, supposed to be drugged. Why is she fighting me, struggling to live? Let go of me, you little bitch. I have to shake off her grasp around my wrist. I'm stronger than she is. I can control her.

Finish the job. Don't let her stop you. Kill her. Kill her now!

A pair of huge hands grabbed her by the arms and flung her backward and away from Jazzy. In her peripheral vision she saw a big blond man jerk the pillow away from Jazzy's face and lift her up into his arms. Gasping for air, Jazzy stared at her with those large brown eyes that looked so much like Farlan's eyes.

"No, dammit, no! You don't understand. She has to die! I can't allow her to live."

"Apparently you're the one who doesn't understand, Mrs. MacKinnon—we won't allow you to hurt Jazzy again."

Veda looked up at a giant of a man who pulled out a pair of handcuffs as he came toward her.

"There's been a mistake, Sheriff Butler," Veda said.

"Yes, ma'am, there has been and you just made it." He turned her around, pulled her arms behind her back and laced the cuffs over her wrists.

"You do know who I am, don't you, young man? I'm Mrs. Farlan MacKinnon. My husband will be outraged when he learns of the way you're treating me."

"That may well be, but there won't be much he can do about it. The chief of police and I caught you red-handed trying to smother Jazzy Talbot. That's attempted murder."

Veda stuck her nose in the air. "If she didn't have such a hard head, she'd have died when I hit her that night on the bridge."

"This is your case since the hospital is in your jurisdiction. Read her her rights before she says anything else," Jacob Butler told Chief Sloan, who did just that.

"Mrs. MacKinnon, you have the right to—"

His voice became little more than a pesky roar. What did she care about rights? About being handcuffed and arrested? Farlan would take care of everything. He'd call Max and Max would have her out of jail and home in her own bed this very night. It wasn't as if she'd done anything wrong. Both of Dinah's little bastards were supposed to have died thirty years ago. She'd handed over both babies to Slim, the MacKinnons' handyman at the time and a person who would do anything for the right amount of money. She'd given him specific instructions to kill both twins and dispose of their bodies separately in two different locations, in two different counties. She had told him that if the bodies were ever found, she didn't want Farlan or anyone else to suspect that those individual babies were Dinah Collins's twins.

"Are you taking me to jail, Sheriff?" Veda asked.

"Chief Sloan will take you to the police station, where you can make a phone call," Sheriff Butler told her. "I'll be staying here with Jazzy."

Veda glanced at the bed where Jazzy Talbot lay. "You were supposed to have died thirty years ago. You and your twin sister. Why didn't you both die then?"

"Get her out of here," Sheriff Butler said.

"Let's go, Mrs. MacKinnon." Chief Sloan grasped her arm firmly. "If you don't cooperate, things could get embarrassing and a lady such as yourself wouldn't like that, would you?"

"No, I wouldn't. Thank you for understanding. I won't put up a fight. I'll go peacefully. But as soon as we arrive at the police station, I'll call Farlan. He'll take care of everything."

He waited until he was reasonably certain no one would see him. With the loud music and rowdy fun inside Jazzy's Joint, there wasn't a chance anyone would hear him. The side street where the policeman was parked was semidark. The young officer, positioned so he could see anyone who approached the steps leading to the apartment above the honky-tonk, was keeping watch over Reve. Shadows cast from the streetlight on the corner illuminated only the back half of the black-and-white car.

He'd never killed anyone with a gun before, but there was a first time for everything. He preferred strangulation. A black braided ribbon had always been his weapon of choice, ever since he'd killed Dinah with the ribbon she wore around her neck. When he'd first seen that little gold heart attached to the ribbon, he'd wondered about it. And when he'd removed it and taken it with him after he'd killed Dinah, he'd been almost afraid to hold it in his hand. But he'd examined the eighteen-karat gold locket thoroughly, and when he opened it, he had discovered two pictures inside. One of Farlan. The other of her twin babies.

Damn Farlan. Damn him to hell.

He had to make sure the policeman didn't hear him, didn't see him coming. All he had to do was get close enough to the car to aim and fire. With a silencer on the gun, it shouldn't make much noise. And at close range, he couldn't miss.

CHAPTER 29

Dallas spoke personally to Judge Earl Ray Stillwell, who issued a warrant to search the MacKinnon property tonight. He called in Lieutenant Tommy Glenn to oversee the search, wanting his very best man for this particular job. Although Veda MacKinnon had talked nonstop since he'd brought her in and had even told him where she'd put the hammer she'd used to attack Jazzy, Dallas didn't want to risk losing any evidence that might show up at her home.

Max Fennel arrived five minutes after Veda called him, which she'd done when she couldn't reach her husband. "He's probably off in Sevierville with Dinah," Veda had said. "She's his mistress, you know. He keeps her in a fine apartment over on Hyatt Street."

"Veda, stop talking," Max advised.

"Oh, shut up yourself, Max. It's not like everyone doesn't know about Farlan and that slut." Veda smiled at Dallas. "He's going to acknowledge those girls as his daughters. He's already met with Reve. I can't allow that. You understand, don't you? I have to protect Brian. I can't allow Farlan to give away my son's legacy to Dinah's children. It wouldn't be right."

Dallas figured Max wouldn't have a problem proving

Veda MacKinnon was insane. If she wasn't certifiable, then she was a great actress. The best he'd ever seen.

"Veda, honey, I do wish you'd be quiet," Max told his client. "All you're doing is digging yourself into a hole that I won't be able to get you out of."

"Nonsense." She dismissed him with a wave of her hand. "I'm Mrs. Farlan MacKinnon. There's no one who can touch me. My husband would never allow anyone to harm me. He'd do absolutely anything for me."

Dallas shook his head. He'd seen cases where people faked insanity, some quite cleverly, but his gut instincts told him that Veda wasn't faking. She was the genuine article. A crazy woman who had tried to kill Jazzy because, according to her, Jazzy and Reve were going to disinherit Farlan Mac-Kinnon's legitimate son.

"Where is Farlan anyway?" Veda asked. "Did you tell him about my little problem?"

"I've left messages for him at home and at the club and I've tried his cell phone repeatedly," Max told her. "I'm sure it's only a matter of time before he gets one of my messages."

As if on cue, the outer doors to the small downtown police station swung open, and Farlan MacKinnon came storming in. Dallas left the interrogation room and closed the door behind him. He met Mr. MacKinnon, stopping him dead in his tracks.

"Where's my wife?" MacKinnon demanded.

"She's with her lawyer, Mr. Fennel."

"Is it true—did she try to kill Jazzy Talbot tonight?"

"Yes, sir, it's true. Sheriff Butler and I caught her in the act."

"God help me. This is all my fault. I should have done something years ago, but—" He paused as if realizing he was voicing his thoughts aloud. "Is Jazzy all right?"

"She was unharmed tonight, but because of the head injury she received, she'll have to undergo months, perhaps years of physical therapy." When MacKinnon hung his head and said nothing, Dallas reached out and grasped his shoulder. "Your wife has confessed to beating Jazzy with a hammer that night on the old covered bridge and dumping her into the creek below. She's told us that she had to kill Dinah's children. And she says Jazzy and Reve are your daughters."

"My wife has severe mental problems," MacKinnon said. "Far more serious than I've allowed myself to accept." He looked Dallas right in the eyes. "I am Jazzy and Reve's biological father."

"Does Reve know?"

"Yes. I met with her this afternoon and explained to her about her mother and me."

"Well, that's another matter," Dallas said. "Right now, I'm going to have to book your wife for attempted murder."

"I understand. I assume she'll be sent to the psychiatric ward of County General as soon as possible."

"Yes, possibly as early as tomorrow. You can probably pull a few strings and—"

"Maxwell will handle things tonight, but by morning I'll have Quinn Cortez here, if I have to send a goon squad to find him. Veda may have tried to kill my daughter, but I'm the one to blame. It's my fault. It's all my fault."

"You should know that Judge Stillwell issued a warrant for us to search your house and grounds," Dallas explained. "Your wife has already told us where she hid the hammer she used to bludgeon Jazzy."

Farlan MacKinnon crumbled right before Dallas's eyes. A proud old man almost literally brought to his knees by guilt and regret. When he swayed, unsteady on his feet, Dallas grabbed his arm. "Come on into my office and sit down for a few minutes."

"I should go see Veda."

"That can wait." Dallas motioned toward his closed office door. "If you'd like, you can use my private line to contact Quinn Cortez. I guess everybody knows he's one of the best trial lawyers in the country. Your wife is fortunate that you're not only wealthy enough to afford Cortez, but that you're willing to spare no expense to help her."

"You're wondering what sort of man I am, aren't you? How could I be concerned about a woman who wants to kill both of my daughters, who probably tried to kill them when they were babies and also probably killed their mother?"

"It's not my job to judge anyone, Mr. MacKinnon."

"You've seen Veda. Surely you see how emotionally fragile she is."

"If you mean crazy—"

"Yes. She's suffered with mental problems all her life. Inherited from her father, who killed himself when she was a young girl. I thought I did the right thing thirty years ago. I told myself that for Brian's sake . . ." MacKinnon's voice cracked. "I believe I would like to use your office for a few minutes, if that's all right with you, Chief Sloan."

"Go on in," Dallas said. "No one will bother you. Make what calls you need to make, and when you're ready to see your wife, let me know."

"Thank you."

Reve put on her silk pajamas, then wrapped the matching robe around her as she slipped into her house shoes and headed toward the kitchen. She intended to go to bed early and get a full night's sleep. Tomorrow she'd meet with Dr. Cornelius to discuss Jazzy's therapy. If her sister would receive the best treatment in Nashville, then that was where she'd go. Or if it was California or even somewhere in Europe, it didn't matter. The only thing that was important was helping Jazzy return to her old self.

After filling a mug with water, Reve popped it into the microwave to heat, then removed a bag from the box of Earl Grey tea she'd brought with her when she moved into Jazzy's apartment. She pulled back the curtain over the sink and peeked out into the dark night. Just seeing the police car still parked below, although she couldn't actually see the policeman from this vantage point, reassured her that she was safe.

The microwave beeped. She removed the hot water, dumped in a tea bag and timed it for a minute, then discarded the bag. Carrying the mug into the living room, she decided that she'd drink her tea and watch the late night news before going to bed.

She placed the mug on a coaster atop the coffee table, then curled up on the sofa and grabbed the remote control. If she wanted local weather, she'd have to watch WMMK. As she put the TV on that station, she couldn't help thinking about the fact that Farlan MacKinnon, owner and chairman of the board of MacKinnon Media, was her father. Her father was one of the wealthiest men in Tennessee, actually in the Southeast, probably as wealthy as her adoptive parents, the Sorrells.

"But don't forget that your mother was a teenage prostitute," Reve said aloud.

She hadn't been paying much attention to what the TV reporter was saying until she heard the name Veda MacKinnon. Reve turned up the sound and focused on the television.

"We don't have all the details, but we're camped out here in front of the police station and will update you when we know more," the reporter announced. "What we do know is that earlier this evening, Veda MacKinnon was seen being brought to the police station in handcuffs. Chief Sloan has not made an official statement, but we're told that Farlan MacKinnon is with his wife, as is Maxwell Fennel, a member of the MacKinnon family and a Cherokee Pointe lawyer."

As she absorbed the information, Reve sat up straight and scooted to the edge of the sofa. Trying not to assume anything, she told herself to wait and call Dallas to find out what was going on before she allowed her imagination to spin some fantastic scenario.

Too late. Already she was thinking about Farlan Mac-

Kinnon's reaction earlier today when she'd asked him if he knew anyone who would have wanted to harm her mother or would have wanted to see Jazzy and her dead. What more likely suspect than his wife? Veda MacKinnon had known about her husband's affair with Dinah. What woman wouldn't have hated her husband's mistress? And if she'd hated Dinah, then she would have hated Dinah's twins. But had the woman been vicious enough to try to kill two innocent babies?

Stop tormenting yourself. Call Dallas and ask him what's going on.

Before she made it to her feet, she heard a repetitive knocking at the front door. Could it be Jacob? Her heart raced wildy as she stood up and rushed across the room. Remembering to be cautious, she looked through the peephole and saw a uniformed policeman. His cap was pulled down over his forehead and his gaze cast downward.

"Ms. Sorrell, it's Officer Graves. I'm just checking on you. I thought I saw someone in the alley behind Jazzy's Joint. Is there any way somebody could have gotten in through one of the back windows?"

"I don't think that's possible."

"If you'd like for me to, I can go through the apartment and make sure everything is secure."

"All right. Thank you."

She unlocked and opened the door. And only then—when it was too late—did she realize that the man in the uniform, standing on the stoop, was not young officer Graves.

"What are you doing—"

He put a sinister-looking gun to her head and grabbed her arm. "Let's go back inside, Reve. We have some unfinished business to take care of."

Caleb stormed into the hospital, straight to Room 310. Jacob rose from where he sat at Jazzy's bedside and headed him off before he woke a peacefully resting Jazzy.

"She's asleep," Jacob warned as he motioned for Caleb to follow him out into the hall. "Whatever you have to say to me, you don't want to upset her." When Caleb did as he'd requested, Jacob followed him into the hall and closed Jazzy's door. "Okay, let me have it."

"I just heard on a news break on WMMK that Veda MacKinnon has been arrested for the attempted murder of Jazzy Talbot." Caleb glared at Jacob. "Want to tell me what's going on? According to the reporter, who'd just been issued a statement by Dallas Sloan, Mrs. MacKinnon tried to kill Jazzy earlier this evening."

"That's right. Dallas and I caught Veda MacKinnon in the act." Jacob knew it would be only a matter of seconds before Caleb put two and two together and came up with the inevitable four.

Caleb stood there for several minutes, his eyes glazed, his mind whirling. "You son of a bitch! You sorry ass son of a bitch!" He lunged for Jacob, who effectively held him off by grabbing his shoulders. "You used her as bait, didn't you? Was Dallas in on this? Dammit, tell me, was he?"

"Calm down. Jazzy is all right. Dallas and I were right across the hall and came in behind Mrs. MacKinnon as soon as she entered the room. Jazzy was never in danger."

"The hell she wasn't! How could you have—"

"Jazzy agreed to our plan. She understood that if we could trap her attacker now, she and Reve would be safe, but if we waited—"

"Then Dallas *was* in on this?"

"Caleb, stop and think. It's over. Jazzy and Reve are safe from Veda MacKinnon. Mrs. MacKinnon is in custody, and my guess is that she'll wind up in the loony bin somewhere."

"If it had been Reve, would you have risked her life the way you did Jazzy's?"

"I have loved Jazzy like a second sister just about all my life," Jacob said, struggling to remain calm and in control of his temper. "Do you honestly think I would have put her in harm's way if I'd thought I couldn't protect her?"

"You didn't answer my question."

"If it had been Reve, she would probably have been the one who'd have thought of the plan and insisted on setting a trap."

Caleb nodded and Jacob could see him relax. "You can leave now," Caleb said. "I'm staying the rest of the night with Jazzy."

"All right. I should head on over to the police station to give Dallas a little moral support. I imagine that Farlan MacKinnon and Max Fennel are giving Dallas a hard time, not to mention that asshole Brian."

When Jacob arrived at the police station, he had to fight his way through a horde of reporters, all clamoring for more details about Mrs. Farlan MacKinnon's arrest. He was surprised that neither Farlan nor Brian had put a stop to the WMMK and *Cherokee Pointe* Herald reporters. But maybe they were a little too busy at the moment to realize what was happening.

As soon as Jacob finally got inside the station, Lieutenant Glenn, motioned to him. Jacob met him just outside Dallas's office. "The chief is questioning Mrs. MacKinnon again. When we found a bloodstained hammer hidden away in the MacKinnons' attic, exactly where Mrs. MacKinnon said it would be, we figured we had our murder weapon. As soon as the lab can ID the blood as Jazzy's—"

"I know y'all did a thorough search," Jacob said. "So, did you find anything else?"

"Odd that you should ask. It just so happens that we found a small gold, heart-shaped locket in a drawer along with a fifteen-foot roll of black braided satin ribbon in a hidden box."

"The hell you say!"

Black braided satin ribbon! The serial killer's weapon in every murder, a fact not known by the general public. Was it possible that the man who had brutally raped and murdered countless women over the past quarter of a century was a member of the MacKinnnon family? Maybe Farlan Mac-Kinnon himself? Or even Max Fennel or Judge Keefer? Both were known to spend a great deal of time at the MacKinnon mansion. It would have been easy for either man to have kept the ribbon there for safekeeping. Of course there was Wallace, too, whom he instantly ruled out as a suspect. After all, Wallace was a gentle giant, with the heart and soul of an innocent child. And since discovering that the first murders on record with the Redhead Killer's MO dated back nearly twenty-eight years, when Brian would have been just a kid, no more than fourteen, it was highly unlikely he was their guy. Of course, children had been known to kill, but in most cases their crimes weren't sexual in nature.

"Has Dallas confronted Mrs. MacKinnon with the locket and the black ribbon?" Jacob asked.

"She claims she knows nothing about either."

"How did she explain the black ribbon being in her room?"

"We didn't find the ribbon in her room."

"In whose room did you find it?"

"We found both items in a locked box at the bottom of Wallace MacKinnon's cedar chest."

"Wallace?"

"Yeah."

"No way could Wallace be connected to the serial killings. The man's a child. And a gentle child at that," Jacob said. "I'm going in there." He pointed to the interrogation room. "I suppose Dallas has his hands full dealing with old man MacKinnon and Brian, too."

"Actually Farlan MacKinnon is cooperating completely," Hendrix said. "And Brian's not here."

"You mean that mama's boy didn't rush down here the minute y'all told him his mother had been arrested?"

"We didn't tell him anything. He wasn't home. Apparently no one knows where he is."

CHAPTER 30

Jacob lifted his hand to knock on the door of the interrogation room, but his fist never made contact. The door flew open and Dallas came close to running into Jacob in his hurry to exit the room. Screeching to a halt when only inches separated them, Dallas grunted.

"Damn, man, what's your hurry?" Jacob asked.

"I had to get out of there for a few minutes," Dallas said. "Mrs. MacKinnon has finally wound down and is crying quietly now." Dallas rubbed his forehead. "I'll be damned if I've ever seen a case like this one."

"Glenn told me she's confessed to trying to kill Jazzy and even told y'all where you could find the hammer she used."

"Oh, that's not the half of it." Dallas motioned to his office. "I could use a cup of coffee. We might as well take a breather until the doctor gets here." When Jacob looked at him questioningly, he explained, "I sent for Dr. Cory, the psychiatrist in charge of the psych unit over at County General. We're going to do all we can to get Mrs. MacKinnon admitted tonight."

"Then there's more to this case than two attempts on Jazzy's life," Jacob said as he followed Dallas toward his office.

"Yeah, a hell of a lot more, but some of it's still a mystery." Dallas opened the door to his office, entered and headed straight for the coffee machine on a stand next to his desk. "It's not fresh," he said as he lifted the half-full pot. "But it's hot and wet. Want a cup?"

Jacob shook his head. "Glenn told me about finding a roll of black satin braided ribbon and a gold locket hidden away in the bottom of Wallace MacKinnon's cedar chest. What do you make of that?"

Dallas poured himself a cup of coffee, sat behind his desk and lifted the mug to his lips. After taking several sips, he replied, "That's the mystery. My gut's telling me that someone associated with the MacKinnons is our serial killer. And we know it's sure as hell not Veda since our killer is definitely male."

"I don't think it could possibly be Wallace," Jacob said. "I've spent a lot time with him ever since I was kid, and the man is as harmless as a fly."

"I agree. Someone hid the ribbon in Wallace's cedar chest. But who?"

"What about Farlan MacKinnon? Maybe he killed Jazzy and Reve's mother. Maybe she was his first victim."

"It's possible," Dallas agreed. "But once again, my gut tells me it's not Farlan."

"Then who? And if you say Brian, I'd agree. I despise that son of bitch. I think he's a mean, vindictive jerk. But if the murders actually began with Jazzy and Reve's mother, then it's unlikely Brian's our man. Brian's forty-two. He would have been only twelve years old thirty years ago."

"In all her rambling, Veda kept talking about her brother having been in love with Dinah. And she even ranted at Max, accusing him of being involved with the woman, too. She kept telling her husband over and over again that there was no way he could be certain he's Jazzy and Reve's father because there were so many other men in Dinah's life."

"If there's any truth to what she said, then Max Fennel or Judge Keefer could have killed Dinah, right?"

"We're making some huge assumptions by thinking Dinah was the serial killer's first victim, especially when we have no real evidence to back up this theory."

"It's as good a theory as any," Jacob said. "And if it turns out we're right, I say we look closer at Judge Keefer."

"Why him?"

"Because I honestly don't think Max Fennel has it in him to kill anybody. I believe he'd cheat, lie and steal, but not kill. On the other hand, Judge Keefer is a quiet, solitary man. And you know the old saying about still waters running deep. Besides, if he was in love with Dinah and she rejected him in favor of—" Jacob's cell phone rang, effectively halting him mid-sentence. "Damn!"

"You'd better get that," Dallas told him.

Jacob retrieved his phone from its belt holder, flipped it open and said, "Yeah, Butler here."

"Jacob . . . help her. Help her now."

"Genny?"

Dallas's eyes widened and he mouthed the words, "Is she all right?"

"You have to get to Reve. Right now. He's going to kill her." Genny's voice was weak, each word a struggle.

"Who's going to kill her?" Jacob's gut knotted painfully.

"I had the vision over twenty minutes ago, but I passed out and just now came to. You have to hurry. I didn't see his face, but he was trying to rape Reve. And he had a black braided ribbon in his pocket. I saw it. He's going to kill her."

"I'll send Dallas home to you right away." Jacob closed his phone and stuck it back in the holder, then turned to Dallas. "Go home. Genny's in a bad way. She had another vision. This time she saw Reve being raped and murdered."

"I'll contact Graves and warn him to be especially careful," Dallas said. "Then I'll head home. Call me as soon as you—"

"I'm heading straight to Jazzy's apartment." Jacob was halfway out the door when he spoke.

* * *

Reve did everything he told her to do. She had to buy time and hope that someone would discover Officer Graves's body and realize she was in trouble.

This crazy idiot had killed that poor young officer. He'd bragged about how easy it had been to sneak up on the policeman and kill him.

"Putting a bullet through that cop's head was almost as easy as renting this police uniform," he'd told her. "I've been outsmarting the law for thirty years. Dallas Sloan isn't much smarter than that stupid Jacob Butler, so there's no way they'll ever catch me."

Jacob! Oh, God, Jacob, help me. If there is such a thing as telepathy, I wish you could hear my thoughts. I wish you could feel my fear.

Holding the gun in his steady hand, he forced her into the bedroom. She knew the serial killer's MO, knew what lay in store for her if she wasn't able to figure a way out of this situation. Bottom line, he was going to kill her, so she actually had nothing to lose. But she had no intention of acting hastily. She would do whatever it took to stay alive for as long as possible. Where there was life, there was hope. And she was going to live!

"Why are you doing this?" she asked as he motioned for her to move closer to the bed.

"Why do you think? Isn't it obvious that I can't let Dinah's daughters live?"

"I just found out that Dinah Collins was my mother. And Jazzy's mother."

"She's a slut just like Dinah was. I'll bet you're probably a slut, too, aren't you? It's in your blood."

"You hated my mother, didn't you? You hated her because—"

"Because she loved Farlan MacKinnon and not me."

That had been the last thing she'd expected him to say. "I don't understand. You wanted her to love you?"

"Sit down, Reve. Sit right there on the bed." He brandished the pistol, waving it around in the air.

Obediently sitting, Reve's mind went into high gear trying to figure out why he would have wanted Dinah to love him. She could understand why he would have hated Dinah and wished her dead, but why—?

"I knew all about them. Farlan never realized that I knew. But I did. I had Slim take me and follow him one time when he left the house. He went to see her in her apartment over on Hyatt Street in Sevierville. I went up to see her, to beg her to stop seeing him."

"Who's Slim?"

"He was our handyman and a real sleazeball, but he was good at following orders if you gave him enough money. He's the one who got rid of the twins for us."

Reve's heartbeat accelerated alarmingly. "Where's Slim now?"

"Dead. I killed him. He blackmailed me for years, so finally I had to get rid of him. Nobody missed him. He was just worthless trash. A lot like your mother."

"You ordered Slim to kill Dinah's twins?"

"No. It wasn't me. I'd forgotten all about the babies, but when I told Slim what I'd done to Dinah, he called her, and she's the one who told him to handle things, to dispose of Dinah's body and to kill the babies."

Nausea churned in Reve's stomach. "You're talking about Veda MacKinnon, aren't you?"

"She hated Dinah. And she hated those babies far more than I did. Besides, we're family, and family always takes care of their own. She cleaned up Farlan's mess, and we never spoke of it again. She thinks I don't remember. She thinks I blocked it all out. And it's been to my advantage to let her keep on believing that."

"Did you love Dinah Collins?" Reve asked, suddenly beginning to suspect the gruesome truth.

"Of course I loved her, and I thought she loved me. She

made me believe she loved me. I visited her quite often, and she was always so sweet to me. She treated me as if she cared. But it was all lies. That day when I told her how I felt, she laughed and said how flattered she was and that she cared for me. But she didn't. She didn't want me." There were tears in his eyes. Honest-to-goodness, genuine tears. "She didn't laugh for long."

"You killed her."

"Of course I killed her. I had to. She should have been mine, but she loved him and not me. She'd led me on, made me believe she loved me, when all along—"

"Oh, God," Reve said in a whispered plea, realizing what must have happened all those years ago, how he had misunderstood kindness and caring for something more. "She probably did love you, just not the way you wanted her to love you."

"I remember that very first time when Slim took me to the apartment on Hyatt Street. I went up and rang the doorbell right after Farlan left. When she opened the door, she knew who I was. She said he'd shown her pictures of me. I thought I'd hate her, but I didn't. She was the most beautiful thing I'd ever seen. And she was sweet. So very sweet.

"I went back to see her again many times, but it was our little secret. She promised me she wouldn't tell him, and she didn't. And I always made sure no one saw me entering and leaving her apartment. Slim always kept watch for me. I started looking forward to going to see her. I loved talking to her, loved listening to her laugh. She was always so cheerful. She would listen to me, really listen to me. She made me feel important."

"You really were in love with her, weren't you?" If he wasn't holding a gun on her, if he wasn't going to rape and kill her, Reve could almost feel sorry for him.

"I loved her more than he did."

"If you loved her, how could you have killed her?"

"Even after I found out she was going to have his babies,

I still thought she loved me, too. But when I finally got up the courage to tell her how I felt . . ." Again, tears misted his eyes.

"You told her after the twins were born."

He glared at Reve. "Yes, after the twins were born. You and Jazzy were only a few weeks old when I went to see her. I wanted her so much. I'd dreamed of what it would be like with her. I thought since she let him fuck her and she'd let a lot of other men fuck her, she'd let me make love to her. But she said no. How could she have said no?"

"So you raped her, didn't you? You raped her and then killed her."

His gaze narrowed, his nostrils flared. "Take off your robe. I want to see you naked."

Reve shivered. Slowly, playing for time, she removed the robe and let it pool around her hips on the bed. He was going to rape her, and if she tried to fight him, he might shoot her in the head. God, what was she going to do?

"You're almost as beautiful as she was," he said. "I'm going to enjoy screwing you almost as much as I enjoy screwing her. And once I kill you and Jazzy, then both of you can play the game, too."

Every nerve in Reve's body rioted, every muscle tensed. "What—what game?" She hated the way he looked at her and knew it was only a matter of time before he touched her.

"I kill Dinah and then she comes back. She always finds just the right body to possess so that I can rape her and kill her all over again. You and Jazzy can do the same thing, and then I'll have three redheaded beauties who'll be all mine whenever I want them."

Salty bile rose in Reve's esophagus and threatened to choke her. How many women had Dallas and Jacob said the Redhead Killer had murdered? Well over twenty, and that was only the ones whose bodies had been found. And this killing spree had all begun with Dinah Collins. A woman who'd been loved by many men. A woman who had given birth to her lover's babies. A woman who had befriended a lonely and confused little boy.

He came toward her. She inched backward, but halted when he ran the tip of the gun between her bare breasts. "If you give me any trouble, I'll shoot you." He pointed the gun to her head. "I'd prefer not to shoot you, but I will if you force me to. Do you understand?"

"Yes, I understand."

"Lie down and spread your legs."

She did as he'd instructed. Fear clawed at her insides. Adrenaline pumped through her body like a fast-acting poison.

Keeping the gun at her temple, he hovered over her. "Reach into my pocket and remove the condom and the black ribbon."

She reached out, slipped her hand into his pants pocket and retrieved both items.

"Lay the ribbon aside for now." She tossed it on the pillow. "Now unzip my pants." She did. He wasn't wearing any underwear, so the moment she unzipped his pants, his small, hard penis popped out. "Put the condom on me."

She hated touching him, but she did it. She took the condom from the foil packet and stretched it over his erection.

"This won't take long," he said. "It never does with Dinah. I'm always so excited that once I'm inside her, I come right away."

Reve closed her eyes, clenched her teeth and prepared to defend herself. But not yet, not until he was a bit more vulnerable. Not until she felt she could overpower him without him shooting her in the head.

She felt him between her legs, felt the scrape of his slacks against her bare thighs, felt his hot breath on her neck. He slid his penis up and down, over her mound, rubbing himself against her, then he lowered his head and suckled one breast.

Reve opened her eyes and looked right and left. The gun he held in his hand was no longer pointed directly at her temple. The barrel faced straight up, toward the wall. She had a fifty-fifty chance right now. And it was probably the only chance she'd get before he raped her.

Jacob discovered Jimmy Graves slumped over inside the black-and-white, a large, ugly hole in the young officer's head. He'd been shot through the window, which was now shattered. A hard knot of fear clutched Jacob's stomach as he ran up the steps to Jazzy's apartment. The door was shut. He grabbed the knob, turned it and the door opened instantly. Not locked. *God, please don't let me be too late.*

Going immediately into warrior mode, Jacob entered the living room, his movements silent and deadly. When he heard a man's voice coming from the bedroom, he didn't slow his pace nor did he rush into action.

"Take the ribbon and tie it around your neck," the man said. "After I've enjoyed your body, I'll show you how I killed your mother."

Jacob's heartbeat thundered in his head. *Stay calm. Remember your SEAL training.*

The bedroom door stood open, so he was able to see inside the room. Naked, the black braided ribbon around her neck, Reve lay on the bed, Brian MacKinnon poised over her. Jacob couldn't tell if he was buried inside her, if he was raping her, but the guy wasn't moving. Everything went black for a split second as pure murderous rage consumed Jacob. It took every ounce of his willpower not to charge into the room like a raging bull.

Instead he crept into the room. As if she sensed his presence, Reve turned her head sideways and stared at him, her eyes wide and pleading. But she didn't let on in any way that he was in the room.

"I'm not going to let you rape me and kill me without putting up a fight," Reve said.

Brian laughed. "Fight all you want. My intention is to

fuck you and then kill you, but if you'd rather, I can blow your brains out and then fuck you."

In one quick, lethal move, Jacob came up behind Brian, circled his neck with masterful precision and twisted, breaking his neck as if it were a small twig. He pulled Brian's body back and away from Reve, tossed him onto the floor, and then reached down and lifted Reve off the bed and into his arms.

"Did he hurt you, baby? Did he—"

She flung her arms around Jacob and buried her face against his neck. "He didn't—didn't rape me. But God, Jacob, I was so scared. He killed my mother and . . . oh, dear God, he killed all those other women, too. Brian MacKinnon was the Redhead Killer."

"Thank God you're all right. If anything had happened to you . . ." He held on to her for dear life.

CHAPTER 31

After Jacob helped Reve into her robe, he called Dallas to tell him what had happened; then he carried Reve into the living room and sat on the sofa with her in his lap until Lieutenant Glenn showed up. Then Jacob took her to the hospital, where she underwent a thorough exam by the ER doctor, who assured Jacob that other than a few bruises and mild shock, she was fine physically.

She wasn't fine. Perhaps physically, but not emotionally. But she would be in time. The easiest thing to do right now would be to curl up into a ball and withdraw from the world. To let Jacob take care of her and handle everything.

Taking the easy route wasn't her style. There were things she needed to do, other people involved in this nightmare. Veda MacKinnon had ordered Jazzy and her put to death as infants. Their father, Farlan MacKinnon, wasn't entirely blameless. But the most important person in this entire scenario was her sister. Jazzy needed her right now, needed her more than anyone else did.

"I want to stay with Jazzy tonight," Reve told Jacob in the ER waiting room. "I need to be the one to tell my sister about our mother and father. About Veda's involvement . . . and about Brian MacKinnon."

"All right, I understand, but I don't want you to stay alone. The doctor gave Jazzy a sedative earlier tonight, and she probably won't wake up until morning. If Genny's up to it, I'll get Dallas to drive her down here to stay with you."

"Why did the doctor give Jazzy a sedative?"

When Jacob looked down at the floor instead of at her, she knew something was wrong. "It's a long story."

"Tell me."

"Jazzy helped Dallas and me set a trap for her attacker," Jacob admitted, then looked directly at Reve. "I swear to you that she was never in danger. Not for one minute. Dallas and I were across the hall, and the minute Veda MacKinnon—"

"So that's why she was arrested," Reve said. "I heard about her arrest on TV, just a few minutes before Brian—" She shook uncontrollably.

Jacob pulled her into his arms and stroked her back. "It's all over, baby. He's dead. He won't ever hurt you or anyone else ever again."

She shoved against Jacob's chest, forcing him to loosen his protective embrace. "Veda knew Brian killed Dinah Collins. All these years, she's known her son was a murderer and she's protected him. He admitted to me that she's the one who was responsible for getting rid of Jazzy and me when we were babies."

"Mrs. MacKinnon is crazy as a Betsy bug," Jacob said. "My guess is she'll spend the rest of her life in a mental institution."

"You know, as unbelievable as this may sound, I actually feel sorry for Farlan MacKinnon."

"I can't feel sorry for him. Not yet. Maybe not ever. He should have made sure you and Jazzy were taken care of. He should have seen to it that you two and your mother were protected."

Reve caressed Jacob's cheek. "Not all men are like you, Sheriff Butler. Brave and honorable and—"

He grabbed her by the shoulders. "If anything had happened to you tonight—"

"Stop worrying about me." She kissed his cheek. "I'm going to be all right. Go with me up to Jazzy's room. Then you should go to the police station and do whatever it is that you need to do."

"I feel as if I should stay with you."

"I told you, I'm fine. Or at least I will be. I've been taking care of myself for thirty years." She forced a brave smile. "With one minor exception—I didn't do such a good job tonight. But believe me, I wouldn't have gone down without a fight. I had every intention of—" Tears poured from her eyes. Damn the tears! When Jacob tried to pull her back into his arms, she swatted at him. "No, I can't lean on you. I have to find a way to deal with this on my own. It's just how I am."

She could tell by the expression on his face that she'd somehow wounded him. Had he misunderstood something she'd said? Did she need to explain that she wasn't rejecting him?

"Jacob, I owe you my life. That's a huge debt. I'll always be grateful—"

"You don't have to say any more. I understand."

"Do you?" Did he truly understand how important self-reliance was to her? She had never needed a man—not ever—and here in the space of only days, she had not only fallen in love with him, surrendering a huge part of herself in the process, but now she owed him her life.

He raked the back of his hand down her cheek. "Come on, honey, I'll go with you up to Jazzy's room, and then I'll drive on over to the police station and tend to a little business."

As they headed for the elevators, an odd thought crossed Reve's mind. Jacob had called her honey, not baby. On some instinctive feminine level, she suspected that somehow their entire relationship had just changed. And not for the better.

A week later, with Brian MacKinnon buried and Veda MacKinnon under police guard in the four-hundred unit at County General, no one in Cherokee County could talk of anything else except the great scandal. But Reve managed to ignore the stares and whispers, and the family had done their best to protect Jazzy from wagging tongues. Although Farlan had asked to see Jazzy, she had declined, telling Reve she wasn't ready to meet their father. Not yet.

Today Reve joined Jazzy's family and friends at the hospital for a going-away party. Dr. Cornelius had arranged for Jazzy to enter an extensive rehabilitation program at Vanderbilt, starting on Monday. Big Jim and Miss Reba were driving Jazzy and Caleb to Nashville this morning, and Caleb would be living in an apartment near the rehab center.

"With luck, Jazzy should complete the program in about a month, then she'll begin out-patient therapy," Dr. Cornelius had explained. "Her prognosis is good."

Lacy Fallon uncorked a bottle of champagne and the bubbly overflowed, spewing high enough to splatter a few of the dozens of helium balloons floating in the air. After Lacy poured the champagne into plastic cups, Ludie distributed the drinks. Once everyone had a cup, Lacy made a toast.

"Here's to Jazzy's full recovery!"

A resounding rumble of voices echoed that sentiment. Reve glanced over at Jacob, who stood off to himself, as if trying to hide behind Genny and Dallas. Of course it was impossible for a man of his size to go unnoticed. Although he had come by the hospital to check on her and Jazzy every day, he'd acted as if they were only friends, as if they'd never been lovers. He'd been friendly and kind and concerned, but he'd kept an emotional distance between them. And for the entire week she'd been trying to figure out what had happened, why she'd gone from being his baby to only his honey.

When their gazes suddenly collided, she felt the power of his heated glare. But he glanced away quickly, as if he couldn't bear to look at her.

"Miss all of you," Jazzy said, then held out her hand to Reve. "You most."

Reve hugged her sister. "Don't you worry about Jazzy's Joint or Jasmine's. I'll keep them going until I can put a full-time manager in place."

"Talk. Alone," Jazzy said to Reve.

"You heard the lady." Caleb began ushering everyone out into the hall. "The sisters want a few minutes alone before Jazzy and I have to leave."

After everyone had exited Jazzy's room and Caleb had closed the door, Jazzy looked up from her wheelchair to where Reve stood at her side. "You and Jacob?"

"We've already had this discussion," Reve said, recalling how she'd poured her heart and soul out to her sister several days ago.

Jazzy shook her head. "Stubborn."

"Me?" Reve pointed to herself.

Jazzy smiled. "You. Jacob, too."

"How am I being stubborn?"

"Tell him."

"Tell him what?"

"Love him. Yes?"

"Yes, I love him, the big dope. But apparently he doesn't love me. If he did, he wouldn't be acting—"

"Tell him. Love him."

"You think I should tell him I love him?"

"Yes."

"And what if I just wind up making a fool of myself?"

Jazzy laughed.

Reve leaned down and kissed her sister's cheek. "Stop worrying about me and Jacob. You go to Nashville and get well.

I'll drive up often to visit. And in the meantime, if you'll promise not to worry about me, I'll take your advice and make sure Jacob Butler knows that I love him."

"Good. Tell him. Soon."

"I will. I promise."

That night at Jazzy's Joint, while she tried to get some paperwork done, all she could think about was Jacob and her promise to her sister. *Why don't you call him and ask him to come over? Or better yet, you know where he lives. Go to him. And don't put it off. Do it tonight. If he rejects you, you'll find a way to deal with it. But at least you'll know where you stand.*

"Reve, come on out to the bar right now." Lacy Fallon stood in the open office doorway.

"What's wrong?"

"Jacob just walked in and guess who jumped him the minute he came through the door—Mindy Harper."

"Oh, she did, did she?" Reve jumped up and came flying around the desk. "Well, I guess I'm going to have to go out there and tell her to keep her hands off my man."

"You are? Hot damn!" Lacy followed Reve out of the office and down the hall.

After they reached the bar, Reve stopped and surveyed the joint. When she saw Jacob on the dance floor with Mindy Harper, she growled.

"If I'd known you were going to forget you were a lady tonight, I'd have brought my video camera," Lacy said. "After all, you and Jacob might like to have this on tape to show your kids someday."

"That's okay," Reve said. "I'm sure every minute of this night will be recorded in my memory and in Jacob's."

Reve marched out onto the dance floor and straight up to Jacob and Mindy. She tapped on Mindy's shoulder and said, "I'm cutting in."

Jacob halted and stared at Reve. Mindy whirled around and said, "The hell you are."

"Look, sister, I'm only going to say this once, so listen up." Reve planted her hands on her hips. "Take your damn hands off my man and do it right now."

"And if I don't?" Mindy glared up at Reve, who was several inches taller and outweighed her by more pounds than Reve wanted to admit.

"Take a good look at me. I'm twice your size and I'm mad as hell. You want to tangle with me, then bring it on." Reve motioned to Mindy.

Mindy stared at Reve for a couple of minutes, then turned back to Jacob. "Is she right—do you belong to her?"

Jacob shrugged. "Yeah, I guess I do."

Huffing loudly, Mindy turned and pranced off toward the bar.

When Reve thought for sure Jacob would welcome her with open arms, he turned and walked away. She stood there on the dance floor, surrounded by couples as the song on the jukebox ended. Before she had a chance to feel like a total fool, she realized Jacob was punching in a number on the juke box. She waited, holding her breath and praying. Then the uniquely beautiful voice of Pasty Cline filled Jazzy's Joint. Reve's heart went wild. Butterflies fluttered maddeningly in her stomach. He came toward her, slowly, taking his time. And suddenly the whole world exploded in a frenzy of happiness as he took her in his arms. They moved languidly to the rhythm of the old country ballad, "He Called Me Baby."

"You kind of staked your claim tonight, didn't you?" Jacob whispered in her ear.

"I guess I did."

"I guess I was wrong when I figured you wanted me to give you some space because you were having second thoughts about us."

"You were wrong," she told him. "And just so there's no more misunderstandings—" She stopped, reached up and cupped his face between her hands. "I love you. Do you hear me? I love you like crazy, you big country hick Cochise wannabe, and I want to marry you and have your babies and spend the rest of my life in your arms."

"Ah, baby, baby . . ."

"Let's get out of here." She took his hand in hers. "Take me upstairs and call me baby, baby, all night long."

He tugged on her hand, yanked her back and into his arms, then leaned down until his lips touched hers. "I'm crazy in love with you, too, Miss High and Mighty."

And then he kissed her. A loud, joyous roar nearly lifted the roof off Jazzy's Joint when the other patrons cheered Jazzy's sister and the man she'd laid claim to tonight.

EPILOGUE

Jazzy Talbot walked down the aisle at the Congregationalist church on the first Saturday evening in December, a little over a year after being brutally attacked by Veda MacKinnon. In the year that had passed, Veda had committed suicide at the state mental institution where she'd been committed, and the FBI and state and local authorities had closed the books on the Redhead Killer's case, burying the past with Brian MacKinnon. And Farlan MacKinnon had spent the past year trying his best to make amends to his twin daughters. Although the three of them had a ways to go yet, the fact that Farlan was walking his daughter down the aisle tonight made a statement to everyone in attendance. Half the county had been invited to the biggest, most elaborate wedding ceremony in the history of Cherokee Pointe, paid for by the bride's father.

Reve stood beside Genny, the two of them acting as Jazzy's matrons of honor. And on the other side of the minister, Jacob stood beside Dallas, the two of them serving as Caleb's best man. Reve glanced at her beautiful sister as she entered the sanctuary and thanked God that nine months of physical therapy had restored Jazzy to her former good health. Jazzy and Caleb had returned to Cherokee Pointe four months ago, and Miss Reba had immediately begun planning what she called an unforgettable wedding. It had been nothing short of amazing to see Reba Upton happily working with Jazzy to make sure every detail of Jazzy's wedding would be perfect. Perhaps the fact that she was a new bride herself made Miss Reba so genuinely caring. This past summer, Big Jim and she had flown to Reno and acquired a quick divorce, dissolving their long and unhappy union. Miss Reba had flown home and straight into Dodd Keefer's waiting arms, and the two were married in a quiet, private ceremony only two months ago. But Big Jim hadn't waited even one day before marrying his long-time mistress, Erin Mercer, in a Las Vegas chapel, before they spent their honeymoon in one of the most expensive suites in Sin City.

As Reve glanced at family and friends seated in the first few rows, she smiled at Sally Talbot and Ludie, both decked out in floor-length gowns, with hairdos compliments of a local beauty salon. Lacy Fallon had her hands full keeping Madoc Sloan pacified because Genny and Dallas's squirming, six-month-old, blond-haired baby boy had his big brown eyes wide open and was taking in the evening's big event.

When Farlan paused before the altar, he leaned down and kissed Jazzy's cheek, then glanced over and smiled at Reve. She returned her father's smile, knowing that he was remembering walking her down the aisle this past June, on the day she became Jacob's wife.

As the ceremony began, Reve's gaze connected with her husband's, the man she loved with all her heart, the man who made her happy on a daily basis. Instinctively, her hand rested on her rounded belly in a motherly, protective gesture. Only this past week, she'd gotten her first sonogram. Jacob had been at her side, holding her hand, when they saw their daughter for the first time. In approximately four months, little Miss Dinah Butler would make her debut. And unless she missed her guess, Reve figured this old world would never be the same again.

PLAY TO WIN . . .
It's the ultimate game—the adrenaline surge of the hunt,
the thrill of victory, the agony of defeat. For in this
game, the rules are simple: To win, you only
have to kill. To lose, you will have to die . . .

PLAY TO SCREAM . . .
The victims are former beauty queens found with a
single rose beside their bodies. Lindsay McAllister has
seen this signature before, when she was a rookie
detective with the Chattanooga PD investigating
the death of Judd Walker's wife, a murder that sent the
handsome lawyer off the deep end. Now, Lindsay has
the brutal task of telling Judd that his wife's killer has
struck again, and she's going to need his help
to outplay their opponent—because the killer
is getting bolder, faster, and more ruthless.
The game is escalating, and no one is safe.

PLAY TO DIE . . .
Now as the body count rises, the rules are changing.
A killer will do anything to win. And the only way
for Lindsay to stop a madman's twisted game
is to play it herself . . .

**Please turn the page for an exciting sneak peak of
Beverly Barton's
THE DYING GAME
*Now Available!***

The intensely bright lights blinded her. She couldn't see anything except the white illumination that obscured everything else in her line of vision. She wished he would turn off the car's headlights.

Judd didn't like her to show houses to clients in the evenings and generally she did what Judd wanted her to do. But her career as a Realtor was just getting off the ground and if she could sell this half-million dollar house to Mr. and Mrs. Farris, her percentage would be enough to furnish the nursery. Not that she was pregnant. Not yet. And not that her husband couldn't well afford to furnish a nursery with the best of everything. It was just that Jennifer wanted the baby to be her gift to her wonderful husband and the nursery to be a gift from her to their child.

Holding her hand up to shield her eyes from the headlights, she walked down the sidewalk to meet John and Katherine Farris, an up-and-coming entrepreneurial couple planning to start a new business in Chattanooga. She had spoken only to John Farris. From their telephone conversations, she had surmised that John, like her own husband, was the type who liked to think he wore the pants in the family.

Odd how, considering the fact that she believed herself to be a thoroughly modern women, Jennifer loved Judd's old-fashioned sense of protectiveness and possessiveness.

When John Farris parked his black Mercedes and opened the driver's door, Jennifer met him, her hand outstretched in greeting. He accepted her hand immediately and smiled warmly.

"Good evening, Mr. Farris." Jennifer glanced around, searching for Mrs. Farris.

"I'm sorry, something came up at the last minute that delayed Katherine. She'll be joining us soon."

When John Farris raked his silvery blue eyes over her, Jennifer shuddered inwardly, an odd sense of uneasiness settling in the pit of her stomach. *You're being silly,* she told herself. Men found her attractive. And it wasn't her fault. She didn't do anything to lead them on, nothing except simply being beautiful, which she owed to the fact that she'd inherited great genes from her attractive parents.

Jennifer sighed. Sometimes being a former beauty queen was a curse.

"If you'd like to wait for your wife before you look at the house, I can go ahead and answer any questions you might have. I 've got all the information in my briefcase in my car."

He shook his head. "No need to wait. I'd like to take a look around now. If I don't like the place, Katherine won't be interested."

"Oh, I see."

He chuckled. "It's not that she gives in to me on everything. We each try to please the other. Isn't that the way to have a successful marriage?"

"Yes, I think so. It's certainly what Judd and I have been trying to do. We're a couple of newlyweds just trying to make our way through that first year of marriage." Jennifer nodded toward the front entrance to the sprawling glass-and-log house. "If you'll follow me."

"I'd be delighted to follow you."

Despite his reply sending a quiver of apprehension along her nerve endings, she kept walking toward the front steps, telling herself that if she had to defend her honor against unwanted advances, it wouldn't be the first time. She knew how to handle herself in sticky situations. She carried pepper spray in her purse and her cell phone rested securely in her jacket pocket.

After unlocking the front door, she flipped on the light switch, which illuminated the large foyer. "The house was built in nineteen-seventy-five by an architect for his own personal home."

John Farris paused in the doorway. "How many rooms?"

"Ten," she replied, then motioned to him. "Please, come on in."

He entered the foyer and glanced around, up into the huge living room and to the right into the open dining room. "It seems perfect for entertaining."

"Oh, it is. There's a state-of-the-art kitchen. It was completely gutted and redone only four years ago by the present owner."

"I'd like to take a look," he told her. "I'm the chef in the family. Katherine can't boil water."

Feeling a bit more at ease, Jennifer led him from the foyer, through the dining room, and into the galley-style kitchen. "I love this kitchen. I'm not much of a cook myself, but I've been taking gourmet cooking lessons as a surprise for my husband."

"Isn't he a lucky man."

Jennifer felt Mr. Farris as he came up behind her. Shuddering nervously, she started to turn to face him, but suddenly and without warning, he grabbed her from behind and covered her face with a foul-smelling rag.

No. No . . . no, this can't be happening.

* * *

Had she been unconscious for a few minutes or a few hours? She didn't know. When she came to, she realized she was sitting propped up against the wall in the kitchen, her feet tied together with rope and her hands pulled over her head, each wrist bound with individual pieces of rope that had been tied to the door handles of two open kitchen cabinet doors.

Groggy, slightly disoriented, Jennifer blinked several times, then took a deep breath and glanced around the room, searching for her attacker. John Farris loomed over her, an odd smile on his face.

"Well, hello, beautiful," he said. "I was wondering how long you'd sleep. I've been waiting patiently for you to wake up. You've been out nearly fifteen minutes."

"Why?" she asked, her voice a ragged whisper.

"Why what?"

"Why are you doing this?"

"What do you think I intend to do?"

"Rape me." Her voice trembled. *Please, God, don't let him kill me.*

He laughed. "What sort of man do you think I am? I'd never force myself on an unwilling woman."

"Please, let me go. Whatever—" She gasped, her mouth sucking in air as she noticed that he held something shiny in his right hand.

A meat cleaver!

Sheer terror claimed her at that moment, body and soul. Her stomach churned. Sweat dampened her face. The loud rat-a-tat-tat of her accelerated heartbeat thundered in her ears.

He reached down with his left hand and fingered her long, dark hair. "If only you were a blonde or a redhead."

Jennifer swallowed hard. *He's going to kill me. He's going to kill me with that meat cleaver. He'll chop me up in little pieces . . .*

She whimpered. *Oh, Judd, why didn't I listen to you? Why did I come here alone tonight?*

"Are you afraid?" John Farris asked.

"Yes."

"You should be," he told her.

"You're going to kill me, aren't you?"

He laughed again. Softly.

"Please . . . please . . ." She cried. Tears filled her eyes and trickled down her cheeks.

He came closer. And closer. He raised the meat cleaver high over her head, then swung it across her right wrist.

Blood splattered on the cabinet, over her head, and across her upper body as her severed right hand tumbled downward and hit the floor.

Pain! Excruciating pain.

And then he lifted the cleaver and swung down and across again, cutting off her left hand with one swift, accurate blow.

Jennifer passed out.